Dedication

To my Mum, who always said I could do anything.

By the same author

THE WOMAN AND THE WITCH

AIRY CAGES AND OTHER STORIES

The Bookbinder

Amanda Larkman

This is a work of fiction. Names, characters, places, and incidents either are the product of the author's imagination or are used fictitiously. Any resemblance to actual persons, living or dead, events, or locales is entirely coincidental.

Copyright © 2021 by Amanda Larkman

All rights reserved. No part of this book may be reproduced or used in any manner without written permission of the copyright owner except for the use of quotations in a book review.

First paperback edition April 2021
Cover design: Jem Butcher
ISBN: 9798718021981

CONTENTS

Sarah: Five Years Ago	1
Chapter 1: Amber	4
Chapter 2: Liz	18
Chapter 3: Amber	31
Chapter 4: Liz	45
Chapter 5: Amber	58
Chapter 6: Liz	76
Chapter 7: Amber	95
Sarah: Five Years Ago	112
Chapter 8: Liz	116
Chapter 9: Amber	130
Chapter 10: Liz	146
Sarah: Five Years Ago	159
Chapter 11: Amber	164
Chapter 12: Liz	180
Chapter 13: Amber	196
Chapter 14: Liz	209
Chapter 15: Amber	221

Sarah: Five Years Ago	238
Chapter 16: Liz	242
Chapter 17: Amber	254
Sarah: Five Years Ago	280
Chapter 18: Liz	269
Chapter 19: Amber	283
Sarah: Five Years Ago	296
Chapter 20: Liz	303
Chapter 21: Amber	318
Chapter 22: Liz	330
Chapter 23: Amber	338
Chapter 24: Amber	354
Chapter 25: Two Months Later	367
About the Author	374

ACKNOWLEDGEMENTS

Thank you to Paul and my children, Joe and Emily for letting me get on with my writing except when they were hungry or needed a lift. Thank you to Bill Browning, as ever, for your support. And to my ever-growing team of beta readers – Jayne, Helena, Rosie, Una, Carolyn and Claire - thank you SO much for your encouragement, reading through piles of first drafts and giving me such great feedback.

SARAH: FIVE YEARS AGO

She ignored the curious gazes and frank stares of the passengers as the train zoomed through the darkness, deep under the English Channel. Her jaw muscles kept leaping, and she popped another chewing gum in her mouth. Her teeth ground together. The coke she'd taken earlier still sizzled in her veins. She couldn't remember the last time she'd slept.

Sleep terrified her. A dragon whose roars she silenced with a chemical lance. She'd need more soon. Was there enough? Her eyelids thinned and twitched as she closed them, remembering packing her bag and sliding the packet of powder into the lining. It was good and fat, enough to last.

She shivered; the carriage was freezing. Looking around at the other passengers she wondered how they could look so comfortable in their shorts and T-shirts. Her face itched and she scratched it, hard, her nails coming away bloody. Spiders began to tap the hairs of their feet down her arms and wrists, she sat on her hands; once she started scratching, she wouldn't be able to stop.

With jerky fingers she checked her bag. It was wedged next to her body in case she passed out and someone tried to steal it. The thought of losing it made her heart beat faster. Everything she had was in there. The leather belts and jewellery she'd spent the last month making were stored in envelopes and boxes, ready to sell.

The gold on her finger flashed as she spun her grandmother's ring. A man standing in the aisle watched as if hypnotised by the shine, and fear gripped her. She glared at him and pulled off the ring, fastening it into her top pocket of her jeans. For the next few hours, she checked the pocket with obsessive compulsion.

Slumping back into her seat she leaned her head against the window; her hands shook as she felt again for her bag. She looped the straps tight around her wrist.

The train stopped and a mother and daughter bumped down the aisle. The seat next to her was empty and the child clambered on, vivid as a flower in her poppy red coat. The mother took one look at the pale woman with stringy hair, bleached face and grinding jaw, and pulled her daughter away, face creased with disgust. The woman pulled at the neck of her jumper, it was three sizes too big for her and matted with greasy patches.

'Don't worry. I'll move,' she said, the crack of her voice like an engine turning over. She picked up her bag and pushed down the aisle to the end of the train and clicked her lighter into sparks until it flamed and lit the end of her joint. She began to sway as she dragged the pungent smoke down to the soles of her feet. Her eyelids began to droop.

The train rocked her body and she nearly fell, oblivious to the sudden swell of light that marked the end of the tunnel. Her hands, red and raw with chilblains constantly tapped over her pocket. Dropping to an unsteady squat she searched through her bag again. The nearby toilet door crashed open and she threw her arms above her head in fright. A man looked down, puzzled by her cry and she squinted up at him, the joint smoking between her fingers. She started to laugh. The movement cracked open the sores at the corners of her mouth, and her lips began to bleed.

The man shook his head and moved away. She took another deep toke of her dope. It wasn't working, her skin still crawled, and every shadow pulled their eyes open to stare at her. Covering her face with her hands she noticed her empty fingers. Panic scuttled across her face before she checked her pocket again and sagged with relief.

She tried to remember where she was going. It felt like a tongue probing a gaping tooth cavity. Her thoughts jumped over each other and raced into unravelling shoals of glittering fish, or glass. There was writing inked onto her hand and she stared at it but the letters stretched and shrunk and wouldn't stay still, no matter how hard she blinked.

Glancing round to check nobody was coming to use the toilet, she unfolded the cuff of her jumper and licked up a tablet. Her face began to glaze almost immediately, and she gave a dreamy smile. The shadows around her lay flat again.

The paper told her where she was going, she remembered now. It was wadded into the side pocket of her bag. In slow motion she unfolded the flyer and spread it smooth. She tried to read but her head lolled –

CHAPTER 1: AMBER

He watched her through the glass doors as she entered the concourse. The cold light streamed in from overhead, picking out the flashes of blue in her crow-black hair. She looked nervous; her hands twisted together, and he enjoyed seeing her eyes darting about.

Amber leaned against the wall, keeping out of the way of the flood of passengers surging towards the overhead screens. Her pulse skipped a little as she searched for Alex. Where was he? He was right behind her at passport control.

How odd it felt to be standing on her own. Without him a prop had been removed - leaving her side exposed. Amber scanned the faces around her again, still no sign. She was used to spotting Alex straight away, with his height and great shock of white-blond hair. But not now. Had he been held up?

Amber swallowed hard as she remembered leaving the hotel with their pile of bags and Alex joking about hiding some weed in his shoes. Surely, he wasn't serious? She shook her head, imagining her worries splashing onto the ground and disappearing. A trick the grief therapist had suggested, but it never worked.

It was cold. She untangled her coat from the straps of her handbag and pulled it on, zipping it up and nestling her chin in the warmth of the collar. It didn't seem possible it was nearly a month since she'd last worn it. Already the days of blue skies and sands bleached by the hot, white, disc of the sun felt like a dream.

Come on, Alex! Amber debated whether to retrace her steps to passport control but worried she'd miss him, so stayed where she was. For the entire honeymoon she and Alex had been entwined. She didn't like not having him within touching distance; she'd got used to him being close.

The doors to her left gaped open. She kept her eyes fixed forward. Memories of her Mum waving - a beam splitting her face as she welcomed Amber back from school trips, and holidays with her mates - studded bullets into Amber's heart.

How could an empty space feel so solid? These moments were so hard to bear; moments when grief skewered as raw and sharp as the day her Mum died. Amber rummaged for her phone to stop thinking. She smiled to see the lock screen light up. Alex grinning, somewhere in the New Forest. He was holding up a muddy welly.

Swiping up, she clicked the phone off airplane mode for the first time in nearly four weeks. Notifications chattered in so fast she couldn't read them quickly enough.

'Hey! I thought we agreed no phones until we got home.' Alex's voice breathed in her ear and Amber jumped, shoving her phone back into her bag with a blush of guilt.

'Where have you been?' she complained, reaching for him so he wrapped his arms around her. In an instant the noise of the baggage claim disappeared, and Amber lost herself in the clean folds of Alex's shirt. She pressed her nose against his skin.

'Come on, babe, the bags will be here any minute. Go and get a trolley.'

With reluctance, Amber peeled away and headed for the trolleys. There was a queue, and as she waited the exit doors dragged her eyes again. She ignored the emptiness that stood on the other side, fixing on Alex instead.

He was standing by the baggage carousel, having already found a group of people to entertain. A man with a neat beard threw his head back and laughed as Alex finished his story. Grins leaped from face to face as Alex's voice grew louder, his gestures more exuberant.

Amber was torn between impatience and indulgence. Alex's magnetic pull on people drove her crazy. The night they met, he and his best friend Curly had been holding court at the bar. Standing, awkward and slightly distanced from the group she had come with, Amber envied their easy charm and good-natured banter.

Watching him now, pushing the white-blond hair out of his eyes and laughing his big laugh, Amber felt again the shock that he had sought her out that evening. Not just sought her out but told her she was beautiful. He'd kept on telling her she was beautiful until here they were, back from their honeymoon after a courtship and marriage so fast it had left her dizzy.

The queue moved forward, and Amber pulled out the last trolley with a shriek of metal. It had stuck to the fixed bar and she grew hot with embarrassment as she tugged and tugged until it broke free. She rattled across the shining floor to the baggage belts. The group around Alex drifted away leaving him surrounded by suitcases.

'I missed you,' he said.

'I was only gone about ten seconds!' Amber laughed. 'You seemed fine.'

Alex hooked his arm around her waist and swooped her back, so her hair hung almost to the floor. He bent over and kissed her. Amber, aware they were creating a scene, tried to push Alex away but he kept on, smiling against her mouth as passing old ladies and young mothers clucked and giggled.

'Come on! Stop it!' Amber protested with a gasp. 'Let's get home.' Alex gave her a final smacker on the cheek and started chucking their suitcases on the trolley.

'So, listen, babe, I've got something to tell you.' Alex grabbed Amber's hand and pulled her along. Just before they reached the exit he swerved towards the wall, parked the trolley, and turned to Amber.

'OK. Don't freak out.'

'What?' Amber's stomach dropped. 'What is it?' She took a breath, but panic still prickled along her veins.

Alex reached for her. 'Stop it,' he whispered. 'It's nothing frightening. It's a good thing.'

'Just tell me.'

'OK, so I know you wanted me to rent out your gran's house...'

'What?'

'Hang on, listen. The thing is I went to see it and it's amazing, babe. A great, big, beautiful house.'

'It's a wreck!' Amber protested. Irritation flicked across Alex's face.

'But who better to do it up than me and Curly? It's what we do all day every day, after all.'

'Curly?'

'Yeah. We planned a surprise… We're going to be living in your gran's place!' Alex's face was awash with boyish excitement.

Amber struggled to take it in. 'But what about my flat?'

'We'll put it on the market, the money can go towards doing up your Gran's place. Me and Curly have got it all worked out, he's been sending me some brilliant ideas on what to do with the ground floor…'

'But Alex I love my flat!' Amber found the words at last. She had used the money her Gran had left her for a deposit on a tiny apartment in a modern block. It was only two years old when she bought it and she had loved the view towards London, its clean, white walls, immaculate kitchen and ensuite bathroom.

The thought of moving into her Gran's old dust-warren filled her with horror. It had four floors and sat in a grim tangle of a garden right next to the Common. Amber had always hated going there. It was oppressive, with hooded windows that gazed down in disapproval at anyone who walked up the path to the peeling front door.

Her Gran had done nothing to it since her husband died in the late 70s and the house had grown darker and more dishevelled until it was passed onto her Mum and, following her death, onto her.

'I don't understand,' she said. 'You told me you were going to sort it all out with the agency…' Amber's voice trailed away.

'But don't you see? It's the perfect place for us! Curly and I can do it up at weekends and that. You got to remember I'm getting on now…'

'Don't be stupid, you're only thirty-nine.'

'Still, it's a lot older than you, and I don't want to leave it too long. I'm a married man now, got to get ready to settle down.'

Amber smiled. His enthusiasm was infectious. She pressed hard against the cramp of mourning for her pretty flat, remembering the curtains and carpet she had chosen with such care, the little bookshelf she'd found that fitted so perfectly next to the big window.

'I'm not very happy about this,' she managed, wishing she could fight harder.

Alex's face softened. 'I know. It's a shock. But hopefully a happy one. I can't wait for you to see it.'

'What do you mean? We're going there now? But it's a dump!'

'Aha! Well that's the surprise,' Alex said, his black eyes sparking. 'Curly moved in there while we were away, he's managed to replace one bathroom and has done up the main bedroom. We can hole up there until the work is finished.' Still talking, Alex touched Amber's elbow and guided her towards the doors through to where loved ones and taxi drivers held up signs, waiting for the new arrivals.

'And here he is! The man himself!'

Amber was bewildered as she tried to take everything in. With a rush, they were through the doors and she blinked at the sudden blaze of light, and clatter of noise. 'What about my flat?' she asked again, but Alex was gone, marching ahead to where she could see Curly was standing at the rail. When he spotted Alex, he waved.

He looked grubby, Amber thought with a grimace. She wasn't keen on Curly, with his chaotic energy and thoughtlessness; an attractive quality at 19, perhaps, but less so at thirty-eight. Alex had made it clear from the start that if she loved him, she had to love Curly too as they had been friends for years. She gave a tight smile as he pulled her into a hug, trying not to recoil at the musty smell of his long, tangled black hair and the grimy damp of his denim jacket.

'Wait!' he said, tugging Alex so he could join the hug. He held up his phone and beamed into it. 'Come on, smile, you two!'

Alex sighed. 'You and your bloody Instagram. Aren't you a bit old for all of that? How many followers you got – three? Including your Mum?'

Curly chuckled. 'More than you, that's for sure.' He uploaded the picture and muttered as he typed. 'The Newly Weds Return… 'There, all done. So! How was it? Must have been good as neither of you have got much of a tan.' He leered and nudged Amber in the ribs. She pushed him away.

Alex laughed and started chatting, so intent on Curly he forgot about the trolley. Amber took hold of it, catching the case that was threatening to fall off. She suppressed a bubble of annoyance. Why was he here? Alex had said they'd get the train back from the airport, take it easy. Now they were hustling towards the multi-storey car park, dodging cars, and travellers with their careering trolleys and piles of bags.

'I can't remember what floor I'm on,' Curly said. 'Hang on, I'll go and check with the desk.' He slipped away, brandishing his ticket.

Amber felt exhaustion hit her. They'd been travelling all day and she wanted to crash out with Alex curved close against her.

'Great to be back, eh?' Alex turned to her. He looked so happy Amber didn't have the heart, or the energy, to talk about the flat and the house anymore. Maybe he was right, he and Curly were builders, after all.

Alex read her face. 'Trust me, I know what I'm doing.'

She dozed in the back of the car listening to Alex and Curly talking about the holiday and what had been done to the house. Sleep hung weights on her eyes, and she allowed them to close, too shattered to mind how uncomfortable she was, wedged up against the big suitcase on the back seat.

Just as she sank into unconsciousness, she realised Alex and Curly had turned in their seats and were watching her; she was too far gone to wonder why their voices had dropped to whispers.

*

It was dark by the time they drew up outside the house. Getting out of the car Amber stretched her arms above her head, pulling the aches out of her cramped back muscles. The cold air was a shock after so many weeks of balmy warmth.

Apart from looking even more dilapidated, the house was as Amber remembered. If Curly had been doing anything over the past four weeks, it hadn't been on the outside. Ivy had been left to clamber across the face of the house and up towards the roof, sending tendrils winding into the gutters.

Amber gazed up as Curly and Alex unloaded the car. She remembered visiting when her Gran was still alive, and the ivy hadn't been so high. She had learned the little round windows in the roof and above the front door were called Oxeyes. Now they were drowned in the dark green ocean of ivy; nothing remained but three, ragged-edged mouths that gasped for air.

She knew if she looked hard, beyond the rotten wood, the gap-toothed brickwork, and sagging roof, she'd see the fine bones of the house. Turning her back to the front door she could see right across the common; it was very pretty, she acknowledged, but it still gave her the creeps.

Amber longed for car-filled streets, colourful shop fronts, and crowds of people. All this greenery and wet dankness hid all sorts of things. In town you knew where you were, and there was nowhere to hide. No bushes, leaves and trees to shield people who wanted to watch.

'Amber!' Alex's voice made her jump. 'What are you doing? Come on, let's get inside, it's miserable out here.'

Amber moved towards the house. She couldn't shake off the unease cooling her skin.

Alex pulled her to him, and the warmth of his arms was comforting. He was all that was important. He was all she had. And Curly, she thought with a wry smile as he led them up the steps and into the front hall.

It stank of damp and mould.

'Like I told you, mate, I've only managed to clear out and clean up your room and my room…'

'Your room?' Amber asked, surprised.

'You can't expect him to come and work on the house for hours and then send him packing back to his bedsit,' Alex said, giving her shoulders a squeeze. 'He's doing us a huge favour, babe, I owe him – big time. This place is going to be a bloody show-stopper when it's finished.'

Amber looked up at the ceiling, which rose three storeys above her. It disappeared into shadows. Cobwebs swung in the corners and she could hear something pattering about.

'Come on, let me show you your room,' Curly said with a sweep of his hand indicating the stairs; they were littered with wood splinters. 'I've sorted it for you guys, so you've got somewhere to escape all the mess.'

Alex took Amber's hand and they climbed up to the first floor. She had forgotten how huge this place was; how on earth had her Gran coped on her own for as long as she did?

As Alex pointed out the port windows and the mouldings on the ceiling, Amber tried to absorb some of his enthusiasm, but it wasn't easy. She hated old things. In these houses she couldn't help thinking about all the people who had died there. Their ghosts hung about her, smelling of dust and neglect.

She listened to Alex as he explained what he wanted to do, the changes he and Curly would put in place. They would knock down walls and open up boarded over fireplaces. 'It's got a huge basement,' he said. 'I can't wait to show it to you. I reckon we could put in a state-of-the-art gym.'

'But how are we going to pay for all of this?' Amber said.

Alex waved his hands. 'Don't you worry about it. We've got some of your mum's money and I've a few ideas up my sleeve.'

Curly nodded. 'It'll be lit when it's all done, Amber, honest.'

'The trouble with you is you've no imagination,' Alex nuzzled his face into her neck.

'He's right, you know,' Curly said, scratching his mop of hair releasing a drift of what looked like plaster dust. 'Have a look at this. I've got one room done, once you see this, I reckon you'll have a bit more faith.'

They'd arrived at the main bedroom. She took a deep breath. The last time she had stood at this doorway was the last time she had visited her Gran, sickly and frail, who was sent to a hospice soon afterwards. The room had been stifled by great swags of green patterned fabric. Everything matched, the counterpane, the curtains, the cushions on the bed.

The bed squatted big and dark, a heavy wood. Her Gran floated on top of it, a tiny, wizened figure dwarfed by the dark brown furniture that loomed around the room. It had stank. Amber wrinkled her nose remembering. The strange, sweet smell that puffed from her gran's body, along with the sting of antiseptic and cleaning fluid, had made her feel sick. She couldn't wait to get out of there, and now here she was again.

With a flourish, Curly swung open the door. Amber gasped. Everything in it was gone, and the difference was extraordinary. Light filled the room that had been re-plastered and painted white. The patterned carpet was gone, exposing the floorboards. All that remained was a white framed, simple bedstead, a wardrobe, and a pretty dressing table set under the window.

'What do you think?' Curly looked so shy and pleased Amber softened and gave him a hug, despite the whiffiness of his jacket.

'I love it, Curly. It's beautiful.'

'I left it really like, bare, as I thought you could decorate it yourself, you know – put up your fairy lights and that.'

'What did you do with all of the furniture?'

Curly looked troubled. 'I dumped it. Alex said that would be OK?'

'Of course, mate, that's fine.' Alex turned to Amber. 'It was all junk, babe, not worth anything and I know you hated it, so we just thought we'd get rid of it.'

'It's OK!' Amber smiled at Alex to reassure him. He looked so worried, bless him. Seeing the transformed room brought home how hard Curly had worked.

'It's lovely. Really, Curly. I'm so pleased with it.'

It was a good job the bedroom was so wonderful as the rest of the house was in utter disarray. The kitchen hadn't been used for decades and every room was filled with junk. With barely anywhere to sit, let along cook, they decided to walk across the common to the local Indian restaurant and Amber found herself relaxing, enjoying the protection offered by Alex and Curly walking on either side.

Their bulk was reassuring. They were the same height, though Curly was a bit heavier with a belly that Alex – who worked out every day – would never tolerate. They had the same eyes, so dark brown to be almost black, but they were more striking on Alex with his blond hair. Curling her arm around Alex's waist and feeling the quilt of muscles she marvelled again that he was her husband.

'OK, babe?' he said, smiling down at her. 'What are you thinking about?'

'How lucky I am to have you,' she said.

'Ah no, I'm the lucky one.'

'Too right!' snorted Curly. 'Sad old man like you with a babe like Amber.'

'Ah thank you, Curly.' She saw the look on Alex's face. 'He's only joking,' she said.

'Ha ha.' Alex smiled, but the look he threw Curly was stony.

*

Crossing back to the house, groaning she'd eaten too much, and her stomach was going to burst, Amber giggled. Her blood bubbled with happiness though she was drunk and almost blind with exhaustion. Alex and Curly had swapped outrageous stories about their past and Alex never took his hands from hers, twirling her hair, kissing her, telling Curly how beautiful his new wife was and how happy he was to be married.

It had been lovely, and Amber swung Alex's hand in hers as they walked home. Curly seemed happy playing third wheel but had managed to get the waitress's phone number.

'I don't know how you do it,' Alex had said. 'It's not like you take care of yourself, I mean look at the state of you. What's in it for them?'

Curly waggled his tongue obscenely. 'I've got great technique,' he said making Alex laugh and Amber feel slightly sick. She had seen for herself the spell Curly seemed to cast over women. In the year and a bit she'd known him he'd gone through scores of girlfriends, all of them beautiful, all of them trying to domesticate Curly and failing. Amber suspected he was untameable, a wild tom cat.

They were standing outside the front door waiting for Curly to wrestle it open when Amber's phone rang. The ring tone was distinctive, and Alex turned, his face sharp.

'That her?' he said.

Amber shrugged, checking the screen. 'Yeah.'

'I thought you told me you blocked her number?'

'I thought I had.' Amber silenced the call. Again. It was the tenth call she'd received since the plane had landed, along with almost twenty messages.

'Give it to me,' he said, taking the phone before Amber knew what he was doing.

He held it up to her face. 'Look at it,' he said, and the phone unlocked.

'What are you doing?'

'Getting that bitch out of our lives and off your phone,' he said, swiping through the menus.

'I can do it, Alex!' she protested, trying to get the phone back, but he held it out of her reach. 'There. Done,' he said in satisfaction, handing it back to her. 'I've deleted all the texts she's sent as well. You haven't answered her, have you?'

'Don't be silly, of course not.'

'You better not have. She's out to tear us apart, you know that. I told…'

'Yes, yes, I know. God's sake, Alex.'

'What's up with you love birds?' Curly said.

'Nothing.' Alex shouldered past him into the house, leaving Amber standing alone.

CHAPTER 2: LIZ

Ice-cold salty wind bit into the skin of my face as I approached the last climb. The muscles in my thighs tensed and flexed, the pain, sharp as a knife, sliding under my flesh and into the tendons. I relished the deep ache, it powered me on – harder, faster – my rhythm steady, the sound of my feet thudding on the ground a soothing, repetitive mantra.

Barbed thoughts clung on, but I wrenched them free, letting them fall, keeping my head empty and ice-cold clear. A gust of wind echoed my gasping breaths as I pushed further, speeding up towards the brow of the hill. The world around me blurred and I kept my eyes fixed on the path, careful to spot any rabbit holes. I'd turned my ankle badly last year, flaring up an old injury, and hadn't been able to run for months. It had nearly driven me mad.

The wind fought me as I raced towards the cliff. Heart hammering and breath tearing, I battled forward until I reached the top. Like a blind rattling up, the view of the sea and sky was suddenly before me. I bent double and sucked in air, bouncing on my toes until my breathing slowed.

I took a moment to absorb the cold emptiness, stretching my arms up towards the expanse of goose-feather-grey clouds streaming away from me. The pull was so strong I faltered at the edge; I let the dizziness roll through me before taking a step back.

I checked my watch. I didn't have long. Skipping a stretch down, I settled for a long, loose jog back home. This time I hooked in my AirPods, blasting music, any music, into my ears to block out the world until I reached the safety of my flat.

I ran the shower and washed before turning the dial as cold as I could bear. I didn't stop until goosebumps popped up over my body and the skin on my fingertips began to look bruised. I dressed fast. Jeans and a jumper, nothing too eye-catching. My hair needed doing again, I ruffled it with my hands pleased to see the muscles in my arm stand proud; I was getting stronger. I checked my watch, I just had time for coffee.

My laptop crouched on the kitchen table. I ignored it, reaching for my bag of coffee beans, the only thing in the freezer. While I waited for the machine to do its work, I filled a tall glass of water, drank it in a couple of swallows and refilled the glass.

Despite all the sessions with Jenny, years and years in that room with its soothing paintings and neutral colour scheme, the urge was still there. It lay dormant, a sleeping tiger curled deep and heavy inside my belly. I skated my nails over the lid of my laptop, tapping it. I could picture the information flowering beneath my fingertips.

I stood up to pour my coffee and let the mug burn my hands a little. I didn't need to look, I told myself. I didn't need to know. Today, I needed to think about work, about the presentation I was due to make in a week's time.

Piled on the kitchen tables were three of my sketch pads. I always kept some at home otherwise I'd forget my ideas by the time I got to work. I pushed aside my laptop, excitement distracting me from the temptation of typing his name into Google.

I flipped through the pages of my most recent designs. My fingers itched for my pencil, but I hadn't time. The coffee was hot and strong. I reached for the heel of a loaf, which languished on the chopping board. I couldn't remember when I'd bought it and it was hard, so I dipped it in the coffee and took a soggy bite. My stomach contracted, but I kept chewing.

Most of my work was tedious and repetitive. I should be grateful for the business, I know - it's not like I can do anything else - but I'd had my fill of binding mediocre university dissertations. I could do them with my eye closed. But this, this was different. I had a chance to do something creative and I'd been planning and refining ideas for weeks.

Patrick, the man I'd bought the shop from, had tipped me off. He'd called me on a day when winter showed no sign of loosening its icy grip.

'Liz? I've 'ad a call,' he'd said.

'Hello, Pat. How are you? It's been a while.'

'An old mate of mine,' he went on. 'He owns that posh hotel with the funny name. What was it? B something. Can't remember. Anyway. He asked me to do some work for him. I told him I'd retired but I thought you should pitch for it – you still doing them arty things?'

I smiled. 'Yes, Pat, when I can.'

I'd called the manager of the hotel, an expensive boutique place near the cliffs. They were re-branding and wanted exclusive, high quality leather-bound bits and pieces for their guests. I would have to present my ideas for notebooks and journals, menu covers, trinkets – up to my imagination, he'd said – but they must all be linked by a theme, using the best grade of paper and a range of different coloured leather.

As Pat knew, this was the sort of work I loved. I often worked on things at home as a hobby, or to pass the time when the shop was quiet. Over the last few years I'd made some money selling belts and bracelets, sometimes a bit of jewellery. This commission was out of my league, to be honest, and I wasn't even sure I could make everything in the time they had suggested.

And yet. Ideas had spooled from my head from the moment I had put the phone down. The manager's lack of vision was irritating. He spoke for almost half an hour about luxury, and the sea, and being aware of the environment. All rather trite and imprecise but straightway I thought of jewel-coloured threads of silk, the softest leathers in reds, greens, and blues, how I could perhaps use pieces of delicate driftwood, or sea glass.

The parched cracks in my brain began to fill. After years and years in the wilderness of solitude and depression, the thought of working with my paper, leather, and tools to create something beautiful warmed me.

Finishing my coffee, I frowned down at my most recent sketch. I still hadn't got it right. I needed an emblem, a striking motif that would be at the core of every piece I made, something that would pull everything together and reflect the values of the hotel.

I rinsed the cup and chucked the crust of bread into the bin. I needed to visit the hotel, I resolved, walk around, get a sense of the view and the architecture. It made me feel better to have something practical to think about. I'd go round there after work. The thought of how little time I had made me anxious, but I knew once I had the core design everything else would fall into place.

*

The traffic was heavy, and I regretted lingering over my coffee that morning. I'd hit the school time surge and my shoulders knotted with tension as I tried to keep away from the stinking buses and stressed-to-breaking-point mums ferrying their children the half a mile journey to school. I could see their faces, quilted with rage as they shouted at the traffic, late for the registration bell.

My heart thudded as a lorry blasted his horn, he'd nearly hit me as we'd turned left. I felt the whoosh of air as it was sucked away from me by its great, metal bulk. Within minutes I was pulling on my brakes until they shrieked to avoid an idiot child who'd dashed across the road.

By the time I arrived, my nerves endings were so raw I was surprised that I couldn't see them, livid on the surface of my skin. I carried my bike through to the back storeroom and turned on the lights. The workshop was too small really, but I'd learned to order supplies little and often.

I turned the 'closed' sign to 'open' and walked about to check all was well. Tension drained from my shoulders. The space was clean and well-ordered. In Pat's day the shop was always in chaos. He'd pile all his tools in an old wooden box and every countertop carpeted with junk. When I took over, I'd had three walls lined with deep, pale wooden shelves and everything I used, every tool, every roll of leather, paper and buckram, every piece of type had its place.

I could put my hand on what I needed with my eyes closed. My beech workbenches were wide and smooth; I cleared them at the end of every day. I slung my bag onto the main table and took out my sketch pad, hoping to find some time to have another look at my ideas in between jobs.

I put the moka pot on my little gas hob and checked the list of jobs I had written in my work journal. The time of binding dissertations was not for a few weeks, things were quiet, but there were a few repairs to do, one quite tricky.

Pat always used to have Heart FM blaring in the workshop. When I worked for him, I used to hate it, and every day we would be locked in a battle – me turning the radio down, and him turning it back up. I preferred to work in silence listening only to the hush of the sea and the caw of the gulls soaring high above the constant bass thrum of the traffic.

Inside was peace. I could smell wood and dust, the warm tang of leather and the crisp dryness of paper. I had been looking forward to the first repair. A local woman had brought in a volume of poetry.

'It belonged to my mother,' she'd explained. 'She died last year, and my Dad reads a poem from it every day.' She sighed. 'He's read it so often it's worn away in his hands. He's had to go in for an op and I'd really like to get it repaired as a surprise for when he comes out. Can you do anything? I've been told you're very good.' She looked defeated in her ugly anorak and damp, sandy hair.

'I'll have a look,' I said, taking it from her. 'But I can't promise anything.'

Most of my orders come through my website and I dealt with people by text or on the phone. Rarely did anyone come into the light-filled, wood-smelling space of my shop. When they did, I would drift behind the nipping press, keeping its solid iron curves between me and their inquisitive eyes.

This woman was different, I pitied her, and her air of despair spoke to me. I would do a good job, I thought.

I laid the book of poems on my bench. The boards hung loose, ripped from the spine which had almost entirely unglued from the book block. I could see it had fallen apart through being handled so often. It had been treasured but was made cheaply and needed a lot of work.

As the scent of coffee drifted from the little kitchen, I laid my tools in a line, listening to the clink and click as I put them in place. When everything was where it should be, I poured my coffee and rested the mug on the bench behind me.

The book was bound in a plain grey buckram. I ran my fingers along the rolls I kept at the back of the shop. I had a good selection ranging from deep indigos and purples to royal blue and wheat yellow. I decided on a dusky blue I thought would go well with the book's original colour.

My heart rate slowed as I used my box cutter to slice off the boards and trim the loose, torn paper and material. The book block fell into my hand and slivers of the glue scattered across the bench as I plucked, picked and eventually scissored it away. When the block was clean, I put it to the side and brushed the scraps of cloth, paper and twist of glue into the bin.

The coffee was good and hot. Contentment settled around me in this quiet space. My mind stilled, a tranquil, hidden, rockwater pool, as my hands moved to measure the hinge cloth. It felt good to think only about making sure the lines were straight, that the cuts I made with my razor-sharp knife were clean and precise.

Once the hinge cloths were glued to the book block, I picked up the trimmed and clean boards, placed them around the block and put the volume in the hand press. Now for the spine stiffener and buckram cloth. I checked the grain with my fingertips, measured and re-measured the shoulders of the book before cutting.

Working with the buckram always made me think of the book given to me by my Gran. It was a handmade edition of 'The Crimson Book of Fairy Tales' and was the most beautiful thing I'd ever had. It felt so precious I wouldn't let anyone touch it. I loved the heavy white pages that whispered and curled in my hand with a shushing scrape and sigh. The illustrations almost felt etched, they were so detailed and heavily inked.

But best of all was the cover. The deepest, deepest crimson cloth covering, inlaid with a drawing of a wolf who circled out from the branches of a tree; a thread of gold wound around his paws and tipping his tail. I was fascinated by the neat packets of pages I could see when I squinted along the spine; each bunch stitched firmly to the back board. I even loved the woven green and red ribbon tucked within the shell. Later, I learned it was called a head band; I thought I was the only one to notice the secret, hidden detail.

It had blown my fourteen-year-old mind when I realised the book had been handmade by my Gran's friend. Pat. She had taken me to his shop, and I fell in love the moment I stepped through the door. A Rumpelstiltskin of a man stood in the middle of a tangle of strange and mysterious things. Brass posts with letters on the end, strange wooden and metal racks, sharp knives and rolls of paper and cloth.

It didn't seem possible that something as beautiful as my precious book could have been made in a blacksmith's workshop of a room.

'Hello, Mrs,' he'd said to my Gran. He nodded at me as I stood in the doorway. 'She's still got the book then?'

'It's very beautiful,' I'd stammered. 'Thank you for making it for me.'

He'd waved a hand and, seeing my shining eyes, took the time to walk me around and show me everything. I could never have dreamed that, years later, I'd be buying the shop and all its contents from him.

I used my bone folder to run a line along the cloth above the spine stiffener and folded the material neatly, pressing it down with the flat end to prevent any bubbles of glue. It was Pat's tool, inherited from his father. I loved using it. You could find them made of acrylic or bamboo but this one was bone – Pat always boasted it was hundreds of years old and made from the skeleton of a deer. I liked how it warmed in my hand as I cut creases with it, or flattened cloth and leather smooth over boards and spines.

Nearly done, I thought with satisfaction. Sometimes my head would be clouded with memories of the monster, and my ruler would lie at the wrong angle and the cut would be wrong. Cloth – or even worse, leather – would be wasted and I would give up and leave, knowing there was no point in going on until my mind was still again.

Not today, though. The boards, newly connected with the blue cloth, fitted snug around the book block and I'd got the overlap just right. I pressed the bone cutter along the spine until the groove on either side was perfect.

I could see the book would be beautiful. I decided to strip the backing from the original spine, leaving a spiderweb of material only just managing to hold the faded gold letters of the title. With great delicacy, I drifted it onto the gluey cloth of the new spine and tapped it down. It gave the book a roughened, slightly ruffled look and the faded gilt worked well with the blue and grey.

Straightening up I blinked as a dizzy spell rocked me backwards. I clutched the bench and was shocked to see how much time had passed. My head throbbed and my mouth was dry. I didn't want to leave but I had to eat, and I had nothing at home.

Vika ran the café two doors down from the shop and since I had moved in had appointed herself as my adoptive mother. Big, loud and unstoppable, I had discovered if I didn't pop into the café at least twice a week she'd bustle into my shop carrying cartons of soup and sandwiches to feed me up. She'd sit and chat endlessly; I found her bulk, her purple hair and multi-coloured kaftans unendurable after about five minutes.

No matter what I did or said she kept coming. She had been doing this for years now and wouldn't stop, even when I was rude and monosyllabic – occasionally I wouldn't speak at all - but she didn't seem to mind and kept talking away. I suspected Pat had asked her to keep an eye on me.

I was used to her now, and if we had to be together, I'd rather it was on my terms. I'd go and sit in her lively café and chat for a while. I found if I did, she was less likely to burst into my shop and poke around my things.

'Darlink!' she called to me across the scattered tables. It was well past lunch time but there weren't many spaces left. 'You look dreadful! Why do you do this to yourself? Ha? Look! Look at you. A bag of bones. A bag of bones!' She gestured round at the amused customers. 'She say she done like my food. Can you belief?' She wagged her head from side to side and squeezed out from behind the counter and took my hand.

'I have a good quiche today but the chicken? Not so good. Here try the zharkoye, it vill stick to your bones. Fill up that little tummy, ha?' She patted my stomach.

Resigned, I took the bowl and a large hunk of bread. A sudden crash from the kitchen sent Vika scurrying off. I decided I couldn't face staying, so slipped out, carrying the food back to the shop.

With the blind down and the sign turned to 'closed' I ate. The stew was rich and dark, with little white islands of floury potatoes. I dipped chunks of the bread and devoured the first few mouthfuls but within minutes I was full, so pushed the bowl away, half eaten.

I felt better, though and promised myself I would thank Vika and tell her (again) what a great cook she was. 'I know,' she would say, with a shrug.

Home beckoned, but I wanted to work on some ideas while I was there with my tools. There was one trinket in particular I wanted to perfect. I'd reproduced hand-painted maps of the city with all the best restaurants, shops, and high-class attractions clearly marked.

I'd spent days researching origami techniques to work out the best way to fold it. I planned to encase the map in the most handsome, hand-tooled, calfskin envelope. When opened, the map was attached in such a way it would blossom out, unfolding its petal secrets. It had amazed me how the pattern of folds could reduce a good size map into something less than the size of your palm.

It was a bit gimmicky, but I thought the hotel would like them instead of the usual tacky leaflets, dotted with biro crosses, doled out to tourists. I just had to work out how to get the right amount of stiffness in the leather, did it need a heavier card inlay? I thought.

It was dark by the time I finished, and the streets were empty as I cycled home. My body was sore, the muscles knotted along my arms and back, but I was happy. My design was working.

I ran up the stairs into the flat to change. My running gear lay limp on the bed. I was still full of Vika's stew, so only needed a glass of water. I bent to tie my trainers and my head throbbed. I rubbed my forehead, feeling the hollow groove running down its centre. Over the years it had all but disappeared, but my fingertips could still seek it out. It served as a reminder of how far I had come. I had no memory of how I had got so badly hurt, I didn't want to know. I could only make damn sure I never ended up in that place again.

I had no pain killers so I made do with another glass of water. Maybe I was just dehydrated.

I'd left the door to the spare bedroom open. I'd not been in there for months now. I pushed the door open a crack, letting it swing open. His pictures were spread everywhere. Photographs, printout from the internet, sketches I'd scrawled again and again so I didn't forget.

I forced myself to meet his dark eyes. Something I did every now and then to measure how I was feeling, test how much stronger I had become.

They bore into me. I took a step back and nearly tripped. I gritted my teeth and bunched my hands into fists to face him. My breathing hitched up a notch and I forced myself to regulate it, counting to ten and pulling air deep into my chest.

It didn't work. Adrenalin pumped into my blood urging me to run. I had to fight hard to stay calm, to remind myself he was far away and had no idea where I was. I hated the instinctive, fearful response to his face, even after so many years had passed.

I shut the door. Strength was my only defence. I had to keep working, keep hardening my body. With a towel thrown on the floor I held a plank until every muscle twitched and screamed. I kept my eyes on my watch, counting under my breath, not stopping until the stopwatch clicked round to three minutes. Weights followed.

    Sweat soaked through my shirt. It cooled the second I went out into the night, ready for my last run of the day. I made sure the door was locked and I tied the key to my lace. I started to run. My feet thudded on, my rhythm steady.

CHAPTER 3: AMBER

'Babe? Have you seen my make-up bag?' Amber called as she hunted through her suitcases. The pretty room Curly had prepared for them was in chaos. They'd only been back a few days but with so little storage and Amber's refusal to let any of her possessions get infected by the mess in the house, they'd ended up leaving everything in their bags.

'What?' Alex called back, his voice muffled. He was up a ladder with Curly on the top floor looking to see if there was anything valuable amongst the piles of junk her Gran had left behind.

'Oh, never mind,' Amber said to herself. She sat back on her heels and looked around the room for the tenth time. She was going to be late for her first day back. Curly and Alex were due to start a big job soon but until then they were clearing more of the house.

She winced as she heard a great crash as they pulled something free above her. 'There you are!' she muttered, retrieving her bag, which had made its way under the bed.

As she painted her face in the dressing table mirror she felt sick. She'd been away so long she wondered if they would have forgotten her. Shaking off the thought, she concentrated on her make-up. With her newly washed and curled hair piled on her head Amber applied her creams, powders, and highlighters until satisfied she had created an immaculate mask with which to face the world.

As she shook her hair back down and arranged it on her shoulders in front of the mirror, she saw Alex standing in the doorway watching her.

'Gorgeous,' he said softly.

She smiled as he walked forward and put his hands on her shoulders. 'You're all dusty! Don't get anything on my top.'

He tugged at a lock of her hair and gave her a kiss. 'You don't need all that crap,' he said. 'Makes you look like a doll.'

'Rude!' She laughed.

'I mean it,' he said. 'And you're a married woman now, I don't want all those dicks at work eyeing you up.'

'Most of them are gay, so I wouldn't worry.' Amber said, looking back into the mirror and wiping a smudge from her cheekbone.

'I'm serious,' Alex said and leaned closer. He held her face and Amber closed her eyes, expecting a kiss, but Alex stayed still. She opened her eyes in surprise just as he used his thumb to wipe her lipstick off with a sudden movement. It smeared a gash of red across her cheek leaving the pad of his thumb bloody.

'What are you doing?' Amber gave a shriek and jumped up from her seat. 'Alex, what the hell? That took me ages.'

'I don't want you wearing red lipstick to work – makes you look whorish.'

'It never bothered you before.' Amber was bewildered, she could still feel the roughness of Alex's thumb on her mouth. She looked at him in astonishment, her hand to her face. A moment stood still between them until Alex smiled.

'Ah but you weren't a respectable married woman then!' He swung her up into his arms and tickled her until she giggled. 'I can't help it, babe,' he whispered in her ear. 'I get jealous. Saggy old man like me with a young bit of stuff like you – of course men are going to flock round. I don't want you running off with them, that's all.' He rubbed his thumb against his finger until they both were red. 'That colour,' he said with a wink, 'that's just for us. In the bedroom.'

Amber blushed. Memories of what they did in the bedroom overwhelmed her; she'd never had sex like it. 'All right,' she said. 'But you mustn't be jealous. You know I'm mad about you.'

'You'd better be. Now sort your face and get off to work!' He patted her on the backside.

Sighing, Amber checked her phone. She didn't have long. Her Gran's house was a good twenty minutes further on from the salon than her flat had been. She dabbed away the gash of red across her cheek and tried to repair the damage with a finger-full of foundation, but it didn't look right. Her face was unbalanced without the pop of red lipstick.

Still a bit cross with Alex, she didn't call goodbye as she clattered down the stairs, rubbing on some lip balm. She had to walk as they'd sold her car to put towards the honeymoon and Alex needed his van to take more rubbish up to the dump.

It wasn't long before her high heels were rubbing sores into her skin and Amber was starting to limp a little as she reached the salon. Her heart lifted as she pushed open the doors and breathed in the gust of hot air, hairspray, nail polish and chatter.

The salon's bright lights, clean, uncluttered lines, polished counters, and bright mirrors were bliss after the dust, dirt, and mess of the house. How lovely to breathe in essential oils and straightening spray after days of rotten plaster and mould, she thought.

'OhmiGod, Amber!' Brenda leaped up from behind the reception desk and tottered over, gathering Amber up in a clash of gold necklaces and scented cashmere jumper. 'You're back! How lovely! Come on, let's take a look at you.' She pulled back and scanned Amber up and down; her beady little eyes didn't miss a thing. 'You don't look very tanned,' she said.

'Well,' Amber said with a shy smile, 'we didn't get out very much.'

Brenda roared. 'I bet you didn't, you dirty buggers! How is your gorgeous man, is he back to work as well?'

'He's working on the house for a bit with Curly, I…' Her words were lost as the others realised she was back and, exclaiming with delight, drifted over to give hugs and ask about the honeymoon. Customers under dryers or having their pedicures smiled and waved.

Amber had worked at the salon since she was 16, straight out of school with dreams of running her own place one day. The staff and customers were her family and she had missed them. She warmed herself on the warm wishes and congratulations that showered down.

Her first client of the day was waiting, and Amber sent her an apologetic look as the technicians twittered around her. She didn't look impressed, checking her watch and pointedly ignoring the pile of magazines on the table next to her.

Flushed with the embarrassment of so much attention, Amber escaped the gossiping group at last and settled her client in front of the mirror.

'How are you, Mrs Bushell?'

'All the better for seeing you, Amber. That Laura ruined my hair last week, I had to wash it through the minute I got home. She was even worse than the other two girls and as for that boy!'

Amber suppressed a smile as her fellow-stylist, Luke, overhearing, grimaced at her over his tray of dyes. Mrs Bushell was a cow, but as the wife of the owner everyone was expected to treat her like a queen.

'Same as usual?'

'Of course. But don't you go blowing it into a helmet like that boy did. I may be old, but I'm not blind. Why he thought I'd want a rock-hard shell of hair five inches above my head is beyond me. I looked like one of them American footballers.'

Amber hastily powered up the hairdryer to drown out Luke's snort of amusement. Mrs Bushell wasn't very nice, but Amber didn't like it when people laughed at her.

Her mind drifted as she worked away with her brush. Mrs Bushell's hair was wiry and coarse and Amber had to work hard to pull it into the soft curls her client insisted upon. The muscles in her arms ached.

Mrs Bushell never seemed to understand that Amber couldn't hear what she was saying over the hairdryer. She would drone on and on, always complaining about something or other. Amber used to turn the dryer off every time she spoke but over the years had learned there was no point; Mrs Bushell wasn't looking for a response, she just wanted someone to listen, so Amber would keep pulling and drying, smiling and nodding every now and then.

Half an hour later Mrs Bushell was finished, and Amber was proud of the result. She had felt awkward and stiff after so long away from work, but her hands fell into the old rhythms easily enough.

'What do you think? Is it OK?' she asked as Mrs Bushell reached for her bag and pulled at the cloak around her neck.

'It's better than it was,' she replied.

'The roots will need doing fairly soon,' Amber said. She suspected her client had very little idea of how grey her hair was under the bleach and colour. The pretty mix of blondes Amber had worked hard to create had grown out while she had been away and the greys were pushing out from her skull, a wiry army marching towards old age.

'I'm glad you're back,' Mrs Bushell said as she retrieved her coat from Brenda and buttoned it up to her chin. 'You're not going away again?'

'Oh no, Mrs Bushell, I'm not going anywhere.'

'No plans for babies?'

Brenda rolled her eyes as Amber laughed. 'Goodness! Don't you worry, Mrs Bushell. Plenty of time for that, we haven't got any plans. We're only just married!'

'Hmm, and a bit of a whirlwind by all accounts. You didn't even know him a year ago.' Mrs Bushell's face was a picture of disapproval.

'Ah now come on, Celia, don't go throwing cold water on love's young dream. He's a very nice boy – her Alex.'

'Hardly a boy from what I've heard,' Mrs Bushell sniffed. 'Anyway, book me in for a colour if you wouldn't mind, Brenda. After I get back from my holiday.'

It took ten minutes to find a date that suited Mrs Bushell, and Brenda and Amber gave a sigh of relief when the door slammed shut on her retreating figure.

Brenda's eyes were wide as she turned back to Amber. 'I don't know how you put up with that bitch,' she said, lowering her voice as Paul, the owner, passed by the desk. 'I know she's his wife and everything, but she walks all over you.' She opened her mouth to continue and the phone shrilled. 'Hang on.'

Amber turned to look out across the street as Brenda answered the phone; she had a mother and daughter due, but they'd called to say they were running late.

Brenda's face was solemn as she hung up. 'Oh, that poor woman.'

'What?' Amber said.

'Haven't you seen it on Facebook? A few days ago, Katie Brook disappeared. Pauline's daughter? You must remember Pauline, she's been coming here for years – big woman – black hair?'

'Oh my God! Yes, I know her. What happened?'

'She's been working nights as a bar maid at The Two Sawyers. God knows how she does it after her day of her nurse training, but she never got home after her last shift. Pauline had a mani pedi booked, and her sister was just ringing in to cancel. They've got the police coming round.'

'Oh, how awful.' Amber felt sick; she often used to go to The Two Sawyers with her mates, before Alex.

'It'll be in the papers soon, I reckon,' Brenda went on. 'She's a good girl, Katie, not one of those Instagram types, as I call them. Poor Pauline. Christ, I can't imagine what she must be going through, poor cow.'

Amber tried to remember Pauline but could only muster up a vague memory of a woman with dark hair in a bright, red dress that was a little too tight for her. She was sure she'd met Katie, once. They'd ended up together in the bathroom of a local club one drunken night a few years ago. She'd made Amber laugh with her stories of mishaps at the local hospital where she worked.

'She's a nurse, isn't she? Katie?'

Brenda nodded. 'She's just finishing her training.'

'I remember her, she had lovely hair. Luke had persuaded her to go for a Cleopatra bob, he dyed it pitch black.'

'That's right! Goodness, I'd forgotten, remember it looked really odd when it grew out? Dark black with flaming red roots?' Brenda shook her head. 'God, I hope she turns up soon.'

Amber put Pauline and her missing daughter to the back of her mind as she welcomed into the salon the mother and daughter pair, both booked for a cut and colour. The daughter was pink with excitement about her first appointment in a grown-up salon.

Four clients later Amber's feet were aching, and her arms were sore. She couldn't believe how quickly the morning had gone. Brenda had asked her to squeeze in a quick trim over her lunch hour, so she ended up having to make do with a fast, tasteless sandwich perched on Amahle's massage table upstairs.

'So, was it amazing?' Amahle said as she pottered about her room recapping oils and unfolding fresh towels.

'What? The honeymoon?' Amber said through a mouthful of dry bread. 'Yeah. It was great, I can't believe it's all over.'

'Are you super-excited about next week?'

'Next week?' Amber looked puzzled.

Amahle swung round. 'Yes, next week. You bitch, have you forgotten? It's only my hen weekend.'

'Oh my God! Yes, of course. I hadn't forgotten.'

'I should think not.' Amahle arranged towels in a heart shape around a collection of face creams and took a photo, uploading it with quick fingers.

'What are you doing?'

'I'm trying to get a photo up every day, establish my brand. The more followers I get the more likely they are to come with me when I set up on my own.'

'When do you think you'll go?' Amber sat up, chucking the rest of her sandwich in the bin, and crumpling up the wrapper. She swallowed hard at the thought of Amahle leaving. They'd trained together and joined the salon at the same time. A hook of jealousy pulled at her chest. All of them dreamed of setting up their own salon, but nobody had confidence like Amahle.

'I thought you were going to wait, and we'd start up something together?'

'I can't work here forever, Amber – Paul and his cow of a wife drive me nuts. Besides it won't make any difference, the minute you're ready you give me a call.'

Amber smiled. 'I will. If it ever happens. We're so skint at the moment. The honeymoon wiped us out – and Alex's obsession with my gran's house will cost a fortune. We've even got Curly living there, and don't look at me like that, I don't know what you see in him. Alex is much better looking…' Amber slumped back on the table. 'But I don't want to talk about all of that now. Cheer me up - what's the plan for next week then? Who's organising it all?

'If you hadn't disappeared off on your honeymoon for so long, you'd know all this,' Amahle grumbled. 'Shove over.' She nudged Amber along the table with her hip and took a pull on her juul. 'My sister's organised everything. We've booked some rooms in a hotel in town. It's got a spa, so we thought we'd spend Saturday getting glammed up and then dinner and some clubs.'

Amber sat up. 'God, I haven't been out clubbing for ages. I can't wait! It will be so nice to see everyone…'

'And Alex is OK with it?'

'Of course he is! Why wouldn't he be?'

'Have you told him you're going?'

'Yeah…' said Amber. She hadn't mentioned to Alex clubbing was involved. She'd glossed it over as a spa day with a sedate dinner. He'd hadn't been keen on her going without him.

Amber smiled as Amahle chatted on, glowing with the excitement of wedding plans and ideas for the weekend. Amahle's fiancé's family was rich and no cost was being spared. Amber had been staggered to hear how much the designer wedding dress had cost, enough to buy a very nice car, but Amahle was crazy in love with Sigi, and so radiant with happiness, Amber was delighted for her. She was looking forward to being her bridesmaid.

It was a shame the two couples didn't get on very well. Amber shifted uncomfortably as Amahle talked. Alex being a bit older was less of a problem when it was just the two of them, or when out with his friends. But when he came out with her friends – not that he did very often – the atmosphere became stilted, everyone seemed self-conscious. Amber could never work out why.

Now she was home, and everything was getting back to normal she would make more of an effort to see her friends. With or without Alex, she thought with a nervy defiance – she was still cross about the lipstick incident that morning.

'I'm so jealous of you having a big white wedding.' She and Alex had gone for a quiet, simple ceremony at the local registry office. She hadn't long lost her Mum, and had let Alex take over everything. 'Men aren't great at organising that kind of thing. I was a mess, and I couldn't expect him to know about flowers and dresses and all of that.'

'Well, he could have invited a few of your friends,' Amahle said, getting off the table and checking her face in the mirror. 'I only knew it was happening because you texted me!'

'I know, I'm sorry. I was all over the place. I didn't want any fuss. I still can't believe the only witnesses at my wedding were Curly, and Alex's favourite electrician from work.'

Amahle laughed. 'You make it sound terrible, but you were crazy about Alex, I could hear it in the way you talked about him. Besides, you can always have a big party later.'

'Good idea. In fact, that's a brilliant idea. I'll ask Alex. One good thing about the house is that it has a nice sized garden. Well, it will once we clear it out a bit. Maybe we could do something out there.'

Amahle gave her a hug. 'Tell you what, let's pretend next weekend is your hen do as well, eh? We'll go out, get pissed, and flirt with unsuitable men.'

There was a knock at the door and Amber jumped up, brushing off crumbs. She grinned. 'That sounds like a plan. I may not mention the bit about flirting with unsuitable men to Alex, though!'

An odd look flickered across Amahle's face before it opened into a smile. 'No, better not,' she said with a wink. 'Now you get going, my lady's here.'

Heading down the stairs, Amber grinned at herself in the mirror. Already she was planning what to wear next weekend. She had a fabulous new dress she hadn't had the chance to show off yet... She paused before going back into the main salon.

If she was honest with herself, she had to admit that what she was really looking forward to was the chance to be silly and giggly with her mates. She adored Alex, of course she did, but he did tend to roll his eyes when she gossiped with friends about Instagram or make up stuff.

Feeling guilty, she pulled out her phone to send him a quick text. 'You getting on OK?' with a stream of heart emojis. His response was instant. 'Good. Yes. Missing you xx'. Her heart was full in her chest. Funny how thoughts of her friends and the coming weekend became irrelevant when her head was full of Alex. She couldn't wait to finish her shift and get back home to him.

The afternoon dragged. Amber could feel her phone buzz in her pocket and knew it was Alex, but they were forbidden from taking calls on the floor. The skin on her forehead tightened and she kept yawning. A long day of work was a shock to the system after so many weeks of doing nothing.

At last it was the end of her shift and she was just curling up her hairdryer wire and putting the sprays and serums back in the cupboard when she spotted Laura crossing over to her. Amber sighed. This always happened. They were friends, but Laura could be bossy and demanding, often asking Amber to cover for her, or clear up when she couldn't be bothered.

'Amber, angel, could you do me a huge favour? I've got a client who needs her colour taking off and another just arrived early. Could you mix up Carrie's for me? Her card is in the drawer.'

'But I'm just finishing my shift!' Amber protested.

'Ah it'll only take a minute, please?'

'Oh. OK.' Amber knew from experience there was no point in arguing.

'You're a star! By the way...' Laura turned, letting her long, blonde hair swirl around her shoulders. Amber noticed her studying the effect in the mirror behind her. 'Have you spoken to...'

'Emma? No. Look if you want me to do this, I'd better...'

'Hang on,' Laura put her hand on Amber's arm. 'Look. I know you don't want to hear this, but she's really desperate. She keeps ringing and ringing.' She leaned in so close Amber could smell her perfume. 'She just wants to talk to you, Amber. Can't you give her a few minutes? Let her explain? You've known each other for...'

'There's nothing to explain,' Amber said, her voice sharp. Her heart knocked against her chest. 'You can tell her to fuck off, OK?' Laura's eyes widened; Amber never swore. 'You know what she did, Laura. Whose side are you on? I can't believe you're even asking after what she did to me and Alex.' She marched away, conscious of everyone's eyes turning to follow her.

Struggling to stop the tears from falling, Amber searched through the drawer for the colour mix cards. She had to blink a few times to be able to read it and was just reaching for the bottles when Laura appeared behind her again. Amber kept her eyes down, concentrating on squirting in the right amounts.

'I'm sorry, Amber. I shouldn't have said anything, it's just she was so upset…'

'I don't care, let me just finish this and go home.'

'Amber…' Laura waited, but Amber didn't look up, so she huffed a big sigh and walked back to her client.

As she left the salon, Amber shoved her fists into her coat pockets so Brenda wouldn't see her hands shaking as she passed the reception desk. Her look of pity made Amber's skin prickle. She loathed the fact everybody knew what had happened.

Emma's flat wasn't far from the salon and Amber dreaded the thought of catching sight of her when she came back to work. Crossing the road, keeping her head down, Amber headed home.

CHAPTER 4: LIZ

I couldn't find anywhere near the hotel to lock my bike so made do with a lamp post on the other side of the road. I pulled the chain tight to check the lock had clicked into place and allowed a dream to unfurl. If I got this commission, I could buy a much better bike, put it towards a deposit on a bigger flat, maybe even a house – a small one – up by the cliffs.

I pulled my thoughts back with a jerk. Stupid. Pat had said the hotel had contacted design companies big and small, the chances of them going with a self-employed local bookbinder were tiny.

Still, it wasn't like I had anything else to do. The cold wind buffeted against me, but the sky stretched bright and blue overhead. I could see the hotel from quite a distance; it stood at the end of the street, aloof, quite set apart from any other buildings.

I approached, taking my time. I wanted to get a sense of the shape of it, the weight of it. Two whitewashed wings curved to meet a chunky rectangle about 10 metres high with great glass windows wrapped around the top.

It reminded me of a private hospital from the 1930s. The Art Deco type built for rich people wanting to swap the murk of the city for sea air. Its white lines were crisp and sharp against the blue of the sky and the pulse of the sea roared in my ears.

I took stock of all the colours I could see, the smell of the air and the crunch of gravel under my feet. Each sensation slotting into categories, matching them with the threads and cloths, leathers and gilts on my shelves. I could taste salt on my lips, and I pictured holding the tiny cubed crystals up to the light, echoing the shape of the hotel's tower.

I tried to work out how I could capture the way the sun burnished the glass-blue of the sky with gold. I pictured layering feathers of gold leaf, so fine a breath would tear them to pieces, over the softest of calf leathers. A periwinkle blue, I decided, walking up to the main entrance.

But it needed something else. I stared at the door, thinking hard. Something to capture the rough, powdery white texture of the round walls. I ran the palm of my hand across the painted brickwork. Flour dusted my fingerprints, as if I had been baking bread; I wiped my hand on the cloth of my jeans. Chalk, maybe. Smooth lengths that would clink when rolled together.

The door opened.

'Do you have a reservation?' A man with a sharp face, his suit immaculate.

I passed him my card, kept my voice quiet so he frowned and tilted his head to hear me. 'I'm Liz Shaw,' I said. 'I called a few days ago.'

Holding the door so I couldn't see behind him, he took the card and studied it. 'I don't think it was me you spoke to.'

'Perhaps not,' I replied. 'But I did call. I asked if I could come and look around the hotel, see some rooms. It will help me to understand…'

'Weren't you sent a brochure?'

'Yes, but photographs can be misleading.' We studied each other. 'I was told I would be welcome to come and look round.'

He flipped the card between his fingers, back and forth, back and forth. 'OK.' He took a step back. 'It's quiet today so I don't think it will be a problem.'

I had to skip a step to keep up with him. He sped across the enormous lobby, dipping in and out of the lights as he walked through the streams of sunshine criss-crossing the floor.

The glass tower, much bigger than it looked from outside, caught the light and refracted it down in dizzying sheets. The architect who remodelled the building had been clever. I was expecting to find the blues of seas and sky, the use of white and sunshine – the standard repertoire of modern hotels by the coast, and here that had been done very well. But as I walked to the reception desk, I found walls lined with antique oak, and long white-covered benches piled high with jewels of cushions embroidered with gold. A Moroccan market riot of colour.

Ideas were filling my head and I couldn't help a smile. My fingers longed to capture the thoughts on paper, I was already selecting and discarding colours and materials to use.

'It's pretty special, isn't it?'

I nodded.

'This lobby is the central hub of the hotel with two wings on either side.' The suited man's well-practised speech rolled into my ears without a stutter or pause. He had gathered up some papers and a glossy brochure, indicating I should follow him as he walked to an open arch leading to the east wing.

'Each wing is made up of a series of one-storey rooms, each of them with an exquisite sea view. As you know, we pride ourselves on being an 'Eco-Hotel' and we aim to be fully carbon neutral in the near future. Everything possible is locally sourced…'

I let him drone on, peering into as many rooms as he would let me. The quality was indisputable. Everything I saw, from the texture of the curtains to the clouds of grey cashmere throws piled on beds and the backs of sofas, spoke of hundreds of thousands of pounds being spent.

The suited man, who had introduced himself as John Church only after I had asked his name directly, kept glancing me up and down, taking in my dusty jeans and hacked off hair. His eyebrows lifted as I spoke, the weight of my past heavy in my vowels.

'How much for a night in this room?' I asked of one that spoke to me more than the others. It was lined with books, real books, well-made and smug in their well-crafted shelves. He mentioned a figure more than I would hope to make in a year. I resolved to up the price I was planning to ask for my work.

We fast walked back across the lobby and through into the West wing and John Church took me onto the outside terrace. I wanted to take my time, but he made it clear he was in a hurry, with far more important things to do than show me round every room, bar and breakfast table.

It was good to be outside in the sunshine. The terrace was broad, overlooking steps that dropped down towards the cliff. The bottom terrace held an infinity pool. I imagined the view from there would be dizzying.

'I'll leave you to it, let you take it all in.' John gestured to the sea, sky, and cliffs as if they belonged to him. I sat down at one of the tables scattered about and searched my coat pocket for some paper and a pencil. John looked down at me. 'Can I…. er… would you like something? To drink or eat?' The words dragged from him by hospitality training rather than any desire to keep me here.

'Yes, a coffee. Thank you.' I hoped it was on the house.

A cafetière arrived. The coffee steamed, hot and dark, as I poured. I held the mug in both hands, letting the warmth scorch them. The terrace stayed empty and I carried my coffee to the wall to get a better look at the sea. There was a wooded area to the left and as I got closer, I could see the opening of a path. I hated woods; they gave me the creeps. The thought of following the track into the trees made my skin crawl.

'Enough there for two?'

The shock of a man's voice, so close and so unexpected, made me yell. Birds flew into the air with a blurring thrum of wings. My arm jerked, and hot splashes of coffee soaked my sleeve. I pushed away. Hard. Felt a body give beneath my hand and I gasped for air. My vision flickered and I tried to run. Smashing my knees against the wall, I fell.

'Christ! I'm sorry! I didn't mean…' A hand on my shoulder made me freeze, it moved within seconds, but I could still feel its weight. The voice kept talking. 'It's OK, it's OK. I didn't realise… I thought you were…. Are you all right?'

An acid wash of coffee choked me, and my pulse beat so strong in my ears I couldn't hear. I flung up my hands, shielding my head and face.

'OK. OK. I'm stepping back. I'm sorry. I should have thought.' There was a rustle of movement and the air shifted.

I looked up, keeping my fists raised. A man about my age sat two metres away, legs crossed like a child. I forced my muscles to unclench and smoothed my face with the palm of my hand. My arm burned and I had to hold my wrist to stop the shaking.

I flinched when he stood up and he raised his arm in a gesture of peace before turning to the terrace and pouring out a coffee into the mug I'd managed to drop into the grass. He approached me, mug outstretched, stopping short so there was a wide gap between us.

'Thanks,' I said, scrambling to my feet. 'Sorry. You made me jump.' I brushed grass and mud from my clothes and reached for the mug, gulping back the still hot coffee.

'I did more than make you jump. You looked like you thought I was going to kill you!' He laughed but stopped when he saw my face. 'No, it's me who should be sorry. I thought you were someone else. I don't normally accost strangers.' He kept his movements minimal, as if worried I was about to bolt.

'Here, do you want some?' I held the mug out.

'That's OK, I've got a cup.' He pulled a battered tin cup, white with a blue rim, from a pocket and poured the rest of the cafetière into it. 'Lovely,' he said, smacking his lips. 'I'm Will by the way.'

'Hi, Will,' I said, draining my mug and setting it on the wall. My hands had stopped shaking, I noticed. I swallowed hard and attempted a smile. 'I'm Liz.'

'Hello, Liz.'

'I'm sorry about… well, you know. Just now. I overreacted.' Heat crept up my cheeks and I ducked my head, concentrating on pulling a knot of grass growing from a crack in the wall. 'I was a bit tense.'

'So, are you a guest? Come here for some R and R?'

My laugh was a bark. 'Do I look like a guest?'

Will smiled. 'Oh, you get all sorts here.'

'No, I'm not a guest. I work as a bookbinder in town, I'm hoping to win a commission to do some designs for the hotel. Menu covers, maps, door key fobs – that kind of thing. Some luxury trinkets.' I stopped.

'Sounds interesting, I thought bookbinders just bound books.' He smiled again and took a tobacco pouch from his top pocket. I watched as he spun a rollie between his fingers. Lighting it, he took a deep puff before breathing out with a sigh of satisfaction. 'First one of the day – always the best.'

'Are you a guest?'

He shook his head. He had thick, dark stubble and long hair pulled back from his face with an elastic band. His eyes were bright and blue, the whites clear.

'I'm a baker. I've been supplying the hotel for a few months. From croissants and baguettes, to the best olive and oregano focaccia roll you've ever tasted. I'm the man everyone comes to.' He took another drag and the smoke drifted over to me. I couldn't take my eyes from his face. 'A craftsman's hands,' he said, spreading his fingers. A warmth liquified, deep in my belly as I watched the movement. I imagined them touching me.

'They look a bit grubby,' I said.

A white grin flashed.

'And they let you in? Looking like that?' I glanced at his baggy jeans, worn through at the knees with a blue rope threaded through the belt loops.

'Only if I come round the back,' he threw me a smile. 'No, only joking. I'm too good for them to care what I look like. It's a big part of their reputation,' he said, nodding at the building, 'serving high-quality, locally sourced bread.'

'Arrogant as well, then.'

Will shrugged and glanced at me over the remaining stub of his rollie, smoke drifting into his eyes, making him blink. His eyelashes tangled together.

I put my notebook, splashed with coffee, back into my pocket and stood up. Will look surprised.

'Where are you going?'

'I've got to get back to work,' I said. 'I've already been here longer than I was expecting.'

'Did you get everything you needed?'

'I think so. I've got some ideas.'

Will stood, stuck out his hand and I shook it. It had been a long time since I'd touched anyone's skin and my nerves fired mad signals; I had to pull away. With my back turned I curled and uncurled my fingers, giving them a shake to release the tension.

'Bye, then,' I said.

'You married, Liz?'

I looked back at him in surprise. 'No. Why?'

Will shrugged again. 'Boyfriend?'

'No.'

'Gay?'

I smiled at that. 'You're nosy.'

'Not gay then.'

I tutted and carried on walking, skirting the hotel and heading for the gate leading onto the street. Will loped along beside me.

'Let me take you out for a drink.'

'No.'

'Please. To say sorry for scaring you like that.'

'No.'

'I think you need someone to talk to.'

I stopped and rubbed my forehead. 'I'm fine.'

'I didn't say you weren't fine, I said you needed someone to talk to. Look, here's my number. I daren't ask for yours because you look like you're about to breathe fire. Take it. Call me if you want to talk.'

He wrote his number on a crumpled receipt and passed it to me. I put it in my back pocket so he would let me go.

It was a relief to get through the gate. I pulled it shut then looked through the wrought iron. The muscles in my back eased a little to have a barrier between us. Will stood, quiet and calm. His body was lean, strong; he was tall, a lot taller than me. I liked his battered boots and the softness of the worn corduroy of his coat.

'I'll see you soon, I hope,' he said.

'Maybe.' I put my hand on the cold iron, letting my fingers push through the gaps. Surprised, Will took a step forward and, with a grave steadiness, met my fingertips with his own. A shocking heat flared between us, making me gasped.

I snatched my hand away and he chuckled.

It took me a while to find my bike. I couldn't seem to think straight. My throat was full and my eyes couldn't fix on anything, they kept skittering about. Crossing and re-crossing the street, I began to sweat, and my mouth felt dry. I needed to get moving.

I'd walked past it twice before I realised it was there. I crouched to unlock it wondering if I should go to work as I'd planned. The thought was intolerable. Swinging my legs over the saddle I set off, pushing as hard as I could. Faster and faster until the wind whipped across my face and my head was empty.

I'd cycled fifteen miles past the town and out along the coast path before I felt able to go back home. Thoughts of Will loitered. I had to do something. I tore off my coat as I climbed the stairs and slammed the flat door shut behind me.

I forced myself to go into the spare room. A single chair stood by the window and I sat in it, grabbing a handful of photos from the wall. One by one I studied them. Staring into his eyes, making myself remember. My bowels shrank and sweat dripped down my back. Another picture, this time from Facebook, his face split into a grin. I focused on the eyes. Their dead blackness.

Tears blinded me as I stumbled out and into the kitchen. Taking a deep breath, I opened the laptop. I hadn't touched it for months, but it was necessary.

The screen lit up and I began as I always do; I typed in his name. The sky outside the window darkened and went black as I clicked link after link. Twitter. Facebook. I followed all his friends as he didn't post often, but they did, tagging him in their photos.

My teeth were gritted so tight a headache crawled over my scalp. I'd been sitting for too long; my hips cracked as I stood up to make more coffee. I rubbed warmth into my arms and continued my search.

Instagram. Click. Click. There. My stomach plummeted. Three of them. A young woman. My fingers cramped around the mouse, clicking the window shut, making me swear with frustration. I couldn't wait to reload the page, so unlocked my phone and tapped through to the Instagram account again, my chest banging.

'The Newly Weds Return…'

I couldn't take it in. My fingers reached to zoom in on her face. She was so young. Beautiful too. Of course. Her skin shone pearl white. His arm was around her, tight. It hurt to look at him, grinning. As if he could see me, sitting in the dark, watching him.

I checked the date, a few weeks ago they had stood and beamed into a camera. I held a damp tea towel to my sore, gritty eyes, running it over the depressed scar on my forehead that throbbed, before returning to the screen. I was beginning to hear his voice, so I got up and searched for my AirPods, throwing piles of clothes aside, making a mess, before I found them in my coat pocket.

Plugging them in I played the first song that came up on my phone, loud as I could bear it. It didn't work. I could still hear him. I held my hands to my head.

'You're everything to me, Liz. I'm lost without you – you've lit up something inside of me…' The honeyed words, sweet and terrible. I stood, pushing my chair back so it fell with a clatter. The bottle was still in the drawer, half full now. Drink was all I allowed myself. No pills, not even aspirin was allowed past my door, but I kept whisky just in case.

I tipped it into my coffee cup and gulped at it, letting its flame burn away the honey. It helped me to recover the chair and sit up straight. The music stepped forward, drowning his voice. I rubbed my face and clicked back to Facebook.

I hadn't contacted Sarah for years. We'd stayed connected through Facebook, but we'd had no need to communicate. She'd moved on, as had I.

Her face smiled out at me. She hadn't changed her profile picture since the last time I'd looked. She was in front of the foot of a mountain, her arm slung around a man who – judging by the similarity of their colouring and bone structure – was her brother. Sam? No, Dan, Daniel, that's right.

I scrolled through her posts. Odd. She hadn't written anything for ages. Her timeline was filled with re-posts and shares. I scrolled further back. Birthday wishes flickered past. She hadn't commented on them – just the jaunty little thumbs up.

I tried the photographs. Her cover picture was of a beach; I hadn't seen it before. A trail of footsteps walked out to sea but no sign of Sarah. She'd posted photos a while back, but they were of landscapes, dogs, shop fronts, a display of flowers…

I clicked Messenger open. Ignoring the string of messages between us from years ago, I stared at the screen for so long it began to dim. I shook the mouse to wake my laptop and typed.

'Sarah, I hope you are well?' Send.

'Can we talk?' Send

'It's important.' Send.

I sat back. The cursor continued to blink. A few minutes crawled past. The bright screen burned itself onto the back of my eyes.

'Seen'

I leaned forward, knocking my coffee cup flying. 'Sarah Andrews is online' the messenger box read. Her profile picture appeared beside my last message - she'd read it.

'Sarah?' I typed.

'Are you there?'

No response.

I took a deep breath.

'*He's married.*' I wrote.

I waited, my knees thudded against the underside of the table as they jerked up and down. Sarah's picture popped up next to my message. I waited for her reply, imagining her at the other end of our cyber connection, frowning at my message. Another pause.

'Sarah Andrews is offline'

CHAPTER 5: AMBER

Amber pulled at the neck of her jumper as she got to the gate leading to the front garden. She'd had to take off her coat and scarf, hooking them onto her bag. Sweat itched down her back. It was still light, despite her long day at work.

She tore off her jumper with a sigh and sat on the second step leading up to the front door, chucking down her handbag and shopping. The garden was so overgrown the trees and bushes leaned together to form a canopy. Amber stretched her arms, letting the cool air drift along her skin. She closed her eyes.

God, Laura was a pain. Yet again she'd collared Amber as she left, this time to wash her lady's hair as, surprise surprise, she was running late. She shouldn't spend so long flirting with her male clients, Amber brooded. She wished she had the guts to say no.

'What are you doing, sitting on the step?' Alex appeared behind her.

Amber smiled. 'You look gorgeous.' Wearing cut-off denims, his feet were bare. She could see he'd already gone brown in the early spring sunshine. 'Have you been out in the garden?'

'For a bit,' he said sitting on the step next to her. He offered her a sip from his bottle of lager.

'You go brown so quickly.' She leaned her head on his shoulder enjoying the silk of his hot skin. He smelled of summer.

'Work OK?'

Amber rolled her eyes. 'Yes, all fine, just Laura keeps making me late.'

'You're too bloody nice to her. What was it this time? Sweeping up hair? Mixing up a colour? Keeping her clients happy while she finished flirting with the towels guy?'

Amber winced. 'Am I going on about it too much?'

'Nah, not really. You just need to stand up for yourself, she's treating you like a mug. Tell her you have a fit bloke waiting for you, can't let him down – problem solved!' They smiled at each other and Alex ran his finger down her arm, making her shiver. 'You've got to come and see what we've been doing,' he said and pulled Amber up to her feet.

'What? Drinking lager in a sunny garden?'

'Funny. No – come on. Me and Curly have been working all week on this. I wanted to surprise you.'

'Haven't you been on a job? I thought it started Wednesday.'

'Problem with the site – starting next week now,' he called over his shoulder as he disappeared into the darkness of the house. 'Good, though as it's given us more time here.'

Leaving her bag and shopping by the door, Amber followed. She had to admit the house was looking better; at last she could walk through the hall without falling over piles of stuff. She wondered what they'd done with it all – just chucked it up the dump, she assumed.

'Where have you gone?' she said to the empty rooms.

'I'm in the basement!' Alex's voice was muffled.

Amber opened the panelled door under the stairs. She hadn't been down there since they'd moved in. When she was little her Mum had sent her to look for the step ladder as her Gran needed it to pick the apples in the garden; Amber had hoped she would make apple crumble for tea.

The basement had been terrifying. Darkness stretched for miles, and the sound of soft scratching at the edges of her hearing had made her hair stir. She hadn't dared move away from the stairs and didn't know where to begin to find a step ladder. She hadn't been entirely sure what one looked like. Was it a ladder with a step at the bottom? She had wondered.

About to yell for her Mum, Amber had shut her mouth, thinking if anything did lie in the darkness, she didn't want to alert it by calling out. She'd scrambled back up the stairs and her Mum had to go back down to find it. 'Silly sausage!' she'd said. Amber smiled at the memory.

The stairs creaked beneath her feet and she recoiled as cobwebs blew into her face. 'What on earth are you doing?' she shouted, spitting out dusty threads. 'It's like something from a slasher movie.'

'Just get down here!'

She reached the bottom where she could smell fresh wood and sawdust. It was a good, clean smell after the claustrophobia of the staircase.

'Are you going to turn the light on? I can't see a thing!'

'Keep walking forward, that's it. A couple more steps… stop!'

There was a click and the room lit up like a stage set.

'Wow!' Amber gasped then laughed. 'Look at you two, grinning like a couple of idiots.'

Curly and Alex stood in the middle of a room that bore no resemblance to the pit of cluttered gloom Amber remembered. The floorboards were new, and stud walls had been fitted to cover the original bricks. 'It looks like an Art gallery!'

'It's a gym, you daft cow,' said Curly. He pointed to a lone exercise bike and a pile of weights in the corner. 'Can't you tell?'

Their energies may have been better placed getting the kitchen functional – or clearing out the main sitting room – but they looked so pleased with themselves she didn't have the heart.

She walked around, feeling the smooth walls. 'I can't believe it. I feel like I'm in a different house!'

'Curly did the lights and I did all the carpentry,' said Alex. 'It took ages to get it cleared but once we'd got that done, the rest was quite straightforward.'

'It's odd though. I haven't been here since I was a kid, but I remember it being huge.'

'It's hardly small now,' scoffed Curly, exchanging a glance with Alex.

'Of course, it will seem a bit smaller,' Alex said, pulling her to him and burying his face into her hair for a moment. 'Haven't you ever gone back to school or a playground you knew when you were little, and it seemed tiny? I'd imagine you're a lot bigger now than you were when you last came down here.'

'I suppose so.'

'And putting these stud walls in takes off a chunk but better that than those horrible old bricks.'

'Of course!' Amber said, nodding her head. 'Of course, you're right. I wasn't being critical or anything. I'm just trying to get my head around how you've changed it. Was it a sort of L shape before? I thought it was…'

'Anyway,' Curly's voice was loud in the room. 'You going to try it out?'

'Try it out? What do you mean?'

'Do some weights! See the mirror?' Alex said. 'It's just like being at a real gym! I've even put a barre here, see?'

Conscious her role was to admire the work done - 'give the men their jam' as her Mum would say - Amber walked into the corner where she could see they'd put down an exercise mat opposite a wall lined floor to ceiling with a mirror.

Alex slapped his hand against the barre that lined the corner. 'Really strong, that is. You try and pull it.'

Amber gave it a tug. 'Very good,' she said with a smile. 'You've done a wonderful job – both of you. It's like something you'd find in a mansion! I can't believe you've managed to do so much in just a few days. I can't wait to see what you do with the rest of the house.'

Curly beamed. 'I told you she'd like it.'

So, are you hungry? It's getting late. I'd better go and make something for dinner.'

'Microwave again?' said Curly with a grimace.

Amber headed for the stairs. 'Not much I can do if you choose to make a gym instead of a kitchen.'

Alex grabbed her around the waist and swung her around, making her giggle. 'But you like me with muscles, don't you?'

'Alex stop it!' Amber cried, aware of Curly's speculative eyes. 'Come on, I've got to get the dinner on, and I still haven't packed!'

*

'Do you have to go?' Alex sat on the bed fiddling with the zip on her suitcase. He'd been quiet all evening. Amahle was picking her up first thing the next morning and Amber wanted to have everything ready before she went to bed. Much as she adored being married to Alex, she missed her friends. Amahle's hen do was going to be fun and she was looking forward to spending a few days in a nice hotel without building dust and the smell of paint filling her airways. Her favourite dress was hanging from the back of the door and she lifted it down, careful not to catch it on anything. The silk weighed nothing in her hands and glimmered in the light.

'You're not taking that? You'll get it ruined.'

'Don't be silly, it's not like I'll be climbing a mountain in it.'

'It's a bit skimpy, isn't it?' Alex pulled it from her hands and held it up. 'Look! You can practically see through it!'

Amber tried to grab it from his hands, but he held on tight, and she was afraid it would rip.

'I wear a slip under it, you twit!' Amber laughed. Alex's face darkened and he threw the dress to the floor behind him where it puddled into a graceless mass of cloth.

'What do you need a tarty dress for anyway? I thought it was a girls' night in at a spa?'

'It is!' stammered Amber. 'But I want to look nice. They'll all dress up…'

'Oh, do what the fuck you want.' Alex jumped so quickly to his feet Amber fell back and almost lost her balance. 'Not enough for you, am I? You have to go and whore around in that dress, pick up some young, self-satisfied prick?' He flipped her dressing table, so it crashed over, sending perfume bottles, make-up and jewellery skidding across the floor. The door slamming as he left drove nails of tension into her shoulders.

Shaking, she picked her away across the mess, looking for broken glass and cracked jars. Keeping her mind blank, she reset every piece, throwing away anything that was now unusable. Amber gathered up the dress and ran the liquid ripples through her fingers. With a sigh she threaded it onto its hanger and put it back in the wardrobe, before sinking onto the bed. 'Fucker!' she thought. 'How dare he!'

In silence she carried on packing, aware of Alex sitting somewhere in the house, clouds gathering around his head. She could almost hear the clink of the bottle as he poured out a whisky. 'I hope he chokes on it,' she thought.

In a flurry of self-righteous irritation, Amber finished packing her case, hesitating only for a moment before reaching for the dress and folding it into aa tight square. Pausing to listen for Alex's step on the stairs, she pushed it into her bag.

An hour later there was no sign of Alex. Amber had texted Amahle to say she couldn't wait for tomorrow and was looking forward to catching up with everyone. She even sent an uncharacteristic selfie, fingers raised in a defiant gesture.

Sitting in the uncomfortable chair by the bed, skimming through her phone, Amber's spirits sagged. She wondered what Alex was doing. Had he gone out? She hadn't heard him leave. Curly had clunked up the stairs to bed ten minutes ago and she could hear him trudging about in his room. After half an hour he stopped, and silence rung through the house.

Not wanting to be the one to offer the olive branch - she hadn't done anything wrong, after all - Amber opened the bedroom door and leaned her head out into the landing and looked down the stairs. The house was dark. She took a step forward, taking care not to make a sound and leaned on the bannisters, craning her neck to see the ground floor.

Her stomach swooped with worry. What was he doing? Was he still fuming? Amber crept down the stairs, not a crack of light showed anywhere. Navigating by the flare of the lamppost shining through the glass of the front door, she reached the bottom of the stairs.

She shivered with the cold. She was about to turn for the kitchen when a soft sound made her turn. The sitting room.

The door creaked as it opened and at first Amber could see nothing beyond the sheeted bulky shapes of the covered furniture. Glancing around she flinched to see Alex slumped against the wall by the bay window, a glass in his hand. He looked up at her, his face filled with such despair she ran to him, holding his head against her breasts, her hair falling around them.

'I'm sorry,' he said, his voice breaking. 'I don't know what comes over me, I hate myself.'

'Sshh,' soothed Amber, her heart aching. 'It's OK.'

'It's just I love you so much,' he said, his voice raw. 'And I can't bear the thought of you leaving. I'm sorry. I don't deserve you.'

Amber held him close, willing him to feel her love. All traces of resentment disappeared.

He clung to her like a child. 'I don't know what I'd do without you,' he muttered. 'I need you to keep sane. The thought of you being with someone else… it just drives me mad. I can't stop thinking about it.' He looked up at her, his eyes wet. 'Do you have to go tomorrow? Can't you stay here? With me?'

Amber paused, wrestling with herself. She hated it when he was like this – so tortured and full of self-loathing. The temptation to agree and call the weekend off was strong. She took a breath. 'I can't, babe, I've promised Amahle – it's important. I have to, really.' The only thing stopping her from giving in to Alex was the knowledge that Amahle would be furious.

Alex rubbed his eyes until they bloomed red under his fists.

'I know. I'm sorry. I shouldn't ask. Ignore me.' He smiled up at her, his eyes hollow. 'Forget I asked.'

'Don't. Don't talk like that,' Amber whispered. She ran her hand across his head, feeling the cool, blond strands slide through her fingers. She remembered the first time she'd touched his hair, sitting in the pub, having broken away from their friends, absorbed in a world of their own.

The memory of meeting his dark eyes, so close to her own, was still powerful. His voice had been low, urgent, as he'd breathed in her ear. 'I think you're the most beautiful girl I've ever seen,' he'd said.

She'd thought he was drunk and would have forgotten all about her when he woke up, but the next day an armful of red roses had arrived at the salon. 'Tonight?' read the card.

Amber, more used to awkward Tinder dates in high-street chain restaurants had been taken aback when Alex arrived in a designer shirt, smelling expensive. He was a stranger, bearing no resemblance to the T-shirted, dusty-jeaned builder with melting eyes she'd met the night before.

'Are you as nervous as I am?' he'd said, making her laugh. Later, he took her hand, and she felt warm for the first time since her Mum had died.

Crushed together, standing by the bar at a terrible nightclub, holding a drink in each hand, he'd looked down at her.

'I don't know whether to drink my beer or kiss you.'

'You could do both.' Amber had said.

And he did. It was the most romantic moment of Amber's life, her movie moment, she told Amahle, Laura, and Emma. They swooned and screamed in excitement, pleased for Amber who'd had such a shit time of it.

He couldn't see her the following night but was there, outside the salon the next day. This time he took her to a tiny restaurant. With only four tables the atmosphere was intimate and confiding. He drew from her stories of childhood; she made him laugh with stories of her grandmother who'd lived in a big old house filled with junk. After a second bottle of wine, she told him how the loss of her Mum had devastated the landscape of her days.

The next night she'd learned of his upbringing in foster homes after his mother died and his father couldn't cope. He talked of how he longed to create a home, something he'd missed all his life.

'I don't know what it is, Amber. There's something special about you. I feel like a… a connection – don't laugh. Maybe I knew you in another life. You make me feel… like, protective and protected at the same time.' And he'd kiss her again. Kisses that melted her like chocolate, sweet and slow.

She couldn't get enough of him, would be embarrassed to find herself twined around his body as they kissed goodnight, his thigh sliding between hers, her hands moving under his shirt to feel his shoulders. Alex would laugh and move her gently away. 'Don't, babe,' he'd whisper against her open mouth, burying his face into her neck. 'You're driving me nuts, but we mustn't rush things.' And he would leave, sending more flowers so they would be there at work when she arrived. The others would sigh with envy.

'I feel like I'm losing my mind,' she would say to Amahle.

Amber spent every hour away from Alex thinking about him. Making him laugh felt like she'd won the lottery. She dreamed about his big, hard body when she slept.

'I can't stop thinking about you,' he'd say. 'Whenever I close my eyes, I see your face.'

There was never a moment of hesitation or doubt in Amber's heart. When Alex appeared in the salon, just as she was applying Mrs Tytheridge's highlights, and got down on one knee, she said yes before he'd finished asking her to marry him.

The salon had erupted into a storm of applause. Another movie moment.

'But you haven't even slept with him!' Amahle had said, worry creasing her beautiful face.

'I don't care,' Amber had replied. 'He's the one.'

They'd slept together that night and it had been rapturous. They hadn't got out of bed for three days, both phoning in sick and ignoring the knowing smirks of their workmates when they returned.

'I'm so glad I found you,' Alex broke into Amber's reverie as they clung together in the quiet sitting room, sliding his hands up between her legs, making her groan. His eyes had darkened as she held him, all trace of tears gone. With a sudden movement he toppled her onto the sheeted armchair and took her face in his hands, kissing her until all thought was forced from her mind.

In silence, he slid the baggy T-shirt from her shoulders, watching the orange streetlight trace her odalisque curves. Her nipples darkened and hardened. He smiled to hear her groan; she was already lost. She reached for him, but he batted her hands away, folding them together and holding them above her head. Her breasts lifted and he dipped his tongue to their tips, sliding his fingers down her belly and between her thighs.

He never took his eyes from her face as her hips undulated. She threw her head back, mouth open, as he slipped soft fingers through her wetness to the hardening bud. Her throat flushed red, and her pelvis reared towards his probing fingertips. As a punishment he stopped and she froze, knowing his game. His expression was intent, grim almost, as he began to move his fingers again. He let go of her hands to cover her mouth as her moans grew louder.

He played his games until he knew she couldn't take much more. By the time he entered her, driving his hardness in, she was wild. She bucked and twisted under him, allowed him to turn her, pull her on top of him. She clawed his skin, pulled him deeper, held her nipples to his lips, his teeth - screamed as he drove into her with his final thrusts. Only then did he smile, closing his eyes, letting go as she pulsed again around him, knowing he'd marked her as his own.

Gasping, shining with sweat they broke apart. Amber curled her nakedness into Alex, hair a dark veil shrouding her flushed face and swollen lips. Within minutes she was asleep. There was a step in the doorway, Curly's silhouette filled the frame. Alex raised his head, careful not to disturb Amber. A look passed between them. Seconds stretched into minutes before Alex shook his head. Curly nodded before padding away into the shadows.

*

Amber's stomach muscles ached from laughing, the room spun, and she grinned at the swirl of dancing, joyful people around her.

'I'm so glad I came, Amahle,' she said for the hundredth time. 'I wasn't going to come, you know – Alex…'

'Wasn't keen on you leaving him. Yes, you've said, you daft cow. I'm glad you came too. God! It's not like we go out very often. He can't really complain.'

'I think I should text him,' Amber looked down at her phone, but her hair swung in front of it and she couldn't see. Amahle reached across the table and whipped it from her hand.

'No, you don't,' she said, her eyes slightly crossing and her speech staccato. 'You'll just end up getting all lovey dovey with each other. And I'll have lost you. You'll go to bed and do sexy FaceTime when you should be out with me. It's my hen night and I demand that you put your phone away. You can text him later. But for now. You are mine. And we are going to enjoy the rest of the evening. The night is young.'

She was interrupted by the return of Amahle's sister Zola and cousin Vanita, alongside the other two bridesmaids, Laura and Grace. They were giggling and bumping against each other. Laura lurched forward so hard she knocked over a bottle of wine; they all screeched.

Vanita collapsed next to Amber reeking of spilled, sticky cocktails and Versace's 'Woman'.

'God, I'm wasted!' she said, 'You having a good time, Amber?'

'Yeah brilliant, I'm so glad I came.'

'I've heard all about what happened,' Vanita went on, leaning into Amber and misjudging it; her elbow slid off the table.

'What do you mean?' Amber said, retrieving Vanita's lipstick and mobile that had fallen to the floor, along with a pack of tissues and a handful of coins.

Vanita burped into her hand and waved for more drinks. 'You know. About Emma.'

The table fell silent. Amber was conscious of the others glancing at each other, and her face grew hot.

'I don't really want to…'

'What a fucking cow, eh? D'you know she was going to come along tonight? Was still going to come! After all she did.'

'Vanita, now isn't the time,' Amahle said, shooting Amber an apologetic look.

Vanita shook her head and started passing fresh cocktails from the barman's tray down the table. 'I said to Amahle I didn't trust her, didn't I? Eh? Good job Grace was willing to step in as replacement bridesmaid.' Her tone was growing belligerent. 'I can't believe you walked in on them! God, how awful. What happened?'

'Who told you that?' Amber said, checking round everyone's faces and stopping on Laura who wouldn't meet her eyes.

Amber remembered her Mum meeting Laura for the first time. 'I don't know why you like that girl,' she'd said. 'Under that trowel full of make-up, she's got a hard little face.'

It didn't look hard now, it looked mortified, thought Amber. 'It's OK,' she mouthed and Laura who gave a weak smile.

'She's been trying to see me. To explain,' Amber said to Vanita, aware the whole table was listening in.

'What a bitch!' Vanita's eyes flashed. 'Explain? What. Is she gonna say oops sorry, Amb, your boyfriend was lying naked on the bed and I fell onto his cock?'

Amber flushed. 'Maybe she wants to say sorry. And he's my husband now.'

'More fool you for marrying him,' Vanita's expression was scornful. 'Once a cheater, always a cheater. Sorry, girl, but it's the truth.'

'He's not a cheater!' Amber's palms were sweating.

'To be fair,' interrupted Laura, who seemed to have recovered some of her former insouciance, 'Emma had fancied him for ages. She made a bee line for him. I don't think he stood a chance.'

'Didn't she get him drunk?' Zola said, nodding at Amahle. 'Was it you who said that? It was at Dom's party and Alex had gone to bed, passed out he said, and when he woke up Emma was in with him? He thought it was Amber but just as he realised it was too late, as Amber had already come in?'

The eyes of the table swivelled, fixing on Amber. Words jammed in her throat.

'It was all a mistake,' she managed.

Zola shook her head, 'I don't think you should have anything to do with that slag.'

Amber winced at the word. It wasn't right. The Emma she had known since primary school had been anything but. She hadn't gone out with anyone until she was eighteen. She had liked Alex, though. Amber remembered. She used to light up when he spoke to her. He was good at that, focusing the beam of his attention so you felt like the only person alive in the world.

Amber closed her eyes. Emma's face stunned and stupid behind Alex's shoulder. The duvet cover unbuttoned and gaping its innards. She snapped her eyes open and stared at the coloured spotlights until the memories went away. She picked up the brimming cocktail in front of her intending to drain it. She didn't feel anywhere near drunk enough anymore.

'Drink, drink, drink,' they chanted until the glass was empty and they cheered, relieved to break the tension. Amahle stood up and pulled off the comedy veil and L-plates the girls had pressed on her before they left for the club.

'Right, girls!' She swayed, then paused, looking puzzled. 'What was I going to say?' They looked up at her, grinning. 'I know! As you may have heard, Amber got married!' There was a cheer. 'But because it all happened so quickly, she never got a hen night.' A chorus of boos. 'So, I told Amber that we were having a joint hen night, because she missed out – so I've had the first half of the weekend, now it's Amber's turn!'

She lurched around the table holding up the veil and L-Plates and, despite her protests, fastened them onto Amber. 'There!' she said in triumph. 'Now you're ready for the dance floor!' They cheered and, as one, rose to their feet. Hands grabbed Amber and moments later they were staggering into the middle of the moving crowd.

Lights spun, making Amber dizzy as she looked up, laughing at the cross play of colours that pulsed in time to the music. Her body moved fast and liquid. A grin split her face as she watched Vanita take off her shoes to wave them over her head. Amahle and Laura swayed together, yelling the lyrics.

'More drinks?' she called. She was desperate for the loo.

'Nah, don't worry,' Vanita yelled. 'The lovely man will bring them. Hey! Lovely man!' she waved at the barman.

'He's not going to bring them out here, you muppet! It's OK, I'll go. Same again, everyone?'

The mass of yelling people at the bar was overwhelming. Amber staggered back. 'Whoops!' she whispered to herself with a giggle, crossing her legs. She looked round for the loos.

She had to make her way back to the front entrance and ask one of the bouncers, who nodded towards a corridor flanking the main bar area. Amber smiled her thanks and trotted over hoping she wouldn't find a queue.

She realised how drunk she was as she struggled to negotiate removing enough clothes to be able to sit down and pee. Refastening everything seemed to take an age. At last, she was ready and pushed the cubicle door back to go and wash her hands at the sink and retouch her make-up.

She hardly recognised the face in the mirror; her lipstick was gone, and smudges of mascara trailed down her face. Amber laughed, feeling woozy. She wet some tissue to rub away the black marks.

With a start she realised she wasn't alone. In the mirror her eyes met those of a young blonde woman. Shock waves hammered through her – she gripped hold of the sink, wondering if her mind was playing tricks on her. Amber watched in the mirror as the woman twisted her hands together, she recognised the gesture.

'Emma,' she said.

CHAPTER 6: LIZ

'I didn't know whether I would be seeing you today,' Jenny said.

'No,' I replied.

'You've missed the last three sessions.'

'I know.'

'I was worried you had stopped coming altogether.'

I shrugged.

'So. Why have you come today?'

I looked around the room, conscious of Jenny's sharp gaze and reluctant to meet it. The room hadn't changed since my first appointment. I wondered how many times I had sat in this worn, red armchair and stared at the picture of a waterfall hanging behind Jenny's head.

It would have been more than once a week to begin with, I thought. At the start I was coming two, three times a week as I skittered on the edge of darkness. Let's say an average of once a week, then. Over – what – five years now? Fifty-two times five…

'Liz.'

'Sorry,' I said.

She leaned forward, her hands clasped under her chin, her elbows resting on her knees – a characteristic gesture. She wore a pale denim shirt over dark jeans, a narrow green scarf wound round her neck. It suited her, complementing her short grey hair and silvery-blue eyes.

I touched the groove above my eyebrows, tracing the jagged shape until I saw Jenny watching, her eyebrows lifted. I stopped.

'How are the nightmares?'

'They come and go,' I replied. She waited for me to go on. 'They've been quite bad these last few weeks.'

'The house one?'

'Yes.' I bit my lip. 'Well, sometimes. Mostly it's the ones I told you about, dreaming I'm still there, with him.' I chewed the side of my thumb.

'Tell me again about the other nightmare.'

I shook my head. I didn't want to talk about it. They were the worst, more frightening that the ones about him. Houses crashing down and splitting my head open. Running into a wood so impenetrable I was forced to turn back only to find more trees bearing down on me.

'I don't have that one very often anymore.' I was lying. I'd dreamed of the falling house the night before.

'You're always searching for something in that one, aren't you?' Jenny mused, making a note on her pad. 'And you wondered once whether it was anything to do with the accident that caused…' she indicated my scar.

'I don't know if it was an accident,' I interrupted. 'I don't remember anything from then, I told you.'

Jenny nodded, sensing my agitation, and smiled. 'OK. But we need to come back to this at some point. It worries me you are still having these nightmares after all this time.'

'There's no point,' I muttered. Jenny stayed silent, her eyes steady on mine.

'I'm working on a project,' I said at last.

'Oh yes?'

'I got a call. A local hotel is asking designers to submit ideas for a new range of exclusive bits and pieces. I thought I'd have a go, I've already worked on some sketches.'

'Sounds good.' She waited.

'It would be a lot of money if I got it,' I went on. 'But I'd be up against some really big, established companies so it's pointless. But… you know… I thought I should try.'

A silence stretched between us.

'What made you come here today?'

I listened to the shriek of gulls outside, a gust of wind spattered rain on the window. Darkness lifted behind my eyes; I closed them, trying to suppress the wave.

'You're safe here. You know that.' Jenny's voice was calm, neutral.

I nodded and took a deep breath. 'I met a man.'

Not by a flicker did Jenny's expression change. Her eyes remained on me, peaceful and clear.

'I see.'

The urge to stand, leave, get on my bike and fly away was irresistible; I shifted on my seat. My thigh muscles knotted, hard as iron, and I longed to stretch my legs with a fast run along the cliffs. I pictured forcing my body on until everything screamed, nothing around me but sky and sea.

'You came here because you need to talk about this,' Jenny said.

I nod again.

'Tell me.'

My hands clutched at the arms of the chair, pulling at the threads of a worn patch, marking it worse.

'It was at the hotel.' I began. 'I'd gone to look around, get a feel for the place – its colours, the light, what materials were inside.' I looked up and Jenny nodded. 'I was outside, in the garden, and this man, Will, he came up to me and said something. Made me jump out of… out of my skin.' My breathing caught and tore ragged. 'And I… I didn't know he was there and I… freaked out, tried to run. I wasn't thinking… couldn't think. My mind just went blank, there was nothing in my head but that terror …'

I didn't realise my body was jerking, my nail rubbing over and over at my thumb, until Jenny leaned forward and laid a gentle hand on my knee.

'Shhh,' she breathed. 'Take a second. Collect your thoughts.'

She kept her hand there until the sounds of the gulls filled the room, then nodded at me to go on.

'He thought I was mad.' A laugh tore out of me. 'I must have looked mad, scrabbling around on the grass kicking him away. But he waited. Sat there until I calmed down and poured me coffee.'

'Describe him to me.'

I took a moment to think. 'Blue eyes and tied up long dark hair. Scruffy looking. Tall, about the same age… He was kind.'

'You're attracted to him.'

I stared at her. The directness of her gaze hurt, but I didn't look away. I swallowed and smoothed flat the denim covering my legs. 'Yes.'

Jenny didn't move, but the air in the room thickened, made heavy with a sudden tension. I pushed down against the urge to run.

'And how did you feel about that?'

I shook my head.

'Liz?'

I couldn't speak.

'When was the last time you found a man attractive?'

My body forced me from the chair; I was at the window, my forehead pressed against the cold glass.

'Liz?'

I breathed in through my nose and let it hiss from my mouth. The glass clouded. My heart thumped in my chest, hard enough to make me feel sick. I tried to picture my workshop, quiet and sunny. I thought of smoothing my bone folder along a piece of leather, but it didn't help.

In a blink I was there, jostled in a crowded stinking hall. The Freshers' dance. The noise was intolerable, I was pressing through the bodies, aching for fresh air, but just as I got to the door a hand grabbed mine and pulled me back. I turned and there he was, his dark eyes intent. My body responded immediately, leaping at his touch. Our lips curved into identical smiles as he reached for me.

'Liz. Liz. Sit down.' Jenny was behind me, her hands firm as she guided me to the chair. She held both of my hands, her face close until my heart slowed, and my breathing stopped its dreadful, wheezing gasps.

'OK?' Jenny said.

'Yes.'

'That was the last time? With him. What you felt for… Will, was it? Was the first time you have felt that level of physical attraction since…?'

She stopped. Letting her words settle. Letting me absorb them.

'Yes,' I said.

'Good.' Jenny leaned back in her chair; a rare smile flickered for a moment. 'You're waking up,' she said.

I gave a snort, wiped my face with a shaking hand. 'Rubbish,' I said.

'Liz, listen to me. It's been years. Years. You are a different person to that woman who was so… exploited and abused by that terrible man. The woman who used drugs to escape from reality. It's time to move on. You know it is.'

'I can't,' I said.

'You can. You must. You're living half of a life. If that.'

I stared out of the window.

'It's been long enough,' she went on. 'You can't keep that part of you closed off forever. I find it interesting your reaction was such a strong one. He must have been something special, this Will.'

'It's so mixed up in my head,' I said at last, the words prising themselves out of me. 'We had a sort of… connection. God, that sounds fucking trite.' I shook my head. 'It made me feel happy, just for a second, I couldn't breathe. I almost didn't know what it was, I wasn't sure what I was feeling… it was so… unfamiliar.'

I gusted a sigh and slumped back onto the chair. My arms and legs lay heavy and limp. I wondered if I would ever be able to lift them again.

'And then?' Jenny wasn't letting me get away with that.

'I had to leave,' I sat up with a jerk. 'I couldn't stay there with him. It was intolerable.'

'Intolerable? Why.'

'It was too much, I couldn't hold all those feelings together, I thought my head would explode if I didn't move.'

'What feelings? Describe them.'

'Lust,' I said with a reluctant grin. 'Warmth. Then…'

'Then?'

'The usual: Fear. Paralysing panic. Claustrophobia. I thought I was going to die. Suffocate. Or that my heart would beat out of my chest if I didn't get away.'

'It sounds very frightening.' Jenny said. 'It will be less frightening the next time.'

'What do you mean, 'next time'? There's not going to be a next time.'

'Did he give you his number?'

'Yes.'

Another pause rippled into the room. She was letting me think things over. Come to the right conclusion. It used to drive me mad when she did this. 'What am I paying you for?' I used to ask. 'You never say anything'.

'I'm not calling him.' I said.

'OK.' She sat back and made a note on the pad on her desk. It had a beautiful, walnut-brown leather cover. I'd made it for her, tracing her initials in gold leaf across the corner.

'You can take out the paper blocks inside when you finish them and store them in your files,' I'd said. 'Just slot in a new one and the cover should last you for years.' It was the only time I had seen her flustered. I wondered if she brought it out in our sessions so as not to hurt my feelings. The leather was slightly worn already, though, so perhaps not.

'How's the internet searching going?'

My cheeks betrayed me. 'I haven't looked for months but then that day with Will knocked me sideways and I went back to see, you know, make sure I didn't forget.'

Jenny nodded without comment, still writing.

'I found out he got married.'

Jenny's pen stilled.

'I tried to contact Sarah to tell her, but she hasn't replied. It's strange, as I'm pretty sure she read my message. I don't know why she hasn't been in touch. She would have been as shocked as I was, I was expecting her to call me the minute I told her – she knows how dangerous he is. Almost as much as I do.'

'Liz. He is out of your life now. You must leave it. This… obsession – understandable though it is – will destroy you. Who he marries, where Sarah is – none of this has anything to do with you.'

'But I have to do something!' I exploded. 'Warn her! Talk to her! Something!'

Jenny put down her pen and caught my eyes with hers.

'No. Stop, Liz. All of this is another life, another woman, another time and place. It is not who you are, and you must stop defining yourself by his narrative. I'm not telling you anything you don't know. You have a chance to break out of this… bleakness with which you surround yourself. This half-life governed by fear and those damn walls you build… it's a waste. Such a waste.'

We've probably had around 300 sessions over the past five years, I calculated. I've spent more time with Jenny than anyone else in my life, except my Grandmother. It's certainly the longest relationship I've been in. In all that time I had never heard her talk for so long. Perhaps we'd reached the end of our time together.

She took my hands in hers again and gave them a squeeze. 'Time's up, I'm afraid but promise me, *promise* me you'll think about what I've said? Instead of googling that monster and stalking him on Facebook, call Will. OK? Try letting that guard down. Just a little.'

She walked me to the door. 'And we need to look into your nightmares, we focused so much on your relationship we still haven't explored what happened to you after you escaped. I think there is much to uncover.'

*

I didn't think about what she said. I walked out of there, got back to work and spent as many hours as I could in the workshop, keeping my mind blank.

It worried me Sarah hadn't responded to my last message. I kept checking Facebook but there was no change. I jumped through to her brother's page, there were more posts there, scattered every few weeks or so. Scrolling right back I found the picture of him and Sarah together, the one she had used for her profile picture, but she didn't feature in any of his subsequent posts.

After a second of hesitation I opened Instagram, finding the 'newly-wed' post again and looked for any updates. Jenny's words sounded in my head, but I ignored them. A buzzing of dread ran black through my veins. I kept returning to the pale, beautiful woman who smiled into the camera, a dark cloud of hair falling past her shoulders.

She wasn't his usual type. I couldn't stop looking at her, trying to read the expression in her eyes. She seemed very young. And weak. I tutted in frustration, there was nothing new for me to see. Just some boring photos of building sites. I saved the links; it might be useful to know where he was working.

Pushing the laptop away, I stood and stretched. There was an acrid, ashy taste in my mouth. I should stop looking, I thought.

Maybe Jenny was right. Maybe I should let the mess just go, sink into my past. I pictured a weight the size and shape of an anvil sinking through layers of ocean down, down, until it wedged itself into the soft sand at the bottom – half buried.

It made me feel free, lighter. A sensation so unfamiliar I had to pause to absorb it. A tiny flicker of something, something bright and vivid stirred its feathers in my chest. My thoughts, dangerous and sly, slipped to the hotel garden. The memory of Will's face warmed my skin as if I was standing in the sun.

'No,' I said aloud, clearing the table. My voice croaked and I poured another glass of water. I had things to do. Mooning over someone with whom I had exchanged a handful of words struck me as ridiculous, alien.

I turned to my work. It was going well. The hours spent at the hotel were bright in my mind, the brightest being my meeting with Will, but thinking of him led to complicated feelings I couldn't deal with. At least not until the work was done. I sensed a warmth ahead, a bright thread woven into the fog I had learned to live with.

The keystone of my design hung clear and vivid – at last I knew exactly what I wanted. I had the pieces lined up on my bench, the sign on the door turned to closed. My blood hummed as I flexed my fingers.

I touched each piece, feeling their textures. A twisted strip of brown leather, as raw as I could get it, and two knuckles of green-blue sea glass, carrying the light of the ocean. I found them endlessly fascinating and rolled them back and forth on the wood, watching them catch the sun. Three rings of chalk, smooth and white as bone and, the final touch, a small nugget of gold its curves heavy, warm, and liquid in my hand.

The gold cost a fortune, but it added a luxurious weight that would be in keeping with the exclusive, absolute top-end feel of the hotel.

I spent hours experimenting with different combinations of glass, gold, and chalk on the leather strip until it was perfect. In this form it would serve as a key fob and I made ten more to see how they worked attached to other objects.

I'd made suede leather folders in a selection of colours, the softest blues and greys I could find. They could be cut to a range of sizes, some would hold envelopes and writing paper for guests to use, others could contain menus or brochures. I'd made a small one for the discreet presentation of astronomical bills at the restaurant. I loved them, the leather was beautiful, though something wasn't right. They were too plain; but when I stitched the glittering bracelets of leather to the spines they were transformed. They became magical and distinctive, inviting hands to hold them up to the light to see the glass and gold shine.

The origami maps had taken forever to get right. On these I looped the leather strip so they could be hung from the wrist, like old-fashioned fans. As the strip had to be quite short there was room for one nub of glass and a tiny pebble of gold. The leather envelope had to be stiff to hold the map, so I opened and closed it over and over again, rubbing a thumbprint of oil into the creases and folds until the movement was smooth.

The map opening out to reveal the tiny, hand-drawn streets and buildings of the city never failed to entertain me, it was like something out of a fairy tale. I glanced over at the two framed pictures on the shop wall. My illustrations taken from an old Ladybird edition of 'The Elves and the Shoemaker'.

As a child I had read the book so many times the pages had thinned, my eyes staring at the pictures until they were imprinted onto my retinas. I'd gone to an exhibition of illustrations and bought my favourites. In one, the shoemaker is cutting shapes out of a roll of the most lovely, violet leather to make shoes for a wealthy gentlewoman wearing a silk dress lined with ermine. In another he sits at a bench, very like mine, with four pairs of leather cut-outs lined up in front of him: Blue, red, yellow, and black. Tools are scattered across the bench and scraps of different coloured leather lie on the floor.

Is that why I fell in love with Pat's workshop? Because it resembled a book from a fairy tale? Maybe I should make something for the elves, I thought with a snort of laughter, unrolling my stores of leather so I could run my hand over them, admiring their rich colours. I was tempted to use my knife to cut out the shapes of shoes, just like the picture, just in case.

I was being fanciful - I'd been on my own for too long and not eaten well. Vika was away visiting her sister and the café was closed. My coffee pot and bad sandwiches from the newsagent across the road had kept me going. The levels of concentration and focus needed were exhausting, and I had done nothing but work, go home to sleep and exercise before returning to my workbench.

It took over a week to get the prototypes finished and ready to present to the hotel. They were too precious and expensive to cart over on the back of my bike, so I ordered an Uber to take me up to the other end of the city.

My legs ached from hours standing at my work bench. The man I was supposed to be meeting – I couldn't remember his name – was running late. I imagined him schmoozing with fat-cat designer companies from London and tried to brush off the leather crumbs and glue stains from my jeans, unnoticed, until I'd walked through the door into the pristine lobby. I sat down on the sofas, placing the box next to me with care.

Twenty minutes passed. I'd fallen into a doze when a crash from across the lobby snapped my eyes open. Will stood, staring at me. He smiled and took a step forward, stamping so the sound of his boots rang out into the air. To the amazement of the reception staff, he continued towards me with a slow, exaggerated heavy walk, as if he was trying to kill passing ants.

'What are you doing?' I said, smothering the sparks leaping in my blood as he came closer.

'I'm making sure you know I'm here. Didn't want to scare you again.'

'Oh!' I said, trying not to laugh. 'Well, you've made an impression,' I gestured at the reception staff. 'What are you doing here?'

'Meeting with the chef – I come every Friday to talk about orders for the next week.' His hair was untied and fell across his cheekbone, he pulled it back, knotting it with a band. 'So. Mrs. You didn't call me.'

'No.'

'Why not?'

'I've been busy. And I didn't want to talk to you.'

'Oh. OK.' He sat down on the white bench of a sofa to my right, pushing my box along. 'Why not?'

I shrugged. 'Because I've got enough people in my life.'

'Have you now,' he said.

'Yes.'

There was a pause.

'How many?'

'Sorry?'

'People. How many people in your life?'

'That's a stupid question.' The beauty of his cheekbones and the shape of his mouth made me want to close my eyes. I took a breath to see him noticing the box of my designs, he ran his finger under the top flap. 'What are you doing?'

'Are they in here? Your designs? Is that why you've come to the hotel?' He opened the box to find layers and layers of tissue.

'Careful!' I said, reaching for the box. 'Don't touch them.'

'I've washed my hands!' he said, exasperated. 'I'll be careful. Let me just look at one…' He reached for the origami maps, which I'd packed last and laid on the top.

'What is this?' He held up the little, manganese-blue leather envelope.

'Open it,' I said, reluctance salting my voice. I hadn't shown anything to anyone, he was the first; I wanted to know what he thought of it. 'Just press on that tab.'

I watched his face. As the map unfurled, I smiled to see his eyes light up with pleasure. 'Oh my God, Liz this is incredible! Look at the detail!' He ran his fingers along the lines of the paper, weaving in and out of the streets. 'And the way it unfolds! It's like a flower. And so big! How did you fit in in? And will I ever be able to get it back in its case?'

'It's quite easy,' I said. 'But there is a bit of a knack.' I twirled the corners together and they sank back into the wallet. 'It may be too complicated…' I said to myself, frowning. 'It's a variation on a Turkish Map Fold.'

Will was digging into the box again and drew out one of the larger folders. He lifted it to his nose. 'God, this smells amazing, and it's really soft.' He took another sniff. 'Honestly, I love that smell. It feels nice to hold too.' He examined the spine, feeling the bumps of glass, chalk, and gold. 'And this.' He looked up at me and his expression filled my belly with a sweetness warm and heavy as honey. 'I had no idea you were so talented, Bookbinder girl.'

'I'm no girl,' I snorted.

'The craftsmanship,' he went on, studying the stitching. 'You did this all by hand?'

I nodded.

'This must have cost a bomb. What will you do if they don't choose you?'

'I can sell it. I often sell Arty stuff like this on Etsy. Eventually, anyway.'

'You look exhausted, have you been working on this since I last saw you?'

'Pretty much, it's always quiet around this time in the shop and if it pays off, I'll be set up for the next five years.'

'Well I hope they do,' Will said, running his hands over a smoky-grey folder before wrapping it back in tissue paper and closing the lid of the box. 'It's a clever design, it looks modern but also as if you found them at the back of a sea cave, in a smugglers' chest.'

I smiled. 'That's exactly the concept I was going for.'

He bounced up. 'Come out with me.'

'What?' I took a wary step back.

'Tomorrow. Come out with me. It's going to be lovely this weekend, I haven't got anything to do, and you look like you need a break.'

'No.'

'Why?'

'I can't.'

I picked up the box, holding its bulk as a barrier between us. 'He's here,' I said, nodding towards the reception desk. 'I'd better go.'

'I'll wait.'

'Don't,' I said.

*

The meeting took hours. Hours of questions fired at me about my ideas, my materials, whether I could meet the deadlines. I thought there was no hope until the owner of the hotel, a stout Irish man in a shabby suit, finally broke into a grin.

'The contract is yours,' he said. 'Don't let us down.'

I couldn't believe it. Every trace of exhaustion fizzed away in a great rush of elation. I leaped to my feet.

'Thank you! Thank you so much! No, I won't let you down, I promise.' I couldn't stop smiling. I shook hands with everyone in the room.

I walked out into the lobby in a daze. Joy burst like fireworks in my bloodstream. I wasn't surprised to see Will sitting on the bench, his eyes fixed on me.

He jumped up when he saw me. As I walked over, he beamed.

'It went well, didn't it?' His grin was infectious. 'I can tell by your face.'

'Yeah, I got it,' I said, in an attempt to sound casual, but my smile was so wide it hurt.

I was filled with such astonishment, such dizzy bliss I didn't notice him tuck my arm into his as he walked me out of the front door and onto the street.

'Where's your box? All the things you made?'

'I left it with them,' I said, lifting my face up until the sun dazzled everything into a joyful wash of light. 'He wants to show it to some others before they make a decision.'

'But they liked your ideas?'

'They loved them,' I said, and my face felt strange. Tiredness and shock had given everything a delirious quality.

'Well done,' Will said. 'I'm made up for you. It's not often the suits appreciate lovely, clever things like yours.'

I turned away from the sky and sun and looked at him. I could have dived into the blue of his eyes. There was something clean and stripped about him, a raw quality. He was strong, but I could find no aggression. My blood was singing so loud it almost drowned the voice that warned I didn't find aggression last time either.

I shook it off. Decided to listen to Jenny after all.

'Yes.'

'What?'

'Yes. I will come with you. Tomorrow. Into the good weather, where you have nothing to do.' I said.

CHAPTER 7: AMBER

'I don't want to talk to you,' Amber said, picking up her bag and making her way to the door. With an impatient gesture she pulled off the trailing veil and L-plates, dropping them on the grubby floor. The ice of shock had washed away the last traces of fuzzy tipsiness rocking her brain; she'd never felt more sober. The bathroom, which had seemed so glamorous and sleek, smelled of sick, and the tiles were filthy.

Emma looked awful. Shadows carved bruises under her eyes, and she'd lost weight. Her hair hung in lank yellow strands. 'Amber, please. Please, just give me a few minutes. I knew you'd be here, and I've come all this way…'

'I don't care how far you've come!' Amber turned in fury, dropping her voice as two drunks staggered in. 'You shouldn't be here. I've got nothing to say to you.'

She needed to get out of there, she couldn't look at her old friend for a moment longer. Pushing open the door, Amber quickened her step, conscious of Emma close behind. The empty corridor stretched ahead, she needed to get back to her friends. Emma wouldn't dare follow her.

The double doors leading back to the club swung shut, muffling the music and noise of the dancers to a dull throb, Amber's pulse beat crazily in her ears, out of time with Emma's steady, following steps.

Over the past months Amber had demonised Emma into a monster, a lying slut, a sly-eyed bitch who'd gone behind her back to sleep with her best friend's man. But this washed-out wretch? The one who looked no different to the nine-year-old kid in pigtails who'd rescued a squealing Amber from a spiders' nest? She couldn't be more different to the femme fatale Amber had created in her head.

She faltered, and stopped, turning so suddenly Emma walked straight into her. Tears were running down her face and Amber suppressed a swell of pity. Sensing weakness, Emma started to gabble.

'I'm so sorry, Amb, I couldn't think what else to do. You weren't answering your calls and I left loads of messages at the salon and Laura said she tried to talk to you, but you wouldn't…'

'What the fuck did you expect?' Amber said, grateful for the rising rage burning away any softening in her heart. 'You were my best friend. And you slept with Alex knowing we were getting married. What kind of fucking friend does that? I can't believe I'm even speaking to you right now. Just fuck off. I don't ever want to see you again.'

'Amber, I'm sorry. But I need to talk to you, to explain.' A sob convulsed her narrow chest. 'I really miss you, and if we could just talk, I'm sure you'd understand. You have to give me a chance to tell you what really happened. Please. I'm not doing too good without you.' A fresh wash of tears spotted dampness across her top and she ran a careless hand across her face. She took a breath, struggling to regain some composure. 'Look, I know I shouldn't be here, I should never have barged in on Amahle's hen night like this. But it was the only way I could work out how to see you face-to-face. I thought if we met in person, you'd be able to see I'm telling you the truth, I'd be able to explain everything. I thought at the very least our friendship would mean enough for you to give me a fair hearing.'

Amber couldn't help a snort of disbelief. 'You are unbelievable! Fair? Was it fair that I walked into that room to see my best friend and the love of my life screwing like… like animals?' Amber's voice cracked and wobbled; she wanted to slap Emma for making her break down - for hurting her so badly. She scrubbed her eyes to stop the traitorous tears. 'We've been friends for years, Emma, I've known you since before I can remember – you knew how I felt about him and you… you…' She stopped, looked up at the ceiling and let out a pent-up breath, clicked through the well-worn movie of Alex and Emma twined together. Her heart hardened, cold as iron. 'Well come on! What's your explanation? What possible reason can you give me for fucking Alex? And don't pretend you didn't, I saw everything. Come on! I'm all ears. You've come all this way you said…'

Emma gave a helpless shrug. Her hands turned together faster than ever. She was a picture of misery. She opened her mouth to speak then closed it.

'You've got nothing,' Amber jeered, though - despite herself - her heart sank. What was she hoping Emma would say? What could she say? 'You just fancied a bit,' she went on. 'Thought nobody would find out – Alex was too drunk to tell tales, wasn't he? You're just a sad cow who couldn't keep her hands to herself. You crawled all over him, took advantage because he'd passed out, pissed. Well, good to know our friendship meant so little to you.' Stepping back Amber turned to the double doors, the lights swam in front of her eyes. She heard a sob but ignored it. She never wanted to see Emma again.

'Wait! Please.'

'No – it's over, Emma. I told you. How could I ever…?'

'I think he drugged me.' Emma's words dropped likes stones between them.

Amber whirled to face her. 'What?'

'I… I can't remember what happened. I only know because of what Laura told me afterwards. I just remember waking up feeling really sick and…'

'What the hell?' Amber shouted, blood roaring through her body, making her face and hands tingle. 'How *dare* you accuse Alex of drugging you? That's the most insane thing I've ever heard. Is that the best excuse you could come up with? Christ! You can't even take responsibility for what you did.'

Emma was shaking her head. 'I promise you, Amber. I would never in a million years *do* something like that. You know me! I'd never hurt you. Amber, please listen to me. The last thing I remember is Curly bringing me a drink from the kitchen, a gin and tonic, I think. And then nothing! It's like everything was wiped clean. There's something wrong there – can't you see? You must have heard those dodgy stories about Curly?'

'Shut up. Shut up,' Amber snapped. 'I know you fancied him. Look me in the eye and tell me you didn't fancy Alex.'

Emma gazed back at her, eyes luminous in the soft light. She swallowed and straightened her shoulders. 'OK. Yes. I did. A bit. He's very attractive and knew how to make me feel special, I'm not sure many people could resist him.'

'I knew it!' Amber said. 'You couldn't keep your eyes off him, you dirty cow.'

'But I would never have gone to bed with him.' Emma's voice was certain and steady. Saying the words pinkened her cheeks with embarrassment. 'You're my best friend. I knew how much you loved him, and I would never have come between you. The only explanation…' her gaze never wavered, '…the *only* explanation I can think of is that I was out of my mind. I hadn't drunk enough to be pissed – one of them must have put something in my drink.'

A pause stretched between them and for a second Amber saw a flicker of hope dance in Emma's eyes.

'Bullshit,' she said at last. 'Drugs! Where the hell would they even get hold of something like that? They're builders, for God's sake, not gangsters. This is all too ridiculous.'

Emma stared at her, defeated. 'I don't know what else to say,' she said. They both moved against the wall as a gang danced past them to the loos, whooping and laughing. They stood still until the corridor was quiet again.

'You're my best friend,' Emma said at last. 'I hate that I haven't seen you for so long.'

'Yeah, well, you should have thought of that before you screwed Alex.'

'I don't even know if I did!' Emma protested.

'Oh, you did all right,' Amber's voice was harsh but full of pain. Emma was unravelling her defences. Again, she forced the image of them in bed to the front of her memory. 'I saw you. With my own eyes, in bed together at Dom's party. You were all over him.'

Emma flushed again, 'I swear to you, on your Mum's grave, I had no idea what I was doing. He must have given me something – he must have.'

Amber's eyes flashed. 'Don't you fucking *dare* mention Mum, you bitch.' Emma stepped back and held up her hands in surrender.

'I'm sorry, I'm sorry. That was stupid of me. I just wanted you to understand how serious I was. I'd never lie to you. I never have lied to you. Have I?'

But Amber wasn't listening. It had taken her months to get over the devastation of finding Alex and Emma together. Alex had told her how Emma had flirted with him. He'd shown her texts she'd sent – even pictures. She couldn't understand why Emma kept trying to get in touch with her, why rekindle the friendship when she'd worked so hard to destroy it?

Her head ached. Sick and dizzy she slumped against the cool wall. 'Just go, Emma,' she said, her voice slurring with the drink and exhaustion.

'Amber. I want to ask one thing. I understand you cutting me out of your life – but why not Alex? From what you said he was just as involved as I was.'

Amber gave a weak laugh. 'He was pissed, he didn't know what he was doing. I believed him – I know what he's like when he's had a few.'

'But…'

'You want to know why? The real reason why? Because I couldn't bear to lose both of you. So, I chose to lose you. Alex is everything to me. He has to be.'

On impulse, Emma leaned forward and grabbed Amber into a hug. 'OK. OK. I'll go,' she said. 'But I'll always be your friend. And Alex. He's not what he seems, Amber. I think he's dangerous. I'm sure of it.'

With all her strength Amber pushed Emma away. 'Don't you say a word about Alex. Don't even say his name. Isn't enough you nearly destroyed us? Go away. Now. I don't ever want to see you again.'

Amber slid down the wall, her head in her hands as Emma walked away. The doors opened and the Amahle and the others spilled through. Emma, hood up and shoulder slumped, wove through them, disappearing out the other side, unnoticed.

'Amber!' shouted Amahle. 'We've been looking everywhere for you! Where have you been?'

'Are you OK?' said Laura, running forward and tripping over her heels.

'Drunk again!' snorted Vanita, stopping to pull her vape from her bag.

'I'm bursting!' Grace laughed, 'sorry, darling, I've got to go pee – I'll be back in a minute.'

Within seconds, Amber was surrounded by the cooing women who pulled her to her feet. 'What's happened?'

'Emma was here,' Amber said. Everyone's mouths fell open in shock.

'No!' said Laura looking wildly up and down the corridor. 'When? Where is she?'

'She just left.' Amber could barely stand, her legs weighed heavy. 'She followed me into the loos.'

'What did she say?' Vanita's eyes sparked with interest.

'That Alex drugged her – no, let me get it right – she said Curly gave her something and then Alex took advantage.'

Exclamations of shock and outrage clashed together.

'We need to get you back to the hotel,' Amahle said, her face creased with concern. 'You look done in.'

'I don't understand it,' Laura said. 'Why would she come all this way to tell you such rubbish?'

'Because she's a lying whore,' said Vanita.

Amber's eyes filled. 'She said it was all Alex, that he forced her.'

Amahle scoffed. 'Honey, you're being mad. Alex adores you, any fool can see that. There's no way he'd risk what he has with you with some one-night stand. Especially with your best friend. For a start he's not that stupid - he must have been completely out of it that night.'

'Yes,' said Amber, sniffing, 'That's what he said.'

'Well, there you go!' Amahle reached down to give Amber a hug.

'It was awful to see her,' Amber went on, her voice muffled. 'She looked terrible – it was really sad.'

'Shhh, hon. I know. Don't worry. You mustn't blame yourself.'

Amahle kept her arms around Amber as they shuffled her out of the club and into a waiting cab. As they drove back to the hotel Amber fell into a doze, her face pressed against the glass of the window. They were nearly there when she became aware of the whispering, casting glances to check she wasn't listening.

'It's not right. The cheek of Emma! Tracking Amber down on your hen-do, Amahle,' Laura was saying.

'And accusing Alex of drugging her!' Vanita's voice dripped with outrage. 'As if he needed to drug anyone. He's fucking gorgeous – I would, that's for sure.'

They all broke into giggles, quickly shushing themselves, worried Amber would wake up.

'I'm serious!' Vanita went on. 'And just between you and me, Amber's a lucky bitch to have caught him. I mean, she pretty and all that, but not in Alex's league.'

'Shut up, Vanita,' Amahle's voice held a note of warning. 'Amber's lovely.'

'Oh, I'm not saying she's not!' Vanita protested. 'But Alex is, like, proper fit. You know – like something out of a movie.'

There was a chorus of agreement,

'Well, don't go saying anything like that to Amber,' Amahle said. 'Come on, we're here.'

Amber pretended to wake up as Amahle patted her cheek gently. 'Out you get, Amber darlin',' she said. 'Let's get you into bed.'

The night air was cold, and they shrieked and giggled in their skimpy dresses as they streaked across the car park to the welcoming light of the hotel. Amahle held Amber tightly. 'Come on, girl,' she said.

'I want to call Alex,' Amber said, struggling free from Amahle's grip and searching through her bag for her phone.

'Don't be mental!' Amahle exclaimed with a grin. 'It's gone two am! He won't thank you for waking him up. You can call him in the morning. You're too pissed to make any sense anyway.'

Amber nodded, her eyes kept wanting to close, and everything seemed to be spinning around.

'I feel sick,' she said.

'I'm not surprised,' Amahle said, her voice warm and kind. 'The amount you put away. Let's get some water down you, and some sleep – you'll be fine in the morning.'

*

Amber dreaded going home. She knew the minute she walked through the door Alex would read in her face something had happened.

It didn't help that her hangover was so severe she could barely see straight. She couldn't face a morsel of breakfast and had watched in amazement as the others chugged down whole platefuls of fried eggs and bacon. She struggled to keep down a black coffee.

Everyone was in great spirits, screeching about men they'd met the night before, and who'd said what and how cute the barman had been. Not one of them mentioned Emma.

Amber sighed. She knew Alex would go nuts. He'd spend the rest of the day ranting about Emma and how she was trying to break them up. She debated not saying anything but knew it was pointless, he knew her too well.

Amahle dropped her off at home, patting her on the knee as Amber got out of the car. 'You OK, Amber?'

'Yeah, I'm fine. Just need an early night and a handful of painkillers. Remind me not to drink like that again!'

Amahle smiled, looking relieved. 'You into work tomorrow?'

'Of course!'

'Good, I'll see you then.'

As Amber got to the gate Alex burst out of the door and ran towards her, sweeping her up in his arms and whirling her around. Her legs knocked against the wheelie bins waiting to be filled and sent them flying.

'Oh my God! Stop! I'll be sick!' she laughed.

He set her down looking so happy she couldn't help but grin at him. 'I missed you,' she said, picking up the bins and pushing them against the wall so they wouldn't fall over again.

'I missed you,' he grinned back. 'Come on, let's get you inside. Curly's out, got some girl on the go.'

'Nothing's changed since I've been away then.'

'Get yourself up to the bedroom, I'll be two minutes.'

'Alex! It's barely lunchtime!'

'I don't care what time it is, get upstairs.'

They were both starving by the time they'd finished. Amber stood under the shower, smiling to hear Alex cursing the Deliveroo app. He was trying to order them a Chinese but had forgotten his password. She'd have to go away more often, she thought, thinking of their blissful reunion. Amber frowned, the hours in bed with Alex had blasted away everything, but she couldn't stop thinking about Emma. Her words kept circling around her head.

She'd have to be careful, she thought, towelling herself off and wincing as her bare feet caught splinters from the old floorboards. Alex had an uncanny ability to see straight into her thoughts. Resolving to put Emma to the back of her mind, Amber dressed quickly in soft jogging bottoms and a hoodie, the bathroom was freezing.

The kitchen was still a bomb site, so Alex had pushed all the furniture in the front room to the back wall leaving enough space for an old card table and two chairs. He'd thrown a blanket over the table and lit candles. Remembering what happened the last time they were in the room, Amber blushed.

She could hear Alex clattering about in the kitchen, so she curled up in the bay window to wait for him.

'Aw, I didn't hear you come down!' he said as he came into the room carrying a pile of plates, cutlery, wine, and glasses. 'I wanted to make it all nice for you.'

Amber jumped up to help, taking the plates and glasses from his arms before they crashed to the floor. 'It already looks gorgeous,' she said, kissing his cheek. 'You are spoiling me.'

'I've ordered the usual,' he said as they laid everything out on the table. 'But I think I cocked up with the prawn crackers, I may have ordered ten bags rather than one.'

Amber laughed. 'No problem for me,' she said. 'I love prawn crackers.'

He shot her a look. 'You won't keep that lush body if you eat too many prawn crackers.'

She rolled her eyes. 'Rude!'

There was a bang on the door. 'That was quick,' said Alex. 'Can you open the wine?'

Amber felt a great swell of happiness. In this candlelit room with Alex all to herself Emma and her accusations felt very far away. 'Drugs!' Amber whispered to herself, shaking her head in disbelief. How could she ever have believed Emma – even for a second?

'What did you say?' Alex stood in the doorway holding two brown paper bags.

'God that smells delicious,' Amber beamed, grateful that all traces of her hangover had disappeared. 'I haven't eaten a thing all day, so I'm absolutely starving!'

'I wasn't sure whether you were looking at me or the bags with lust in your eyes,' Alex said. 'And it looks like it was the food!'

'Never,' said Amber walking towards him. She took the bags and balanced them on the table before returning to Alex and kissing him, hard.

The bags had cooled by someway by the time they came up for air. 'Phew!' said Alex, the impact of her kiss obvious. 'OK, point taken. But if I don't have something to eat, I won't be any use to you later.'

Sitting at the rickety table they wolfed the food down in silence. Amber groaned aloud, grease shining on her chin, as she worked her way through crispy beef and the best spring rolls she'd ever tasted.

At last, they were finished, the foil trays and plates cleared away and another bottle of wine opened. Feeling woozy and relaxed Amber gazed across at Alex.

'It's nice being here without having to worry about Curly,' she said, reaching her hands across to hold his. 'When do you think he will move out?'

Alex pulled his hands away to refill his glass. 'I need him at the moment,' he said. 'There's no way I could get any of the work done on the house alone, and it's not like you're much use.'

'Do you know how long it's going to take?'

'Hey! I haven't asked you how the weekend went? Did you have fun?' Alex leaned back on his chair and took another gulp of wine.

'Oh! It was great!' Amber said, fiddling with the stem of her glass.

Alex let the chair fall back to the floor with a crash. 'What? What happened? I knew it! I knew something was up.'

'Nothing happened! It was fine! We met, we had spa treatments and we had dinner. That's it. I got a bit drunk, that's all.'

'Oh?' Alex was tapping his fingers along the edge of the table. 'I heard it was a nightclub, but, whatever.'

'We weren't planning to go there, it's just some of them fancied a dance and…'

'It doesn't matter. It's not like I'm your Dad.'

'But I don't want you to be upset about it,' Amber reached for him again, but he moved, running his hands through his hair. 'It was just us. We didn't talk to anyone- just danced together and drank some cocktails.

He stared at her, unmoving, waiting for her to go on.

'And that's it, really.'

The silence that followed lasted so long Amber could hear the drips of grease from the takeaway cartons falling to the floor in the kitchen. The words bubbled up in her.

'Emma came to find me.'

Alex slammed his fist down on the table, knocking over the empty wine bottle. 'What. The. FUCK did she do that for?' he said, his voice controlled but furious.

'She just wanted to explain,' stuttered Amber, leaning away from the grim lines that had appeared in Alex's face.

'What do you mean? Explain?' He was on his feet now and walking up and down. The tension in Amber's shoulders winched them up around her ears.

'I didn't listen to her, Alex…' she was gabbling.

'I said. What do you mean by explain?'

'You know, about what happened.'

'Oh yes? And what did happen?'

Amber shook her head. 'She just wanted to say sorry.'

'And that's it? She trekked all the way over there to say sorry? Then what? Did she sit down with the girls? All tarts together? Have a few drinks, did she? Slag off some men, did you?'

Amber stood, trying to calm him with her body, her arms, and hands, but he kept moving. Back and forth, back and forth.

'She's just trying to get to me through you,' he snarled. 'You do realise that don't you? She'd fucking obsessed. Curly said she'd been hanging around the pub looking for me.'

Amber's mouth fell open. 'What?'

'Yeah, I didn't want to tell you. She can't get enough. Keeps trying to get in touch.'

'But why…?' Amber sat down on the chair, her mind whirling in shock.

Alex's face shifted. He knelt in front of her, tipping his forehead against hers. 'She's trouble, Amber. I've seen it. She'll say or do anything to get what she wants. She's dangerous. We need to keep her away from us, from here.'

'But she said…'

'She's a liar, Amber! Can't you see that! Oh, babe, you're so good, so kind and sweet you can't see it when people are out to get you. Out to destroy everything. She's jealous! Can't you see that?'

'That's what Laura said,' Amber's voice was a whisper.

'And she's right. She's got her head screwed on, that Laura.' He pulled Amber to her feet and held her to his chest, cradling her with the utmost gentleness. 'You tell me, OK? If that bitch comes anywhere near you…'

'She won't,' said Amber. 'I promise you, Alex. I've sorted it. I made it clear to her I never want to see her again.'

They clung together for a moment. 'How about I take you away next weekend?' Alex said, breathing into her ear and making her shiver. 'A dirty weekend – posh hotel – the works. What do you think?'

'Can we afford it?' Amber looked up to meet his smiling eyes.

'Yeah, leave it to me. We don't need to spend a fortune. How about Brighton?'

'Sounds perfect,' she said.

It was gone midnight when something woke Amber up. Alex had curled around her, and she was boiling hot. Her mouth was dry from the wine and the takeaway. She lifted Alex's arms and slid out of bed.

'Where are you going?' Alex murmured.

'I need a wee and a drink,' she whispered. 'Do you want anything?' But Alex had fallen back to sleep.

Amber admired the beauty of his profile for a moment before going downstairs.

She checked the door was locked and paused, leaning forward to get a better look through the window. Curly was there, outside, two doors down. He was shoving something into the wheelie bin of no 14. Cupping her hands around her face, Amber tried to see what he was doing. It looked like quite a big bag.

He let the lid fall with a crash and bounced down the street to the door before she could move away very far. The door opened and he walked in, bringing a wash of fresh, cold air and the blossom of lager.

'Christ, Amber! You made me jump! What are you doing hiding away in the dark?'

'I wasn't hiding away!' she exclaimed. 'I was just coming down for some water.'

'Ah, OK. Sorted.' He sniffed the air. 'You two had a Chinese?'

'Yes, there's some left if you want it. Alex ordered masses.'

'Cushty,' Curly replied, heading for the kitchen, rubbing his hands together.

'Curly?'

'Yeah?'

'What were you doing putting rubbish in the neighbours' bin?'

Curly paused. 'Just getting rid of some crap we cleared this morning. Our bins are full up.' He disappeared into the kitchen whistling.

Amber locked the door, noticing through the window that the wheelie bins in their garden had fallen over again. They were both empty.

SARAH: FIVE YEARS AGO

A phone was ringing. Five trains seemed have disgorged at once and the station was packed. Wedged into a crowd squashed so close together she could smell the cigarettes on the skin of the man behind her, she struggled to breathe. Her wrists were red where she'd held onto them, hugging the bag tightly to her chest. The ringing continued; it was maddening.

The pill had softened everything, the colours around her were marshmallow bright – pinks and greens, olives, and soft blues. She wanted to lean over and take a bite of the pillowy cream square of a coat in front of her.

'Will somebody answer that phone,' she slurred, almost falling into the purple-haired woman in a cream coat who stood in her way. Her hair waved like springs with bright silver roots straddling a seam of scalp, she wanted to touch it, feel the curly bounce beneath her hand. The woman ignored her, inching away from the filthy junkie with vacant eyes.

'Will somebody please answer the phone?' she said again as it continued to ring. 'Oh.' There was a pause as she cocked her head towards her bag. 'It's mine.' She sniggered and tried to catch the eye of the old man standing to her left, but he turned his head away. The crowd wasn't moving, and her arms were pinned to her chest, wrapped around her bag. The ringing stopped, mercifully, but after a pause began again.

She pushed forward, wincing at the pressure of bodies against her sore wrists. 'Excuse me. Excuse me.' Her voice was loud, but it was the emaciation of her face, her smell and gaping pupils that made people draw away. The ringing continued to jangle in her head, and she kept pushing. The noise was becoming unbearable, her head throbbed; she was desperate to make it stop.

Outside, the sun bloomed sudden and dazzling, her pupils cranked themselves shut and a headache threatened to split her skull open. She staggered back against a wall and felt for her phone. It continued to ring, and she screamed with frustration when she couldn't find it, eventually dumping the contents of the bag on the floor.

'Yes?' She kept her head down as she retrieved some boxes and packets that had rolled under a nearby bin. She gave a start when the person at the other end began to speak. She smiled.

'Hey! So good to hear from you! It's been ages. How are… what's wrong? Yes, Paris… how did you know?' She frowned and used her hand to shield her eyes from the sun that was tearing at the skin on her face. 'Is everything… wait, I can't understand you… who will hear? What's going on?... I'm fine, just a bit wasted… yeah, well, I know, but…Can I come? Now? I don't know… I'm supposed to be meeting this guy with my stuff… What? What is it? What's happened? Christ. What? Why are you with him?' Horror stole over her face like a dark mist and she swallowed. 'I thought… Fuck's sake, babe, how?... OK. Yes… I'll come. Of course… Of course I will. Where are you?'

Blinking hard and feeling numb she scrabbled in her bag for something to write on, speaking gently on the phone, reassuring nonsense that didn't seem to be helping. 'Please stop crying… it's going to be OK, I'm coming…'

With a tremendous effort of will she concentrated hard enough to write down an address. She read it back and nodded. 'Right, I've got it…. Yes, I'll come now! But I don't understand how you… wait! Hello? Hello?'

Worry plunged her into ice and she emerged gasping, the scene in front of her suddenly pin sharp. The last threads of the Xanax slipped free and her mind raced. Immediately she called back but the phone rang and rang until the voicemail kicked in. She hung up and dialled again but this time the voicemail started straight away. The phone had been turned off.

Stomach churning, she turned back towards the station, hoping she had enough money for a train out of Paris. Without holding out much hope she tried the ATM next to the ticket office. She had £70 left and withdrew it all, knowing once that was gone, she would be left with nothing.

She shook the thought off, she had to go. She had no choice. The phone call had been desperate. Skirting the crowd still surging towards the exit she looked for a map, or a platform board. The station was huge, and it took many wrong turns before she found the line that would take her to the right village. The next one left in an hour. The adrenalin sparked by the phone call had drained away and exhaustion slowed her steps, along with her thinking.

Fear trickled into her veins as she remembered the conversation. Why was he there? She'd have to keep her brain sharp; he'd sniff her out when she got close, she knew it. The temptation to pretend the phone call never happened was strong, she could sink into the oblivion of a handful of pills. Her thoughts slid to the cuff of her jumper, her mouth warmed at the thought of them but the voice on the phone sounded in her head, loud as the station tannoy. She folded the cuff more securely and sighed.

The station toilets looked clean, but she didn't want to take any risks. She hooked a fingerful of powder and inhaled sharply letting the sparking fingers wipe round her eyeballs and push into her brain. The punch jerked her head back with a snap and she placed her hand on her chest to feel the hammering.

Her thoughts zoomed ahead, fast as a train on silver tracks. She sniffed and wiped her face, smiling at herself in the wall of mirrors. Her eyes glittered.

Too much time had passed. She only had ten minutes. Her feet were swift and sure as she strode out of the toilets. She'd need something to take off the edge and didn't want to risk pills on the next train. She skipped through the crowds and was outside and grabbing two cheap bottles of wine from the shelf of a tiny shop across the road within minutes.

She only just caught the train. The bottles clinked in her hand as she raced down the platform, a hysterical laugh bubbling up her throat. The train pulled away and she twisted the cap from the bottle. Her brain was chattering along too fast, scaring her with what lay ahead. She swallowed too much wine and it splashed red down her chest. It looked like blood -

CHAPTER 8: LIZ

I woke with a scream, my throat raw. This always happened when I saw Jenny. My subconscious presented a reel of horror film to watch through the night. His face bearing down on me, the broken bones, the trail of his victims who'd disappeared. The sheet covering the mattress had pulled away from its moorings and lay in a messy heap at the side of the bed.

    I sat up and breathed deeply until my pulse slowed. My head throbbed but draining the glass of water by my bed helped. I groaned aloud as I pushed myself off the bed and bent to stretch my back, letting my hands brush the floor. The nightmares brimmed, dark and wet, and I moved with care, so they didn't spill. Dressing in yesterday's running gear, which I hadn't washed and stank of dried sweat, I walked straight out of the flat, down the stairs and out onto the pavement where I stood for a moment. The wind was sharp and cold, and I let it blow through me until my face burned and my fingers blued into numbness.

    Only then could I run. Slow at first, then picking up in pace. The blackness began to jolt with my steps and fragments dropped away. I imagine them shattering behind me, blades of dark glass. The thud of my feet awoke the words of a poem I learned years ago. 'I wake and feel the fell of dark not day.' Each step sounded out the syllables of the same line, over and over again; I couldn't remember the rest.

No sun yet, though I could see a pencil-thin line of light unzipping the darkness of the horizon. The nightmares forced their way forward. I wouldn't be able to escape them for long. I sped up a little, but my hips and knees were sore and the faster I went the more they protested.

Ignoring the pain, I thought about the storm of the night before. Jenny would have something to say about why they have appeared again, I thought.

It was one of the worst, the one rooted in the last days of the relationship. Those days when I thought I was going mad. Our house became unfamiliar, I would trip over furniture, forgetting it was there. Texts I sent popped onto my phone screen, jumbled with strange misspellings. I had to keep following them up with corrections and silly emojis.

I sucked a deep breath, the smell of the sea growing strong. I remember learning to be quiet, to pad around so I didn't draw his attention. Rage wove through every hour, hidden, most of the time, but on bad days it would rip through the surface.

'Beauty,' he used to call me. 'My Beauty.' Bitter saliva coated my teeth and tongue. I spat it to the ground and gulped water from my bottle.

My nightmares took a step forward, blocking my path. I tried to run through, but they clung to me as I passed. A series of flashbacks clicking through my head. A bag of shopping on the floor, smashed glass and pasta sauce oozing from it. Dinner with friends and the hand on my thigh reminding me I had drunk enough wine. The look that sent me scurrying to change the dress that revealed too much skin.

I gritted my teeth to stop a growl of frustration escaping. And Sarah. Where was she? Why hadn't she replied? I'd sent a further message and this time it remained un-read.

I picked up the pace, my blood pumped through my veins, flushing out the last of the memories. My muscles flexed smooth and powerful as I raced towards the cliff edge. I was gasping so hard everything was driven from my head.

I would go and find her, I resolved as I neared the cliff, sweat pouring down my chest and back. I couldn't wait to get home and shower away the last of my nightmare-filled sleep. I stopped for a moment to catch my breath, trying to remember the last time I saw Sarah.

The sun peered through threads of gauzy clouds as I turned back. My phone chimed its alarm and I remembered with a tightness across my chest I was meeting Will today.

*

He smiled as he saw me leaning against the wall outside my flat. I couldn't think what to wear. The part of my brain responsible for deciding what was appropriate for a date seemed to have frozen. I didn't have a lot of choice, which helped, and in the end I'd gone for brown moleskin jeans and a soft, crimson polo neck.

Will looked the same as he always did in old jeans and a crumpled cotton shirt under a thick jumper. As he walked towards me, I regretted the last-minute slick of scarlet lipstick and turned away to rub it off with the back of my hand.

'You look gorgeous,' he said. He stepped forward to kiss my cheek but seeing me flinch he stopped. 'Here, put this on. I can't imagine you'll worry about messing up your hair.'

I rubbed the bleached fuzz on my scalp. It was starting to get longer than I liked. I took the motorbike helmet and held its solid black curves in my hand. It was heavier than it looked.

'We're going on a bike?' I said, stupidly.

He grinned, a white flash bright in the dark stubble of his face. 'Well I'm not making you wear it on the bus,' he said.

'Where are we going?'

'It's a surprise,' he said.

'I don't like surprises.' I handed the helmet back to him. He started to protest, then stopped when he saw the look on my face.

'OK, no magical mystery tour for you. I thought we could go for a ride along the coast up to a little village called Ayleswater, my mate runs a café there, I thought we could have lunch and then I'd drive you back. What do you think?'

'How far is it?'

'About two hours, but it's a lovely route, most of it by the sea – and it's a perfect day for it.'

It was one of those freakish days you get in early spring when you remember that winter doesn't last forever. The sun beat down hot on my face. The shadows were still cold, but in the sun, it could have been July.

'I don't know,' I said. 'That's quite far, we won't be back until late.'

He waited; his eyes steady on me. Jenny's voice whispered in my head.

'OK,' I said at last. 'I'll just text my friend where I'm going.'

He nodded and walked over to his bike. It suited him, old fashioned with a worn brown leather seat and chrome pipework that shone in the sun.

I didn't have anyone to text, so sent an email to a client who was late with payment instead. My heart rate ticked up and my hands were cold. I'd never been on a bike before, and the thought of flying away with Will was making me want to turn and run up the stairs to the safety of my flat.

Before I could move, Will was back beside me. 'Put this on,' he said, handing me the helmet again. 'And look, can you see that bar at the back here? You hold onto that. Of course, you can hold onto me – that's probably the safest - but the main thing is to relax, lean where I lean. OK?'

I nodded and pulled on the helmet, immediately feeling more secure. Will slung his leg over the bike, put on his helmet and held out his hand. Ignoring it, I hopped on behind him. The seat felt sturdy beneath me, but as Will began to pull out onto the road, I had to clutch hold of the bar as the movement jerked me back.

'OK?' he yelled back at me, voice muffled.

'Fine.'

With a rush the bike leaped forwards, throwing my stomach up into my throat. I had to stifle a scream as we began to speed up, weaving in and out of the traffic. I kept my eyes shut tight, focusing on nothing but the dip and lurch of the bike.

The thrum of panic began to rise, and I shifted on my seat, fighting the urge to make Will stop. 'Look,' he said.

Holding tight onto the bar, I opened my eyes to a great whoosh of colour and speed. The blue sea and sky, the green of the hedgerows, the yellow sand of the beaches streaked past me, a great smear of the most vivid oils, as if someone had run their hands over a huge painting that hadn't yet dried.

A whoop escaped me; giddy with the rush I laughed out loud. Will drove fast, but with care. I felt safe. I wanted it to go on forever. Eventually, we turned away from the sea and climbed higher, up from a valley dotted with sheep into a pretty village.

When Will stopped and turned off the bike I could see still feel the vibrating hum of the engine in the nerves of my hands and legs. I took off my helmet and we grinned at each other.

'Good?' he said.

'Fantastic! I didn't want it to end.'

He looked pleased but didn't say any more. 'I hope you're hungry.'

I nodded. 'Starving,' I said, surprised to find it was true. Usually, I forced myself to eat. Food crumbled tasteless in my mouth; I only ate when I felt faint. The trip up had blown the matter that choked my mouth and belly clean away.

I followed Will into a long, low building. Inside were tables with benches that reminded me of science labs at school. The look was softened by plants everywhere, hanging from the ceiling, crammed in along windowsills, and trailing their leaves in pots under the serving area. It smelled of fresh basil, and rosemary.

A woman standing behind the till with hair the colour of pink candyfloss caught sight of Will and cried out in delight. 'Jonno, it's Will!'

Behind the forest of plants, I realised you could see through to the kitchen where a huge man with a great shock of black hair was cooking. Seeing Will he pulled off his striped apron and wiped his hands.

'Mate! Long time no see, yeah? Where have you been hiding yourself? And who's this?'

Will introduced me, and the pink-haired woman, whose name turned out to be Coco, directed us out into the garden. 'Go on, it's lovely and sunny out there and you'll be on your own. I'll bring your food out.' Jonno and Will fell into conversation, the way old friends do. Fragments of words dancing into shouts of laughter and shared stories.

There was a tiny courtyard around the back with a view across the fields. Will pulled a chair out for me, tucking the helmets under the table.

'Shouldn't we look at the menu?' I said, sitting down and enjoying the sun on my shoulders.

'Nah, they only have one thing for lunch – whatever they've got fresh in. I'm sure you'll like it – you're not allergic to anything?'

I shook my head.

'My sister's allergic to egg,' he said. 'It's a real pain. Have you got brothers or sisters?'

'No, just me. My parents died when I was very young. I was brought up by my Gran, She's the only family I've known.'

'Ouch, that must have been tough. What happened?'

'My Dad killed himself after my mother got cancer.'

'Christ! How awful.'

I shrugged, 'I never really knew them. It hit my Gran really hard. She never forgave him for leaving my Mum like that, you know, to deal with the cancer on her own. Sorry. Not really the thing to talk about the first time you go out to lunch with someone. I've not done this for a while.'

'What? Go on a date with someone?'

'Here we are, loveys!' Coco appeared with two large plates. She put them on the table and then went to fetch a basket of bread, which she presented with a large pat of creamy yellow butter. 'Not up to your standard, Will, but if you will insist on living so far away.'

Will laughed. 'It looks great,' he said, breaking off a piece of olive focaccia roll and tearing at it with his teeth. Something about the way he ate with such relish stirred a warmth in me.

'I've never seen a salad like this,' I said as I dug in. The leaves were crisp and fresh and dotted with chunks of grilled goats' cheese as well as courgette flowers and glossy red and green peppers. 'The dressing is amazing.'

Will tore another roll in two and passed me half. Our fingers touched. 'So how long has it been?' he said.

'Sorry?'

'Since your last date.'

I stopped chewing and swallowed, my appetite diminishing. 'A few years,' I admitted. 'More than, in fact. Not since university.'

Will's eyes searched my face.

'What happened?' he said, his voice soft.

'Just a… a… bit of a bad relationship,' I said, keeping my voice light. 'It took me a while to get out of. Longer than it should have done.'

'Well, I'm honoured to be your first date since then.'

'You should be,' I smiled, but every muscle in my body had tensed. Talking about those lost years always had that effect.

'So, tell me about your Gran,' Will said, changing the subject, letting me breathe again.

The next few hours passed so quickly I couldn't believe it was gone 5 o'clock. Coco had brought out berry compote with lemon syllabub for pudding and my stomach pushed against the waistband of my jeans. We hadn't stopped talking. He told me stories of his three sisters and harassed father. I envied him his tales of a messy, warm, and loving family. I had little to offer except stories of my strange, lonely life as a child surrounded by the elderly, and my love for my work.

He listened with a quiet intensity, letting me talk. Our heads grew close and every now and then I forgot myself. He had a mobile face; I liked watching his expressions flicker and change. Every now and then his hand or arm would brush against mine and energy would zip through me.

'I suppose we better get back,' he said at last. The café had closed hours ago. Coco had thrown Will the keys, asking him to drop them through their letter box as we left.

'Take as long as you like,' she'd said, with a wink at Will that made him laugh.

'Yes, I'd better get back,' I said, without any idea what I had to get back to. Part of me wanted to sit with Will as the sun went down, watching the shadows stretch across the valley as we talked.

Every minute of the ride home felt like a dream. We hadn't drunk any alcohol, but my limbs felt heavy and liquid, my heart rate slow. Will's driving was unhurried, as if he wanted to take as long as possible. It was getting cold now the sun was down, and it felt like the most natural thing in the world to slip my arms around his waist as the bike flew through the darkening lanes.

For a second the feel of his body under my hands sent a shock wave of anxiety through me, but Will turned, took my hands with absolute gentleness, and folded them firmly back around his waist. 'Do you mind if we stop off at my place?' he shouted. Only for a minute,' he added, feeling me tense at his words. 'I want you to meet my dog.'

My smile was hidden by my helmet. 'Is that a euphemism?'

Will's house was just outside the city, high up on the cliffs, not far from the usual path of my run. It was tiny, made of stone, with little windows that blinked out at you under heavy eaves. As we arrived a huge, white dog appeared, staring through the glass and jumping as if it was on a trampoline.

'That's Dolly,' said Will, pulling off his helmet. 'I'm later than I should be, she'll have been crossing her legs for the past hour or so.'

He unlocked the door and Dolly shot out, dancing around Will and yodelling with delight. She couldn't decide between greeting Will, checking me out, and relieving her bladder. In the end she bounced around Will, greeted me with a quick, polite sniff, and then trotted onto the little front lawn for an endless pee.

I couldn't stop laughing. It was such a joyful thing to watch. 'She's enormous!' I said as she galloped past. 'What is she?'

'She's a labradoodle, and I love her to bits,' Will said. Dolly stopped racing about and leaned her big, shaggy head against his leg, a panting, pink tongue hanging out of her smiling face. 'Do you want to come in? Have a cup of tea?' Will asked, looking up as he rubbed Dolly's neck.

'No, I'd better get home,' I said, adjusting the bag across my shoulder and looking down at my hands.

'Shame,' Will said.

'I'm not far from here, I could probably walk it.'

'Not alone you can't. Dolly needs to stretch her legs, I'll come with you.'

I sat on the wall by the gate waiting as he grabbed Dolly's lead and a long, stripy scarf which he wound round my neck. I held my breath at his closeness.

We didn't talk much as we strolled back down into the city. Dolly stopped at every lamppost to investigate smells, so it took ages. I didn't mind. Every step home was another step towards bad memories, and I wanted to linger in the sunshine for a little longer.

'Here we are,' I said.

Will tied Dolly to a railing and waited as I unlocked the door.

'Thank you for coming out with me.' He said. 'I'm glad you met Dolly. She likes you, I can tell. And she's a great judge of character - never been wrong.'

'Really?' I looked down at Dolly's dopey, grinning face. 'Has she ever taken against anyone?'

'My brother-in-law Chris,' he said. 'And she was right too, he's the most boring man in England.'

I laughed.

A silence fell, heavy with many unspoken things. 'I had a really good day,' I said at last. 'I don't have many of them. So, thank you.' I cleared my throat.

'It was a pleasure. I hope we can do something together again soon.'

'I'd like that.' I couldn't take my eyes from my boots.

'Liz,' Will said.

'What?' I looked up at him. He was very close. I couldn't move. His lips were millimetres from mine and the breath caught in my throat. My body jerked backwards before I could stop it. 'Sorry!' I gasped.

'It's fine,' Will's mouth curled up at one side. 'I can wait. As long as you promise to see me again.'

'Yes,' I said.

I bounced up the stair as excited and stupid as Dolly. I could run a hundred miles, I thought, and the electricity zapping along my veins would carry me along and I would never tire. I was too wired to sleep and too wired to do any work or read. I sat in the kitchen holding a coffee in my hands until it grew cold, replaying the day over and over in my head.

The temptation to text him, to call, to ask him to come over was so strong I turned my phone off before I did something stupid.

I turned the TV on, flicked through the hundreds of channels and snapped it off. There was nothing I wanted to see.

I opened my laptop. I could look him up. He said he had a web page. I wanted to look at his picture. I sighed with impatience, it was flat, and I didn't know where I'd put the cable. I tracked it down in the bedroom. I kept stopping to think about the motorbike ride, or the way Will had smiled when he talked about his new-born niece.

Back in the kitchen, laptop plugged in and switched on, I waited. It took an age to whirr into life and I rubbed my forehead as I waited for it to light up. I was just about to type his name into images when a familiar ping sounded. My body stiffened in a Pavlovian response. It was my internet alert.

I'd set up a number of alerts to keep track of the monster, keeping an eye on places I knew he visited often, or news from the town where he lived.

I paused. I could continue to look for Will, or I could open up the alert. My fingers stilled at the keyboard. Jenny whispered in my ear. What good would it do to open the alert? Did I want to keep trailing the man who had nearly taken me apart? I'd exhausted myself, nearly killed myself, warning people about him and trying to move past our abusive relationship. Nobody had ever believed me, except Sarah. It was time to move on. Jenny was right.

Will was good. He was true. He was opening up something for me I would be mad not to explore. But then I remembered Sarah, the look on her face when she told me she was leaving the monster, the marks of fear ground into her face. She still hadn't replied. I didn't know where she was.

I clicked on the alert.

The text arrived before the photo downloaded. Not for the first time I cursed the sluggishness of my internet connection. A murder. A young woman. She'd been missing for days before her body had been found, thrown into undergrowth. She'd been strangled.

My blood started to freeze, any vestige of warmth from my day with Will cooled and disappeared. When the photo finally appeared, I covered my eyes, shaking my head. My hands shook as if palsied. 'No. No, please.' I muttered, staring at the lovely young face with smiling eyes. Eyes that held no hint of the terrible end she was about to face.

CHAPTER 9: AMBER

There was an odd atmosphere when Amber got to work on Monday morning. It was quiet, not many clients were around, and the chatter was muted.

'What's going on?' she said to Brenda before getting a good look at her. 'Christ, Brenda! What's happened?'

'Haven't you heard? I thought Laura or someone would have told you.' Amber had never seen Brenda without her make-up on. She was startlingly pale, bereft of her usual eyeliner, mascara and orange spots of blusher.

'No. I was away all weekend at Amahle's hen-do and then Alex and I just got a take-away and went to bed. He makes us turn our phones off when it's just the two of us.'

'It's Katie, Pauline's daughter.'

'The one who went missing?' Amber said, hanging up her coat and chucking her bag beneath it.

'She'd dead. Murdered. They found her body yesterday morning.'

'What?' Amber spun round to Brenda, her hands to her face in shock. 'No! How awful. Oh my God.'

Brenda sighed. 'It's not like I knew the poor girl terribly well, but Pauline's been coming here for years. I remember her getting her hair done when she was pregnant with Katie. "I'm not going to look like I've been pulled through a hedge backwards in the photos this time," I remember her saying. "I looked like a drowned rat when Kyle was born." Oh, God, what she must be going through, losing her daughter like that. Jesus, if anything like that had happened to my Susan…'

She started to cry and Amber hustled round to give her a hug. 'It's just awful, Brenda. And she was so young.'

Brenda pulled out a tissue from her sleeve and wiped her eyes, shaking her head. 'I just can't believe it. It's like something off the TV. To think that someone I know…'

'Where did they find her?'

'Up on the common,' A slim shard of ice slid down Amber's back. 'Some kids found her, she'd been thrown into the bushes like rubbish.' Brenda's shoulders heaved. Amber hugged as hard as she could.

'Christ! We're right next to the common. Do they know who did it?'

'No. Not yet. But when they do, I hope they hang the bastard.'

'How do you know? I didn't hear anything on the radio this morning.'

Brenda clocked the time and started tidying herself up. It was pointless, as grief and shock had hollowed her face into a haggard mask. Without her bright cashmere jumpers, gold jewellery and trails of Opium, Brenda was diminished – looking all of her 60 odd years.

'Jacquie called me last night.' Jacquie was Brenda's much hated sister-in-law. 'Her son's a copper and he told her. She must have rung everybody I know, couldn't wait to spread the bad news,' Brenda said, her mouth pursing in disapproval. 'Bitch.'

Amber sat down with a thump next to Brenda. Her legs weren't strong enough to hold her up any longer. Katie wasn't much younger than me, she thought. She remembered the larky woman she had met in the nightclub loos and sadness hung heavy in her throat.

Katie's murder hit the news a few days later. Amber couldn't stop thinking about it. They'd used an awful photo of Katie - a silly selfie intended to make her Instagram followers laugh - and scatter-gunned it across all the front pages. Her pouting face was all over Amber's feeds, and every time she saw it her heart sank a little; it didn't look anything like the funny, straightforward woman she had met. Scrolling through her phone Amber grew sickened by the comments gathering pace under the stories and posts.

'How can they write this stuff?' she'd asked Alex one evening as he and Curly watched a football documentary. A programme Amber had found so boring she'd picked up her phone and disappeared down a cyber rabbit hole, chasing the trail of Katie's story.

'Wha?' Curly said, trying to light his cigarette the wrong way round. He'd been out drinking with the chippys from the new site and was halfway to passing out on the stinking bean bag he'd brought down from his room.

Amber read out the comments, the glowing screen lighting up her face in the darkness. '"She deserved it, dressing like that. What does she expect? Girls should know not to go out late at night".' Amber sighed in frustration. 'Who are these people? Who says these kinds of things? She was a trained nurse, not some YouTubing Instagram star – not that that matters - they're talking about her as if she encouraged her killer. Just because she posted a selfie where she's pulling a sexy face. Oh, it's so awful.' She threw her phone down.

'Can we stop banging on about it?' Alex said with a yawn. 'Bloody hell, babe, you're talking about her like she was your best mate.'

'Well, I did meet her once. I think.'

Alex reached over and settled his arm around Amber. 'Look, I'm not saying it's not sad. Of course it is. It's awful. But these things happen all the time. No point getting upset about it. Now, how about going and getting me another one of these?'

He held his ice-cold beer bottle against her arm, laughing when she jumped and pushed it away.

'I'll have another an' all,' said Curly. His hair was over his face and he hadn't bothered showering when he got in, so he was still dusty and smelled of wood shavings.

Amber got to her feet. It was stuffy and hot in the room and a sudden yearning to sit in the cool air was overwhelming. Winding through the junk in the kitchen she forced open the back door and sat on the step, looking up at the moon that sailed overhead. Katie's face hung before her.

A step behind her made her turn.

'What you up to, Amb? Fuck me! It's freezing.'

'Come and sit down, warm me up.'

She leaned into him, enjoying his warmth and the smell of his leather jacket.

'Why've you got your coat on? You going out?'

'Yeah, Tony just rang, got a problem with a radiator that's sprung a leak.'

Amber pulled away from him. 'Alex! It's gone nine o'clock in the evening!'

'Sorry, babe. I can't leave him in the lurch. I won't be long.' He stood up and slapped his jeans free of the dust from the step.

'Is Curly going with you?'

'Nope, he's out for the count.'

Amber held out her hand for Alex to pull her up. 'Do you really have to go?'

'Christ! How many times do I have to tell you?' He shook his hand free from hers. 'Do you think I want to get up and go out to fix some poxy radiator?'

'I'm sorry, Alex – of course you don't want to go. You're so good to your friends, you should try to say no more often.'

'You're probably right. I best be off. I won't be longer than an hour.'

Shutting the door behind Alex, Amber thought she might as well go to bed. She was halfway through the latest Lisa Jewell and wanted to take her mind off things. Curly appeared in the doorway as she started up the stairs. His wild hair made him look crazy, and he was having a good scratch around the crotch of his bagging jeans.

'Where did you all go?' he yawned like a cat, not bothering to cover his mouth.

'Alex had to go, got a call from Tony.'

'Tony?' he replied, rubbing the stubble on his face with the same hand he'd had down his trousers.

'Something about a radiator,' Amber said, going up the stairs.

'That's weird.'

'What?'

'He hasn't taken his tools,' Curly nodded at a big box by the front door. He waved his hand and shuffled towards the kitchen. Amber heard the fridge open and close and the clink of glass as he helped himself to another beer.

Alex wasn't back for hours. Amber had dropped off with her book, the lamp still shining, when he returned. She jerked awake with a start as he came in.

'Sorry, darl,' he said, pulling his shirt over his head and kicking off his shoes. 'Took fucking ages, Christ, it's cold! I'm freezing, you need to warm me up.' He jumped into bed, his high spirits so infectious she giggled, and forgot about asking why he didn't take his tools.

He kissed her, sliding his cold hands under Amber's shirt, making her gasp. 'Oooh, you're lovely and warm,' he said. 'Oh! And I nearly forgot – I've got everything booked for the weekend.'

Amber struggled upright, shoving a pillow behind her back. 'What weekend?'

'Remember? I told you I thought we haven't spent much proper time together, not since we got back from the honeymoon. What do you say? You and me, train down to Brighton. Nice hotel – well, B&B – happy?'

Amber grinned. 'Very. And just the two of us? No Curly?'

'Nope,' he said, pulling her back down under the covers. 'Just the two of us. Now come here, woman!'

*

The start of the weekend was blissful. Amber, feeling resentful, stuck at the back of the salon mixing up a quick colour for Laura's client again, gasped in delight when Alex appeared, waving through the big windows that looked out onto the street.

He'd marched in with a nod at Laura. 'Still got her doing your dirty work, Laura?' he'd called, a broad grin softening his words. Laura had laughed in protest. 'She did offer!' Dropping her hairspray and comb she'd danced over to Alex. 'Hello, stranger! I haven't seen you for ages!' She gave him a hug and Amber smiled to see him roll his eyes behind her back.

'I hope nobody minds if I take my gorgeous wife away for the weekend?' he'd called round. There was a chorus of ooh and aahs from the old dears sitting along the wall waiting for their shampoos and sets.

'I reckon you've got a good one there, Amber!' Mrs Evans had shouted. Dirty weekend, is it?' She and her elderly neighbour descended into school-girl giggles and Amber blushed.

'I'll see you on Monday, everyone,' she said, with a shy wave. 'Laura, I haven't finished mixing up…'

'S'all right,' she said. 'I'll do it now. Go on, you go enjoy yourself.'

Alex couldn't have been more loving. From the moment they'd arrived at the station Amber felt like a princess. They'd drunk champagne on the way down and she had grown tipsy on alcohol and the warmth of Alex's attention. They'd held hands like teenagers, gazing out the window as the city flickered by.

There was a tricky moment when they arrived as the taxi Alex had ordered wasn't there.

'It's fine, babe!' Amber had said as Alex marched up and down outside the station yelling into his phone. 'Look, we can just grab a minicab from that place on the corner.'

'That's not the point!' Alex shoved his phone back in his pocket looking furious. 'I ordered it so it would be waiting for us, so we didn't have to hang around this SHITHOLE of a station.' His roar pulled Amber's shoulders up to her ears.

At last, the cab arrived and Amber sat silent in the back as Alex fumed, playing with his phone, stabbing away at the screen.

'What are you doing?' She peered at his phone, but he angled his body away.

'Making sure this driver never fucks up again,' he growled.

'Oh, come on, Alex, I'm sure it wasn't his fault.'

'Whose fault was it, then? Mine?'

'No of course not… I just…'

But Alex was glaring out of the window, tapping his thighs. It was a familiar gesture and Amber knew to leave him alone until he calmed down.

The B&B was gorgeous. Amber had to repress an excited squeal as she bounced up the steps. The honeymoon had been the first time she had stayed in a hotel and she'd loved every minute. Her Mum used to take her to the caravan park at Reculver Bay most summers and she'd always looked forward to them, but they didn't compare to the luxury of a proper hotel.

Alex couldn't understand it when she told him on their honeymoon. 'Your Grandma must have been loaded to have that great big house,' he'd said as they lay on the beach, sipping mimosas and staring at the sea. 'How come you didn't go live it up in Ibiza with all the other rich kids?'

'Dunno,' Amber had laughed. 'We were always skint when I was growing up. I've never really thought about it. I don't think Mum and her got on when she was young, she didn't approve of my Dad – turned out she was right, as it happens. But anyway, Gran never worked – she lived off my Granddad's pension, after he died. It wasn't like she had loads of money.'

Now here she was, her second hotel of the year. It wasn't nearly as grand as the one Alex had chosen for their honeymoon, but it was striking, with a huge piano in the front lobby. Amber chattered away, exclaiming at everything, her face lit up with excitement.

All the rooms had a theme and Alex had chosen the 'Hamptons Room'. Amber loved the way it transported her from a chilly, wet evening in England to a beach house by the sea. The stripped floorboards were covered with sky-blue cotton rugs and the bed was wide and low. An old wooden chest that looked like it had been dragged from the sea served as a side table. Behind the bed the wall was panelled with reclaimed oak, giving the sleeping area the cosy feel of a ship's cabin. Best of all was an enormous claw-footed roll top bath placed in the floor to ceiling window that looked out over the sea.

'It's a bit cheesy,' Alex said, tossing the room key onto the bed.

Amber ran over to the bed and bounced on the crisp, white sheets. 'You hush, it's the best room I've ever seen in my life. You've got two minutes to get into that wonderful looking bath with me.'

*

Amber groaned with delight as Alex carried a huge tray over to the bed. Crowned with two silver cloches and smelling deliciously of fresh coffee, it was the most indulgent and glamorous way to wake up. 'You ordered breakfast in bed?' she said. 'When did you do that?'

'Only the best for my woman,' he replied. 'Now hurry up. I've got lots planned today,' He poured himself a coffee and bounced onto the bed next to her. He lifted a cloche to release a billow of bacon-scented steam. With a clatter of knife and fork he began to eat.

'Oh, my goodness, this is fantastic,' Amber grinned. 'Just what I need, I'm starving – we hardly had any dinner last night.' She lifted the other cloche, her mouth-watering in expectation. 'Oh.'

'What is it?' Alex leaned over and pinched a strawberry from her bowl.

'I was expecting the full English!' she exclaimed, careful to keep her voice light. 'I mean, this is lovely but…'

'You can't have too many carbs,' Alex explained, giving her leg a squeeze. 'And bacon, sausage and egg? All that fat? Not good for you.' He dunked his sausage in ketchup and took a bite.

'But it's all right for you?' said Amber, comparing his laden plate with her bowl of fruit and single croissant.

'I'm a bloke,' he shrugged. 'It's different.' He wiped his plate clean with a piece of fried bread and burped in satisfaction. 'Right! I'm getting up. Don't be long.'

They walked along the beach for miles. Amber couldn't stop smiling. Alex kept his arm tight around her, and the blast of cold, salty air brought the blood thrumming to the surface of her skin. He took her shopping in the Lanes, and for once Amber didn't worry about where the money was coming from

Smiling, he encouraged her to try on tops and dresses, running his hand over the skin of her shoulders when she came out of the changing room to show off a gold-green halter neck number. 'You're a beauty,' he whispered, his eyes darkening.

They explored the little shops until Amber's feet ached, her hands full of bags. Alex was on a mission, money burning a hole in his pocket, and only stopped when Amber ground to a halt outside a coffee shop and demanded a hot drink and a sit down.

'I can't believe you took a whole weekend away from the house,' she said as they drank their coffees. 'You haven't stopped since we got back from the honeymoon.'

'It's going to look amazing, babe,' he said. 'Honestly, at first the changes won't be obvious because so much of it is boring stuff like the electrics and the floors, but soon you're going to really see a difference.'

'I hope so, it's horrid living there with all that mess.'

'I promise, you, hand on heart…' Alex's phone rang, and he reached to check who was calling. He turned it face down. 'Honestly, you won't recognise the place – we'll be living the high life, babe.' His phone rang again, and he frowned in irritation.

'Who is it?'

'Nothing, nobody.' He opened his mouth to speak and was interrupted again by the phone's insistent ring. 'Fuck's sake!' he exclaimed.

'You'd better answer, it might be important,' Amber said.

'Fine!' Alex snapped and got to his feet. She watched him go out of the café, phone to his ear, before crossing the street. He was agitated, his hands jabbing into the air, his face looked drawn. After a few minutes, the call was over and Alex was back at the table lifting his coat from his char. 'Come on, I've got a surprise for you.'

'Who was that on the phone?' Amber said, knocking back the last of her coffee and picking up her bags.

'Oh, a guy I'm working for. Prick doesn't listen to what he's told. He's moaning because I haven't been in touch – Christ! It's only been a few weeks.'

'Are you behind on a job?' Amber said as she hurried after him.

'Nothing for you to worry about.' Alex strode on, hands in his pockets.

'Where are we going?'

They'd walked from one end of the street to another before Alex stopped. 'There they are!'

Amber's heart sank to see Curly and an over-dressed bosomy woman about her age sitting at a garden table outside a busy looking bar.

'I thought you said it was going to be just the two of us?' said Amber, but Alex had gone, jogging across the road and greeting Curly with a slap on the back as if he hadn't seen him for weeks.

Amber trailed behind, forcing a welcoming smile to her face.

'This is Brianna,' Curly was saying. 'We met on the train down. We've booked a room at your place, though it's nothing like yours.'

'You saw our room?'

'It's lovely, Amy.' The woman stood up to hug her, kissing each cheek leaving a greasy print of lipstick. Amber tried to work out what was off about her, then realised she had overdone the lip filler, so her mouth protruded forward before puffing out into two mushroom smooth pillows. Her breasts were glossy, dusted with a shimmering powder, and hoiked to chin height by a tight, low cut t-shirt. Her best feature was her hair, the colour of polished chestnuts it fell in perfect waves halfway down her back.

'I said to Curly – why couldn't you have got us a nice room like that? He spoils you, that Alex.'

'We could have just gone and stayed at yours,' Curly protested. Amber watched them in amazement, they'd only known each other a few hours and they were bickering like an old couple already.

Brianna turned to her and winked a heavily mascaraed, false-lashed eye. 'From what I hear, you're a lucky girl, Amy.'

'It's Amber,' she corrected. As Brianna chatted, Alex and Curly fell into a quiet conversation on the other side of the table.

'How did you get on?' Alex said, keeping his voice low. Amber could barely hear him over Brianna's prattle about 'what club they should go to later.'

'Good, man!' Curly replied. 'All of it went, you wouldn't believe how much…'

Alex put up his hand to stop him. 'Amber, babe, what do you want to drink? How about a cocktail?'

'Oooh lovely,' Brianna said. 'Can you see if they do a passion fruit daiquiri? Extra rum!'

'No problem,' Alex shot her one of his charming smiles. 'What about you, Amb?'

'Oh, just a glass of wine, thanks.'

Amber dropped her bags with a sigh and sat down. Her legs and ankles throbbed, and she wanted to go back to the hotel with Alex. She couldn't believe Curly had appeared; why hadn't Alex told her his friend was coming down?

Everyone except Amber seemed intent on getting as drunk as possible. Alex made it clear he found Brianna attractive and didn't take his eyes from her cleavage the whole evening. As Brianna grew more and more flirtatious, sucking on straws with her puffy lips and flipping her hair from one shoulder to another, Amber wondered why Curly didn't say anything.

By the time they ended up in a club Brianna was lolling about between Alex and Curly. Amber could see he was enjoying her attention but couldn't read his face when he looked over at her. Something nasty flickered at the edge of his smile.

Curly went to get more drinks. Amber asked for water, but he just laughed, and she knew he'd set before her some revolting concoction. Her stomach heaved at the thought. Alex had his hand on her thigh, but his other was twining a hank of Brianna's hair around his fingers. She was looking up at him as he spoke, hypnotised by his words.

Amber couldn't sit still a moment longer. She peeled Alex's hand from her leg and stood up.

'I think I'm going to go home,' she said, a rock of pain lodged deep in her throat. 'Alex? Shall we go?'

He eyed her with a lazy smile. 'What do you think, Brianna? Shall we all go back to the hotel?'

'Nah,' she hiccupped. 'Look, Curly's just brought more drinks! It would be rude not to finish these off.'

Amber didn't move. Curly slid past her with the drinks and sat down. She looked down at their sloppy, drunken faces and shot a pleading look at Alex. He shrugged and reached for his drink. He wasn't going anywhere.

She couldn't stay a minute longer but didn't want to go without Alex. She waited, passing people bumping against her as she tried to catch his eye again. She was desperate to connect with him, to make him see how bewildered she was, how lost. What was he doing? Was he angry with her? Was he trying to test her in some way?

Despite the sweaty heat of the club, Amber shivered. Alex had slammed the door on her, leaving her alone, shut off from the sun. She ran her hands up and down her arms. 'Alex,' she called again.

'Are you going or staying?' he replied at last, turning his head away from Brianna but sliding his hand under her hair.

'I'm going,' Amber said, trying to meet his eyes.

'Fine,' he replied. 'I'll see you later.'

She swallowed hard. 'Right, OK.' A blade of pain twisted in her side, but she stood up straight, blinking to stop the tears. They didn't even look up as she left, Curly watching Brianna and Alex with eyes that glittered.

Only when she reached the safety of the taxi did Amber let herself cry. Sobbing hard she waved away the concerned clucks from the driver. She kept checking her phone to see if Alex had called but there was nothing.

Back in her room, she left the curtains open so she could see the moon shining. She called Alex's phone over and over again, but he didn't answer. Eventually, she fell asleep, stretched across the bed where they'd made love so rapturously the night before. When she woke in the cold hours of the morning, the bed was still empty.

CHAPTER 10: LIZ

I knew as soon as I saw the photograph. Without any doubt. Even so, I scrolled through my years of saved articles to find the one I wanted. There she was. So much time had passed the photo looked dated. I had been unaware of any changes in fashion and hairstyle, but must have known enough, as the woman already looked as if she belonged to a different time.

This one had never been found. But I knew his type.

This is why I couldn't move on. It was the only thing I kept from Jenny. After years of being mocked and dismissed I'd given up my crusade, thrown myself into my work and cut myself off. It was too hard. Nobody took me seriously. The internet alerts had been quiet for months. I thought he'd stopped. Prayed he'd stopped. And now this.

I didn't know what to do; but I knew I had to do something. My thoughts kept turning to Sarah. A survivor like me, we'd become friends. Though we stood on different sides of the line. Me his past, and she his present. Well, she was then.

I saved Sarah's life. The knowledge of that was one of three good things I carried in my core. That, my work, and the memories of my Gran. They weighed good and heavy, keeping me from flying away from the clifftops. When I thought of them, I saw my Fairy Tale book, and the careless princess who lost her golden ball. Stupid woman to throw away her glittering gifts.

Sarah was the first, after me. As I lay, broken and mad on the floor, he'd moved on. Quick to charm another fool with his lazy smile and dark eyes. It didn't take me long to track him down. Hour after hour I would huddle in my car watching their relationship develop through light-hearted flirtation in trendy bars, to hours-long meals in restaurants

He knew I was there. I could tell by the way his shoulders hitched, wanting to turn. No matter where I hid he would recognise me, he could snuff me out – his muzzle lifted to the winds.

Once, only once, I'd crept into her house when I knew she was at work. Sifting through her things I looked for evidence he was doing the same to her as he did to me. Looking back, it was stupid. It made me weak, vulnerable. If she'd found out - if he'd found out - I'd have been locked up. I certainly came close to it. I hadn't found anything, anyway. Not then. He was too clever to leave a trace.

I needed to talk to Sarah. Not just to make sure she was OK, but I needed her clear, straightforward way of thinking. She hadn't been damaged as I had. My scars remained, a crazed glaze of fine cracks, but she'd escaped in time. She was a woman of action, once her mind was made up, she was decisive and certain.

I could call the police. Ring up the detective in charge of the investigation of the poor, strangled woman and tell him what I knew. But the moment they heard my name and looked me up, they'd find a bulging file detailing all the accusations and demands

I'd thrown at the police over the years. I pictured the file, stained with coffee, hand-written pages sliding from it – every line damning me as unhinged, desperate: a stalker.

It was a stupid vision. Everything would be digital now – no bulging manilla folders. And digital files were easier to share, easier to cross-reference. All the calls I made would be logged, the many visits to the station where I was constantly fobbed off. No. I needed Sarah. I needed her calm assurance. People listened to her when they didn't listen to me. She was the one who thought to keep records. She made notes, laid out her experiences in a neat, detailed sequence of events.

I thought of the two of us in that horrid little room. Me, hair wild, twitchy with nerves, a scrabble of pages covered in jerky snatches of sentences. Sarah, cool and still, her hair tied back in a neat ponytail, unsnapping an elastic band from a handful of notebooks. Not that it did any good.

There would be more. I knew it in the marrow of my bones. If I could just find them and present the evidence to the police, they would find the link themselves. There would be something, some thread, some fragment he would have overlooked. It had to be irrefutable though, I thought. I knew too well how able he was to spin a convincing story.

Hands clicking across the keyboard, I broadened my internet search, and created alerts using more key words. Reading news article after news article. Scanning through paragraphs of tiny text made my eyes dry into spongy wedges of tissue, and I had to push my thumbs into the lids to make them close.

*

I didn't remember falling asleep. The crash of glass from the pub outside woke me up with a jerk on Sunday morning. My face ached from being pressed against the cold wood all night.

Grey light at the window told me it was early; confusion jangled bells in my head and my eyes hurt. As the coffee brewed, I stretched my back and powered up my phone. A stream of texts pinged in, all from Will.

There was also a missed call from the hotel; they must have phoned when I was out flying around on Will's bike. Three voicemails had been left, one from the hotel and two from Will. I ignored them. I had to talk to Sarah. I needed her to help me gather my thoughts, decide what do. Most important, with Sarah by my side I knew I'd be believed.

I woke my laptop and went straight to Facebook to check my messages and Sarah's page. No change. My only lead was her brother, Daniel. His page was active; I could see he'd shared a movie recommendation only a few days before. A chirpy string of comments under his post discussed the film. Opinion seemed to be divided.

Life moved on it would seem. Even though young women were lying in morgues and more were missing; women who slipped quietly through crowded streets and disappeared.

Daniel was the only way I could think of to contact Sarah. I couldn't remember if we'd met, I didn't think so, but I didn't remember much from that time.

'*Hi Daniel,*' I wrote in the message box. '*You don't know me, but I was very close to Sarah in the past. I'm trying to track her down as she hasn't been in touch. Do you have a number for her? Thank you. Liz.*'

The blinking cursor burned itself onto the back of my eyes as I stared at the screen. Five minutes passed. Ten. I didn't move. I was gripped with a superstitious certainty that if I looked away, he'd never answer, and all would be lost.

My patience was rewarded. Suddenly his profile picture appeared next to my message, just as it had done when I messaged Sarah. But this time, three blue bubbles danced at the corner of my screen. He was writing back! I had to take a breath; I hadn't realised I had been holding it for so long.

'*Hello, Liz. How do you know Sarah?*'

I flexed my fingers, I had to get this right. '*I'm an old friend,*' I typed with great care. '*We've lost touch, and I'd love to see her again.*'

'*I'm afraid I can't help you.*' Daniel's smiling profile photograph belied the terseness of his words.

'*Oh dear,*' I forced myself to sound calm. '*Why is that? I don't mind waiting if you'd like to check with Sarah before passing on her number, or maybe you could give her mine?*'

The blue dots bubbled again. Stopped. Then bubbled. But no reply. I rubbed my head as I waited, holding myself back from typing a load of questions and demands.

'*I don't have Sarah's number,*' he wrote at last. '*I haven't seen her for years.*'

Shock smacked me in the face as I stared at the screen, not able to take in the meaning of the words. Had he misunderstood what I meant? I thought. How could he not have seen Sarah for so long? My fingers started to type then faltered when I realised I had no idea what to write beyond 'WHY?'

My hands fell away from the keyboard. Sarah and Daniel were close. Over the short time I'd spent with her she'd spoken of him often. He'd been living away. A memory sprang into my head – fully formed. Sarah and I, facing each other in a Starbucks.

'I wish Daniel was here,' she had said. 'I don't want to worry my Mum and Dad with all this crap. He'd be all right, though. Probably laugh about it all. Just what I need right now.'

The strength of the memory rocked me. I could picture every line of Sarah's face, the length of her lashes and the pinched corners of her mouth. Daniel was studying in Spain and she was going to go and see him when the mess was all over.

And now he hadn't seen her in years? In the quiet of my kitchen I shivered. Someone had stepped on my grave. Something was wrong.

Clicking away from Facebook messenger I scrolled through Daniel's profile, gathering information. Where he lived, where he worked. I studied his photographs looking for clues, familiar landmarks. Anything that would tell me where he was as I knew nothing about him. Despite the brief intimacy of my relationship with Sarah I knew none of the details of her life.

Cambridge. He lived in Cambridge. I flicked back to the messenger box where the warp and weft of our conversation wove down the screen.

'*Hi Daniel. Funnily enough* (I cringed as I wrote the words) *I've got a meeting in Cambridge tomorrow,*' I wrote. '*I'd like to talk to you about Sarah in person. Would that be possible?*' Daniel didn't reply for almost half an hour. I had nothing to do but wait.

'*It's not really very convenient,*' his response spooled across the screen. '*I'm at work and won't be finished until late.*'

'*That's fine,*' I typed as fast as I could; I sensed an opening and I wanted to get through to him before it closed. '*More than happy to see you after you finish work – it doesn't matter how late it is. I'll buy you a drink?*'

Another pause. More blue bubbles.

'*OK. Send me your number and I'll text you the details. I warn you, though – it might not be until after 7.*'

'*Perfect,*' I wrote, sending him my mobile number. Then he was gone. My coffee was cold, but I drank it anyway as I brought up the train times on Google. Not having a car didn't usually bother me, the city was small, and my bike got me round well enough, and there was always Uber. But to get to Cambridge there was only the train. A hire car would be too expensive, and I still didn't really trust myself behind a wheel.

It took me a frustrating 40 minutes to find my rucksack. I shoved in a change of clothes and a bottle of water. It didn't take long to check the flat was secure and I sat down to wait. It was only eleven in the morning and the day stretched empty ahead of me. I couldn't settle to anything. Even a long run and a punishing strength work out couldn't stop the itch feathering against my skin.

'Fuck it,' I said at last and picked up my rucksack. I'd just have to find somewhere to stay in Cambridge. I didn't have much, but probably enough for a room if it was somewhere cheap.

The train was delayed twice, and it took just over three hours. I took my sketch book and tried to work on some ideas as countryside flickered past my window. I was working on something new, a sculpture of paper using pages from old children's books. I thought they'd be something nice for a nursery, but the inspiration kept disappearing. Sarah's face appeared under my pencil, a slight frown between her brows and shadows under her eyes. I couldn't remember what her smile looked like.

*

I had to get it right. I'd rehearsed my lines over and over on the journey to Cambridge; I didn't want to sound mad, or paranoid, or too desperate, though I was all of those things. My phone buzzed in my pocket, Will again. Regret landed on my skin, light and clinging as a cobweb.

I'd managed to find an Airbnb right next to the station. It was cheap and uncomfortable, and my bones ached from a night in a cold room on a damp sofa bed. From my window I could see a corner of Parker's Piece and in the dawn light there were already runners jogging across the grass, their breath clouding in front of them. I longed to join them, my legs needed to move after the hours on the train, but I hadn't brought my running gear.

Push up, dips and squats in the tiny bedroom had to do, and I scrubbed off the sweat as best I could at the sink, avoiding my white-faced reflection as I thought again what I would say to Daniel.

Monday passed slowly. Walking around the streets until my feet were sore, I'd seen as much of Cambridge as possible without money. We'd arranged to meet at a pub called The Mill, which was close to where Daniel worked. I arrived at six with an hour to wait. Nobody noticed me; was I invisible? The streets were busy and more than once people walked straight into me as if I wasn't there. Maybe I wasn't. Maybe I didn't survive, and I was some terrible wraith that haunted the earth looking for revenge.

Ghosts don't have to take trains, I reminded myself, and tried to remember the last time I had spoken to anyone. Sometimes weeks would go by and I would feel my throat closing with disuse and I would clear it loudly, shocking myself with the noise.

Leaning against the wall by the kitchens in the bar, I looked down at my legs and my hands, making sure my bag was firm across my shoulders. I checked my face looked normal in the glass of the window and practiced a smile.

Daniel's colouring was different, but I could see Sarah in the slant of his eyebrow and the shape of his mouth. I waited a moment to study him as he entered the bar, impatiently checking his watch and scanning the crowd.

'Daniel? Hi!' I said, reaching out to give him a firm handshake.

'Liz? Good to meet you. Would you like a drink?'

'I'll get them, what are you having?' The hearty words doughy in my mouth.

'I'll have a pint of Symonds.'

'OK, do you want to grab that table and I'll bring them over?'

I could see his discomfort, despite the genial grin. He sat at the table flicking a beermat between his fingers.

I carried over his drink and my coffee and waited as he took a deep swallow. 'Needed that,' he said, licking his lips.

'Long day?'

He shrugged and tilted the glass to his mouth again.

'Look, Daniel, I know this is weird, and thank you so much for agreeing to see me. I don't normally chase down people like this.' I attempted a laugh.

He rubbed his head. 'He warned me you'd come and speak to me.'

'Sorry?'

'Sarah's husband. He told me he had some crazy ex who kept stalking him. Said you tried to ruin every relationship he'd ever had.'

I clutched the edge of the table to stop my reeling head throwing me backwards. Shock punched the thoughts from my head and my mouth opened as I struggled for words. 'I don't understand,' I said at last, 'Sarah's husband? They got married? But that's impossible.'

Daniel shook his head. 'None of this makes sense,' he muttered.

'Why the hell would she have married him if she went to the police to report him for abuse?' I scratched at my neck and tugged at the roots of my hair. 'And don't tell me she didn't because I was there.'

As I sat across from Daniel seeing my shock mirrored in the white of his face I remembered sitting with Sarah, holding her hand as she sobbed and tried to light a cigarette at the same time.

'He repulses me now,' she'd said. 'I know you told me to wait, but I can't do this much longer. I can see through everything he does. The lies he tells me,' she gave a cough of a laugh, 'how the fuck did I not see them before? He's made me feel shit about myself for two years, I thought I was going mad. And you're right, money has gone missing…'

'…That's why I agreed to see you.' Daniel's voice broke into my memory and Sarah's desperate face disappeared.

'Sorry, what?'

'I'm worried about Sarah,' Daniel repeated. 'When I saw your name on Facebook, I knew you were the one he'd told me to watch out for but…'

'Daniel, I can't get my head around this. You said she married him?'

He sighed. 'Look, I was away when they fell out.'

'Fell out?' I couldn't believe it, Sarah marrying the monster after all we'd went through was as impossible as me being able to fly out of the window. The idea refused to settle in my head, my body rejected it as preposterous.

'I never found out the details. She wouldn't say anything to Mum and Dad, he told them...'

'He told them?' I said. 'Not Sarah?'

'Well, no. She'd already gone off and got married by the time I got back from Spain. Mum and Dad were so upset they'd just shot off and got married somewhere ridiculous on their own.'

I stood up with a jerk, knocking my chair against the wall. 'I can't take all of this in. I don't understand.'

'What's the matter?' Daniel half stood, trapped behind the table. 'Are you OK?'

'Can we walk?' I said, pulling at my hair. 'I can't stay in here, it's too... small, I need to get out.' I looked around for the door and headed for it, pushing aside a group of old men with dogs at their feet.

'Hey! Wait!' Daniel called, but I was out and taking deep gasps of air, my heart thudding.

'It's freezing out here,' he complained, pulling his coat around him.

'Let's walk,' I said. A fence strung with bikes stood in front of me and a lake of boats to my left, knocking against each other with a hollow wooden sound. I turned left and almost jogged along the road until I saw a gate leading to a path that ran alongside the river.

Once I'd got past the buildings and could see the water, my breathing began to calm down. I could hear Daniel behind me, trotting to keep up.

'What the hell is going on?' he said. He looked ridiculous, red-faced in his grey suit, his sandy-blond hair awry.

I slowed down. 'OK, I'm sorry, I know this is all very strange, but I got to know Sarah well.' As I talked, my steps paced faster, in time with my words. 'Alex was a very dangerous man, you're right, I was his ex – for a long time, we met at uni – and the relationship nearly killed me. It took me a long time to recover, longer than I would have liked. There were other women, but I was too fucked up to do anything about them, but I did do something for Sarah. It is one of the few good things I have ever done.'

I looked over at Daniel who looked bewildered. I tried to stop my face twisting. How could Daniel possibly think Sarah had gone on to marry him?

'When was the last time you heard from Sarah, what happened?'

'Can you slow down a bit?' he said, his breath starting to puff. Worry was replacing the bewilderment in his eyes. 'So, it was a few years ago now, maybe five or six? I was studying in Spain so I only heard about what was going on with Sarah through Mum and Dad and the occasional message or phone call when Sarah could be bothered. I thought it was a bit odd at the time as we'd always been so close. Mum thought it was because she was head over heels in love.'

'Sounds familiar,' I said, remembering with a strange yearning the early days when I was mad with desire.

'Anyway, she called me to say she was engaged. I'd never heard her so happy – I was so pleased for her. She was a bit older than me and I could see she was desperate to settle down and have loads of babies.' He smiled, and my heart wrung to see Sarah in him. 'You've reminded me of how much I miss her,' he said.

'I think this is where I came in,' I said. 'I knew he'd proposed as he made a great show of setting it all up. I saw the whole thing.'

'You watched them?'

'I was trying to protect her! I needed to warn her! When I saw him propose in that stupid, over the top way I knew I had to do something.'

'What did you do?'

'I kept on watching, then I managed to talk to Sarah. I explained everything, we went to the police… So where is she now? None of this makes sense!'

'They married abroad,' Daniel said, his face creased like paper. 'Mum said he'd got a job in France, Sarah went with him, he called me from there a couple of times.'

'Why did he call you? Why not Sarah?'

Daniel blew out an exasperated sigh. 'I don't know! She'd fallen out with Mum and Dad over going away for the wedding and not inviting them, I assumed she didn't want to speak to me either. In fact, I remember thinking what a good bloke he was keeping us up-to-date.'

'A good bloke?' I could see Daniel was irritated by my incredulity. I was losing him, so I pulled up my sleeves and thrust my wrists towards him, turning the soft inner skin so he could see.

He stopped and I watched his eyes run along the weals that ribboned up from the join of my wrist stretching towards my elbow. 'They're called keloid scars. They're from old wounds.'

Daniel frowned. 'Did you do this?'

'No,' I said. 'He did.'

SARAH: FIVE YEARS AGO

A sudden clatter woke her. Bleary eyed she looked round. She chafed her hands rubbing her empty ring finger in concern. She began to search her bag with terrible intensity before finding what she was looking for in her jeans' pocket. For a moment she gazed at the ring. A quick polish on her jumper made it shine and she ran the coolness of the metal across her top lip. She held it there for a moment before shaking her head and buttoning it back up.

The train was empty. Puzzled, she stood and looked from one end to another. Nobody. This wasn't the Eurostar. This train was old and smelled bad. It had none of the slickness of the one she had taken from London.

She used the windowsill to get to her feet, stumbling twice, and pressed her face against the glass to see if she recognised anything. Two empty wine bottles rolled back and forth under the seats, clanking softly against each other.

Against the light of the window her wasted body was clearly visible, holding up the filthy jumper like a pair of wire coat hangers. She bumped back down on her seat – it was no good, she had no idea where she was.

Frowning, she tried to remember the name of the village. She'd been pretty wasted by the time the train pulled into Paris. Black holes had eaten away at her brain over the last year and great chunks had fallen into darkness, never to be retrieved. She banged at her skull to knock the memories free.

She began to mutter to herself, picking through her bag and examining the leather pieces she found there. She was going to sell them. She needed the money. But why in France? She found the flyer. A festival. That's right. She was hoping to sell what she'd made at the big musical festival.

But this wasn't Paris. She stood up again and scanned the landscape. All she could see was green fields and woods. Her head ached. What had happened in Paris? She ran her fingers into the hem of her bag until she found some pills, swallowing them dry. She pressed the heel of her hand hard against her forehead.

The phone call. Her pulp of a heart contracted painfully. Fear - clean, cold, and sharp as a knife - cut through the thick matter clogging her skull. She remembered the voice, panicked, whispering she needed her help. Would she come? Would she come?

Like a rocket shooting hot sparks, the pill took effect. Lying her head back against the seat rest, skin so sensitive she could feel every bump and seam of the faded blue cloth, she closed her eyes to stop them jerking from side to side.

She remembered writing the address on a piece of paper. She found it, folded over and over into a small packet. It took her three goes to make sense of it. Her tongue lay thick in her mouth and a strange sound rang in her ears. The writing was smudged, she must have written it in a rush, it slid across the page and fell off the corner but there was enough to read the address. Her head reeled as the view from the window blurred into smears of colour.

'Madame! Madame! Se réveiller! Wake up. We have reached the terminus.'

She awoke to find herself slumped against the train window, a guard shaking her shoulder. Despite her protests he grabbed her jacket and pulled her to her feet, pushing the bag into her arms. 'That's my bag,' she slurred. 'I've got everything in there, very important things. Hey! Stop pushing me! I'll go, I'll go. Wait!' She looked at her hand in terror. 'Where's my ring? What have you done with my ring?'

The guard tutted and, with a shake of his head, hustled her onto the platform. She stumbled and fell, scraping her knees and the heel of her hand. 'It's my Gran's ring – it's gone. Wait, you have to stop the train!' She turned to the porter standing by the gate, but he looked away. It started to rain.

She gathered up the things that had bounced crazily along the platform and put them back in her bag. A wrap of blow fell out and without a moment's hesitation she shook some into her fingernail and took a deep, wet sniff. The needles fired into the front of her skull and she blinked. Her pocket. She patted her hip. Of course. The ring. To keep it safe.

It was starting to rain. She looked round blinking as the drizzle slid down her face in sheets, like tears. Outside the tiny station, holding onto her bag, she looked left and right. The road was deserted. Two bungalows with white faces and red roofs leaned against each other across the way. Something flickered in the corner of her eye, a sudden movement and she turned, almost falling as her legs shook. A young guy was watching her. He was unshaven and his face was scabbed.

'Can you take me here?' she said, holding out her paper. A gust of air almost tugged it out of her hand and snatched the words from her mouth. 'I need to help my friend,' she tried again, throwing her voice across the wind. 'She called me but… I can't remember what she said… I wrote her address down and I must find her. Can you help me?'

The man threw down his cigarette and blew smoke into the night air. 'Let me see.'

'Oh, you're French.' She waited, shivering, as he examined her paper. His eyes wandered across her grey face and traced the marks on her throat and hands. He passed the paper back to her.

'Yes. I know this place. It is a walk away. Perhaps a drink first?' He jerked his head to the end of the road where a square of light laid a yellow path across the gathering gloom of the evening.

'Yes. Please. Thank you.' She slung her bag across her body and held it tight as they walked to the bar. She stumbled a few times and the young man took hold of her elbow. She tried to focus on his face, it looked like he was smiling.

'What's your name?' she said as he guided her to a table in the corner. It was empty except for a fat old man with a dog who huddled over a pastis at the bar.

'Marc,' he replied. 'I will get you wine? Yes?'

'Please.'

More of his friends arrived as the evening wore on. Dressed like Marc in tracksuits and beanies they filled the bar with noise. She couldn't understand anything but didn't care, Marc had slipped her some pills as she went to the toilet and she was happy riding the rush.

She showed the creased paper with the address to everyone, they nodded and smiled, and Marc would wave his hand. 'Later. We go later. I'll show you. Have a good time now, poulette, OK?'

She gave up, sitting back and letting the incomprehensible chatter wash over her. She smiled at the ribbons of colour that wreathed around the lights and hung in the air. A blue-haired woman across the table smiled back, piercings winking from her lips and nose.

A blink and she was giggling, arm in arm with a man called Felix, the blue-haired woman behind her. Gravel crunched beneath her feet and Marc's torch light bounced crazily along the road as they walked towards a house that loomed dark ahead of them.

He opened the door with a rattle and a strong smell of diesel and cowshit billowed out, it was freezing, and she rubbed her arms –

CHAPTER 11: AMBER

'You're getting too thin, hun.' Amahle pushed the second half of her Snickers Duo across the massage table at Amber. 'What's up with you? You're not dieting, are you?'

Amber shook her head and cracked some of the chocolate shell away, placing it on her tongue. The sweetness turned sticky in the dry cave of her mouth. 'I'm just not sleeping very well, off my food a bit.'

'Fuck! You're not pregnant?'

Amber shook her head again and swallowed. Amahle looked at her friend with concern. Amber's glorious cloud of dark hair was dry, and her collar bones rose sharp as knives; her skin gleamed so pale it had a greenish tinge.

Sensing the weight of Amahle's gaze Amber straightened and ran her hands through her hair, smoothing it and flipping a slither of fringe over her eyes.

'What is it? What's happened?

'Nothing, Amahle. I promise. Stop fussing. I'm probably just coming down with something.'

'And Alex is OK?'

'Of course! He's fine. Why wouldn't he be?'

Amahle gave a gesture of surrender. Packing up her lunch she stood and gave Amber a quick squeeze, smacking a kiss on her cheek. 'You know I'm always here, babe. If you need me.' Her voice was soft.

'I'd better get on,' Amber rubbed her nose and sniffed. The temptation to blurt out everything was intolerable. Things had gone so badly wrong in Brighton and now Alex had gone missing.

He hadn't apologised. When he finally turned up, stinking of beer and dry-eyed with exhaustion, Amber expected sorrowful tales of broken-down taxis, tears of regret and sad bunches of flowers snatched from a garage forecourt.

But there was nothing. He'd fallen into bed and a deep sleep, only waking when she'd poked him awake to remind him they needed to check out.

The journey home from Brighton had none of the larkiness of the trip down. Alex stared at his phone the whole way while Amber looked out of the window, refusing to talk to him. Curly, who'd had the sense to sit a few rows behind, slept with his mouth open, his face squashed against the glass of the train window.

Amber's stomach churned. Whenever she thought of Brianna with her knowing smile and fleshy curves, she wanted to be sick. Had Alex done it with her? she thought, her heart thudding. How could he? She refused to believe it, couldn't believe it. They'd only just returned from their honeymoon.

She turned the rings on her finger as the landscape jittering past darkened. She longed to be back in her cool, white bedroom where she could talk to Alex properly. Explain how hurt she was, how angry and upset that it looked like he'd spent the night with that awful woman.

Avoiding her solemn reflection, Amber looked up at the sky. She knew, deep in her heart he couldn't have cheated. He loved her too much to go that far. But she'd upset him; he'd been cross with her for not being more pleased to see Curly, for being a party pooper when he wanted to stay out late drinking. He hadn't said anything, but she'd seen it in the tightness of his jaw. She hated it when she saw that muscle jumping, livid, reminding her of clenched fists.

Amber sighed, risking a glance over at Alex but his head stayed low, his rapid fingers dotting over the screen. Who was he texting? she wondered.

You've got to be calm, she told herself, eyes turning back to the window; there's no point in being emotional. Alex always hated it when she got upset with him. He'd grow so angry and defensive a small complaint would blow up into a row. She resolved to apologise for not being happier that Curly had come down, and to show how grateful she was that he'd made such an effort to find that gorgeous hotel. With a frown she tried to work out how best to tell him that he couldn't just go off with his friends all night. They were married now and…

With a sudden, shocking feeling of air being sucked from her ears the train plunged into a tunnel. Amber touched her eyelids to check her eyes were still open. In the darkness a tear slipped past her fingertips.

*

Back at the house Curly pushed past them up to his lair. Alex, carrying two bags with one hand, eyes still fixed on the phone in the other, walked into the sitting room.

'Tea?' asked Amber, her voice cracking after so many hours of silence. Alex grunted in response. She washed her hands in the stained, green sink and ran water around the back of her neck. Her skin felt grimy and she dreamed about soaking in a foot-deep bath with Alex after they'd had an honest talk.

Feeling better, she carried the mugs out of the kitchen along the hall to the sitting room just as the front door slammed shut.

'Alex?' she called, putting the mugs on the floor and running to the window. 'Alex!' she shouted, pulling the door open. The stone path was cold under her bare feet as she picked her way past the thistles and nettles thronging the front garden to the gate. Feeling the wrought iron pressing into her hips she leaned forward looking left and right down the street. There was no sign of him.

Blinking back tears and breathing deep to control her panic she went back inside. She managed to knock over the mugs and gasped as tea splashed burning hot across her feet and ankles. She cleared it up, keeping her mind blank. Her heart continued to thud in her ears. What if he didn't come back?

Pulling her phone from her back pocket she stabbed at his number. They had to talk. She wasn't going to take no for an answer.

Amber let the phone ring out three, four, five times. She would leave it for five minutes, then do the same again. Hours passed as she waited in the hall, leaning against the wall so she could see out of the window if he returned. She toyed with the idea of going to find him, but her ears burned with humiliation at the thought, and she was frightened of what she might find. Curly would know what pub he was in, but there was no way she was going to let him know she and Alex were having troubles. She could imagine the knowing look he'd give her.

The rest of the day dragged. With her phone by her side Amber stared, unseeing at the television. Curly clanked in and out and spent the afternoon working on stripping out the kitchen, chucking the ripped-up units and strips of lino into the back garden.

Then he too left, and Amber tried to ignore the emptiness of the house. No matter how much she turned up the volume on the TV the echoing silence thrummed at the corners of the room and she grew cold. Her thoughts banged from one side of her brain to the other. The sense of outrage at Alex's treatment of her in Brighton was hard and burned hot. But the longer he stayed away, the longer he didn't answer her calls or respond to her increasingly desperate texts, the greater the fear grew.

What if he'd done something stupid? She thought. Or had an accident, got too drunk and fallen into the road? Amber stood, knocking the collection of remote controls to the floor. They flew everywhere and she couldn't find the one that turned off the television.

The squawking of a ludicrous game show made Amber's skin itch. After a fruitless search under the sofa followed by an attempt to find the off button on the new flatscreen, she eventually ripped the plug from the wall, almost weeping with frustration.

She couldn't sit still. She knew she should eat but the thought of pushing food into her mouth was inconceivable. Again, she brought up the 'find my' app. Amber's eyes watered as she focused on the screen, refreshing and refreshing, but Alex's icon on the map didn't change. It still showed his location as in the house over eight hours ago. Had he stopped sharing his location?

Another gulp of panic pushed Amber up the stairs and into the bedroom. She stood at the window with the lights off, pressing her face against the cold glass searching left and right up the lamplit street, desperate to see Alex's returning figure.

The hours ticked by. At four in the morning Amber could barely move, she was so cold. Shivering and wretched she slid under the covers, clutching her phone, calling Alex one more time before sleep knocked her unconscious.

*

Amber called in sick the following day. She was unable to do anything but sit on the sofa in a strange, blank limbo, waiting for Alex to return. She scrolled through the news on her phone, not taking it in but recognising Katie's photograph. The investigation was still ongoing, but no arrests had been made. Two more plumply pretty faces linked to Katie's article. One looked familiar and something shifted in Amber stomach. Her finger hovered over the link but jumped as the phone shrieked in her hand. Amahle.

Amber let it ring, her thoughts racing. Maybe Amahle knew something about Alex? Indecision paralysed her, and by the time she answered the call Amahle had rung off. Pushing her hands through her hair, wincing at the knots and lankness of it, Amber imagined calling Amahle back, knowing she would sense something was wrong the moment Amber spoke and would pick and pick until she found out what had happened. But if she knew something about Alex…?

No. Her head was too full of worry about Alex to even think about talking to Amahle. She would call back if it were important. It was just because she didn't go into work. She'd have to go in tomorrow; she couldn't risk taking too much time off.

She'd felt half-crazed with lack of sleep when she arrived at the salon the following day. She'd lain in bed until gone two when her whirring head forced her to get up and walk around, phoning Alex over and over again. By four am she had gnawed her fingers to bleeding and started to ring hospitals.

Curly, pulling on his boots and dropping his phone in the hall, jerked Amber awake. She had fallen into a head-nodding doze on the arm of the sofa and the noise made her head ache. Her lips had chapped into flakes; her eyes felt strange: gritty and wet.

'Curly!' she called, grabbing the arm of her sofa as dizziness pulled her down. Her voice cracked and she called again. 'Curly?'

'Yeah?'

He was so heavily wrapped in a coat and scarf Amber couldn't make out his face, He looked big and menacing in the hallway. Only his shock of dark curls assured her it was him.

'Do you know where Alex is? I... er... he said something, but I can't remember where he said he was going...' Amber cheeks grew red with the lie.

Curly stopped and looked at her; he took his time buttoning up his donkey jacket. 'Done a bunk has he?'

'No! No! Nothing like that, it's just I thought...'

Curly's eyes softened. 'Don't you worry, Amb, he's a funny bloke. He gets moods like this, always has done. Needs to get away every now and then. Clear his head. He'll be back. He told me he was going up North, something he's hoping to pick up from the house.'

'He's called you?'

'Nah, just a text. Sorry, love, I've got to go. I'll be late.' He tucked his phone away and lit a cigarette, going out into the dark and letting the door slam behind him. Amber's shoulders slumped but she was aware of a boiling fury bubbling up from her stomach. Was Alex playing some kind of game? The bastard. Leaving her to worry like this when it was obvious he was fine.

It was anger that propelled her into work, despite her exhaustion, where she was grateful for the extra load of clients she had to see. She refused to stop for lunch and kept on her feet all day forcing away any thoughts of Alex, though she kept her phone close in case he rang. She must have radiated a fierce energy as nobody approached her beyond asking meekly if she wanted a cup of tea.

Amber was aware of the pointed glances going on behind her back, but she ignored them. She leaned heavily on her anger to push back the pain and worry that left her stomach gaping. It was gone six by the time she finished, and she thanked God Amahle wasn't in that day as she would have beetled straight over and not let up until Amber told her everything.

*

It was a week before Alex returned. In that time the fierce, white-hot rage that crackled across Amber's skin had faded. She couldn't eat, and the house echoed hollow as a drum every evening when she returned from work. Curly hadn't come back either and an apathy had stolen over her. She wished she could shake it off, go out and look for Alex, but she didn't know where to start and besides, with no car it was hopeless.

After staring, unseeing, at the television until her eyes burned, Amber sat and drank glass after glass of wine, waiting for the gnawing teeth of anxiety to retreat a little. An idea struck. Holding a second bottle by its neck she walked into the bedroom, an electric wire of nerves that felt like excitement twisted in her guts. She would search his things.

It didn't take long. It shocked her how little Alex had stored in his cupboard and drawers. The bedside cabinet held nothing but a pair of old chargers and a sticky, oozing puddle of what looked like cough syrup in the bottom corner; tissue and fragments of paper had stuck there.

Amber ran her hands through his clothes, exploring his pockets, skin prickling at the familiar smell that drifted from the jumpers and jackets. He'd never said anything, but she knew he'd hate the thought of her going through his stuff. She shrugged off the thought, she had to do something.

With a sigh she gave up and sat on the bed. She'd found nothing beyond clothes and loose change. It struck her as strange that a man of Alex's age hadn't accumulated more junk, but perhaps he wasn't the kind of man who kept things.

Unlike Curly, Amber thought as she stood in the doorway to his room. She'd locked the front door from the inside in case he made a sudden reappearance before she'd had a chance to look around.

Clothes were everywhere. Piles of trainers tossed into the corner were the source of a smell so pungent it made her gag. A small TV and a games console were piled high with discs that had slipped and scattered like coins over the desk. She couldn't see the floor, hoodies and jeans clambered over the carpet in a chaotic mess of arms and legs like dismembered bodies.

Amber rubbed her arms again. She knew she should eat, but some part of her seemed to be waiting for Alex before allowing her to carry on as normal. Curly's drawers were pulled open, out of which spilled more clothes. She tentatively pulled open the smaller, top drawer but it was stuffed full of different coloured wires and she didn't have the energy to explore further. She kept thinking she could hear Curly returning and her heart would thud with panic at the thought of him catching her prying through his things.

She didn't really know why she was here. The smell was now overwhelming, but something was keeping her in the room. She looked around again, resisting the temptation to rattle open the big window to let in the cold air.

Trying hard not to move anything, she made for the door, but her bracelet caught on the woolly edge of a blanket and it slithered behind her and something thudded to the floor.

'Shit,' Amber whispered softly and crouched to pick up whatever it was to put on the bed.

It was a small, square laptop. Pausing to check there was no sound of someone trying to get into the house, Amber opened it. The screen was so bright in the dark room it made her wince. Blinking she waited for her eyes to adjust.

Curly had left his laptop open on Facebook. She was surprised, he didn't seem the type, bit old-fashioned, she thought. She didn't know the girl on the page. Maybe Curly was stalking an ex? Amber thought with a small smile. She checked through the other tabs but there was nothing very interesting: just a local building supplier, eBay and Gumtree.

Feeling weak with tiredness Amber put the laptop back under the blanket noticing with revulsion how dirty Curly's sheets were. A battered grey box file lay in the middle of the bed filled with so much paper the clasp had bulged open. Rubbing her eyes Amber pulled out a sheet to see it was a bank statement.

A sudden awareness of how intrusive she was being filled her with scarlet-cheeked shame and she pushed to her feet and left the room, closing the door quietly behind her. Cross with herself for prying, particularly as she hadn't found anything of any use,

Amber returned to her bedroom where she gulped at the second bottle of wine until it felled her into sleep.

It was four more days until Alex came back. Days in which Amber swung from fury to despair. It was exhausting. It felt like madness. Rage would swamp her, and she longed to scream down the phone at him, asking why he would put her through this. And then her heart would thump and lurch with horror wondering if he had left her and was never coming back.

Her mobile grew hot in her hand as she refreshed and refreshed, hoping his location would appear so she could go and find him. An endless stream of unanswered texts scrolled down the right-hand side of her screen. She called him constantly.

She should just walk, she'd think with a surge of courage. Go and stay with Amahle. Give him something to worry about. But then… Amber's heart would give a lurch, if she left the house, she might miss him. She had to wait.

After a few warm days, the temperature dropped and a spiteful wind followed Amber home from work, snatching at her hair and throwing handfuls of icy water into her face. The house felt strange as she slammed the front door behind her. She ran her hand along the hall radiator to find it stone cold.

'For fuck's sake,' Amber sighed. She let her coat fall on the floor and wrapped the woolly throw from the sitting room around her shoulders and went to make a cup of tea. The cold air prowled around the kitchen, breathing into her face. The darkness of the top floors of the house had never felt so oppressive.

She stared out into the back garden, pitch black except for the tops of the trees that gleamed in the electric fizz of the streetlamps. With a shock Amber realised the tea had gone cold. She poured it down the sink, undrunk, it would have been vile anyway, she'd run out of milk a few days ago.

A soft click made her turn. She held her breath, her heart banged in her ears. Was someone breaking in? Curly had texted to say he was staying a few nights with some new girlfriend and wouldn't be back until the morning. Amber swallowed and stepped back towards the kitchen wall, sliding through the door, keeping her feet flat and soft.

Her body knew before she did.

'Alex?!' A great, gushing wave of glorious relief swept over Amber. Tears rose in a sobbing gulp, and warmth turned her limbs fluid and supple. Within seconds she was in his arms. Every word of her carefully rehearsed speeches of reproach and outrage fled from her head. Alex cradled her, crooning endearments in her hair. The feel of his skin was a deep, visceral comfort. His arms a hot water bottle on a freezing night, a glass of cold water when dying of thirst, a hot meal after starving.

Without speaking, he lowered her to the floor and took her with such tenderness Amber's heart broke.

'I'm sorry, I'm sorry,' he whispered, at last. Amber held onto him, her heart still hammering in her chest. Relief warmed her blood like a drug, her muscles relaxed, and the band strapped around her lungs began to loosen.

'Alex. I have to ask... Did you... did you sleep with...that girl...?'

Alex rolled away and sat up. The silence stretched for so long Amber's ears began to ring. Then, to her astonishment, she realised he was weeping. Head in hands, his shoulders heaved.

She reared up and wrapped her arms around his body that was as clenched as a fist.

She murmured words of comfort as he cried.

'Amber,' he said at last. 'I can't bear it. You're so good and true and I'm such a…'

'No, no, don't say that,' she cried with him.

'I love you, OK? Nobody else. Of course I didn't sleep with that filthy… tart. I just wanted to… I dunno… I couldn't…'

'You were angry with me,' Amber said. 'You wanted to punish me.'

'It was that bloke at the bar, you smiled at him and it was just like…' He thumped his head, hard. Amber pulled at his arm to hold him still. Her mind raced as she tried to remember what man Alex was talking about. She couldn't think straight. There was no man, was there?

'I can't handle it, babe. There's something in me that just can't… bear it. The thought of losing you. I just lash out. You should leave me.'

'Shh shh, don't be silly. I'm not going to leave.'

It took hours to calm him down. Hours that stretched into the darkness. Amber strained her ears as he whispered of his foster parents' cruelty, his foster brothers' blows. A household filled with menace and fear. She hated the thought of that little boy crushed and rejected. She held him close until he slept then turned away and watched the cold light of morning creep across the floor.

*

When Alex woke nothing was said of the night before. It dizzied her, the change from the vulnerable, broken man to the brash geezer who brought in tea with a wide grin, smelling of aftershave.

'I did bloody well up north,' he said, putting the mug on her locker. 'I've made loads of new contacts and some big work coming. Check this out.' He reached into his jeans pocket and pulled out a bundle. He tossed it in the air, and it separated into piles of £50 notes that landed red and crackling on the duvet.

Amber sat up, weariness tugging at her eyelids. 'What? How much…?'

'Enough,' Alex replied.

'Alex…' Amber sorted through the piles. 'There's thousands here. Where did it all come from?'

'Ah. Now that will be telling. It's a surprise.'

He grinned at her, excited as a little boy. His blond hair fell into his eyes and Amber couldn't help it; her body thrummed with pleasure just looking at him.

'And you know what else?' He jumped so heavily onto the bed Amber almost bounced out of it. 'I've been thinking. I reckon it's time we had a baby.'

'A baby?' Amber looked at Alex in astonishment.

'Yeah!' He lay on the bed his arms behind his head. 'I think it's time. Why not? Money's coming in and when we finish this place and sell it, we'll be wadded. Why not hand in your notice and we can start right away?' He trailed his hand over her hip.

'You want me to give up my job?' Alarm bells began to ring, and panic rattled, this was all too soon, too rushed. She'd only just accepted the reality of his return.

'Why not? I'll be bringing in enough for you to stay at home.'

'But I love my job!' She opened her mouth to continue but saw that familiar pinched look in Alex's face and stopped. 'Well, let's not talk about it now.'

'But you'll think about it?' She couldn't help it. His eyes were so bright, so full of eagerness and hope she couldn't resist him. Reaching to feel the heavy silk of his hair under her fingers she pressed her lips against his cheek.

'I'll think about it.'

'Now hurry up and get dressed. I'm taking you up town. You deserve a treat. I'm going to spend a bit of money on you. Get you some decent clothes.'

Listening to Alex whistling in the bathroom as she put on her face Amber stared at her reflection. The piles of cash worried her. What had he been up to? She could imagine what Amahle would say about Alex disappearing without a word. But then she remembered the broken man who whispered in the dark and pity soaked away the last stains of misery and anger that had lingered.

Alex was a good as his word. He wouldn't accept Amber's protests and swept her up to the city where he trailed her in and out of shockingly expensive shops until he found a long dress in rose madder that gave Amber an ethereal beauty; a dressing gown that shimmered with embroidered peacock feathers, which cost more than a month's salary; and three pairs of wild, sky-high heels in red, green, and oyster silk. They were utterly impractical – Amber could barely walk and had to cling to Alex's arm as she wore the red pair to lunch – but she loved them.

Sunday lazed by, Curly was back and full of silly stories about escaping his girlfriend's husband. He'd unexpectedly turned up when a neighbour tipped him off about Curly's presence. Alex cooked roast chicken, feeding Amber the odd mouthful declaring she needed fattening up. He never took his hands from her skin.

They left early Monday morning for a new job. Amber was up and smiled as they joshed and heckled each other, Alex laughing and Curly pulling faces. They bundled out of the door, shoulder to shoulder, their breath gusting white mist in the darkness. She waved them goodbye, hugging her new dressing gown tight around her body. She couldn't help a grin of pure happiness.

The slam of the van door was loud in the quiet street. Amber waited until they'd pulled away then saw with a start someone standing by the gate.

It was a woman. Slight, and dressed in black with a hoodie pulled over her hair. Amber shivered. The woman was staring right at her, eyes dark shadows in her white face. Amber took a step into the house but before she could close the door the woman shot towards her at a speed that didn't seem possible. She was so quick Amber couldn't help a little cry of fright escaping. She moved backwards into the lighted hall and began to pull the door shut but the woman was in the way. Suddenly. So close Amber could smell her, an acrid, goatish smell of fear and sweat.

'I need to speak to you,' the woman said, her voice cracked glass. She pulled her hood back and gave a ghastly smile. Her skull of a face and her brutally short, bleached fuzz of white-yellow hair made Amber rear back in horror. The woman was painfully thin, and her eyes scorched in their intensity.

'I'm sorry, I can't...' Amber tried again to push the door shut but the woman whipped her hand up to stop it. No matter how hard she tugged, Amber couldn't wrest the door from her grip; she was phenomenally strong.

'I need to talk to you about Alex,' the stranger said.

CHAPTER 12: LIZ

I lost Daniel the minute he saw my scars. I could see it in his eyes. I'd frightened him and he didn't trust me to begin with. I didn't care, to be honest. At least I'd made him question what had happened to Sarah. I was increasingly convinced it was something awful. My head ached and I couldn't think straight. Worry drove away any sense of calm I had developed over the past few years. Something kept nagging at me, something that skittered away when I tried to retrieve it.

Standing by the river, holding my arms out to the cold air, I struggled to keep my voice steady.

'You let your sister disappear and you never tried to contact her? You just swallowed what he told you without question?' I dropped my arms and pulled my sleeves down. 'She didn't tell you, did she.'

'None of this is your business,' he said defensively. 'I wasn't there. She said there was something she wanted to tell me but that it would wait until I get back from Spain.'

'Didn't you wonder why she suddenly stopped talking to you?'

He shrugged. 'Of course, but Mum and Dad were so upset she just left, making it clear she didn't want us at the wedding... I did try to call. Of course I did. But I couldn't get through, I'd leave messages, but she never got back to me. We just... gave up.'

'I don't believe it!' I was horrified.

'What about you? Why didn't you stay in touch? I thought she was your friend.'

There was nothing I could say. He was right, I was as guilty as he was. 'I'm going to find her,' I said and started walking away. Mist rolled in from the river.

'Leave it!' Daniel shouted after me. 'I'll call the police and explain what's happened. They'll know what to do.'

I didn't stop.

'I don't want you mixed up in this!' He looked around to see if anyone was watching. He dropped his voice, but I could hear him loud and clear. 'And those aren't scars, you lying bitch,' he hissed. 'They're track marks. You're just a fucking junkie.'

I covered my ears and kept walking.

*

The train arrived at King's Cross before dawn. After seeing Daniel I'd waited at Cambridge station for the first morning train. I couldn't afford another night in that horrible little room and at least the station had a heated waiting area. His words rang in my head and my face burned with shame.

It was only as I saw Old Street and Moorgate pass that I realised what I was doing. Whether or not it was the right thing to do I was too exhausted to work out. Closing my eyes for a second, I must have dozed off. Doors slamming open jerked me awake. I'd arrived already – too quickly. I hadn't had time to think. In my imagination all I'd need to do would be to stand in front of Alex's wife, mute, and she – understanding without the need for words – would call me in and hear my story and together we'd finish the monster once and for all.

It didn't work out like that.

I horrified her.

She'd lost weight and looked tired but was still infinitely more beautiful than her photograph. "Cover her face; mine eyes dazzle." I thought as I stood in the dark watching her waving from the honey-lit hallway of a tremendous house.

I didn't look at the men as they slammed into their van and drove off in a billow of noise and smoke that ripped through the silence of the street. I daren't let them see me.

My feet didn't make a sound as I darted across the street. There was nothing in my head but the need to talk. To contact another one of his victims. Perhaps I'd lost Sarah, but please, God, let me save this one.

'I need to talk to you about Alex,' I said. She tried to pull the door shut but I held on to it.

'Who are you? Go away!' Her voice was musical. I saw the soft flesh of her throat, the luminous pearl of her skin and shuddered at what I knew he would do to her. Desperation rose from me like a rancid perfume.

'Look, you don't know me, my name is Liz.' I rattled out the words and saw the girl flinch as I spoke. 'I know Alex. I know him very well and he's dangerous. Amber, isn't it? He's dangerous

Amber, he nearly destroyed me, and I know he's done awful things to women.'

I relaxed my hand on the door as I spoke, and she nearly pulled it away from me, so I tightened my grip. 'No! Please! You have to listen to me! There's a girl. Sarah. The one he met after me. She's gone missing and…'

'Stop! I'm not listening to you,' Amber's eyes flashed. 'I don't know who you are but get away from my house.'

The door began to close, and tears of frustration made my eyes swim. 'Please, Amber! I'm telling you the truth. He hurts women, and he'll hurt you. The minute he's got what he wants he'll drop you, or worse. Please, Amber… You have to listen.'

The door slammed. I hammered on it, but she didn't respond. My fists began to bleed but I kept on until the pain was intolerable and I leaned against the door, my breath ragged. 'I'm going to go and find out what happened to Sarah,' I pressed my mouth close to the door. 'I wanted you to come with me so you could see with your own eyes what he is. But he's got you fooled. He's good, isn't he? In bed? The best fuck you've ever had. But watch him, Amber. Please. That's all I ask. Watch him. And be careful.'

Was she listening? Could she hear me? 'I'm going to come back, Amber. When I find out. But if you need me. If you get scared call me, OK? I'll come get you. I'm strong. He doesn't frighten me anymore.' I winced at the lie, but I needed her to believe me. 'I'm putting my card through the letterbox. Any time. OK? Any time.'

The letterbox was stiff and old; the hinges creaked as I slid my card through the dark slot. The lights had been turned out and I pictured Amber sitting in the hall watching my card fall to the floor.

I stuffed my hands into my pockets, my face was wet. Despair threatened to overwhelm, but I forced it away. I'd just have to do it on my own.

*

'Are you sure about this, honey? I know what this book means to you.'

'Oh, don't go on about it, Lucy. Just tell me how much you can sell it for.'

It was over a week since I'd seen Amber. She hadn't called, I don't know why I ever expected she would. I could see it in her eyes, I knew what it was because I'd seen that look in my own, years ago. Blinded. Bewitched.

Everything was on hold. I was starting to turn my beautiful prototypes into real objects that I hoped would be held and admired by guests from around the world. They made me happier than I could have imagined but learning about Sarah had blasted everything away. I couldn't concentrate on the hotel contract until I had contacted Sarah.

Lucy's shop was one of my favourite places. The last of the independent book sellers in the city. Watching her inspecting my Crimson Book of Fairy Tales, the red and gold cover gleaming in the light, tore at my heart.

'It's just I've got a lot of people after this to complete their collections – it'll get snapped up the minute I update the site. If it goes, you can't get it back.'

'Yes. I know,' my stomach turned upside down with grief, but I wanted it over and done with. 'How much?'

'Well, give me a few days…'

'I haven't got a few days, Lucy! Just get me a fair price, it doesn't have to be top whack, I don't care what you do with it. I just need the cash.'

Lucy paused from examining my book and looked at me with a frown. 'Liz, if you're stuck, I can lend you…'

'No. Stop. I'm not borrowing money from you. Look, if you don't want to sell it for me, I can try Terry down the road.'

'All right, all right.' Lucy looked at her watch. 'I haven't got enough in my till, can you keep an eye on the shop while I pop over to the bank? I'll be closing in twenty minutes, so you won't have anyone coming in now.'

She shrugged into her coat and left, the shop bell giving a sharp ring as she walked across the doormat. My nerves were wound so tight the noise made me jump.

I took a minute to hold the book in my hands, tracing the illustrations with my finger and smiling at the heft of the pages in my hand. Wonderful stories so beautifully bound by a man who'd meant a lot to me, and my Gran. A tear splashed onto the cover and I rubbed it away with the sleeve of my jumper.

It was the only way, I told myself as I waited for Lucy to come back. I was absolutely skint, and the hotel money wouldn't hit my account until I'd delivered the first batch. My fairy tale book was the only thing I had of any value and I needed the money. I had to go to France to try and find Sarah. Nothing else had any importance. If I didn't find out what had happened to her I would go mad.

'Sorry I took so long!' Lucy's cheeks were red, and she brought in a breeze of air that smelled of grass and growth. She must have cut across the park. 'Last chance to change your mind,' she said forcing me to meet her eyes; they were too sharp. I looked away.

'Thanks, Lucy. That's kind of you but it's the only way.'

She sighed and took the book from me. 'It's so beautiful, I'll look after it – make sure it goes to a good home.'

I gave a weak smile and folded the notes Lucy had given me into my back pocket. It was enough for a return train ticket and a few nights somewhere cheap. Marching fast down the street I started to plan. The only useful detail Daniel could offer was a village name in France. It had flashed up on his phone when Alex had called a few weeks after the wedding.

I would start there. Chauron. I'd never heard of it. Everything I knew I'd gathered from Google and Wikipedia. It wasn't very big and although it was only a couple of hours from Paris it looked a quiet, sleepy place. Was Sarah there? I thought. After booking my ticket I leaned against the wall and opened Google street map to walk around a sunlit village 250 miles away.

I slid my finger along the houses with their pastel shutters. Some looked very run down. Was Sarah behind one of these windows? One of the women in the butcher's shop, her face blurred? Jitters made my hands shake. I should eat. Something hot. And maybe some tea. A good night's sleep before I left to discover what had happened to my friend.

The thought calmed me. Doing something stilled the terrible creeping sense of fear that shadowed my footsteps.

Seeing the warm lights of my shop spilling out onto the road as night fell was cheering. I'd pick up my sketch books and work on the train. As I drew close, I stumbled. Something crunched under my feet. I looked down. Broken glass glittered.

My heart began to pound. Now I was near, I could see the window at the front of the shop was smashed and shards hung crazily. Before taking another step, I scrabbled for my phone and called the police. 'My shop's been broken into…' I gasped.

While giving out the address I pushed open the door, the lock had been prised out and hung like a broken tooth. Once inside I covered my eyes in an instinctive, pointless gesture.

All the angles were wrong. My beautiful shelves had been pulled forward and had crashed and splintered on the floor. Unrolled leathers and cloth hung like grotesque tongues with slashes through them. But the worst was to come.

At the back of the shop my locked cupboards had been torn open and all the work I had done so far for the hotel, every folder, every delicate origami map, every carefully tooled manganese-blue wallet, had been wrenched from their shelves and thrown to the ground. Bits and pieces lay shredded and smeared across the floorboards. The violence and chaos made me cry out; I couldn't stand.

Fragments of my beautiful sea glass, now smashed into dusty smithereens, imprinted my skin. Nothing had been left untouched. As I sat on the floor weeping hard, desperate tears, waiting for the police to come, I knew it was hopeless. I would never be able to afford to buy replacement materials and the thought of doing all that time-consuming, intricate work again was unbearable.

Understanding I would never be able to go into that stunning hotel and see my work, my art, being used and admired, hurt almost as much as selling the last solid link to my past. A storm of rubbish, as if a hurricane had blown through my shop, littered every surface. The most expensive and lovely calfskin leather had been scissored into ugly tufts. Who would do this?

And then the door to the kitchen swung shut and I understood. Painted across it in neat, black capitals I read his message: "Stay Away, Bitch."

Feathers of black swooped over my vision as horror drilled into my bones. Was he here? Was he waiting for me? Animal instincts took over and I whimpered as I slid backwards, kicking away the rubbish. Panic drove me frantic.

I bumped from surface to surface trying to find the door. My mind screamed with the fear he was in the room, slithering along the floor, reaching for me. At last I was on the street. I couldn't breathe. I thumped at my chest, trying to force in air. I was going to die. My heart stuttered into a blur so fast I could see my pulse jumping in my wrists, could feel it hammering in my neck.

And then a voice, kind and low began to talk to me. Holding my hands. Letting me lean on him. Will.

I didn't recognise him. The shock and fear wiped my mind clean and in that mad chaos my body began to flail in his arms, beating him away like a madwoman. He held me as the police arrived and waited until I began to calm down. I felt him nod them into the shop as he walked me away, never stopping his calm stream of nonsense, grounding me, soothing me until my breath stopped hiccupping in my chest.

As the police lumbered in and out Will walked me back and forth, back and forth eventually settling me on a low wall across the road. I was shivering; he took off his coat and hung it around my shoulders. Dimly conscious of his spicy, sandalwood smell and grateful for the warmth, I tried to smile up at him, but my mind was racing.

'What are you doing here?'

'I was out walking Dolly and saw you on the street.' He pointed across the road where Dolly stood, tied to a lamppost.

I nodded but my mind was miles away. How did Alex find me? Did Amber show him my card? She must have done. I thanked God it only showed my workshop address, but now he knew what city I lived in and that was enough to terrify.

Will had found a cup of coffee and he pushed the mug into my hand, sitting next to me and putting his arm around my shoulders.

'You OK?' he said, then gave a hollow laugh. 'Stupid question.' He squeezed my shoulders. 'I'm just going to pop over and see what's happening. Will you be all right waiting here? I won't be long.'

I nodded and watched him lope across the road and catch hold of one of the police officers. They looked back at me then carried on talking. Will followed her into the shop and returned after a few minutes.

'There's nobody in there, the police reckon whoever did it is long gone. When was the last time you were in the shop?'

'A couple of days ago,' I said. 'I wasn't in over the weekend and I worked from home in the morning as I don't normally open on Mondays.'

'It could have happened a few days ago then.'

I shook my head. 'No, someone in the street would have noticed.'

Will looked over at the destroyed front window. 'Let's leave them to it, I've given them my phone number. They want you to go in tomorrow to make a statement. I didn't think it would be a good idea for you talk to them tonight, you're in shock. Come on, I'll drive you home.'

I looked up at his dear face, lit by the soft fall of the nearby lamppost. I felt again that strange pull and let him take my hand. He untied Dolly and she jumped into the back seat, curling round and round before falling asleep, paws crossed over her nose.

We didn't speak. I wound down the window and rested my head back, breathing in the cool air. I sensed Will looking over at me every now and then but was grateful he seemed happy to let the silence hang.

I handed him his coat at the door of my block.

'Do you want me to go up and check? Make sure nobody is there?'

I stared at him. I hated the fear that made me weak. I had nothing left to lose, and if the Monster waited for me in the flat, I would face him – no longer the frail little girl who hung on his every word, his every touch. But not yet. I owed it to Sarah, I couldn't live not knowing where she was and whether or not she was OK.

Will smiled and touched my cheek when I gave a quick nod. 'Give me your keys,' he said.

'I'll come up as well. You can go first though.' My smile was shaky.

The flat was clear but seeing it through Will's eyes was strange. It looked as if nobody lived there. I should buy some colourful cushions or throws. Something. Will walked quickly into every room. I know he checked the spare room but didn't comment on what he saw there.

I walked him back down to the street and he gave me a hug. I was ashamed to find I couldn't help clinging onto him and pulled back quickly.

'I've missed you, Liz.'

He leaned forward and kissed me just to the side of my mouth; his lips so gentle, so soft, my heart melted – just for a moment. And then I moved back, letting cold air step between us.

'Thanks, Will. For being there. You've been great.'

'But?'

'There's something I need to do. I don't know how long it will take but if I don't sort it, well, I can't move on. I wish I could explain properly but… well, I can't. Not yet.'

Will smiled, his blue eyes grave. 'You don't have to do this alone, Liz.'

I couldn't speak. The longing, oh, the longing to just forget about everything: To take Will's hand and lie with him, safe in his little house. He must have seen something in my face because his eyes softened, and I saw his mouth open to speak.

Sniffing to stop the tears I shook my head and tried to smile. 'I'll come find you,' I said.

He looked up at the sky and back down with a sigh. 'OK. But if you don't, I'll come find you.'

'Deal,' I said, my voice shaking. I reached for the door before I weakened, climbing the stairs to my flat without looking back.

*

I didn't look at my phone until I was on the train coming out of Paris towards Chauron and Sarah. The police had called, I had missed my appointment. A number I didn't recognise had called twice and there were messages from Will and the hotel manager, again.

It hadn't taken me long to gather what I needed. A force propelled me forward. To stay still was intolerable, my pulse only slowed when I was moving. Whenever I paused - waiting in the kitchen for the kettle to boil, or stood in my workshop, my back to the devastation, looking for Vika to give her the keys - my heart would race with panic.

Before I left my flat I stripped the spare room of every piece of evidence I had. The articles and photos along with my notes were copied, three times, and I left the originals in a pile on my kitchen table. I'd written a letter, 'to whom it may concern…' conscious as I wrote how melodramatic my words sounded.

As I pulled the door shut, I wondered what sort of person would be next to open it. Would it be me after an unsuccessful, pointless journey? Would it be him? Maybe the police? I dithered. He knew about my workshop. It wouldn't take him long to find out where I lived. I quailed at the thought of posting a package labelled 'in the event of my death…' It sounded ridiculous, a cliché from a bad novel.

The destruction of my workshop untethered me from the city. My flat had always been just a shelter, there was nothing of me there. It didn't bother me as much as it should, perhaps, that I had no one to whom I could entrust my file of papers. There was only Will.

The thought of explaining anything to him was exhausting. I could only think about travelling to the station, getting onto the train and then walking from one end of Chauron to the other, not stopping until I had found Sarah.

So, I stood in the dark, the sea at my back and watched as Will left his cottage to turn on his ovens and make his bread. The envelope was bulky but I managed to squeeze it through the letterbox. As I walked away, feeling rain dampen my face, I thought of what I'd written: 'Will, please look after this for me. I'll explain everything when I get back.' It didn't matter if he opened it, I'd be hundreds of miles away by the time he got back from work.

Everything was falling away leaving me light and clean. I checked the ticket was safe in my pocket, everything else was packed in my rucksack. As I moved, I heard the crackle of the last envelope. That, I was saving for her. I would make sure to see her once more before I left. I didn't care anymore if she believed me. Finding out what happened to Sarah was what I had to do now. I pictured handing over the envelope before moving on, uncluttered and clear-minded. I thought of my fairy tale book with a pang of grief but remembering the knights, with their grave faces filled with purpose, brought me comfort.

*

On the train the glimpses of the sea were such a bright blue I could almost feel the jewels of blue-green glass I had threaded onto my beautiful designs in my hand. Tipping my head back so the tears slid into my hair I thought of the things I had made and the amazing contract I never thought I'd win. But the monster had made a mistake. He'd taken everything from me so there was nothing left. My work, my memories – all gone. I was beginning to feel untouchable. He could kill me, of course, but I found I didn't care much about that either. Everything I loved was destroyed. What was there to live for?

Finding Sarah and putting the monster away. I decided. Putting him away so he would spend the rest of his life rotting in jail. I smiled to picture it. That was worth living for.

I'd slept most of the way to Paris, so exhausted the guard had to shake me awake and I staggered, disorientated onto the platform. As I walked from one end of the station to the other something tapped at my memory. Something that made me swallow hard. I was overcome by a deep sense of unease as I bought my ticket. I had to run to catch the train and almost stumbled as I had what my Gran would have called a 'funny turn'. What was the matter with me?

I hadn't eaten since the day before. Thinking it might help, I bought cup after cup after cup of good, strong coffee and worked through two buttery croissants. I thought of Vika and her stew and wondered if I'd ever eat in her café again. The food warmed me, and I felt a little better. But something still knocked at the back of my mind and no matter how much I probed I couldn't work out what it was.

I hadn't packed much. A change of clothes, my running kit, a toothbrush, and some cream for my sore, cracked hands. I'd changed the last of Lucy's cash into Euros and most of it disappeared into the hands of Madam Betty - a bonny woman in her fifties, cleavage tanned to a freckled butterscotch - who was renting me a room at the top of her house.

There was a world of difference between the cramped digs I'd rented in Cambridge and Madam Betty's loft. It smelled of clean sheets and sunshine. The flowers and greening trees on the journey down had been astonishing; France was much further into spring than England.

A tray by the window held a cafetiere and a single, delicate bone china cup which glowed teal blue in the light. Despite still feeling stuffed from the croissants on the train I couldn't resist a square of thick, homemade shortbread, scattered with crystals of sugar. I stood and gazed out over the garden, the tickle of unease disappearing at last.

I washed quickly and swapped my jumper for a thin cycling jacket. Madam Betty didn't speak any English, but I'd communicated my needs well enough for her to sketch me a map of the village.

My GCSE French identified a café as well as the local butcher's and bakery. I remember seeing the woman with the blurred face in the butchers on Google street view. That was as good a place to start as any, I thought.

The shop fell silent as I walked in, announcing my arrival with a jingling bell that reminded me of Lucy's place. I'd scanned every face from Madame Betty's on the way, desperate to find Sarah but saw nobody even close to her age. The village seemed populated with cross looking middle-aged women in scarves. I felt like I'd time travelled to the 50s.

The chatter of French was machine-gun fast, and I failed to pick up a single word. I began to worry this would be a wild goose chase. Nobody seemed to speak any English. As I waited, I breathed in the smell of meat, blood, and sawdust. It zoomed me back to shopping trips with my Gran and I remembered the day's meat being wrapped up at sixty miles an hour in thin, red and white striped plastic bags.

'Bonjour. Madame?' The butcher was gruff, and impatient.

'Oh. Yes. Hello.' The women loitered, tucking their purchases into large brown handbags. Their mournful eyes frisked me before exchanging glances with each other.

'I am looking for a friend. An English friend. A couple in fact. They were here a few years ago. Can you help me? Her name was Sarah.'

CHAPTER 13: AMBER

'But who was she, Alex? Why was she here? Do you know her?' Amber had waited all day for Alex and Curly to get back from work. Again, she had called in sick. That awful woman had frightened her so terribly she couldn't leave the house. 'And why didn't you answer your phone? I've been calling you all day.'

'Amber, babe, I told you – we turn them off – the boss would have our guts for garters if we had our phones on site. Isn't that right, Curly?'

Curly walked into the sitting room holding three bottles of beer with an enormous packet of Doritos wedged under his arm. He handed round the drinks and sat down, prising off his boots and resting his socked feet on the coffee table.

Amber turned to Alex. 'Shall we go upstairs?'

'I want to watch this,' Alex protested as Curly switched on the TV and clicked to a football match.

'I can't believe you!' Amber's voice rose and Curly looked over in surprise. Amber never took her eyes from Alex. 'Some bloody madwoman comes to the house saying all sorts of horrible things…'

Curly sat up, his feet landing with a thump on the floor, beer forgotten. 'Not Lizzie?' he said in astonishment to Alex, who nodded.

'I'm surprised it's taken her so long to find us. I hoped this crap was all over with.'

'Will you please tell me what the hell's going on?' Amber cried, looking at them both, aghast. 'How can you be so… flippant about it? She said you…' She couldn't bear to say the words. 'Just tell me who she is.'

Alex cracked the top off his beer and passed the opener to Curly who did the same. 'She's someone we know from way back,' he said before stopping to take a long swallow of beer.

'She's a fucking nutter,' Curly chipped in.

Amber shivered. 'I thought she was going to attack me.'

Alex put down his bottle and pulled Amber into his arms, shooting a look at Curly across her head as he did so. 'Oh, babe. I'm sorry. I should have warned you. It's just we hadn't seen her for so long I thought she'd given up.'

'Given up what? For God's sake tell me who she is.'

There was a pause. Amber sensed something darting between Alex and Curly. It unnerved her sometimes, their closeness.

He sighed. 'We met her years ago, at university. I'd just moved to Bristol and didn't know anyone. I was sharing a flat with Curly and she started following us around.'

'Yeah, right little puppy dog,' Curly said. 'We both had her at one point, didn't we?'

Alex tensed, but his voice stayed light. 'She picked me in the end, thought, didn't she, mate?'

'Thank fuck,' Curly picked up Amber's bottle and took a swig. 'Talk about mental. Good in bed, though. Great tits.'

'You can't use words like that, Curly.'

'What? Tits?'

'No – mental. It's an awful thing to say.'

'But she was! She even got locked up at one point, didn't she?'

'So, what happened? Just start at the beginning.' Amber's voice tightened.

'It's no big deal OK?' Alex jerked out of the sofa and disappeared into the kitchen. Amber and Curly sat in silence until he returned with more bottles clinking in his hands. 'It's ancient history all right? Just some crazy bint who lost the plot. She couldn't handle it when I dumped her and made up all sorts of shit. Even went to the police.'

'Oh my God. What did she say?'

A strange expression tugged at Alex's face, Amber was surprised to see unhappiness shadow his eyes. 'She said I hurt her.'

'She'd hurt herself,' Curly interrupted. 'Would slash at her arms and bash against things to make whacking great bruises and then say it was us. Fucking bitch. Caused a mass of trouble.'

'That's awful.'

'Yeah. She was fucked up all right. But I didn't want to do anything because she'd had a hard life – she didn't know what she was doing half the time.'

'She was off her face, that's why.' Curly chucked the bottle opener so hard towards the table it bounced and skidded under a bookshelf.

'Was she a druggie?' Amber couldn't believe what she was hearing. But that made sense. The woman who'd accosted her had that emaciated, burning-eyed look she'd come to associate with heroin addicts on TV.

'And the rest,' Curly snorted. 'She was super intense, into everything. Was a bit wild. It was a relief when she hooked her claws into Alex – she'd worn me out.'

'Why's she going on about you hurting woman, Alex? And who's Sarah?'

Something shifted. A charge cracked the air. Amber studied Alex's face but his expression didn't change. Curly made a fuss of retrieving the bottle opener. 'Well?'

'An old girlfriend. That's all. Lizzie had real problems. After we split, she loathed the thought of me being with anyone else. She's tried to break up every relationship I've had and now she's come to you with her lies and bullshit.'

Curly leaned over and lightly punched Alex's shoulder. 'It's all right, mate.' He sighed. 'I don't bloody believe this. After all this time.'

'Why didn't you tell me this before? We're *married*, Alex.'

Alex opened his hands in an ambiguous gesture. 'You're right, babe, I should have done. But it was like I started again when I met you. I couldn't believe I'd even find someone so sweet and good. I wanted a fresh start, a new beginning without any of this crazy… mess clouding things.'

'And why shouldn't you?' Curly's voice was hoarse. 'You deserved it, mate, after all she did. All those hours being questioned. God, if I could get my hands on her…'

'Stop, Curly.' Alex's voice was soft. 'She couldn't help it could she?' Curly opened his mouth to protest but a look from Alex made him drop his eyes to the bottle opener he was rolling between his hands.

'You've always been a soft twat.'

'It was all made up? She was just trying to destroy us?'

'That's exactly what she was trying to do. I'll have to get back onto the police now she's found where we live. Curly and I had to take out a restraining order when this kicked off. I'm sure it's still in place. Fuck's sake. What a pain. She's harmless, but I don't want her hanging around scaring you.'

'And where's this Sarah she kept going on about? She said she's going to go and look for her.'

'I don't know!' Alex, angry now, pulled away from Amber and stalked to the window, looking out into the dark street and the common beyond. 'Fucking hell, Amber. She was an old girlfriend who dumped me because she believed all of the shit Lizzie spooned into her. I haven't seen her in years. Last I heard she scurried home to Mummy and Daddy in their big fuck off mansion!' He turned back to face Amber, his eyes haunted. 'And you believe her! Don't you? She's going to do it again. Fucking crush everything…'

He looked so haunted, so bereft, Amber jumped to her feet to hug Alex with all her strength. 'Of course I don't believe her. I just freaked out because I didn't know what was going on. I understand now.'

They stood, tightly enfolded.

Curly coughed. 'I'll er… order a takeaway, shall I?' He left the room, closing the door softly behind him.

'It must have been awful,' Amber said, settling Alex beside her on the sofa. 'I can't believe you went through all of this on your own.'

'I had Curly. He got me through it, to be honest.'

'Well, now you've got me,' Amber said, holding his hand. 'You can tell me anything. I love you, remember? In it together - forever.'

Alex leaned his forehead against hers. 'I don't deserve you.'

'Don't be thick.'

He smiled. 'It's actually a bit of a weight off my shoulders. I hated not telling you stuff. Especially since we got married. I should have been more honest. I'm sorry.'

'I understand, really. It all sounds horrid. I can see why you wouldn't want to tell me. Especially when she's saying such awful, awful things.'

He ran his fingers down her back, sliding them into her jeans, making her shiver. 'Now stop that! Curly's just outside. She patted his leg. 'I'd better go and get the plates ready. The food will be here soon.' She kissed him on the cheek, inhaling the warmth of his skin.

'OK. thanks. And look, if you see her again you call the police straight away.'

'I thought you said she was harmless?'

'She is, but for her own good she needs help. It sounds like she's off her meds and the police will have a file on her. They'll know what to do – don't worry.'

'OK, I'll try. You're so good, you know. Not many people could be so kind and understanding. Must be why I love you.'

*

Curly looked up from the basement door in surprise as Amber came down the stairs dressed for work the next day.

'I thought you weren't going in?'

'Of course I am! Why not?'

'I just thought after yesterday with that weirdo Lizzie…'

'Well, you and Alex have explained all about that – poor woman. Besides, I've missed too much work recently. I'll get into trouble if I do it again. What are you up to? Don't normally see you up so early if you've not got a job on. Alex is still asleep.'

'I've been using the gym.'

He looked a bit sweaty, Amber thought. 'In your jeans?'

'Er, yeah. I was just doing some weights, doing cardio with Alex tomorrow.'

'OK, I'd better be off. See you later.'

The morning passed quickly. As she worked Amber daydreamed about the night before with Alex. He'd never been so loving, her heart swooped at the memory of it. She couldn't stop the smile dancing across her mouth.

Every now and then the memory of Lizzie's desperate voice pleading through the door would make her forget what she was doing but she brushed it away. The woman was clearly deranged. Poor Alex!

It was funny, even though she'd only been away from work for a few days she was already feeling disconnected from the salon, more so than she did after returning from her honeymoon. Maybe now *was* the right time to have a baby? After talking to Alex, late into the night they were closer than ever. He'd opened up to her far more about his childhood, and later the terrible impact of Lizzie's lies.

'Hey! Are you listening to me? She's away with the fairies,' Amahle laughed with Amber's client.

'Oh, I'm sorry! I was miles away.' Amber blinked and dabbed a sheen of serum onto Mrs Evans' lovely white hair.

'Amber, I've got a break and Brenda says you haven't got anyone after young Mrs Evans here. I just wondered if you fancied popping out for a bit of lunch? Treat ourselves!'

Amber leant down to unplug her hairdryer, hiding her face from her friend. She was happy with Alex's explanation about Lizzie, but she wasn't quite sure how to explain it to Amahle. She suspected she wouldn't understand. Amahle didn't know Alex the way she did. Amber sighed. She wished she could have a proper talk with Amahle, explain how mixed-up she was feeling, but it felt disloyal to Alex. He hadn't said anything, but she knew he didn't like her much.

'Sorry, Amahle, I'd love to, but I've missed a few days and I need to catch up. I'm not very hungry so I'm just going to work through. Rain check?'

Mrs Evans, engrossed in her *Hello!* Magazine, didn't see the worry on Amahle's face as she walked away across the salon floor. Amber sighed with relief, but her heart was heavy.

'Don't forget you've got Mrs Bushell coming in to have her roots done this afternoon,' Brenda called as Amber helped Mrs Evans on with her coat and saw her out of the door.

'I know. She's back from her holiday, then?'

'Yup. Let's hope it's put her in a better mood.'

Amber glanced over Brenda's head to the window that looked out over the road. She couldn't help checking to see if Lizzie was hanging around. She could have followed her to the salon. God, it was bad enough when she had to worry about bumping into Emma.

Amber was conscious of a circling dread. As if danger paced at the edges of her vision. She tried to shake it off. It was all the nasty stuff with Emma, she thought, and now this poor, haunted Lizzie. The house didn't help either; the thought of it and the work to be done made her shoulders sag. She couldn't wait until they could sell up. If they made the figures Alex bandied about it would be enough to move somewhere new and set up that salon she'd promised herself for so many years.

Crossing to the colouring station, Amber found Mrs Bushell's card and pulled down the bottles, checking the numbers with care. Maybe she could persuade Amahle to move with her? she thought with a smile.

She looked up to see if Mrs Bushell had arrived, and her mouth fell open in astonishment. 'Alex! What are you doing here?' She grinned and whipped around the counter and let him give her a hug as she held her gloved hands above her head.

'Got bored stuck at home. No work until Monday and couldn't face doing any more in the house. You all right?'

'Yes! Busy! Oh, it's so nice to see you here.' He followed her as she slipped back behind the counter.

'Any chance you could sneak off? Come with me up town?'

'Oh, Alex. I'd love to. But I've got Mrs Bushell coming in any minute and she only likes me doing her hair…'

'Oooh hello, handsome!' Eyes alight, tossing her hair so it shimmered, Laura wiggled over to Alex.

'Hey, Laura, good to see you.' Alex bent to kiss Laura's cheek.

She listened to them chat while she measured out powder and was just reaching for the developer when Alex spoke.

'What do you think, babe?'

'Sorry? I wasn't listening! I need to concentrate on this.'

'I was just saying that I'm sure Laura wouldn't mind doing the old woman for you.'

'Oh, no. I can't expect Laura to...'

'Well, you've done it enough times for her, hasn't she Laura? She's often been late home as you'd asked her to mix up a colour or clean up after you.' Alex was smiling but the words were sharp; Laura blushed to hear them.

'Yeah of course, I don't mind, Amber, if you want to get away early.'

'I don't think…'

Laura pulled Amber towards the loos leaving Alex at the counter. 'Amber, come on, I really don't mind. The old bag will be fine with it – I'll just tell her and Paul you didn't feel well and had to go home. Besides,' she gave Amber a wink 'Alex slipped me a hundred quid to cover for you.'

'You're joking! Bloody hell, Laura. I can't believe he offered you money.'

'Sssh!' Laura tugged Amber further down the corridor so no one could hear them talking. 'I swore I wouldn't tell you. Come on, I could do with the money and you get to skip work and go out on a hot date with your husband. Besides,' she softened, 'I'm worried about you. Coming in, looking like shit – missing days. Not like you at all. Go spend some quality time with him.' She gave Amber a little push.

'You sure?'

'Absolutely.'

'OK then.' Amber was uncomfortable but it didn't seem she had much choice. Alex must really want to take her out to go to all this trouble. 'Let me just finish mixing up Mrs Bushell's colour, I've finally got it how she likes it.'

'Fine, hurry up. I'll tell Paul and Brenda after you go.'

Telling Alex to wait outside, Amber finished Mrs Bushell's colour. For a panicked moment she couldn't remember if she'd added all the developer. She could hear Mrs Bushell chatting to Brenda in reception and her nerves began to tighten. She'd better get this done. With shaking hands, she stirred everything together. It smelled a bit strong. Shit!

Laura settled Mrs Bushell in a chair and slipped round the back to Amber. 'Come on, she's here. I'd better get started.'

Amber peered down at the mix.

'Come on!'

'I'm not sure it's right,' Amber said frowning.

'Oh, it's fine. Come on. Off you go.' Laura took the bowl and the brush and nodded at the back door. 'See you tomorrow – have fun!'

*

It was nice spending time with Alex without Curly hanging around, thought Amber as they caught the tube into the West End. She wished he'd given her a chance to change her outfit and refresh her make-up, but he'd told her she looked beautiful and who cared anyway in the dark of the cinema?

Amber got a little drunk after the film, Alex took her to a hotel bar and ordered champagne, pretended they'd never met and chatted her up until she giggled.

He had to hold her up as she tottered up the path to the front of the house. They'd run to catch the last train and she felt like a teenager as Alex opened the door putting his fingers on his lips to shush her, so they didn't wake up Curly.

As Amber shut the front door, light flooded the hall.

'Curly?' she said, holding her hand up to shield her face from the dazzle. 'Why are you up so late?'

'Where have you been? I've been trying to get hold of you! I've called and called.'

Squinting, Amber opened her bag to look at her phone. 'My phone's flat. Why didn't you call Alex? What's happened?'

'I did try Alex, most of the evening.'

'Sorry, mate, had mine on silent so I could concentrate on my lovely wife.' He slid his arm around her waist. 'What's up?'

'It's your boss, Amber. Something happened at the salon. He was fuming, wanted you to call him straight away.'

The room suddenly felt very cold and a sense of foreboding prickled the hairs at the back of Amber's neck. 'What did he say happened?'

'Something about one of your clients.'

Amber thudded up the stairs into the bedroom to plug in her phone. 'Come on, come on,' she urged. It seemed to take for ever. Finally, it lit up and a stream of missed calls from Paul appeared on the screen. There were three voicemails.

She was listening to the third when Alex came in with two glasses of water. 'What is it? What happened?' he said, alarmed by her white face.

'It's Mrs Bushell, Paul's wife. The one who came in this afternoon. There must have been something wrong with the colour I mixed. It's wrecked her hair and burned her scalp so badly she had to go to hospital. I feel awful. I don't understand how this could have happened. Oh, Alex, he's furious. He's threatening to fire me.'

CHAPTER 14: LIZ

The longer I stayed in Chauron the more hopeless I felt. Within days I had become an oddity. The local women pointed me out to their friends, gossiping in their rattle of exclamations and bursts of laughter.

I visited every shop, both cafés, and the restaurant with its old-fashioned formality and faint whiff of soup. I'd questioned mothers in the playground, accosted dog walkers, and talked to old men who waited at bus stops. I had stayed three days, longer than I had planned, and was running out of money.

I got nowhere. Nobody knew who I was talking about. The photographs I showed went unrecognised. Hopelessness threatened to pull me under. I'd wake up at four in the morning wondering what I was doing. Pushing myself out of my bed, I'd go out in the dark and run down the centre of the empty lanes, breathing in the air that smelled of damp earth and the woods.

Blasting music into my ears, pushing myself so hard every muscle screamed, glaring at the brightening horizon, I couldn't stop seeing my smashed and broken workshop. My beautiful designs in pieces. A sob rose to my throat and tears were blinding so I'd have to stop, gasping. Bent double and coughing out my grief.

My rage had abandoned me. This fools' errand had left me with nothing but fear, and a dangerous lassitude. Untethered, with little money left, a phone that didn't work in France and nothing to go back to, my resolve faltered. If I didn't find Sarah I had no idea what to do next.

I remembered the cliffs back home, the emptiness of sky and sea, the cold air that froze the breath and promised oblivion. I'd propped my sketch of Sarah on the little table next to the bedroom window. It was her gaze I met when I woke, and guilt soured my stomach so I couldn't eat the hot, fragrant bag of croissants Madame Betty left me every morning.

Brushing my teeth, I spat blood into the sink. My jeans smelled stale, but I couldn't think of a way to get them clean. There was no washing machine and although I could wash them by hand it was too cold to hang them out to dry.

There were only a few notes left in my wallet and just over a hundred pounds in my account with no prospect of any money coming in. I could afford a couple more nights and that would be it. I tied my laces tight and pulled on a thick jumper. It had been very cold that morning as I ran, the temperature had dropped a few degrees since the sunny day I arrived.

I pulled the door shut and wrapped a thick wool scarf high around my face and ears. I was going to knock on every door, I decided. Show them my photos of Sarah and the monster. If I did that, I'd know I'd done everything I could, and then I could meet Sarah's gaze without shame.

The gravel crunched under my feet as I walked along the little alleyway that led from Madame Betty's house out onto the street. Checking I had the photos ready on my phone, I tucked it back into my coat pocket and set off into the village.

A banging made me turn my head. I was standing by two handsome pillars framing a wrought iron gate higher than my head. Beyond the gate a short drive led to a house set well back from the main street. It was solid and square with grey stone walls and tall windows. At one of them stood Madame Betty, banging on the glass, gesturing I should come in.

I opened the gates with a creak and a clang that made me thing of Pip entering Satis House to meet Miss Havisham. The door swung open as I approached and Madame Betty exclaimed over my cold hands and rubbed them in her own, an intimate gesture I found curiously comforting. It made me miss my Gran.

She guided me into a warm kitchen in which sat a slim, elderly woman with the big, blown out hair so favoured by rich French females. She wore well-cut trousers with expensive looking boots and a tweed tailored jacket into which she'd tucked a beautiful silk scarf.

'This is em, how do you say… my friend,' said Madame Betty. 'My good friend. Madame Heurteau. This is Elizabett, she stay with me...' She finished the rest of the sentence in French.

Madame Heurteau rose to shake my hand. I looked for somewhere to sit as Madame Betty bustled into another room and returned with a tray loaded with a cafetiere of delicious smelling coffee, and a basket of cakes. She began to speak in her warm, rushing torrent of French until the old woman laid her hand on her arm and she stopped.

When she spoke, her English was good but so heavily accented I had to concentrate hard to work out what she was saying. She tended to elongate the vowels in the wrong place; it sounded beautiful, though, like music and I had to force myself to listen to the content. 'You are staying with Betty, I 'ear?' she said.

'Yes. That's right.'

'And the villagers tell me you are looking for someone?'

'Yes,' I sipped my coffee. It was so strong it made me gasp.

'Betty wondered if I may be able to 'elp. I have lived here all my life and seen many things. You have searched very carefully from what I have been told?'

I shrugged, the coffee had splashed into my empty stomach and up behind my eyeballs, giving me a shot of energy. I sat up straight. 'I have. I think I must have come to the wrong village.'

'Do you have a picture I could look at? Names?'

'Her name was Sarah, and she married a man called Alex. Very tall with dark eyes. Here…'

I picked up my coat and looked for my phone as Madame Betty and Madame Heurteau waited politely, drinking their coffee. I found the picture I had of Sarah. I'd taken it on a beautiful day when we'd walked along a beach for miles, weaving together the early threads of our friendship.

I held up the screen and both women leaned in to have a look. Betty shrugged and returned to her cakes. Madame Heurteau gave a quick shake of her head, she reminded me of a bird with her little bright eyes and feathered hair. 'Non,' she said decisively. My heart sank.

'The man? Alex you say?'

I scrolled through my phone, I couldn't bear to store photos of the monster there, so I swiped over to Instagram and found the shot of him with his new wife. 'The Newly Weds Return...' I read again.

With a shiver of shock, I saw Madame Heurteau's face immediately change. She turned to Madame Betty and asked her a question. The reply was fast and incomprehensible. Madame Heurteau took the phone from my hand and peered at the photo. With agonising slowness, she searched for, found, and put on a pair of spectacles and looked again.

There followed a lengthy conversation in French with Madame Betty. Madame Heurteau kept tapping on my phone screen with her glasses as she spoke. She then held up the photo to her friend who just shrugged. The older woman tutted with irritation.

Waiting was unbearable. I strained my ears but couldn't make out a word of what they were saying. Did they recognise him? The monster? Had he been here? Did Madame Heurteau know where he stayed? I felt sick with impatience, but I daren't interrupt them. When silence fell at last, I stood, almost knocking my coffee cup to the floor. 'What is it? Do you recognise him?'

*

I couldn't believe it. Madame Heurteau knew him. She wasn't exactly sure, but she thought she may have rented her gîte to him. She didn't remember if there was a woman. Madame Betty kept shaking her head. It had been a long time the older woman explained. She hadn't rented it for years as the roof had fallen.

Something in me stirred at her words. A shiver rippled across my shoulders. 'Someone standing on you grave,' my Gran would have said. I tried to shake it off but the cold lingered, slipping up my neck and prickling the hairs on the back of my head.

Madame Betty looked at me in concern and I attempted a smile. I turned back to the older woman. 'Was this man the last guest?'

'Perhaps,' she shrugged.

I peppered her with questions to which, frustratingly, she had no answers. She certainly didn't recognise Sarah, but she was sure she had met the man. 'But only once, you see? He was a strange man, very intense with dark eyes. That's what I recognised on your phone.'

Madame Betty interrupted with a question and Madame Heurteau nodded. 'Betty has reminded me, and I think she is correct. This man you are looking for, 'e stayed in my gîte for quite a long time. 'e paid in full but left before the end of his tenancy. At the time I wondered if it was because the roof was beginning to leak – it collapsed soon after - but 'e didn't say anything. No note.'

'Did he leave anything behind?' I said. My heart was racing.

'I'm not sure. I don't think so. But the roof was very bad. After the surveyor went in and confirmed it was very dangerous we secured the 'ouse and...' She lifted her hands in an elegant gesture. 'My 'usband died and I was left with very little. It is a great shame, it is a pretty cottage but I cannot afford to have it mended.'

'I'm sorry about your husband,' Madame Heurteau inclined her head. I let a silence fall for a moment. Grief still painted lines on her face. It took all my strength to hold my body still and quiet. Urgency was hammering in my head until I had to speak. 'So, nobody has been in since this man...' I lifted my phone. 'Since he left?'

'If it is the same man, then that is correct.'

'Madame, I know this is very rude of me, but would you mind if I went to your cottage? I'm very worried for my friend and I'm sure this man brought her here. Maybe there is a note or an address that can help me find her.'

'But of course, however, I don't think there is anything to be found. I will ask Betty to find the keys. Do be careful, Elizabett, the roof is very bad and more may fall.'

'Yes, I will. Thank you. I'm very grateful.'

*

I couldn't think straight. Madame Betty had given me a key ring upon which swung two keys, one was large, heavy, and black – a key from a fairy tale. The other, a more prosaic brass Yale. I weighed them in my hand as I walked to the other end of the village. I wanted to run but settled for a fast trot.

There would be nothing, I told my heart, which jumped in my chest. It may not even be him who stayed there. The houses on the street passed in a blur, I ignored the villagers who nodded and waved. There was the church. Madame Heurteau had told me the gîte was on the other side. I was to look for a track running a little way into the woods.

I stopped as I heard the susurration of the trees. I could picture the branches moving in the wind, their ends clattering together. I put my hand on my stomach, it had lurched as suddenly as if I had rocketed down in a lift. Where had this sudden jolt of fear come from? There was nobody watching me, the street was empty, the solid bulk of the church was comforting. But I didn't want to move. I didn't want to get closer to the whisper of the woods.

Clenching my fists I thought of Sarah. Her kindness, her strength. I had to try. I kept my head down as I skirted the church and reached the rutted lane. The gîte had been part of a bigger estate that was destroyed in the war, Madame Heurteau had told me. As I stumbled on thick ridges of mud, I caught a glimpse of the building.

It wasn't a cottage, more of an outbuilding that had been added to using the stones remaining from the old house. It was pretty, though, with windows peeping out from behind the ivy that clung to the walls. The faded lavender shutters complemented the soft greys of the stone and the green of the woods behind. The roof looked as if a giant had sat on it; it bowed terribly, and many tiles had fallen to the ground.

As I looked up at the roof an invisible shockwave rolled towards me and sent my brain reeling. I felt as if I was going to faint, and with a gust of breath I flopped forward, letting the blood rush to my head. Something was dancing at the back of my mind, screaming at me to focus, listen to what it was saying. I concentrated, but my probing thoughts bounced back as if trying to push against a rubber wall.

It felt isolated. I shivered a little in the damp cold air. I knew the village was only a short walk away, but it felt like I was in the middle of nowhere. The clink of the keys sounded loud in the emptiness of the wood. No birds sang and the peaty earth swallowed up the sound of my steps. From where I stood, I could see nothing but trees. There was something about them that made me feel uneasy. Again, a memory tugged at my mind but it sunk before I could grab it.

The door was swollen with damp and I had to tug hard to get it open. It wouldn't shut behind me, so I left it open. The sitting room was small, plastered white, with a large fireplace; two wooden chairs angled towards it. A narrow flight of wooden stairs led up to the next floor and a small kitchen lay beyond. My eyes snagged on the stairs and I studied its length, but there was nothing odd about it.

Upstairs, one tiny bedroom had disappeared under the sunken roof. The other was empty except for a brass bed and a wardrobe. From the top window I could see a small extension had been built onto the back, presumably the bathroom. I couldn't shake off a horrible feeling of dread. I had to force myself to explore the cottage properly when every nerve seemed desperate to leave.

There was nothing to be found. Every drawer, every shelf, every cupboard was empty. I could find nothing that proved Sarah and Alex had been there. Beginning to grow desperate, I tapped walls and lifted dusty rugs, ever conscious of the broken roof weighing heavy above me. The disappointment was choking.

I looked again in the large pantry in the kitchen. A faint smell of vinegar stained the air, telling old tales of pickling jars. The wooden shelves reminded me of my workshop and a sudden pang cramped so hard it bent me double.

A breath of air touched my face.

I looked around to check but, as I thought, there was no window in the pantry and the one in the kitchen was firmly shut. I held out my hand and felt the puff of air again. From the floorboards? I thought.

I sat on my heels and laid my hands on the floor of the pantry. There was definitely a draught. Excitement rose, dispelling the shadow of unease that had stalked me since I entered the wood.

I tapped the torch on my phone. There. A fingerhold in the corner, a notch channelled out of the edge of a floorboard. I pulled on it and a square of wood popped up. Underneath was a metal ring.

Tucking my phone into my pocket, I stood and pulled it up. The whole floor lifted. It was a trap door. Cold air billowed into my face and I saw roughly made steps leading down into what must be some kind of cellar.

Adrenalin coursed through my body. Judging by the dust, nobody had been down here for years. Did Madame Heurteau know this cellar existed? She must do, I told myself.

The stairs were steep and the rungs narrow. It was more like a ladder and I gripped tight to the edges as I went down. An image of the roof collapsing, trapping me beneath the house made me sweat with horror. I stopped and swallowed hard, concentrating on my breathing until my heart rate slowed.

The cellar was pitch dark. I clenched my hands, letting the nails cut into the skin of my palm to stop panic rising. I turned on my torch. It was icy cold and stank of damp and rot. I followed the light as I moved it over the earth floor and across the whitewashed bricks. It seemed empty until I reached the corner.

My stomach swooped with a sickening lurch. What looked like an old futon mattress lay unrolled on the ground. There were terrible stains. A thick chain hung from a heavy ring, bolted securely to the wall.

Hardly breathing, I followed the length of the chain to the end with the torch. My hand shook so hard the light jerked crazily, but it was enough to see the handcuffs lying open and glinting in the darkness.

*

The police brought huge spotlights on frames that they ferried efficiently down the steps. In their white dazzle the room was exposed. Black earth greened with moss at the edges, white walls gleaming with condensation, and the foul mattress. The black ring and chain tore at the eye, dreadful graffiti on the blank wall.

It all happened so quickly I couldn't gather my thoughts in any kind of cohesive pattern. I wasn't sure what this meant. Someone had been kept here. That was certain; the bloodstains on the mattress spoke a foul story. I wondered where the young man was. The lone hiker I'd grabbed hold of as I staggered out of the cottage, urging him to call the police. He thought I was mad but made the call on his mobile, glancing at me in concern as he did so.

A serious young officer touched my arm, I was leaning against the wall furthest from the mattress, the damp soaked into my coat. I thought of the police examining my ruined workshop back home and felt sick. Had the same person been here? And who had lain on that mattress?

The officer was guiding me to the stairs but as I stepped round the cables, I heard an exclamation. A bulky officer in his forties was kneeling uncomfortably on the mattress, poking at the wall with the end of a pen. White flakes fell and sparkled in the bright lights. Everyone in the room paused to watch him.

The sound of scraping was loud and at last, with a grunt of satisfaction, the man pulled at something that had been wedged into a gap between the bricks. Using his pen, he hooked it out. Something slithered into his hand.

The hairs on my neck rose. My head gave an involuntary shake. No… My chest was tight, and I took a step forward. The officer tried to hold me back, but I had to see what was in his hand. I was already reaching into my jacket for the folded sketch I'd drawn of Sarah.

Pulling himself up by leaning on the wall, the officer stepped away from the mattress and looked beyond me to my companion who nodded. Swallowing hard, I rubbed my eyes and held out my hand. He didn't want to let go of it so held it up. A long, gold chain with a pendant in the shape of a butterfly. I began to cry.

I was too late. Tears spilled too fast for me to rub away. My throat filled with a great ache of sadness. The gasps of my breath echoed loud in the room.

Fumbling, I opened the sketch of Sarah. I couldn't see through my tears, but I knew what was there: strong eyebrows, a slight frown, that full mouth. But I knew the police in the room weren't looking at Sarah's face. Their eyes were fixed on the necklace that lay on her breastbone.

CHAPTER 15: AMBER

Amber had never felt so humiliated in her life. Paul dressed her down in front of the whole salon. He was red with rage and kept running his hands through his grey hair until it stood on end.

'How COULD you be so careless, Amber? Her hair is ruined!'

'I... I don't know what to say, Paul. I don't know what could have happened,' Amber stammered as her heart kicked at her chest. 'I'm so sorry, I can't believe this...'

'Our clients need to trust you. Trust the salon. Celia is devastated. How could you have done this to her?'

Amber shook her head, weeping. 'I didn't do anything different... I'm so sorry,' she rubbed her eyes with a ball of tissue, already soaked with tears.

'You must have used a 40 volume developer!'

Amber's mouth fell open. 'But that's not possible, I always check so carefully...'

'Well what the hell else do you think could have burned her scalp and broken her hair off like that? It was coming off in her hands!' Paul roared. It was early morning, before the salon opened. The staff who'd come in to set up their stations stood frozen as Paul paced up and down.

Amber stared at the floor; she couldn't bear to see the look on everyone's faces.

'But Amber didn't put the colour on Mrs Bushell's hair,' Amahle protested. She had appeared on the salon floor, drawn by the raised voices. She reached for Amber's hand and held it tight. 'She told me Laura put it on!'

'Amahle, don't,' Amber protested. 'It's not her fault…'

'Let's call her in, shall we?' Amber and Amahle flinched at his tone. 'Laura!'

Silence hung in the salon; nobody dared move. Heads turned to the staff room door as Laura appeared, pale in the face of Paul's wrath.

'You put on Celia's colour?'

'Yes, I was covering for Amber as…'

'And when did you notice something was wrong?' Paul's controlled questions was more terrifying than his anger, Amber thought.

'Well, pretty much straight away, I thought something wasn't right but I trusted Amber…'

'Amber mixed it up? You didn't do anything to it?'

'No! Of course not.'

'Definitely Amber who mixed the bleach?'

There was a pause. Laura glanced over at Amber then back at Paul. 'Yeah, it was. Sorry, Amber.'

'It's OK,' Amber tried to smile.

'Pack up your stuff,' Paul turned to her. 'You're fired.'

'You can't!' Amahle was horrified. 'Amber's been here for years, she's a fantastic stylist. It was obviously an accident…'

'You want to join her?'

Amber could see Amahle was about to do something stupid, she knew how hot-headed her friend could be and was terrified she'd get sacked too. 'No, Amahle!' she hissed, pulling her behind her.

Paul hadn't finished. He raised a meaty, mottled red finger. 'And don't go thinking you can take any of you clients with you. If I hear you've made contact with any of them, I'll sue you. Understand?'

Amber blinked. Shock was making her dizzy. 'I understand. I'm sorry, Paul. And please can you tell Mrs Bushell how upset I am by all of this? I just can't understand what happened. Do you think I can visit to apologise in person? If there is anything I can do to make up….'

'Don't be bloody ridiculous. Haven't you done enough? Get out of my sight.'

*

Amahle helped Amber gather her things. The staff were tactful enough to leave them alone as Amber, inconsolable, emptied her locker. Amahle passed tissue after tissue as Amber wept.

'What's he going to say to all my clients?' she sobbed. 'I've worked with some of them since I was sixteen. I can't believe I'll never come here again.'

Amahle gave her a fierce hug. 'You'll be OK, darling. I promise. He's a shit, and you're better off out of it. Maybe it's a good thing? You can go and have your babies and then we'll set up that salon we've always promised ourselves. Maybe I should go and tell him I quit – he can stick his job up his arse.'

'Oh, Amahle you can't! Not with the wedding coming up so soon. You're so lovely to say that, but it isn't worth it, really. I'll be fine, I'm sure,' she sobbed and Amahle passed over another wodge of tissues.

'Do you think you misread the bottles, or something?'

'I don't know. I've gone over and over it. The only thing I can remember is it smelled a bit strong. Why didn't I toss it and make up another batch? I'm so stupid!'

'Come on, let's get you an uber home. You can't carry all this home on your own. Have you told Alex?'

'No, not yet. What am I going to do, Amahle? I love this job. I love coming here. I love seeing you each day catching up – the house is such a mess and here it's so… clean and everything smells nice. Of course, Alex and Curly are doing all they can – they've been brilliant, and the house looks better every day – but they've got to keep working to pay for all the materials and everything and so they can really only do stuff at the weekends.' She took a great, shuddering sniff. Her hands shook and Amahle reached to hug her again.

A lump rose to her throat as she watched Amber, white-faced and trembling, place her box of belongings in the boot of the cab. A teddy bear holding a red satin heart wobbled on the top and

Amber squashed it down. Amahle remembered Alex handing it to Amber the day he proposed, along with armfuls of roses. She frowned as Amber gave a jerky wave, swallowed up in the dark cabin of the taxi. Her skin shivered across her shoulders and she hugged her arms around herself, trying to shake off the strange feeling this would be the last time she would see her friend.

*

'What a wanker! Do you want me to go see him? Tell him what I think?' For once they were eating dinner alone. Curly was on a rare visit home to see his family and Alex had the following day off thanks to a delivery delay that had held up the entire site.

'There's no point.' Amber piled his plate with pasta feeling guilty she hadn't had the energy to cook him something decent. 'Once Paul's made up his mind there's no going back. I've seen it before.' She sat down and curled some spaghetti around her fork, too wiped out with nausea to swallow anything.

'Maybe it's a good thing,' Alex spoke through a mouthful of food, chewing quickly.

'You're right, maybe it is time for a change.' Amber's voice was brave, but her heart sunk at the thought of starting again somewhere else. 'I've had a look at jobs in some other salons, but nobody will take me on without a good reference, and there's no way Paul will do that now. Maybe I could get Amahle to write something…'

'I meant, you not working.' Alex took his plate over to the sink and ran it under the tap, his back to her.

'What do you mean? Not working?'

'I just thought it'd be nice having you here when I get home. Not having to work weekends, leaving me alone on Saturday mornings. I hate that.'

'Do you? I thought you liked having the day to yourself.'

'Nah, I was just being nice. I'd much rather be with you.'

'Oh, Alex,' Amber said, touched.

He turned round from the sink, his eyes bright. 'Honestly, Amber, I know this is awful for you – nobody likes being fired, especially over a stupid mistake, but we have been talking about having a family and this way you can have a couple of months of peace and quiet, get some vitamins down you, look after me as well – like a proper wife!'

'You don't think I'm a proper wife?'

'Don't be stupid! Course I do. It's just I'm bringing in enough to cover us both. It's not like you earned very much anyway. Then when we sell the house we'll be loaded.'

'And I can start my own salon?'

Alex laughed. 'Don't get carried away, Amb. You'll have to wait until the kids are at school. I want them to have their mother with them until then.' A familiar expression crossed his face and Amber moved to hug it away. It broke her heart to think of Alex motherless at such a young age, left in the care of money-grabbing foster families.

'You'll be a great mum,' Alex whispered into her hair and Amber's heart began to lift with happiness.

*

Spending all day in the house was a depressing business. Whenever she thought about the salon and what she would normally be doing at that moment, Amber was crushed with such a monumental weight of sadness she felt like she'd never recover. So0 she stopped thinking about it. She couldn't even bear to take calls from Amahle or an apologetic Laura. Grimly, she focused on

Alex. Making elaborate, three course meals until Curly protested he couldn't cope with 'posh food' anymore and made Alex order a takeaway.

By the time Alex and Curly got back after work Amber felt like she'd spent the day swimming in an endless pool. They brought with them the outside world; their jokes and noise banished the emptiness in the house for a few hours, but every morning it returned: Cold, filled with echoes and the press of silence.

Within days Amber thought she would die of boredom. From a child she had school or work, never had she spent so much time on her own with nothing to do beyond mindless chores. Loneliness wound round her like a starving cat as she walked from room to room. She missed the way work gave structure to her days. It didn't help that the weather was so bad. Endless days of rain sheeted the windows, darkening the house into a damp, grey gloom.

On a day when Amber woke from a dream of her Mum that made her heart break she decided it was time to visit her grave. This was something she had avoided. Alex and the speedy wedding had filled the gaps grief had clawed into her body, but now the holes gaped again.

She unearthed rubber boots from the back of an unopened storage box, one of many that had arrived from her flat a few weeks after they returned from the honeymoon. She really should find the time to unpack them all, but not today. She had nothing waterproof so wrapped Alex's parka over a thick cardigan and leggings and opened the door to the wet world outside.

It was a long trip, halfway across the outskirts of London and Amber felt strange; as if a layer of protection had been shaved away when she lost her job. The lack of work to go to alienated her from the frowning, purposeful faces of the others swaying on the bus. She kept looking around, thinking Alex had jumped on the bus with her and was staring at the back of her head.

Maybe she should have told him she was going out to see Mum, she thought. Perhaps she should text him in case he got back early and was worried? Amber swiped open her phone but then put it back in her pocket. This wasn't anything to do with him, she reasoned. There was no possible way he could accuse her of doing anything wrong, besides, she'd be back before him.

At the entrance to the crematorium a flower stall bloomed bright against the dull brick walls. Amber stopped. Her mother hadn't approved of cut flowers, but she couldn't go and see her empty-handed.

She ended up spending far too much on a bunch of fat, pink tulips that were handed to her wrapped in brown paper. They looked pretty, and their brilliance warmed Amber as she followed the path to where her mother's remains lay behind a gold plaque in the ground.

Amber bent to wipe her mother's name clean and laid the tulips next to the stone. A crunch on the gravel path made her turn and she leaped to her feet to see Lizzie standing still, watching her, eyes burning.

*

'What are you doing here? Did you *follow* me?' Amber stammered, searching her pockets for her phone. 'Get away from me...'

The rain drenched them both as they faced each other, the names of the dead stretching to either side. Amber wiped away the water stinging her eyes and took a breath. She felt her Mum's presence close beside her, and it helped her to stand a little straighter. 'I'll call the police. I know you need help.'

'Give me five minutes,' Lizzie said. She was different. Energy didn't jangle about her in the crazy way it had done when she'd shouted at Amber's door. She stood, slim and straight as a boy, the planes of her face sharp.

'To do what? Alex has told me everything. I know what happened.'

Lizzie held up an envelope. 'It's all in here. If you'd just give me some time to explain... I could just leave it, but it might not make any sense.'

Despite everything Alex and Curly had told her, the sight of the brandished envelope made Amber curious. There was something compelling about this woman.

'Look, I'm leaving soon. I'll be completely out of your hair. I promise you'll never have to see me again. I'm not really sure why I'm here, I need to find out what happened to Sarah.' Amber saw a shiver of desperation, a frightening intensity cross Lizzie's face and it made her heart thump in fear again. She opened her phone and got ready to call Alex's number.

Lizzie held up her hand and took a step back. 'Sorry. I know I messed up last time, I freaked you out. I'm sure... He's said some things...' Amber saw she couldn't say Alex's name. 'OK.' She took a jerky breath. 'I should probably go. I'll leave this for you.' Lizzie held out the envelope.

Amber couldn't speak. She listened to the sound of rain pattering onto her hood. The envelope dampened in the wet and she tried to pull her eyes away, but curiosity made her fingers itch. 'Five minutes?' The tension eased from the other woman's face.

'Thank you. Yes. There's a Macdonald's just across the street. We could go there… for a coffee. I can barely hear you over the rain.'

'Lizzie…'

'It's Liz.' Amber, who'd started to feel almost motherly towards this fragile figure, was struck cold by the rage that crackled like lighting across Liz's eyes and mouth. 'Lizzie is what he called me. I'm not that person anymore.'

'Oh, OK.' Amber wondered if this was a good idea. She looked down at the phone again, but Liz had started to walk away, back down the path towards the main entrance. She was so tiny she couldn't possibly pose a threat, thought Amber.

It was a relief to get out of the sheeting rain and into the chip-fat-warmed air of the restaurant. Amber was thankful it was packed with a coach load of French students. The plastic easy-wipe tables and familiar branding was reassuring after the strange encounter in the crematorium.

Liz indicated Amber find a seat, so she slid into a booth at the window, far enough away from the chatting students but visible, in case anything went wrong.

Liz returned with two mugs of coffee; Amber was surprised at how good they smelled - rich and nutty.

'I didn't know if you took sugar,' Liz tossed a variety of sachets onto the sticky table.

'Thanks.' Amber chose a packet of brown sugar and snapped it back and forth, the practised movement slowing her heartrate further. She eyed the envelope in Liz's hand and wished they could just sit, warm and dry, and drink the good coffee without having to talk.

Her phone buzzed in her pocket. Alex. He'd sent a few texts that she hadn't seen and was now calling her. He'd be furious if he found out she was here, with Liz and her envelope of evidence. A flash of defiance rolled up from her stomach. There was no threat coming from Liz. Loneliness and curiosity kept Amber in her seat. The phone lit up again and, after hesitating only for a moment, Amber turned the volume off.

'I'm going to be quick as I've got to catch a train soon.' Liz took a deep sip of her coffee, though it must have been scalding, and ran her thumb under the flap of the envelope. 'These are all copies, right? I have left the originals with a friend.'

Amber pressed down an urge to laugh, this was all so ridiculous. Liz was so serious, so intent. She'd pulled off her soaking beanie and her shaved head was shocking.

'I met Alex at uni…'

'Yeah, he told me.'

'I didn't really notice him at first. He and his friends didn't mix with the people I hung out with.' She paused and Amber saw Liz's hands had curled into fists so tight the knuckles stood out, bone-white. She was finding it very hard to tell this story, Amber realised.

'But then I caught his eye. He started to follow me around, ask me out on dates. He was charming. I liked him but I… well, I was quite popular and was already going out with someone, but that didn't seem to bother him. But then I heard my boyfriend was sleeping with someone else, so I chucked him out. Alex was great. He came round a few days later and took me out for breakfast. He said he was going to tell me jokes until I smiled, and that's what he did. They were stupid, Christmas cracker jokes, but before long I was laughing. He looked like he'd won a million pounds.'

She smiled at Amber's look of astonishment.

'Not quite what he told you?'

Amber shook her head.

'We started going out and that Christmas he asked me to come and meet his family, I thought he was rushing things but…'

'Wait. What? Alex hasn't got any family, his mother died when he was young. He was brought up by foster homes.'

Liz gave a tight smile. 'He tells different stories,' she said.

Amber made to stand up, this was crazy. She wasn't talking about her Alex. Liz leaned over and held her arm. 'When you go back, look around. See what you can find. But please stay, I've barely started.'

'OK, but I don't think this is right.'

'We grew closer, only a few months in we were mad about each other. He seemed besotted, said I made him a better person, I was his Beauty.' She gagged on the word and took another sip of coffee to burn away the taste. 'But then things began to get dark. He'd get angry if I went out with friends, didn't like me going back home to see my Gran. After a year it was like everything I did was wrong. And then he hit me.'

Silence fell between them.

'What did you do?' Amber's voice cracked. Her mouth was dry.

'I left him,' Liz watched her fingers running around the mouth of the coffee mug. 'He came after me, begging. Said he was sorry. All the usual bullshit. So, I went back.' She gave a weak shrug. 'And then he wouldn't let me out of his sight. He'd walk me to lectures and then be waiting when I came out. I persuaded myself it was romantic. My therapist helped me to see they were red flags. But that was later.'

'I don't understand this,' Amber put down her empty mug with a bang. 'None of this makes any sense.'

'Just listen, OK? Then you can make up your own mind.' She took a breath, memories shadowed her eyes. 'It took him three years to break me completely. I had no sense of who I was outside him. He took away every yard stick, so I no longer knew what was normal. He threatened to kill himself if I left, and later he'd threaten to kill me.'

'Christ,' said Amber, able now to empathise as she knew this woman couldn't possibly be describing her Alex. Liz was delusional, just as he and Curly had said.

'By the end I thought I was mad. I would forget things, lose my phone, find my books torn and destroyed and he'd tell me I'd done it in my sleep. He'd said he was worried about me, that I went into a fugue state.' She laughed, but tears were sliding down her cheeks. Amber fought an urge to hold her hand, Liz's pain was raw and burned, it was unbearable to watch.

'You don't need the details. But I got out. That's the main thing. And then I stalked him until I saw him with another woman, Sarah, and I told her what he was, and I saved her. Well, I thought I did. Turned out I didn't. God, I wish this was gin.' She said, gesturing at the coffee mug. Amber didn't smile.

'So, what's in the envelope?'

'I started to realise I wasn't the first victim. He'd hurt others and he'd go on hurting.' With a glance around the restaurant she opened the envelope and emptied its contents. Clippings from newspapers, photographs, scrawled notes and printouts slithered onto the table.

Amber began to sort through them. She focused on the articles, checking the dates and putting them in order. Everything else looked like a crazed mass of crap pulled from a tramp's shopping trolley, she thought.

Each article featured a missing girl. There must have been fifteen, stretching back over more than ten years. As Amber leafed through them, she slowed as she noticed something. 'They all look…'

'Like me,' said Liz.

Amber couldn't help a bark of shocked laughter. 'They don't look anything like you! I was going to say they all look like each other, big girls with red hair.'

Liz pulled a polaroid from her rucksack and held it up for Amber to see before lying it, face up, on the table.

'That's you?' Amber was incredulous as she held the photo in her hand, studying it closely. The colours had faded, but they were clear enough to see a smiling girl in a green dress. Her red hair corkscrewed past her shoulders, her figure a generous hour glass. She looked over at the shaven headed wraith of a woman who perched, rigid with tension, on the plastic chair. 'This can't be you.'

'It's me. Just before I met Alex.'

The pack of students had left. The restaurant was empty except for a bored teenager in a baseball cap and a drab uniform who skidded a bucket along the floor with his mop.

Nothing could have told Liz's story with more eloquence than the horrific contrast between the polaroid photo and the woman sitting before her.

'I'm sorry.' The words weren't enough, of course. What else could she say? Amber wondered. Her heart broke for this damaged woman, and she knew there must have been a mistake, it wasn't her husband Liz was describing. That knowledge allowed her sympathy to rise unchecked, and she put down the articles. 'What can I do? How can I help you?'

'I don't need your help,' Liz was brisk as she gathered up the papers and pushed them into the envelope. 'I'm going to find my friend. Sarah. I need to know what happened. You keep this, do what you want with it. I can see you don't believe me. I've not changed your mind about Alex. But don't be the fool I was. Watch him. Someone stole these girls. They've disappeared from all over the country. Nobody has seen the link between them except me. I see it, because they all look like me, or, should I say, the first girl who broke his heart.'

'What do you mean?' Amber stood as Liz pulled the woollen beanie, which glittered with rain, down over her eyes. She shrugged into a heavy pea coat, it swallowed her up and Amber could only see the white of her long hands and the oval of her face. Liz walked out but lingered in the doorway, sheltering from the rain that continued to fall.

Amber grabbed her handbag and followed; standing side by side they looked out at the rain as Liz continued to speak. 'I met a friend of his, an old school friend. It was just before we dated properly, I didn't think anything of it at the time. He came over to talk to me at a bar one night because he thought I was this girl he'd gone to school with, Lisa. He said I looked just like her. Flattered me. Said she was the most popular girl at school and Alex had fallen head over heels in love with her. Obsessively so. They'd joke about it. Something bad happened between them but this guy wasn't sure what as he'd moved schools. I told him Alex was there, but he didn't want to meet him. I thought it was a bit odd at the time but didn't push it. Probably pissed.'

'What, and you think he's got an obsession with hurting pretty girls with red hair?' Amber tone was mocking. She felt terrible for Liz, but the story had nothing to do with her.

'I do. Yes. Sarah was the same. I'm going to prove it. I'm going to find the evidence that's going to put that monster away forever.'

'But if any of this is true it doesn't make sense. I don't look anything like those girls.'

Liz, whose eyes were fixed on the street shining in the rain turned back to Amber. 'You need to ask yourself what you've got that Alex needs. When he no longer needs you… well, that will be the end. You're in danger, Amber. Make no mistake. I don't know why he chose you to marry but he's a twisted fuck with a strange obsession. You're not his type. I don't know why he's with you, but there will be a reason. You need to find out what it is.'

'I'm sorry, Liz. Sorry for what you've been through, but I can't believe any of this can be about my husband. It's all so… crazy.'

'I have to go. Take care, Amber. I hope to see you again.'

And she was gone. So fast Amber lost sight of her within seconds, as if she was a ghost. On the way to a bus stop she passed a bin and was tempted to shove in the envelope, hiding it beneath the junk food cartons and bulging plastic bags. But something stopped her. She folded it over and pushed it deep into her handbag, just as her phone began to vibrate.

Alex again. Suffused with a longing for the reassurance his voice would offer, she answered.

'Amber? What the fuck are you doing? Why are you on the other side of London?'

SARAH: FIVE YEARS AGO

She woke, still dressed, lying on a concrete floor. Sleeping bodies lay everywhere and she was desperate for water. She groped through the dark into a kitchen and ran the tap. The water ran brown, but she was so thirsty she scoped handfuls into her mouth, soaking her clothes. Shoving her head under the freezing flow of water rinsed away the last of the sticky residue of pills, leaving her mind clear. Her eyes were gritty and red, and she rubbed at them.

She crept about the room looking for her bag, careful not to disturb anyone. Marc was nowhere to be seen. A man was using her bag as a pillow and she inched it out, holding her breath as his head fell back with a thud, but he didn't wake.

She left the room and followed a corridor to find Marc rolling a joint. He was crouched over an iron bucket in which smoked a small fire.

'Good morning,' he said.

'Can I have some of that?' He passed it over. They smoked in silence. 'Can we go now? I am worried about my friend. Do you remember the address I showed you?'

He scowled. 'It's a long walk through the woods.'

'Please.'

It was clear he had no intention of going anywhere. He looked bombed, she thought.

'Make it worth my while?' he said with a nasty smile.

She shook her head to shake off the memory of the voice on the phone, pleading with her. Marc had to help; she couldn't think of what else to do. Despair made her want to weep as she handed over the last of her blow and all but €20 of her cash. Marc got to his feet and brushed down his filthy tracksuit bottoms with a sigh.

'OK. We go now.'

The woods were dark and wet; she kept tripping over roots and stumbling into rabbit holes. The earth was soft and crumbled down slopes in little peaty rushes of soil. Marc stalked ahead faster and faster and she panted to keep up.

Above her the trees knotted into a dense canopy that blocked out the sky. For a horrified moment she felt like Orpheus following Hades into the underworld. What was she doing? Panic dried her throat and she tried to ignore the faces that mouthed at her from the crooks and hollows of the wood.

Her ankles were aching by the time they finally saw light brightening ahead. Marc stopped at the start of a rutted track that led out of the trees. He stopped and pointed down it.

'Down there, not long. Two or three minutes.'

'Can you give me anything?' Her lungs were tight, her breathing shallow. A tight band squeezed round her chest. She didn't want to keep walking, now badly frightened at the thought of what she was going to find. She tried to remember exactly what her friend had said on the phone, but her mind fell into a jumble of jigsaw pieces and she couldn't fit them back together no matter how hard she concentrated.

'Only this,' Marc said, holding up a capsule. 'But it's strong.'

'Yes, that's fine.' She reached for it, but he clenched his hand into a fist. 'What do I get for it?'

He repulsed her with his scrawny body and unshaven grey face. But she needed something to soften the edges.

'How about these?' She unhooked her earrings. 'They're gold.' They weren't, but she assumed he was too stoned to tell.

Marc nodded, took the earrings, and passed her the pill. Within seconds he was gone, and she was alone in a wood that seemed to be breathing. Feeling in her pocket for her Gran's ring she pushed it securely onto her finger, needing the reassurance. She tried to imagine her Grandmother standing in the wood, encouraging her on, but when she looked, there was nobody there.

She held the pill on her tongue for a moment until the casing began to soften, then swallowed. She waited until she imagined it liquifying in her blood before moving forward.

It wasn't two or three minutes; it was half an hour before she got to the end of the track and saw a cottage ahead. Marc's pill was stretching her brain like elastic and the woods moved closer and closer snapping back into place when she turned to look. She laughed at the distortion and held up her hand to see the light shining through her skin, the fingers elongating until they vanished.

Her laughter rippled up into the air, shimmering oily fronds which moved as she stirred them. She slowed as she got closer to the building; her smile dying as she saw black shadows leaking from the brickwork. A crash and a rattle boomed loud, making her jump. She stumbled to hide herself in the hedges in the garden at the back of the house.

Rapid footsteps echoed but she couldn't work out where they were coming from. She crept through the tangled undergrowth and peered around the side of the cottage. Shoving her fist into her mouth so she didn't make a sound she pulled back.

Alex! Alex was walking away down the track. What the hell was he doing here? Terror ballooned and adrenalin pushed her heart into a frantic thundering. Disorientated, she began to run in the opposite direction but somehow ended pushing through a wall of overgrown bushes, tripping over a step and smashing headfirst into the stone frame of the back door.

Her brain exploded into stars and for a moment she watched them fall. She held the wall and looked down, marvelling at the splashes of red ink appearing in slow motion on the concrete. The palms of her hands glittered with shards of glass; she pulled them out wondering why she felt no pain.

Like a police light flashing, her mind kept up its urgent message: He's near! He's near! The words pounded with her heartbeat. She had to leave. But a flicker caught her eye, it made her think of a swimmer thrashing through water. The dizziness was getting worse, but she had to see. She moved to look through the back-door window and froze in horror.

A body swung in the shadows, the legs kicking with desperate force -

CHAPTER 16: LIZ

'Sarah left her necklace, I know she did. She wanted someone to know she was here.' I couldn't stop crying. I wasn't sure the officer by my side understood anything I was saying, but she offered me a pack of tissues. I wondered if all police officers carried them. They must see a lot of pain, I thought.

Outside the cottage on the track stood a small huddle of villagers. My landlady stood next to Madame Heurteau whose face was blank with shock. She was shivering in the cold, and an official in a Hi-Viz jacket approached and wrapped a thick red blanket around her shoulders.

'She didn't know the cellar was there,' the police officer said, seeing my glance. 'They've owned the cottage for years, but they never knew.'

'Oh,' I said, sniffing and wiping my face; the skin felt raw. 'I didn't know you spoke English. My name is Liz.'

'Ondine,' she replied. 'This is a bad time. Chauron is a quiet village, we are not used to crimes such as these.'

We fell silent, watching officials move in and out of the cottage in their white protective suits. The man in the Hi-Viz jacket was unrolling tape to stop the villagers coming closer. Reading the words 'SCÈNE DE CRIME: PASSAGE INTERDIT' I felt faint. I began to sway and Ondine put her hand on my shoulder to bend me forward.

I closed my eyes and rubbed my fists into them, but I could still see Sarah. The courage I'd admired when reporting Alex to the police. The kindness she'd shown me in my desperate madness and addiction. I couldn't work out how she had ended up marrying Alex, going to France and then hiding her necklace in that cellar wall. Whenever I tried to move from one step to another a great vacuum appeared. It was too impossible. She would never have gone willingly.

I stood up, feeling better. Rage was beginning to beat up from the ground, thrumming into my blood. The synapses in my brain firing up. The vacuum was gone. Of course. How could I have been so stupid? I should have thought better of Sarah. No wonder every part of me violently rejected the idea that she had married him. What evidence did we have that even happened? Just Alex's word for it in a phone conversation with her brother.

'Are you OK?' Ondine looked concerned. I realised I was muttering out loud. Anger was sparking off me, I couldn't contain it.

'I need to speak to someone. I know who did this…' But as I spoke, the words faltered. Ondine was looking back at the cottage and I turned to see why. I cried out in despair as I saw two policemen carrying their big lights into the garden. A third officer had already started digging.

*

By the time the police had finished with me I was utterly exhausted. Even Madame Betty's delicious bowl of steaming garbure, heavy with tender chunks of meat and thick with vegetables couldn't dissolve the ball of ice I was holding inside. She urged me to rest, her eyes full of the horror at what the police had discovered in that overgrown garden, but I couldn't. It took all my focus and concentration to sit still enough to eat.

I would have refused it, but I had seen in the mirror that morning I was wasting away. My face had acquired that gauntness that looked simian, downy hair had appeared on my arms and the back of my neck. This was it. The French police would find something. Some hair, some thread that would link him here and it would be the end of him.

I needed to be strong and certain and sane, so I could help them gather those trails of evidence that would lead back to England and the other girls I knew lay hidden in silent graves.

I thought of Amber, shivering in a coat too big for her, eyes wide as I told her my story. How much danger was she in? I hope she had the sense not to tell him she'd seen me again. I wished I had her number so I could tell her to leave. Who knows what he'd do when the police came knocking? And they would. I'd make sure of it.

*

The next morning Madame Betty drove me to the local police station where I was to make a witness statement. The breakfast she'd forced down me churned in my stomach and I swallowed hard to keep it down as we swung round the curves of the narrow lanes. Every now and then she would reach over and squeeze my hand, offering me strength. I wished my French was good enough to express how grateful I was for her care.

Two officers were waiting for me and led me past the reception area to a room empty except for a table and three chairs. As I sat, I saw Ondine standing by the door and she gave a small smile as I caught her eye. Rain continued to spatter against the window, and I remembered with a shiver the white-suited police carrying lights into the muddy garden of Madame Heurteau's little cottage.

They brought tea that was undrinkable; I abandoned it after the first watery sip. I'd spent the night planning what I needed to stay and in what order. I had to be clear, reasoned and calm. I couldn't mess this up.

A burly man who introduced himself as Laurent squeezed behind the table and sat down. His coffee looked better than my tea. With careful precision he took my details. His English was impeccable.

'Perhaps the best thing would be for you to explain why you are here. You were looking for your friend?'

I watched his hand move across the paper as I spoke. I wondered why it wasn't done electronically. I'd expected a laptop or an iPad. It took an hour. An hour of staying focused and collected, my hands shook with the effort.

'And you recognise the necklace? You are certain?'

I nodded. 'Absolutely. If you look at my sketch...'

'Yes, I have seen your drawing. We are hoping to be able to identify the body soon, to be sure – you understand?'

'It is definite... the body you found...' I didn't want to say the words, sweat cooled along my hair line. 'I was told it was a woman?'

He nodded, darting a sharp look at Ondine.

'I have her brother's details. You must call him. And I know who did this, I can tell you his name too, and where he is. You must get onto the UK police to arrest him right now. If he hears Sarah has been found he'll disappear. You'll miss him. He's married, I'm pretty sure his wife is in danger too.' I stopped. Pillars were folding and collapsing in my head, crashing against each other, I could see white dust rising. My mouth was dry.

Laurent's face shifted, closed. I clenched my fists under the table to keep myself under control. Madness had my brain between its teeth and was giving it a good shake. I reached for my tea with clumsy hands, knocking it flying. As Laurent exclaimed and dabbed at the mess with a pile of napkins, I got myself back under control.

'I'm so sorry. What a mess! It's all so upsetting, Sarah was a close friend, I'm… not quite myself.'

'I understand,' Laurent replied, he looked at me with pity, I railed against it. I needed him to listen, not dismiss me as a fantasist. 'I need you to stay close by Madame Shaw,' he went on. 'We may have more questions for you.'

'Yes, of course. That's fine.' I stood up and the chair shrieked, an ugly sound that made my teeth ache.

*

They came for me earlier than I had expected. A car pulled up outside Madame Betty's house just as we were finishing lunch. I opened the door to find two officers on the step. Madame Betty elbowed me aside and assailed them in her machine gun fire French, her arm around me.

'We need you to come in to answer some more questions,' an unfamiliar young woman spoke to me over Madame Betty's dramatic exclamations and dancing hands. I didn't need to speak

French to know she was telling them we'd only just finished lunch, that I was exhausted and needed to rest – no more questions, couldn't they see how pale I was? Didn't they know what I'd been through?

'It's OK, it's OK, Madame Betty.' I stepped past her and out of the house, patting her back as she hugged me, letting her warmth seep towards my sharp bones. I felt like crying.

'Where are we going?' I asked as we whipped past the village police station and signs appeared for the autoroute for Paris.

'We just need to go through some questions with you,' the driver spoke without looking back, his companion never raised his eyes from his iPhone.

'In Paris?'

'Yes.'

I sat back, my mind racing. What was going on? What more could I tell them? I knew it was Sarah whose body they'd found, and I knew who'd done it. Why was I being driven to Paris?

I don't know what I was expecting, but I was surprised by the classical beauty of the building when we finally arrived. I had no idea where I was. I looked left and right as we crossed from the car park to the main entrance but could see no familiar landmarks. No Eiffel tower. My sense of dislocation grew stronger. Utterly rudderless, I longed to escape to my work bench with the lovely reality of wood and leather under my hands.

I stood, passive, as the officers checked me in, a lanyard was handed to me and I looped it over my head. There was lots of noise and chatter, it made my head spin and I had to think hard to remember enough French to ask for water. It wasn't necessary, everyone I met spoke impeccable English, but it was shaming how little I knew, how much I relied on everyone speaking my language in their country.

The building was modern inside, lots of clean white spaces. Nothing like the cosy, slightly run-down police station in Chauron, where I'd been interviewed that morning. It felt like years ago. Nobody seemed able to tell me why I was there. I sensed they were waiting for the person in charge of the investigation. In the meantime, I was directed to wait in an open plan common room which had a coffee station dominated by a complicated looking machine.

After an hour an officer approached and walked me up two flights of stairs and through a pair of doors into a spacious lobby with a reception desk. My heart began to thump. Two men were talking, their backs turned. One had the unmistakable dark hair, large moustache, and small stature of a man from the south of France. The other… the other. It couldn't be. Panic rattled at the back of my eyes and I sucked in a breath with a gasp. The officer next to me glanced over in concern.

There was a chair to my right, one of two placed either side of a window. I grabbed the back as tightly as I could to stay upright.

The men moved, separated, and walked towards me. How could this be possible? How could he be here, in France? I dug my nails deep into the palm of my hand. Was I dreaming? My belly cramped and a hand seemed to grab at the muscles of my chest and twist them into a hard knot.

'Madame Shaw? I am Inspector Cadieux, thank you for coming all this way.' His handshake was warm, his face open and intelligent. I fixed my eyes on him. 'And this, as you know, is Detective Inspector Cartwright. He has kindly flown over from the UK to help us with our enquiries.'

I risked a glance. He hadn't changed. Slim, with close cropped gingery hair and a narrow face. I didn't meet his eyes. I already knew that assessing, calculating gaze - one that had the power to turn your guts into ice.

'Mz Shaw.' I shivered at the sound of his voice. The urge to bolt was overwhelming. Sarah. I thought. Focus on Sarah. You know you're right. My pulse eased a fraction.

'Shall we?' Inspector Cadieux opened the door to a room with one wall of glass through which filtered the sound of Parisian traffic. I breathed deep to still the quiver in my chest.

They sat me in the chair opposite the window and when they took their seats they morphed into threatening, faceless silhouettes.

'Madame Shaw, you have given a statement to my colleagues about the body that was found in Chauron.'

'Yes, that's right.' I had to clear my throat.

'And you think this is the body of your friend, Sarah Andrews?'

'Yes, and I have also given you the name of the man who killed her, I told them this morning. You must get to him and have him arrested before he hurts anyone else. He's going to hear about this on the news and he'll disappear. I know he will – he's done it before…' I stopped. I was sounding desperate again. I took a deep breath through my nose, allowing the silence to stretch. 'I know he's responsible for other murders, I have proof.'

I unzipped my rucksack and rummaged for my envelope of evidence. I handed it to Inspector Cadieux who shook out the contents.

'Ah, now, this is the problem.' Cartwright's pedantic tone made every cell in my body itch with hatred. 'Inspector Cadieux, I'm afraid to say Mz Shaw has rather an obsession. It's a good job you got in touch, I think I can add some, er, context, which may be of use.'

I glared at him with defiance, but my heart thudded. I hated not being able to see Cadieux's expression as he read through my notes.

'She's been coming to the police for years with her accusations about this man, an ex-lover of hers. It became so upsetting he had to take out a number of restraining orders, many of which she broke, resulting in some hefty fines and the threat of prison, I'm sorry to say.'

Inspector Cadieux was quiet, his head tilted as he listened, but he continued to study my notes. I remembered Amber as she sorted the newspaper clippings into date order as I saw him do the same.

'Mz Shaw's mental health is not good and though her… issues… are treatable, occasionally she will stop taking her medication and her obsession appears again.'

'Not anymore,' I said sharply. 'That was a long time ago.'

'And you have investigated these disappearances?' Cadieux slid the packet of articles across to Cartwright who gave an impatient sigh.

'Of course we have, we're not completely incompetent.' As he continued to speak, he lifted each article from the pile and placed it on the table, like a croupier dealing cards. At all times his air of long-suffering patience made me want to punch him. 'This girl sadly committed suicide. Something Mz Shaw refused to accept. This one was killed by her boyfriend, he's in jail. This one?

Murdered by her husband,' he shook his head. 'A terrible thing. Another suicide,' he lay down the article with its photo of a smiling girl with a flourish. 'And this young lady disappeared for a few weeks but was found dead of an overdose in a public lavatory. Need I go on?'

'This is all bullshit and you know it!' I cried. 'I've told you he's clever, he's making fucking… fools of you. All of you. You don't know what he's capable of. Anyone who was arrested was set up! He knows exactly what to do - how to lead the police round by the nose – he's got them exactly where he wants them.'

'Every one of these cases have been investigated and solved. Not one of them have a connection with the other…'

'Look at them!' I pleaded with Cadieux. 'Look at their faces! Can't you see? They look like sisters!'

'There is a striking resemblance…' he said.

'A coincidence,' Cartwright waved his hand. 'I can assure you we found nothing to prove Mz Shaw's accusations. Not a shred of evidence connecting these women to each other or the man with whom she is obsessed.

'But what about Sarah?'

'Ah, yes, Ms Andrews. You convinced her, right enough – almost drove her mad with your warnings and allegations – but she didn't believe you in the end. I hear she married him?'

'She couldn't have married him. He must have… kidnapped her or something. And now she's dead!' My heart sank as I saw them exchange glances.

'We don't yet have confirmation of the identity of the body…'

'But it's a woman, yes? Around the same age as me? And a necklace identical to Sarah's was found where she'd been imprisoned? Seems pretty fucking obvious to me!'

'There's no need for such language, Madame Shaw,' Cadieux voice was soft but held a heavy rebuke.

'I'm sorry.' Helpless, I rubbed my face. 'It's just so frustrating. Sarah was my friend, I thought I'd saved her…' Tears spilled through my fingers.

'Yes. Sarah.' Cartwright's words were sharp and dangerous as a poisoned dart. 'Quite a strange relationship going on there, wasn't it?' He looked over at Cadieux. 'She was arrested for breaking into Sarah's house.'

'I can explain that… I was looking for…'

'She made up lies about being beaten,' Cartwright was remorseless. 'Obsessed with putting away her ex she would do anything, say anything to get him investigated. To begin with we took her seriously, but it was obvious pretty soon this was nothing but a jealous woman seeking revenge. Intent on destroying the man who'd left her, any way she could. Nothing could convince her, no matter how strong his alibi.'

'I left him! And he made people lie for him! He was able to do that, he has some sort of weird charm…' I protested, but already I could see the darkness flickering at the corner of my eyes. The room stretched away from me like a grotesque fairground mirror. Voices echoed in my head and I clamped my hands over my ears.

'If the body you find is Sarah Andrews, I think you need to look very carefully at Mz Shaw's movements. Quite a coincidence she was the one to find her, isn't it?'

'You can't think I... you can't think I had anything to do with this?'

Cartwright shrugged. 'Inspector Cadieux all I can tell you is that I have read all the reports on Mz Shaw. Her lists of accusations as well as the arrests and prosecutions. Still getting high, Liz?'

I shook my head so hard my ears rang. 'No, no, that's not me...'

'She was arrested many times for possession of class A drugs,'

'That was years ago! I haven't touched...'

'It would work well for you, wouldn't it, Liz? A murder with all the clues pointing to your ex? That would put him out of the picture for good. Isn't that what you want?'

'Well, yes, of course that's what I want,' I stammered. 'But I didn't set anything up... I came here looking for Sarah. Call her brother, he'll tell you. How long has the body been there? I'm sure I can prove I wasn't anywhere near when she died...'

A cloud passed over the sun and shadows swung into the room. At last I could see their faces, no longer in silhouette. Inspector Cadieux's expression was grave.

'I think it would be best, Madame Shaw, if we took a break. Is there anything we can collect for you from your lodgings? Medication perhaps?'

I shook my head. 'I'm not on any medication,' I stared at Cartwright; he gave a light, scoffing laugh.

'I suggest you ask for her medical records,' he said and Cadieux nodded. I was filled with despair.

CHAPTER 17: AMBER

'Have you been tracking me?' Amber said, suddenly furious. Her nerves were all over the place after visiting her mother's grave and meeting Liz. Hearing Alex snarling down the phone pushed her into defiance.

The bus swayed, throwing Amber against the window so she banged her shoulder, hard.

'I just want to know where my wife is, what's wrong with that? I came home early to see you and you'd gone. No note, nothing. I was worried sick!'

Amber took a breath. 'You're right, I should have texted you. I thought I'd be back before you.'

'What were you doing?'

'Does it matter?'

Amber could sense Alex trying to get a grip on his temper. 'I'm just asking. I'm not accusing you of anything.'

'I went to visit Mum,' Amber's throat closed with the ever-present grief.

She heard him sigh with relief. What did he think she was doing? she wondered. The folded envelope in her handbag seemed to glow with a radioactive menace. Suddenly frightened Alex would sense it the minute she got home, Amber tugged it free, folded it twice more and slid the little packet inside her coat pocket.

'Are you coming home? I miss you.'

'Yes. I won't be long.'

As the bus jerked forward Amber tried to forget Liz sitting, taut and desperate, with her package of papers. On a deep, instinctive level she knew Liz had got it wrong. She was obviously messed up, an obsessed stalker whose paranoia had made her delusional. But something was going on with those girls, something weird. She resolved to read through the notes properly the next time she was alone.

*

Any pretence at patience and concern was ripped away as Amber opened the front door to see Alex waiting for her, swollen with rage.

'Where's Curly?' she asked, slipping off her coat and bag and hanging them on the hook in the hall.

'He's out.'

Amber walked past him to the kitchen. 'Shall I make something for dinner? I didn't realise how late it was.' She kept her voice steady but felt like she was carrying a bowl of cold water in her stomach and took small steps, so it didn't spill.

They were low on food. She checked the boxes lined up on the makeshift counters and found some pasta and two tins of tuna. Alex's looming presence stopped her from thinking straight. A strange high thrumming sound rang in her head, ratcheting up her nerve endings until they were on the verge of snapping.

'So, you went to see your mum?'

'Yes, I hadn't visited since she died, and I wanted to see her grave…'

'So why the *fuck* did you need to spend an hour in a shitty Macdonald's?'

Amber gritted her teeth. She knew these rages came from depression and they'd pass, like bad weather, but she hated them. Hated the weight of violence hanging in the air, sliding tension into her shoulders and scalp. Her mind flickered to Liz and her pile of notes, the photographs of smiling girls.

Amber's heart gave a sudden lurch. Had Katie Brook been a face in that pile? She couldn't remember. Desperately she tried to think. She remembered laughing with her about her bright red roots as her black hair grew out. 'I look like I'm radioactive!' she had joked. Amber remembered advising her to use Head and Shoulders to get rid of the black dye so she could show off her lovely red hair again. The same hair that had made Liz so beautiful before her life exploded.

'Amber I'm talking to you!' Alex grabbed her shoulder and turned her to face him. 'Who were you with?'

'You've no right to spy on me like…'

'I have every right!' His face was so close she could smell his skin. Her body instinctively responded to its heat even as her mouth dried and her brain raced to find the words that would calm him.

'Alex, please. It's nothing. I went to see Mum and while I was there I met a client.'

'Which one? What was her name?'

'Uh, you wouldn't know her, she moved on before we met, I haven't seen her in years.'

'What was her name?'

'Jesus! Does it matter? Alex, please.'

With a shocking, sudden movement he gripped her arms and shook her twice, so violently her head snapped back.

'Alex! Don't! You're hurting me.'

'Tell me the name.'

'It was Mrs Jenkins. She was one of my first clients.' Fear added fluency to the lies. 'She moved away years ago. I bumped into her leaving the crematorium and she was so pleased to see me I couldn't say no – it was just a quick coffee. A catch up. That's all.'

He pushed her away so hard she banged against the counter.

'Don't you ever go out and meet people without telling me first. There's some freak out there and I don't want you getting hurt.'

'What freak?'

'Dom was telling me on site this morning. Another local girl has disappeared, it's all over his Facebook, he said. They think its linked with the girl you were talking about, the one from your salon – Kayleigh.'

'Katie,' Amber corrected rubbing her neck

'Yeah, that's the one. It's why I came home early, I tried to call you and when you didn't answer…'

'Alex. Look at me. You've got to trust me. I can't have you flying off the handle because I'm having coffee with a friend.'

He stared at he, searching her face. A long pause passed before the tension left him. 'I can't help it, babe. I was so worried.'

Amber let herself be drawn into his arms, her neck was still sore but it was so nice to be close, protected by the strength of him. She forced down the dark misgivings which were chiselling cracks into the certainty of her love for Alex.

*

'Babe, have you seen my phone?' Alex and Curly were chatting in the kitchen, the smell of frying bacon curled up the stairs, making her mouth water. Amber leaned over the bannister trying to see into the kitchen.

'No, sorry.'

'Can I have some bacon?'

Curly stuck his head out and looked up at her his cheeks bulging. 'Sorry, love. We've eaten the last of it – there's some cereal?'

'No, it's OK. Can you get Alex to call my phone?'

'Sure.'

Amber went back to the bedroom, hoping to hear Alex's ring tone. She was sure she'd left it charging by her bed last night.

'Are you calling it?' she shouted.

'Calling now!' came Alex's muffled shout.

She sighed in frustration; she couldn't hear anything. She'd have to look downstairs.

'We're off!' Curly called.

'Wait!' Amber finished buttoning her jeans and tugged an old t-shirt over her head, wincing at the soreness in the muscles of her neck and shoulders. She skidded in her thick socks to the top of the stairs. 'Alex, I can't find my phone, I'm sure I left it on the locker to charge – have you seen it?'

'No, sorry babe. Maybe in the sitting room? Better go, Dom's picking us up any minute. You stay inside, OK? Make me a nice dinner.' He blew her a kiss and Curly laughed.

But Amber wasn't listening. Horror flashed through her. The coat! But it was too late. Before she could speak or even think of anything she could do to stop him, Alex shrugged into his parka. As she watched him, her heart beating so hard it was a roar in her ears, he sniffed the collar and smiled.

'It smells of you, babe! You been pinching my clothes?'

'Yes, sorry, it was raining and…' Amber replied weakly.

'It's nice. It'll be like I'm taking you with me. Love you!'

'Love you.'

The minute the door slammed shut Amber slid to the floor her head in her hands. Christ! What was she going to do? If he found that envelope in the pocket, he'd go mad, he'd know she'd spent time with Liz. It wouldn't matter that she hadn't believed any of Liz's accusations; he'd see it as betrayal enough that she'd accepted a coffee from his strange ex-girlfriend.

Amber's mind darted to and fro. There was nothing she could do – the thought of following the men to the site and looking through wherever they put their coats was laughable. She didn't even have her bloody phone to call an uber.

Still shaking, she used the bannister to pull herself to standing. I'll just have to explain to him, she thought. I'll be calm and honest and make him understand what happened. I didn't go looking for Liz, she found me. I never believed for a moment he had anything to do with the disappearance and murders of those poor girls, the idea was absurd.

If only she'd taken the envelope out of his pocket before he left! She could easily have slipped down in the night and hidden it somewhere while he slept. What an idiot. Amber wished she'd looked more closely at Liz's clippings. Was Katie there? The thought was haunting. The girls whose stories Liz had collected were from all over the country, all the way from Scotland down to Cornwall. None of them were near London, Amber was sure of it. But Katie's body had been found less than a mile away from the house she, Alex and Curly shared. And now another had stepped into the shadows, reappearing in lurid posts shared across Facebook by desperate loved ones.

In the kitchen, Amber stared at the mess from dinner the night before, Alex and Curly had brought in their dishes but then left them in the sink with a scum of water and washing up liquid squirted over them. She felt too full up with panic and fear to find the space to care about clearing up. Her heart buzzed against her rib cage and she ran her wrists under the cold tap to try and dispel the strange numbness that squatted behind her eyes.

Perhaps he wouldn't check the pocket? Amber tried to reassure herself. He always kept his wallet and phone in the back of his jeans, no need for him to unzip the inside space that held a folded envelope filled with terrible things.

She needed to find her phone. That was something she could concentrate on; she'd worry about Alex finding the envelope later. She'd turned the bedroom upside down with no luck and there was no sign of it in the kitchen. The pipes gave a rattle, making her jump. The radiators probably needed bleeding again. She reached for her phone to text Alex before realising how stupid that was.

The pipes banged again as she finished searching the obvious places. The front drawing room Alex had knocked through to the garden room was now completely cleared and her footsteps echoed as she crossed over to the front window. The light was watery but enough to make the new, oak floorboards shine with a dark light. Curly had built neat shelves around the new fireplace, sourced by Alex on one of his journeys up north.

The plaster was smooth, the rotten window frames replaced. Amber found she was planning how to place a rug so the light from the window would make the colours sing. She pictured big squashy sofas in cream with bright throws. The shelves could be filled with the pictures and ornaments they would collect on her travels.

By contrast, the sitting room smelled of spilled beers and the fustiness of a space left too long with the door and windows closed. Cups lined the sofa arms, and beer bottles lay on their side next to the overflowing wastepaper basket. Jerking the curtains open and cracking open the window Amber felt again the stir of resentment that she was stuck at home, jobless, with the expectation she should spend her days cleaning up after Alex and Curly.

Grabbing a bin bag from the kitchen, she chucked in every bit of rubbish from the sitting room. Once it was clear, the bulging bin bag dumped into the hall, Amber searched in earnest for her phone. Her shirt was soaked with sweat by the time she'd finished.

All the cushions had been thrown onto the floor and she'd run her hand down every crease, groaning in disgust at the crap she found wedged down there. She dropped tangled messes of hair, coins and bits of take-away food onto the floor.

But still no phone. Amber wanted to scream. They didn't even have a landline and she couldn't remember any phone numbers except her mother's. She ran up the stairs to check the bedroom one last time. The bottom of the cupboards, under the mattress, behind the radiator – nothing. Where the hell was it? Chucking the duvet back on the bed, not bothering to straighten it, Amber remembered Curly's laptop. She could use it to track her phone.

His room was as revolting as she remembered it, even the doorknob felt sticky. How could he live like this? she thought. Perhaps that's why he worked through girlfriends the way he did, preferring to sleep in their presumably tidy houses rather than in his bedroom which looked like it belonged to a junkie teenager. What was wrong with him? He's a grown man and he still couldn't be bothered to bring down his mugs and glasses, leaving them stacked on the windowsill, flourishing with grey mould.

The laptop wasn't on the bed. The curtains were drawn and she couldn't see anything in the gloom, she also couldn't inhale the fetid air a moment longer, so she shoved the window, banging on the wood, until it slid up in a rush. Fresh air blew in and Amber took a moment to cool herself down, breathing in deeply.

Grimacing, she picked through bits of clothing and damp, foul smelling towels until she found his laptop. She then had to search for the charger. She couldn't bear to stay in Curly's room for a minute longer, so took it out onto the landing and plugged it in. As she waited for it to start up, she looked around to see how well he and Alex had done. It had taken so long the changes were imperceptible, but now she could see the banisters was clean and oiled, the walls replastered, and room by room space and light had been carved from the rubble of her grandmother's things.

Curly's face grinned out at her from the opening screen, it was an old photo. In it he had his arm slung around Alex's shoulders. Amber smiled to see them looking so happy and relaxed, and a little bit pissed – judging by the empty bottles ranked on the table in front of them. He must spend a lot of time on Facebook, she thought as she couldn't resist scrolling through his feed. Lots of silly memes and reposts of videos from Ladbible.

He had over 500 hundred friends. Clicking on the link, Amber saw an awful lot of them were women. She wanted to see more pictures of Alex from the days before they met. The photos on Curly's Facebook page served as a modern version of old albums she remembered from childhood. Her Gran would press photos on the pages and then cover them with sticky plastic sheets, holding them in place.

Curly's photos went back years. Clicking on 'your photos' Amber tapped the right arrow key and scrolled through hundreds of pictures Curly had uploaded. In a dizzying rush she flicked back in time through parties and hikes and pub crawls. Alex featured often and Amber would linger on them, admiring his white smile and thick, blond hair. Curly didn't change much. His black nest of curls grew longer and longer the further back she went, ten years before they were matted dreads that reached towards his elbows.

Amber thought it looked awful, but it didn't seem to put off the women who clung to his arm in numerous selfies. She tapped left to her favourite photo. It must have been about five years ago, she thought – checking the date on the right-hand side to confirm. Before Alex even knew she existed.

It was a candid shot, taken outside at what looked like a beach party. Alex and Curly, dressed warmly in thick coats, sat on a bench with the remains of a fire glowing like jewels in the sand before them. Alex had his head thrown back in laughter, the picture so vivid Amber could almost hear the sound. Curly was grinning at him, holding his right arm in an awkward gesture of protection.

That must have been when he broke his arm. Alex told the story over and over despite Curly's protests. A stupid accident when drunk, he'd challenged some big bloke in a pub to an arm wrestle, broke his arm in three places – had to have pins put in. Alex thought it was hilarious and would repeat it when introducing Curly to new people. Amber used to think it was funny too, but the more she saw Curly's reaction the more she saw how cruel Alex was being.

She shook off the thought, looking again at the picture and smiling at the joy on Alex's face. I must get a copy of that, she thought. Could she send it to herself? She right clicked it, there – save as. She saved it to Curly's desktop then opened her Gmail and emailed it to herself. It was such a lovely picture of Alex, looking so young and untroubled. It made her realise how he'd changed; it wasn't very often she saw him so open and relaxed.

Opening a new page, Amber logged into her iCloud account, and tapped her fingers in impatience as it loaded up. It seemed to take ages but eventually the screen cleared, and a green dot appeared on a white road. Where was that? She clicked on hybrid and looked for anything she recognised on the satellite image. The street name wasn't familiar, and it certainly wasn't where she was sitting at that moment.

North London. The green dot lay next to an extensive building site dotted with cranes and skips. Something in her head clicked. Maybe Alex was working there. Of course! She smiled with relief. He must have picked up her phone by accident.

She logged out and closed the laptop, unplugging the charger and putting it back where she found it. Curly wouldn't mind her using it, she was pretty sure, but there was no point in advertising she'd been rummaging around in his room. She pulled the window shut and closed the curtains again.

Walking down the stairs, holding tight to the newly polished bannister, Amber tamped down hard on the voice wondering if Alex taking her phone really was an accident.

*

Amber could tell the moment Alex walked in the door with Curly that he hadn't found the envelope. The wires pinning her shoulders to her ears and pinching her stomach into a crimp of metal were cut free. Thank God, she thought.

The house was clear, sofa cushions restored, bin bag outside, and the comforting smell of roasting chicken drifted into the hall. Curly and Alex sniffed with appreciation.

'God that smells good,' Curly said. 'I'm bloody starving. Is it nearly ready?'

'Ten minutes,' Amber replied. 'And I've set up a table in the knocked through room, it looks so lovely in there I think we should make the most of it. I didn't realise how much you'd done!'

Alex smiled as he took off his coat and gave her a hug. 'Yeah, I'm really pleased with it, we only finished it a few days ago. I was keeping it as a surprise, was going to do a big reveal but you jumped the gun.'

'Sorry, babe, I was looking for my phone and searched the house top to bottom.' She kept her eyes on his face, watching his expression. 'But it wasn't here, was it?' A smile played across her lips, he was going to feel like such a numpty when he realised.

'Sorry, love?'

'My phone. It wasn't in the house.'

'Wasn't it?'

A chill slid into her stomach, the smile falling from her mouth. 'No. Do you know where it might be?'

He gave an easy shrug. 'Nope. Sorry. I told you this morning I didn't know where it was. I'm going to grab a quick shower before dinner. You said ten minutes?'

Amber, rocked, blinked and refocused. 'Yes, ten minutes,' she said faintly.

'You OK?'

'Um, yeah, I'm fine.'

'I won't be long.'

'Alex,' she called up the stairs as he bounded towards their bedroom.

'Yeah?'

'Where were you and Curly working today?'

His head appeared above her. 'Up near Wembley, bloody big job. New shopping centre, it's been going on for years. Guy kept running out of money. Why?'

'Just wondered.'

Alex and Curly were in high spirits as they ate in the room Amber thought of as the family room. They didn't notice she wasn't eating, just pushing her food from side to side. Their behaviour bordered on manic. Alex kept laughing too hard at Curly's jokes. They tried to tell Amber a story about something that had happened at the site, but they kept interrupting each other, exclaiming and hooting, so she couldn't work out what they were trying to say.

'Have you taken something?' she whispered to Alex while Curly popped out to answer a phone call. Alex lurched towards her, his elbow slipping off the table.

'What are you on about?' His eyes were rimmed with red and his pupils so stretched she could barely make out the irises.

'You're on something, I can tell.' She knew he'd taken drugs in the past but thought he was over all of that.

'It's nothing, just a little bump for fuck's sake. How else do you expect me to work all day and then come home and work on this place?' His attention switched to Curly as he came back into the room. 'Mate! Come on, your glass is empty!'

Amber watched them with a sinking heart. Alex had that glassy, over excited look he sometimes got when out with friends he wanted to impress. Had that been drugs too? She thought about her phone, he must have taken it, she thought. Why is he lying? She looked at Curly, unless he took it? she thought watching him as he laughed and opened another bottle of wine.

They made the room feel small with their shouts of laughter and broad-shouldered bulk. Their stories excluded her and Amber felt herself diminishing into a sliver between them, they didn't feel like her protectors any more.

Later, in the sitting room Curly and Alex, well on their way to full drunkenness, argued over what to watch. The South East news was just starting. The dramatic, pounding music pulled their attention and the room fell silent as the headlines appeared.

'Police are appealing for anyone to come forward who may have information regarding the disappearance of Brianna Templeton who has been missing...'

Amber looked in horror at Alex and Curly who sat, frozen, on the sofa. Their faces were white with shock.

'That's… That's the girl…the one from Brighton,' she stammered.

'Shut up!' Alex roared.

CHAPTER 18: LIZ

I wasn't under arrest, but where could I go? The police had taken my passport 'as a precaution'. That fucker Cartwright had obviously told them I was a flight risk. I wished I could talk to Inspector Cadieux on my own, I'm sure I would convince him, but with Cartwright around I knew it was hopeless. He knew too much about me, well the me of years ago. I wasn't that person anymore, I told myself over and over again as I waited, watching the city from my window.

I was a mess, losing my purpose. Cartwright had muddled something that had been clear and true, and I had lost the thread to find my way back to the path. He thought I killed Sarah! A rational part of my brain told me that it wouldn't take long for them to establish the time of death and I would have an alibi. I wouldn't even have been in the country. And Daniel, Sarah's brother would back up my story. I just had to wait.

But then I remembered Cartwright, and everything in me sagged. He hated me. He'd written me off as a drug-addled fantasist. I wasn't strong enough to prove him otherwise. I didn't know where to start. Just knowing he was in the building made me clench my jaw to stop from whimpering.

There was nowhere for me to go. I couldn't even afford a hostel. The only thing I had was my train ticket; I thanked God I'd left the return journey flexible otherwise I had no idea how I would have got back home.

How long would it be before they called me back in? Inspector Cadieux had asked for a break as he could see I was becoming incoherent, losing the thread of my sentences, getting hysterical. Signalling the officers standing just outside the door, he asked them to take me out for 'une pause' and they led me downstairs to the ground floor to an empty waiting room with another complicated coffee machine and wide sofas upholstered in a rough looking green tweed.

A young woman entered and explained Inspector Cadieux had asked for me to be checked over. Her gloved hands were cool on the heat of my forehead as she introduced herself as Dr Rogier. She seemed very young with her unlined skin and clear blue eyes. She took my blood pressure, listened to my heart, checked my eyes and ears and tutted when she felt the boniness of my upper arms. She touched the scars on the inside of my wrists, running her thumb over the ridges.

'Your blood pressure is low. You're undernourished and dehydrated. I will ask them to send in some food.'

'Thank you.'

'You should call a lawyer.'

The door shut and silence pressed against my ears again. I wanted to run after this composed young woman and explain I didn't need a lawyer. I hadn't done anything wrong.

An hour passed and despite the thoughts circling around my head I managed to fall asleep. The nervous tension of the day had been draining and I tumbled gratefully into the dreamless dark.

I woke up when the door opened. Saliva rushed into my mouth at the smell of the food being brought in by a thin man in his 60s. He nodded at me and placed his tray carefully on the table before disappearing backwards out of the room and closing the door with a soft thud.

I swung my legs round and sat up, suddenly ravenous. My phone was flat, and I had no idea what the time was, but it must have been very late – darkness had fallen a long time ago. The food was nothing special, a slice of pizza, a plastic packet of salad and a bottle of water, but I wolfed it down, enjoying the burst of fresh, cold tomatoes against my tongue. I drank the water in two deep swallows.

The food made me feel better, stronger. I was ready for them.

*

By the time I was called in to resume the interview I was well-fed with two cups of strong coffee zinging along my bloodstream. My mind was clear and I determined to stay focused and in control.

It was the same room and my heart sank to see Cartwright there again with his smug smile. Inspector Cadieux looked tired and was apologetic for keeping me waiting for so long.. I nodded in acknowledgment. I didn't really care, it wasn't as if I had anywhere else to be.

'Have you identified Sarah?'

Inspector Cadieux gave a sigh. 'Madame I am very sorry to tell you that we have just been informed that the body discovered in Chauron *has* been identified as that of Sarah Andrews. We are trying to contact her family but there have been some problems tracking them down.'

Stupid. I already knew this to be true, had known since the moment my torch tracked across the mattress in that cellar, but the words still hit me like a wave of iced water so cold I blinked and gasped with grief. My body buckled in on itself. Tears spilled through my fingers and I tried to press them back. Poor Sarah.

They gave me a moment to recover myself. Cadieux pushed a bottle of water and a box of tissues across the table. I took a handful of sheets and held them to my face, sniffing back the tears. My mind raced. I had to be careful. I had to get this right. Cartwright would be watching my every move. Finally, I straightened, unscrewed the lid from the bottle of water and took a sip.

'How did you identify her? How can you be sure?'

'Her fingerprints,' Cartwright interrupted, 'the minute they were scanned in they found a match to records held in the UK.'

'Yes, of course. She got arrested at university on a march for women's rights.' I paused and swallowed. 'She was pretty political, I think.'

Cartwright leaned forward and clicked the end of his pen. 'Mz Shaw, how did you find the cottage?'

'I told the police at Chauron,' I said, looking at Cadieux. 'It was luck really, I just asked questions of everyone I met and…'

'Luck,' said Cartwright, jotting a note in his book. 'And how did you know the cellar was there?'

'Why is he asking the questions?' I searched for Cadieux's eyes. 'I don't understand.'

Cadieux gave a very gallic shrug. 'It is felt DI Cartwright has valuable background information that could help us with our investigation.'

'Do you mean background information on me?' I laughed. 'How does what he knows about me help with finding Sarah's killer?'

Silence filled the room.

'Surely you don't still think I have anything to do with it?' Incredulous, I pleaded with Cadieux. 'I promise you I have nothing to do with what has happened. Nothing.'

'We have to explore all options,' Cadieux said at last, his voice was sympathetic but resolute. 'Please answer the questions. I assure you we are investigating this murder with eyes that are completely open and without bias.'

'How dd you know the cellar was there?' Cartwright said again.

'I didn't. I noticed a breeze that seemed odd, and when I looked closer, I saw a notch in the wood. I pulled it back and saw the ring that was fixed on the trapdoor. How long has she been there? Can you tell?'

'Many years,' Cadieux replied. 'She had been buried in peaty earth which preserved the... ah... remains better than we might have expected. Enough to identify her without too much difficulty.'

'How did she die?' I balled my hands into fists to steel myself for the answer.

Cadieux and Cartwright looked at each other.

'We have only the preliminary findings but as well as a severe head injury it appears she was strangled.'

I held my hand to my mouth, I thought I was going to be sick. My stomach rolled in protest. Something about those words…

'I don't understand, how did she get a head injury…?' A picture was flashing at the back of my mind. Cartwright never took his eyes from my face as I faltered and stopped. Cadieux's pen stilled. He, too, was trying to read my expression and I rubbed my forehead, hard, keeping my face neutral. My head hurt as I tried to reach for the thought that was nagging me.

Cartwright began to talk but I was so focused on hooking out the memory his words had triggered I couldn't hear him.

'Sorry, what did you say?'

'I said,' he replied in exasperation, 'it was about five years ago you were found in Sarah's house, isn't it, Liz?'

'Er, yes. Maybe. About that.'

'And then somehow you convinced her there as something wrong with her boyfriend. She went to her local police station to report him for abuse. And you went with her.'

Cadieux cast a sharp glance at me.

'Yes, that's right.'

'But he wasn't abusing her, was he, Liz?'

'He was! He was starting to do all the things he did to me!'

'Like what, Madame Shaw?'

I turned to Cadieux. 'He'd stop me seeing my friends, told them lies about me, stopped me leaving the house without him. He took my phone…'

'But he never abused Sarah. Did he?' Cartwright interrupted.

I stared at him, mute with hatred.

'In fact,' Cartwright went on, 'it turned out you'd made up quite a lot of lies to try and convince Sarah to split up with him.'

I shook my head. 'That's not true. She was in danger. I knew she was. Maybe he hadn't got as far as hurting her, but he was going to. He'd done it to loads of women. I told you. I pieced it together. I followed it up, all those girls. He was linked with them all. I'm sure of it.'

Cartwright's voice was remorseless. 'You manufactured a friendship with Sarah because you hated the idea of the man you were obsessed with to be with anyone else. You did everything you could to split them up – even to go so far as to accuse him of murder. You'd do anything, wouldn't you, Liz, to destroy him. Did you follow Sarah to France? Was she trying to end her friendship with you?'

'No, that's ridiculous! I...'

'What about Ellie Richardson?'

I stopped.

'Remember her?' Cartwright's voice warmed with satisfaction. I could imagine him smirking. I kept my eyes down, my mind galloping with calculations underscored with a bass note of fear.

'That was a mistake... A long time ago...'

'Inspector Cadieux, shortly after Mz Shaw was abandoned by her lover she ended up in a very bad place.' As he spoke, his level gaze traced acid hot lines across my face. 'She started taking drugs, a few recreational bags of weed – nothing serious to begin with – but she became more desperate. Didn't have anywhere to stay so ended up drifting from one friend's house to another, until the friends were no longer friends…'

I struggled to stay impassive as Cartwright outlined the darkest years of my life.

'She attempted suicide a number of times and was hospitalised. When she came out, she discovered her man had moved on to another woman: Ellie Richardson.'

'This has nothing to do with…'

'You weren't very nice to Ellie Richardson, were you, Liz? Dog shit through the letterbox, paint stripper thrown over her car, abusive messages sent to her work colleagues…'

Blood rushed to my face, burning my skin. 'The thing is I don't remember doing any of those things. I'm not saying I didn't do them. I wasn't well and I was fucked up on drugs for a while, it wasn't anything to do with…'

'Ah, but it tells a story, don't you think? Of how far you're prepared to go.'

'It tells a story of how far someone is prepared to go.'

Cartwright gave a harsh, mocking laugh. 'You're saying Alex set up some weird campaign of abuse against his *own* girlfriend?'

'I don't know, OK? I can't remember. I just can't. I've tried but…' I took a deep breath. 'Besides. None of this is relevant. It certainly doesn't have any bearing on what happened to Sarah.'

'But you did lie to the police. You lied to Sarah, terrified her, made her leave the man she loved and none of it was true! You manipulated her into thinking Alex was a psychopath who was going to kill her. But when the police investigated, they found absolutely no evidence of any physical abuse whatsoever.'

'OK I lied!' I stood up so quickly they both leaned back in shock. 'Of course I did! I had to! Nobody would believe me. Nobody would believe what he was capable of. I never tried to commit suicide. HE DID THIS.' Sobbing, I ripped up my sleeves and presented my terrible scars. 'He couldn't stand me leaving him. He was the one who had to do the dumping. Not me. When I left something cracked in his head. Even when he was with Ellie he kept following me, threatening me. He'd leave stuff in my flat. Make sure I knew he'd been there, so I was constantly terrified. If he couldn't have me, he wanted to make damn sure I was thinking about him all the time, even if it was with absolute horror and fear. That's the kind of man he is, and nobody will believe me. I knew. I KNEW he was going to do to Sarah what he did to me, and I suspected he'd already murdered at that point. Every time he got away with it, he got more powerful. I had to say anything I could to get Sarah out of that relationship.'

'Sit down, Madame Shaw.'

I crossed my arms to try and still the terrible shaking. I couldn't hold the bottle to my lips and put it back on the table. Memories I'd suppressed over years were exploding out of the depths of me, a sickening lava swallowing everything up in its terrible wake and pushing it to the surface.

Cadieux waited a moment until my breathing calmed. 'This... Alex. This is the man whose name you gave to the police in Chauron?'

'Yes. Yes. It's him. I promise you. He was the one who killed Sarah. It's because she tried to leave him. He won't ever let that happen. He'd rather kill than let his possessions go. That's how he saw us. Possessions. You have to arrest him now. Before the news gets out because the minute he sees it he'll be gone. He'll disappear. Off to find another women to exploit.' I wished I could claw away my skin to show him the truth of what I was saying. They were both repelled by my desperation, I knew, but I couldn't control myself.

'I have to say, Madame, that at the present time we have no evidence to link the crime scene with this man you describe. We have only the testimony of Madame Heurteau that a man rented the gîte, but she is old and cannot be sure the dates match.' His voice was slow and kind, but the expression on his face frightened me. A file had appeared on the table and my eyes were drawn to his fingers as they tapped on the cover.

'We have, however, found some evidence which seems rather conclusive.'

He opened the flap and slid out a plastic evidence bag.

'Could you tell me, Madame Shaw, whether you recognise this?' He upended the bag and a gold ring fell into his hand. 'The reason I ask is because it has your initials carved into it as well as a name, Adah. Your grandmother, I believe?'

'Oh my God! It's my grandmother's ring!' I reached for it, but he held it away from me. 'Where did you find it? I lost it years ago, it's very precious. I don't understand…'

'It was discovered in the earth beneath Sarah Andrew's body. Have you any idea how that could have happened?'

Shock punched every ounce of breath from my body. Black dots swarmed like terrible flies in front of me, I could hear their buzzing in my head.

'He must have planted that there for you to find…' My words were a whisper. The room was zooming in and out of focus.

'Elizabeth Shaw, I am arresting you on suspicion of a connection with the murder…'

But it was no use. No matter how hard I tried I couldn't make sense of what he was saying. I looked up at the ceiling and tried to breathe, frowning as I couldn't move my head. Then the table shot up towards me, hitting my jaw, and the pain catapulted me into darkness.

SARAH: FIVE YEARS AGO

'Sarah!' she screamed. Alex forgotten. She slammed herself forward and the door popped open. Her body was slow to respond to her frantic commands but eventually she managed to get to the top of the stairs where Sarah hung from a rope looped over a high beam.

Sobbing, she grabbed Sarah's body and tried to lift it to take the terrible pressure from her neck that was already turning her face purple. She wasn't strong enough. 'No! Please!' she cried.

There was a terrible creaking sound and she looked up. Cracks were running across the ceiling like streams of ants fleeing a fire. She tilted her head; she couldn't work out what was happening. A breaking noise followed by a deep groan made her want to cover her ears. It was as if the house was howling the grief that stopped up her throat.

The roof! The roof was cracking open. She could see a chair in the room to her left. Letting go of Sarah for a horrific second, she dragged the chair to the landing and used it to climb up and balance on the bannister. For a moment she swung forward and nearly fell onto the floor below, but with a huge effort she just managed to catch hold of the beam.

Tears and dizziness blinded her, and she blinked. She didn't know what to do. Sarah's body was still; the kicking had stopped. She had to do something. Holding onto the beam she leaned forward and reached for the rope. She could feel the wood jumping in her hands as the roof continued to move. She couldn't untie the rope; it was too tightly knotted.

Instead she jumped and grabbed the rope, so the beam held her weight as well as Sarah's. For a moment nothing happened, and she screamed at it, tugging on the rope to try and snap the beam. It wasn't very thick, surely it couldn't hold them both. She pulled again, and again. With a deafening crash the beam dropped about a foot, hit the stone shelf of the chimney stack on the other side of the landing and snapped.

They fell in a cloud of masonry dust and smashed to the floor. Plaster and stones were falling all around as she got to her feet. Agony lanced through her, she couldn't put any weight on her left ankle and her elbow throbbed. She dived towards Sarah's body.

'Please, please, please God,' she gibbered pulling at the rope around her neck. Finally, it tore free. 'Sarah! Sarah! Wake up. Sarah! It's Liz. Please.'

To her incredulous joy the appalling purple and blue stains across Sarah's face began to fade.

'Yes, Sarah! Breathe. Breathe.'

She felt for a pulse, noticing the bracelets of bruises and bleeding welts on Sarah's wrists. What had he done to her? Sarah began to move, she coughed dust from her mouth and Liz tried to help her to her feet.

'We have to get out of here, Sarah,' she said. 'I don't know how far away he is.' Her voice was slurred, her tongue felt too big for her mouth and her skull blazed with pain as if it had been split open. She touched her forehead and yelped with pain as she touched a raw, softened bruise which gave under her fingers. Fresh blood spilled and she had to rub it from her eyes. Sarah stirred again and gave a soft moan.

Liz tried to hook Sarah's arm over her to pry her up from the ground, but she just wasn't strong enough. 'You have to help me, Sarah.' There was no response. She stepped back to look for anything that could help when, with a sickening, splintering rush, a landslide of rubble cascaded from the roof above and Sarah disappeared beneath it –

CHAPTER 19: AMBER

'How did it go? What happened?' she said as Alex and Curly arrived back home just before lunch time.

Amber had spent the morning sick with nerves. After the bombshell on the news the night before, she'd insisted Alex and Curly go to the police to tell them what they knew.

'You've got to!' she said. 'You might be the last people to see her alive!'

Curly was shaking, Alex, stony faced, stared at the TV. They'd rewound the news piece and watched it over and over again,

'They're linking it with the other missing women,' she said. 'How did you meet her, Curly?'

'I just picked her up on the train on the way down to Brighton,' he said. 'I don't fucking believe this, it's all we need.'

'What do you mean?'

'Well, it's obvious isn't it? It looks like I was with her just before she went missing. They're going to think I did it.'

'Don't be fucking stupid,' Alex said, getting up and snapping off the television. 'You've got nothing to do with it. You picked her up easily enough didn't you? A tart like that would go with anyone.'

'Alex!' Amber reproved, but he ignored her.

'Fuck, man,' Curly started pacing up and down. 'What am I going to do?'

'You'll have to go in,' Amber said. 'People would have seen us with her, they'll think it strange if you don't – you'll look guilty.'

'She's right,' Curly looked at Alex, 'don't you think?'

Alex pushed his hair out of his eyes and nodded. 'Yeah. You should go in, it's not like you've got anything to worry about, you've not done anything wrong. I'll come with you, let Dom know we won't be able to get to work until late, we'll go in first thing, OK?'

'I'll come too.'

'Don't be stupid, Amber. There's no point in us all sitting around waiting for three hours to give a five minute statement.'

'Where will you go?'

'The local nick. Fucked if I'm going all the way down to Brighton.' He looked over at Curly who was still dazed with shock. 'It'll be fine, Curly. Mate, honestly. Don't worry about it.'

That night Alex had been terse and uncommunicative, the news had sobered him up and he batted away Amber's worried questions and optimistic reassurances. She lay beside him, knowing he couldn't get to sleep either, but couldn't find the words to get through to him.

Dawn was just lighting the curtains when he got out of bed and went downstairs. Curly joined him shortly afterwards and she listened to their soft murmurs as the room brightened. Yawning with tiredness, Amber sat up and stared at the wall before pulling on her slippers and dressing gown and going downstairs.

'We're off,' Alex said. 'We want to get it over with.'

'OK. Hope it all goes all right. I'm sure it will.' She gave him a hug, feeling the rigidity in his muscles. He didn't respond to her touch.

They left and as Amber closed the door her heart sped up when she saw Alex's parka still hanging on the coat hook. Checking he and Curly hadn't forgotten anything and were coming back down the path, she took it down and walked into the kitchen, feeling the crackle of the envelope still in the pocket.

Trembling with relief, she retrieved it and hung the coat back on the hook. Tucking the envelope under her arm she made a mug of coffee and carried it up to the bedroom. Chances were Alex and Curly wouldn't be back for ages, but just in case they returned early she opened her locker drawer so she could shove everything in there until she could find a better hiding place.

The articles first. The older ones were faded as if photocopied from paper softened with constant reading. The pipes thumped and rattled again as Amber read. The earliest clippings were a few years apart, but as they grew more recent, the gaps were shorter. Eight women in total and Amber's heart swooped as she recognised Katie in the last article. Again, she read through the details, although she already knew most of them.

It made her shudder to think of Katie's body being dumped in the undergrowth of the common. She wished she had her phone to look up more on the other victims. She'd had a quick look in Curly's room but couldn't find his laptop. The cuttings only detailed the women's disappearance, there was no follow up or indication whether they'd ever been found or if anyone had been arrested.

Amber read through the cuttings again and made notes. All the women were between around 20 and 30. All had long red hair and curvy figures. Amber couldn't see anything to connect them in terms of their work – one was a teacher, two were students, another a secretary, two worked as shop assistants, and two nurses including Katie. Only one was married. As Liz had said, they were from all over the country.

Amber sighed, she hadn't really learned much more. She was reluctant to turn to the rest of the notes as they looked chaotic. A folded map of the UK had been marked with the places the missing women had lived, alongside dates written in biro. Amber remembered Liz mentioning a Sarah, but none of the clippings had a victim with that name.

The final pile contained sheets of paper absolutely covered in cramped scrawls. Liz had written down the margins and along the top and bottom on both sides as if terrified she would run out of paper. No numbers, so it took Amber ages to try and sort them into order.

Most of it was incoherent, and some lines illegible. There were dense crossings out and parts had been ripped where the pen had pressed so hard it had torn the paper. Amber was glad she was looking at photocopies as she suspected the originals would have smelled bad. Drops of what looked like blood or wine were dotted all over the pages.

She turned on her bedside lamp to see more clearly. There was no order to the notes, Liz had jumped from victim to victim, her thoughts a jumble as she tried to make connections. Over and over Amber kept reading phrases like, 'where was he then? Working here. Close enough?' Scrawled asterisks and crosses seemed to refer to places on the map but Amber couldn't make sense of them.

In one corner a paragraph drew her eye as Liz had framed it in a square. 'Drugs? All out drinking. Maybe in their glass/bottle? Rohypnol? Best as leaves bodies and he keeps them. Where did he get it? Where does he keep them?'

The mention of drugs struck Amber, it reminded her of something that made her uneasy. What was it? It was if her mind didn't want to give her the answer, but she persisted, and it came to her. Emma. Her pleading face as she spoke above the pounding music at the night club. 'I think he drugged me.'

Agitation drove Amber from the bed and, clutching the pages, she walked up and down. Liz was right, in the clippings all the victims had last been seen at pubs or clubs. Easy to slip a drug into their drink as they looked away. 'Haven't you heard the stories about Curly?' Emma's voice, clear with a truth Amber had refused to accept, telling her Curly brought her a drink just before she felt odd and passed out.

Her heart thudded, skipped another beat, and started to race. For the tenth time that morning she reached for her phone, this time to call Emma before remembering, again, it was lost. Or taken.

Pushing the thought aside, Amber folded the pages back into the envelope and after dithering for a few minutes, she dug out her suitcase and hid it under the zipped lining. Sliding it under the bed she checked her watch. She had no idea how long Alex and

Curly would be at the police station, but they could be back any moment.

Brianna had disappeared. But Amber remembered her as bright and loud – no signs of being drugged, she seemed really into Curly, they couldn't take their hands off each other. Amber remembered the way Alex had looked at Brianna with a shiver; It was as if he wanted to eat her up.

Of course they didn't have anything to do with what happened to her, Amber reassured herself. Why would they be so happy to go in to talk to the police if they were guilty? They may even be able to help the police; they might have seen something important. Brianna was comfortable enough when Amber had left to go back to the hotel but who knows what happened after she'd gone, leaving them to it?

Pushing open Curly's door she took a deep breath. She would have to search properly. She didn't know what she was looking for but had to try. Amber found it shocking how reliant she was on looking things up on her phone. Without it, she felt utterly disconnected from the world.

A clock was ticking in her head as she looked, careful to put everything back as she found it. A bag of weed under the mattress, some wraps of cocaine in plastic bags, a stack of £50 notes wrapped up in a sock in his bedside table along with lots of expensive looking gadgets. She sighed with frustration, she didn't even know if she was looking for a tablet or something liquid.

A noise downstairs made her run to the landing, mouth dry, but it was just the post arriving. Was she being ridiculous? Paranoid? Did she really think these missing women had anything to do with Alex? She'd already searched though his things looking for her phone but hadn't seen anything like drugs or medicine.

The shared bathroom hadn't been touched since they arrived except Alex had ripped out the disgusting carpet to expose the floorboards. There was a large mirrored cabinet over the sink, but first Amber looked in the three toiletry bags lined up on the deep windowsill above the bath. Curly's held nothing but old deodorant sticks and a rolled up tube of toothpaste.

Amber paused again to listen to the sounds of the house. All was quiet. She unzipped Alex's bag and took out the bottles that clinked as she put them in the sink one by one. Expensive aftershave, a pot of top quality moisturiser Amber knew cost over a hundred pounds, matching cleansing cream, hair serum, whitening toothpaste and deodorant. Nothing she hadn't seen before and nothing sinister.

Feeling like a character from a police drama, she checked the cistern. Nothing. The clank as she put the lid back was deafening and sweat began to slide down her back. The bath panel had peeled away, and it only took a little tug for her to pull it back far enough to see there was nothing there but rust and damp. Relief started to steal into her bones. She had dreaded finding anything that would shake her faith in Alex.

Her face in the cabinet mirror was pale; she looked small and vulnerable. Remembering Liz, scrawny and desperate, Amber straightened her shoulders and stood up straight. She didn't want to look like a victim. She opened the cabinet, holding her breath, even though the rational part of her brain was telling her that a bathroom cabinet would be a stupid place to try and hide anything.

Amber grimaced at the smell of damp. The three shelves inside were corrugated and looked soggy. A green bottle of something called Vosene that looked a hundred years old leaned drunkenly against the corner of the cupboard. A dark sludge lay at the bottom. Amber pulled off the cap and took a sniff. Immediately she put the cap back on. The smell was so strong it made her eyes water. Coughing and spluttering she threw the bottle into the bin.

There was nothing else on the shelves but just before she closed the door her brain flashed a warning. What was it? Was Alex back? Standing stock still Amber listened hard; the house was silent. She opened the door again and looked at the shelves. An oval stain marked where the Vosene bottle had rested. Amber rubbed at it with her finger, the mark was sticky.

Grabbing a wodge of tissue Amber wetted it and rubbed at the stain again. The shelf moved and tipped forward. There was a space behind it. Heart jumping Amber leaned forward, wishing she had her phone so she could use the torch. Was there anything in there?

The shelf was in two parts, she realised. The left side firmly attached to the back of the cupboard, but on the right a separate part acted as small door. As she lifted the shelf piece out, a hole was revealed; a hole that had been cut into the wall behind the cupboard.

Gritting her teeth, Amber rolled up her sleeve and reached into the darkness. The thought of cobwebs and spiders landing on her hand made her want to scream. She stretched her fingers as far as they could go. It didn't seem like there was anything in there. The sink pressed hard against her hip and Amber shifted position so more of her arm could get into the hole. She stretched her fingers still further, her face pressed against the stinking shelves. How far back did it go?

A clink. The very tips of her fingers touched something cold and glassy…

'Amber! Where the hell are you?'

The voice shouting up the stairs made her jump so hard she bashed her head against the top shelf. She reared back, pulling her arm out so quickly she scraped her wrist on the edge. 'I'm in the loo! Won't be a sec!' she shouted back. With hands that shook as if palsied she replaced the shelf. It didn't look right – too clean. Where the hell had she put that green bottle?

Amber's heart thudded so strongly in her head she could barely see. At last she found it in the bin and put it back where it was. She wasted precious seconds arranging and rearranging the bottle until it looked right.

'Amber!'

She flushed the loo, grateful for its thundering noise that covered the sound of her closing the cabinet. Scanning quickly around the bathroom to check nothing was out of place, Amber took a deep breath and ran down the stairs.

'How did it go? What happened?'

*

'Bloody waste of time,' Alex said, shrugging off his coat and kicking his shoes towards the door.

'You've been ages!' Amber gave Alex a quick hug, hoping he wouldn't feel her heart racing. 'So, what happened?'

'I'm starving, any chance you can knock something up for lunch?' Curly said, 'I couldn't eat any breakfast, felt sick.'

'I can do eggs and oven chips, we haven't got much in – I'll have to get out to the shops later.'

Amber watched them as they ate, both buttering bread and stuffing down chips as if they hadn't eaten in days: Curly with his dark curls and soft face, Alex's blond beauty with muscles that pushed at the lines of his shirt.

'You not eating?'

'Oh, yes. I'm not that hungry but I'll have a bit of bread.'

Amber sat down at the table and poured out more tea for them both. She struggled to keep her face without expression as she relived, over and over, the brush of glass against her fingertips.

'So, are you going to tell me what happened?'

Curly sat back and belched, wiping egg yolk from his mouth with the back of his hand. 'All fine, wasn't it, mate?' he said looking at Alex.

Alex finished wiping his plate with the last slice of bread. 'Yeah. Good job we went in as I think they were looking for us.'

'What did they say?'

'The main thing was we could prove she was still around after we left. She showed up on CCTV after we'd got the train.'

The breath Amber didn't realise she was holding gusted out of her. Thank God, she thought. 'Oh, that's good. What a relief!'

'What do you mean?'

'Well…'

'You think Curly had something to do with her disappearing?'

'No! Of course not…' Amber stammered. 'It's just good to know that you don't have anything to worry about.' There was a pause. 'Do they…' she cleared her throat. 'Do they think Brianna is linked with those other girls? Like Katie?'

Alex shrugged. 'They didn't say. We waited for fuck knows how long, got called in, they made some phone calls and then they asked us what time we left Brighton.'

'And you don't have to go back?'

'They took our numbers in case they need to call, but otherwise that's it.'

Alex was studying Amber from across the table, his eyes roamed over her but for the first time she didn't feel her body leap in response.

'We'd better get going if we want to get to the site before the end of the day,' Curly said, getting up with his plate.

'I'm not going in,' Alex said, eyes still on Amber. 'I've got stuff to do here.'

'Well, if you're not going in, I won't bother either.' Curly called back from the kitchen where he had dumped his plate in the sink with a clatter. 'I might go down the pub. Do you fancy it?'

'Not right now, mate. May join you later.'

Within seconds of the front door slamming Alex was at Amber's side, pulling her to her feet and reaching around to unbutton her jeans. His hands were cold and stiff against her flesh. 'Alex!' she protested, half-laughing, but her head was filled with missing women and Liz's pages, covered in lines and lines of research she'd done to prove her husband had something to do with what happened to them. It made her feel sick.

'Stop talking,' he whispered in her ear. He grabbed at her breasts under her shirt, pressing himself against her back. 'Take this off.'

He pushed Amber forward, his body like a vice around hers. She was glad he couldn't see her face as he bent her over the table. Holding onto her hips so tightly she could feel bruises flowering beneath his hands, Alex pushed into her. He'd never treated her like this before. Her passivity seemed to excite him, and he moved more quickly.

Amber wanted to call out, say something, make him stop, but before she could find the words he was finished. He stepped away from her, doing up his jeans and breathing heavily. Amber didn't move, waiting to see if he would say anything. Apologise perhaps. If he noticed her stillness he didn't comment. Whistling, he bounded past her up the stairs, smacking her on the backside as he went. Within a few minutes she heard running water. He'd gone for a shower, Amber realised with a pulse of shock.

Sitting on the bottom step Amber felt breathless with loneliness. She longed and longed to speak to her Mum, to be reassured that things like this happened in a marriage, that men could be selfish but it didn't mean anything. Haunted by Liz's notes and the stories of those missing woman, disquiet fell around her shoulders, a soft cloak of shadowy feathers. Amber rubbed her face to try and dispel the sense of dread that weighed so heavy, but it wouldn't shift.

But the police had dismissed Alex and Curly as having anything to do with Brianna's disappearance, and she'd found nothing suspicious in the house. Perhaps that strange space behind the bathroom cabinet was just some odd leftover from when her Gran had lived here.

This was Alex she was thinking about, Amber banged her forehead with the heel of her hands. If she really thought he was capable of such awful things she should leave. Now. Call the police. She imagined sitting in the police station, trying to articulate her vague sense of dread, bringing out the notes that had already been dismissed by everyone Liz had shown them to.

She needed to know. Be sure. She couldn't cope with this creeping sense of doom all the time. As soon as she could, she would explore that space behind the bathroom cupboard properly; she'd use a torch and find out exactly what was in there.

Amber stood up and carried the rest of the lunch things into the kitchen. She heard Alex crossing the landing upstairs and imagined him, bare chested, with the towel wrapped around his waist. He should look vulnerable, half dressed like that, but Alex never did.

'Amber! Get ready, we're going to the pub,' he shouted down at her.

'OK,' she called back, frozen at the bottom of the stairs, looking at the door leading to the cellar. She hadn't been down there since Alex and Curly had shown her the work they'd done. The pipes rattled and she remembered the heating failing. Part of her brain reminded herself to tell Alex to have a look at it, while another part of her brain was wondering if he was killing young women with red hair. Her head throbbed and she held it tightly between her hands. Tomorrow. After Alex and Curly had gone to work. She'd go down and find out for sure if anything was hidden in the roots of the house.

SARAH: FIVE YEARS AGO

Liz don't know how long she sat beside Sarah's body, cradling her poor, bloodied head in her lap. She no longer cared if Alex came back, in fact she longed for it because it meant she could kill him for what he had done to her friend.

Her fingernails were ripped and bleeding, every movement triggered such pain in her head she worried she'd pass out. The dizziness was now constant. The chunks of stone that had fallen, killing Sarah, lay by her side. She hadn't been able to save her.

Liz got up and limped into the kitchen for water. She was caked in powdery dust and her throat was parched. There was something on the table. She struggled to focus on it, a piece of paper. A suicide note. But a strange one. It was Sarah's writing but only a fragment of a few sentences.

Green-black puddles were clouding her vision and a strange numbness disconnected her from the surrounding chaos. But she knew one thing. Alex had murdered Sarah and set it up as a suicide. He'd tried to do the same to her.

He wouldn't get away with it this time, she thought, through the clanging in her brain. Teetering on the edge of passing out, Liz pressed wet hands against her cheeks. She tore the fake suicide note up into pieces and shoved them into her pocket. Holding onto walls, Liz lurched around the house looking for something, anything she could use to prove to the police what had happened. Of course, there was nothing, he was too clever for that.

It was difficult climbing the rubble-strewn stairs, but she made it to the top bedroom. The smaller one was impassable; the roof had collapsed onto the floor. She thought of Sarah's crushed skull and swallowed hard to keep from throwing up.

Her body was on the verge of collapse. She kept whiting out and clicking back into place in different parts of the cottage. She'd searched everywhere, nothing to incriminate Alex, not even a hair. The clouds behind her eyes were thickening. It was hopeless, she thought.

Over and over Liz saw Sarah, hanging from the beam, her legs kicking. Burying her head in her hands she pictured the colour returning to Sarah's face in that blissful moment when she thought she hadn't been too late. If only she'd dragged her clear more quickly - got her up to her feet before the roof collapsed. Despair knocked her into a rage of weeping. Her face and hands stung as she cried. She couldn't bear it. This was all her fault.

The sky was darkening. Liz sat up and wiped her face on her sleeve. There had to be something. Something he'd overlooked that would prove he'd been there. Sniffing deeply, she stood and walked back up the stairs, picking carefully around fallen stones and smashed bricks.

The small bedroom was the only place she hadn't searched. She began to pull away stones using one hand as her left elbow was now grossly swollen. When she'd cleared a space, she lay on her stomach and wriggled through the hole until she could see a clear patch at the far end of the room. Pushing herself forward through the tunnel of stones and fallen brick, she could see the edge of a pink rug and a dressing table. Its legs had given way and the whole thing had fallen forward.

Liz stretched out her arm and scrabbled at the drawer, coughing on the clouds of dust that rose from the floor. A creaking above her melted her bowels into ice and she froze in horror, expecting the ceiling to fall at any second. Every cell of her body screamed at her to hurry but she daren't move in case she released something in the overhead beams.

Eventually, all was silent, and she crept forward, millimetre by millimetre until she reached the dressing table. What if there was nothing there? What then?

Using the very tips of her fingers, she pulled the drawer open and her heart dropped with disappointment. Empty. She rolled onto her back and stared at the buckled ceiling, tears sliding into her hair. She was about to slide herself back out when she saw the foot of the brass bed to her left, the ceiling had fallen onto it but as the bed was so high there was a good amount of space under it.

Wincing as she knocked her elbow and knee, she used the bed leg to pull herself under the frame. She prodded at the mattress from below, but nothing fell out. That was it. No use. She slid her hand along the frame until her hand touched something plastic.

Heart thudding, she twisted and turned until she could tweezer her fingers to pull it out. She held it in front of her face blinking in disbelief. A thin card wallet. She flicked it open. Alex's Oyster card! She recognised the crack across the face.

Full of energy, ignoring the protests of her sore head and sprained joints, Liz pulled herself out of the rubble, clutching the card wallet in her hand. This was it. This was what she needed to prove Alex was here.

Standing in front of Sarah's body at the foot of the stairs Liz couldn't bear to look at her poor smashed face a moment longer. She fetched a towel from the kitchen and laid it gently over her. Shame tore her apart and guilt flowed into the cracks, filling her to the top of her skull. This was her fault. She should have kept in touch with Sarah more often. Made sure she kept away from that bastard Alex. How had they ended up back together? Her mind reeled.

She couldn't think about that now. There was no time to mourn Sarah. She had to make sure Alex didn't get away with it. Again. As gently as she could, she lifted the edge of Sarah's shirt and tucked Alex's oyster card wallet into the waistband of Sarah's jeans. The police couldn't miss it, she thought.

Liz splashed water onto her face, gritting her teeth against the pain in her head, arm, and ankle, which was now a constant throb. Sarah's body had to be moved. If it was found buried under the wreckage of the roof people would assume it was an accident. She kicked a path through the rubble to the back door and looped the rope under Sarah's shoulders, shivering with horror.

Twisting the ends together she pulled Sarah through the kitchen and out to the back garden. She was shocked to see night had fallen. Liz had to keep wiping tears and blood away from her eyes. It took all her strength to move her; Sarah was small but in death her weight seemed to have doubled.

Liz couldn't bear to look at Sarah's body any longer. Just past the back door she discovered a garden pond, long since dried up and half-filled with leaves. With the last vestiges of energy, she rolled Sarah's body into the hollow and dug handfuls of the soft earth to cover her up, piling it more and more thickly until she couldn't see her anymore. Covered in dirt, tears streaming down her face Liz dragged two flagstones over, one by one, then added more earth. She didn't want any animals coming to find her before she'd tipped off the police. She'd call them as soon as she could reach a phone.

The blackout hit her out of nowhere –

*

She woke as dawn was breaking, slumped over a mound of earth. Her consciousness splintered out of a darkness so impenetrable she was utterly disorientated. She'd never known a headache like it. Nothing came close to the pain ricocheting around her skull, the bones of which felt as fragile as eggshell. She turned her head and agony exploded sulphur-yellow behind her eyeballs and she vomited.

She dragged herself to her feet and cried out as her ankle gave way beneath her. As she tentatively touched her forehead a shower of pills fell from her cuff. She grabbed them and ate them hungrily, crunching them down. She didn't care how many. Anything to numb the pain.

A shaft of sunlight lit a track behind the garden. Throwing her bag over her shoulder she limped towards it. She began to walk, a memory faintly stirring. She passed out again in the thick of the woods and came round to feel the heat of the afternoon swaddling her, heavy as a duvet.

Liz kept walking, incapable of thinking of anything beyond putting one step in front of the other. When she reached the end of the track she stood still. Bewildered.

'Fuck, man! What happened to you?' A man was sitting on the doorstep of a big barn of a house, the light from inside casting him into shadow.

'Can you help me?' Liz mumbled, swaying. 'I need Xanax, or a benzo.'

'You need a doctor not drugs,' he said, looking at her strangely. 'Did you find your friend?'

She squinted at him, pulling back her hair with a shaking hand. 'Do I know you?'

'Come here, poulette,' he crooned. 'Marc will look after you…'

She looked back at the woods, the trees were trying to tell her something, but she couldn't make it out.

It took a week for her head to heal. She drifted in and out of sleep for days, waking up screaming with terrible nightmares. She vomited for hours until Marc was moved enough to bring her water as well as the drugs she begged for. Liz thought he was being kind but discovered later she'd paid for them with her passport. He must have taken it when she was unconscious.

Later, Liz woke up in Paris, in a park, with the Eiffel tower looming above her. Marc had driven her there and left her to make her way home. Tourists drifted past in colourful groups and she looked round, dazed by the unfamiliar sunshine after days in Marc's dank barn. Her bag was gone. Her arms and legs were covered with bruises but at last the terrible headache had faded into a dull throb.

Desperate to get home, she loitered at the bus station. It took hours before she saw a young woman with short hair disappear into the toilets. She was older and darker, but she would do. The stolen passport was in her hand before she could think about what she was doing. In the end the guards barely glanced at the photograph and she managed to slip through the crowds onto a coach heading for Dover. She slept most of the way, a sleep troubled by dreams of houses falling and shadows kicking, and it was only when the bus pulled into Dover that she realised her grandmother's ring had gone.

CHAPTER 20: LIZ

They must have carried me into the cell. Seeing my grandmother's ring had been too much. My brain had just… shut down, and I'd passed out. When I came round, I wanted to beg them for pills, anything to stop the locked box of my memories from cracking open.

How could I have forgotten? I wept as I realised how stupid I'd been. And I'd left Sarah there, poor, tortured Sarah. I'd left her in the earth and then blown my brains out with drugs and that, along with what must have been a bad concussion, had wiped my memory clean and I'd never called the police.

And because of my idiocy, Alex would get away with it. They'd think it was me and the real killer would never get the punishment he deserved. Rage and despair were a toxic combination and I wept and smashed against the walls of the cell, much to the consternation of the officer standing at the door.

Again and again I retraced my steps through the woods down the rutted track to the cottage where I'd seen that terrible, terrible scene. Sarah. Hanging. Her legs kicking desperately.

I vomited. My body rebelling against the memory. My forehead throbbed as if it wanted to crack open.

I wiped my mouth and forced myself to remember every detail. To confront my shame and desperation. They may as well arrest me, I acknowledged. I was to blame for Sarah's death. If I'd pulled her clear she'd still be alive.

I couldn't stop crying. The doctor was brought in to try and calm me down.

'Elle a besoin de sedation,' the guard said.

'No!' I screamed, terrified. The Doctor whispered soothingly as she approached, and I scrabbled back onto the bed. The temptation to give in and stick out my arm for the needle was overwhelming and I fought it with every cell in my body. 'No, please. I can't. I'm an addict. Please… no sedative.'

She stopped and stepped back, muttering to the guard who nodded.

'I can give you something mild,' she said, kindly.

I sniffed and sat up. 'No. I can't risk it… you understand?' I longed and longed to take whatever she could give me, but I'd worked too hard and too long to get off the drugs and I couldn't handle even a taste.

She nodded in understanding and they left me alone.

It was a terrible time. My jaw ached from my fall and I checked it with my fingers, wincing at the pain. With nothing to distract me from my thoughts I was forced to face up to what I had done. Sarah's death was on my hands, and the sadness of it would be a part of me for the rest of my life.

Cartwright's questions had left me skinned raw, but he was describing someone who didn't exist anymore. Jenny had helped me to come to terms with what I was and his words, though painful, I could deal with. It was the sight of my grandmother' ring that had torn me apart.

I had to focus. Yes, I'd done some terrible things, but I had survived, I was here. Unlike poor Sarah. I had to do everything I could to make sure that bastard paid for what he did. I had to plan what I would say with great care. They mustn't find out I was there, in Chauron. Alex planned to murder Sarah. He wanted to frame it as a suicide, something I knew he'd done before. If I hadn't discovered her the police would have been none the wiser.

I wondered what he thought when her body hadn't been discovered. Did he think of her at all? Daniel had said the family continued to pay Sarah's allowance; I would bet my workshop Alex had worked out how to get his hands on her money.

I sat up on the bed. Surely that would link Alex to Sarah? I had to think hard. Cartwright had Cadieux believing I was untrustworthy. They would interview me again soon, I had to make sure my story was convincing, not just to convict Alex of Sarah's murder, but all the other lost women as well.

*

Cartwright had told Cadieux that every one of the women in my clippings had nothing to do with Alex, but I knew better. He was clever. I knew only too well how clever he could be. His ability to manipulate was something I saw every day we were together.

Those victims had to be connected, they just had to be. The resemblance to Lisa, the obsession from his school days, was just too marked to be a coincidence. I'd only seen her photo once, but it was enough to convince me. When I met his mate from school, I hadn't thought anything of it, it was just a story about Alex's past that didn't seem important. But then a while later, when Alex and I had got a place at uni together, I found her photograph.

I wouldn't have thought if significant if he hadn't gone to such great lengths to hide it. He'd slipped it into a crack behind the skirting board, next to his bed. It had appeared when I knocked against the wood with the hoover. She was quite breath-taking. When I pulled the photo out I assumed it was something left by the previous tenant, but I stopped short when I had a proper look.

It had been taken in a school hall, a string of fairy light across the stage and a tree in the background marked it as a Christmas party. The flash was unforgiving and bathed the whole scene in an artificial, bleaching light. It had turned everyone's eyes red except for hers. I remembered how strange it felt seeing myself in her face. We shared the same colouring, the same full breasts but, I acknowledged I was a poor copy - a palimpsest - compared to this glowing beauty.

Thinking nothing of it beyond the strange feeling of seeing an almost twin, I turned to chuck it in the bin when something caught my eye. Alex. Alex was in the corner of the photograph. I was about to call out to him to ask about it when I saw the expression on his face. It was awful. Haunting.

He was leaning against a wall at the back of the photo, almost out of the frame. Most of his body was hidden behind the crowd, but his face was clear. He was looking at the girl with an expression I struggled to identify. A sort of tortured hunger, was the closest I could get. His eyes large and dark, he was much thinner then and his cheekbones curved high and sharp – too thin, really, but it gave him a gothic glamour.

It was the vulnerability I saw in Alex's face that stopped me calling him in so I could tease him about it. His vulnerability, but also there was something in his eyes that was so frightening my body responded instinctively; I turned cold.

I flipped it over. 'Lisa' was written in Alex's neat black capitals. The corners of the photograph were softened and grey. He'd held it many times. It was a picture of obsession, clear as day. There was nothing in that room of any interest to Alex except that girl. And it was killing him. I could see it in the tightness of his jaw, the way his fists were balled, and the tension that filled every line of him as he unconsciously leaned towards her, eyes burning.

In that horrid little cell, I shivered to remember it. I wished I still had it, had thought to make a copy, I was sure it would convince anyone who saw it that Alex was capable of evil. But I'd been a fool, I thought. Too madly in love with Alex to question what I'd seen. I tucked the photo back behind the skirting board and when I looked again a few days later, it had gone.

Thinking back, he knew I'd found the photograph. It wasn't long after that that things started to change. I should have left then, the minute I'd seen Alex's unguarded face. It was the face of a monster; I should have realised. I thought of Amber with her delicate beauty, her eyes still full of the blinding stars Alex had put there.

Alex. I had to use his name. He wasn't some devil, he was a corrupt, obsessed, and dangerous man who has stalked and murdered young women, I didn't care what Cartwright said. I wondered if Amber had looked through everything I left and whether it would have made any difference to her feelings. Would it have made a difference to me?

I had to admit it probably wouldn't. Alex could break my heart with his vulnerability, make me feel like the most incredible person he'd ever met, and the sex was unbelievable. I'd never had anything like it before or since. It was like no drug I'd ever taken;

for years and years afterwards, I'd wake up throbbing from dreams reliving our time in bed together.

However, every one of those dreams were accompanied by others that were far darker, the ones where Alex was trying to kill me. Towards the end we'd got wasted together and I'd woken up in the bath, my wrists cut and bleeding into the water. It was only by rolling myself out and banging on the floor, alerting the tenant below, did I manage to survive.

My mouth curled as I remembered Alex's tears. How desolate he was that I would want to kill myself. How solicitous he was about feeding me my anti-depressants. Bewildered, I would swallow them dutifully, never questioning what had happened. I thought I'd done something stupid while off my head. It never occurred to me to think otherwise.

Agitation rose as I remembered my blind stupidity, pushing me to my feet to pace back and forth in the little cell. I reminded myself of desperate zoo animals in too small enclosures.

There was no point in remembering the past. It was gone. I had to convince Cadieux Alex must have planted that ring. A cramp of grief pinched my heart at the thought of it lying under Sarah's body all those years. I didn't know if the Oyster card I'd tucked into Sara's jeans would still be there, perhaps it would have rotted.

I swallowed at the thought. If the ring was the only evidence they had I could be facing a murder charge. If the card I'd planted had rotted I needed something else to convince them. I banged my hands against my head in frustration. There must be something else, some other piece of evidence that would link Sarah's death to Alex. They couldn't charge me based on the ring? Surely? Wouldn't that be circumstantial evidence?

The door opened and a tray of food was brought in. The surface of the soup was already curdling; the thought of eating made me feel sick. But then I remembered Alex's face and the women he'd killed, and a flame began to burn bright in my chest. I remembered the doctor tutting over my low blood pressure and dehydration. I couldn't beat him if I let myself wither away.

I began to do press-ups. At first, I wanted to scream with frustration at the weakness that had stolen into my body over the past month. But I kept going, and they got easier. Then squats, then pull ups using the frame of the door. I kept going until black dots fizzled across my vision and I was panting for breath. Only when the sweat poured did I sit and eat.

Everything was cold but I forced it down, washing it back with a bottle of water. I had to stay strong. I warmed myself on the flame of rage that continued to grow. I would do everything I could to get him put away. Finding out about Sarah had thrown me off course, but not any longer.

*

I was escorted upstairs for further questions the following morning. I had spent a miserable night unable to sleep on the hard bed and with the constant clanging and shouting that echoed down the corridors. Thankfully Cartwright wasn't there, and it was Cadieux who sat at the table, flanked by an officer and a middle-aged black woman in a suit.

'This is Madame Génin, she is the duty lawyer who is here to protect your interests, I suggest you see her now in private to discuss your case.'

I shook my head. 'No. Thank you, but that won't be necessary.' I tried to smile at her, but she didn't respond. She looked tired as she gathered up her things and moved to sit next to me.

Madame Génin took notes throughout the interview and once or twice placed her hand on my arm to stop me talking, or to ask me to clarify something, but generally she faded into the background. I closed my eyes for a second and pictured that flame inside me burning away all the sediment of the past stirred up by Cartwright. I pictured my muscles hardening and growing in strength. I needed to focus on Alex, everything else had to be stripped away.

'Madame, as you know we have evidence that points towards you being involved in the murder of Sarah Andrews. You are under arrest but not yet charged as we continue our investigations. Do you understand?'

I nodded, taking a slow breath. Cadieux's partner handed him a file which he opened, shuffling through the pages. He extracted one and looked across at me. I liked his face, the creases around his eyes and mouth made it easy to imagine him laughing in the sunshine drinking wine. I could almost feel the Provençal heat soaking into my skin. The thought made me giddy.

'Madame?'

I snapped back into the room. Madame Génin leaned towards me. 'You need to concentrate, Madame Shaw. This is very serious.'

'I know,' I replied. 'Yes. I'm sorry.'

'You knew Sarah Andrews before she came to France, that has been established and you have confirmed.'

'Yes.'

'Did you come and visit her while she was here?'

'No,' I said carefully, raising my eyebrows in surprise. 'I only found out she'd gone to France recently.'

'What contact did you have before then?'

I shifted in my chair. 'Well, I hadn't really. We were very close for a while but over the years we kept in touch over Facebook, just the odd message. She seemed really happy and I was getting back on track, I started my apprenticeship and was in therapy. We talked about meeting up, but time passed and it didn't happen.'

'So, what made you come to France?'

'I found out Alex had married again. I knew Sarah would want to know as we'd made a sort of pact to follow Alex online. We knew he was dangerous but apart from hunting him down and stalking him there was nothing we could do. He didn't show up anywhere on the Internet until I saw the Instagram post.'

'Instagram post?'

They had taken my phone but Cadieux's partner passed over an iPad and I found the post and passed it back. Cadieux frowned, studying the screen carefully. He handed it back to his colleague and turned to me.

'And what happened then?'

'I couldn't get hold of her. She didn't reply although I could see she'd read the messages. I thought it was really strange she didn't respond so I contacted her brother.'

'You say she read your messages? On Facebook?'

'Yes, that's right, her picture appeared next to what I'd written so it shows she must have read…' I stopped.

Excitement began to swell as I realised this was how I would destroy Alex. Why didn't I think of this before?

'Wait.' I held up my hand. 'Sarah was already dead then, wasn't she? Of course she was.' My mind raced with a crystal-clear rush. 'That was only in the last few months. How could she be on Facebook? Oh my God, that's it!' I made to rise out of my seat, but the lawyer held me back.

'Can you show me?' Cadieux gestured to the iPad again. Grabbing it, my hands shaking, I typed the address into the search bar and brought up Facebook. For a horrified moment I couldn't remember my password but then it came to me and I logged in. I brought up my messages to Sarah.

'Look, see? Those questions have been read, but not these last few. Can you see her profile picture here? That means whoever is on this account has read my message. How is that possible?' I had to make an effort to stop shouting in his face. 'Who was reading my messages? And look…' I scrolled through the conversations going back and forth since we first met. 'If she was dead and buried in France, who was talking to me over the past few years?' I forced back the tears that were threatening to fall. I had to keep calm. I had to keep calm.

Cadieux gave the iPad to his colleague and with a nod at me and my lawyer left the room. We sat in silence trying to work out what was being said on the other side of the door. I couldn't make out anything and looked over at Madame Génin. 'Can you hear what they are saying?'

'Inspector Cadieux is asking for your Facebook account to be investigated…' She was about to say something else but stopped when Cadieux returned, accompanied by a different officer. I searched their faces but couldn't read anything in their carefully neutral expressions.

'What's happening? What did you find? Anything? I bet it's him. Alex. It has to be. Search his IP address! You'll find the location of whoever was logged onto Sarah's account.'

'All in good time, Madame. If we could continue, please?'

Impatience twitched tension through my body, but I nodded and sat still.

'Sarah Andrews, you say her brother told you she had married?'

'Yes, and that's what started all this,' I gestured round the room. 'I couldn't believe she'd gone on and married him, it didn't make sense.' I remembered what I'd realised the night before. 'Oh! Daniel... her brother... he also said she was still collecting the allowance from her parents! That's why they didn't worry too much about her. You must check that too. Ask him!'

'We are trying to contact her family.' He made a note, his colleague read it and nodded. He picked up his phone and sent a message. I tried to read it, but he placed the phone face down before I could see.

'The thing is, Madame Shaw, there is no record of a marriage. It never happened.'

'I knew it. I knew that was a lie.'

'There is something I find of a concern.' He picked up the paper lying before him and read it before looking up. 'I have here a passenger list for Eurostar journeys between Paris and London covering a broad period around the time Madame Heurteau thinks her tenant left. It is a lengthy process but thanks to the digitisation of records, we are able to track down registered names with surprising rapidity.'

'Did you find his name? I bet it's there. Surely that's proof I'm right?' Hope lifted my heart. I craned my neck to read the list.

'We didn't find the name of the man you have accused…'

'He probably used a fake name,' I said. 'Pass it over to me and I'll have a look, I bet I'll be able to work out which one is him…' I reached for the paper, but my lawyer held me back.

'Wait,' she muttered.

'We didn't find his name,' Cadieux watched me as he spun the paper round. 'We found yours.'

*

I made sure to look stunned with shock. My pulse hitched up a notch. I had to be very careful. 'How is that possible?' I said.

'The facts are irrefutable. This has been checked and double checked. We have, with difficulty, retrieved CCTV footage from the station and we can place you on the Gare de Nord platform.'

I shook my head. 'Wait, let me think.' I pressed my head into my hands and tried to remember. 'Those years were difficult for me… I can't remember clearly.' I allowed the silence to lengthen as I calculated what to say. 'I think I came to Paris for a festival. Was there one around that time? I'd been working on some leather designs…' My voice was becoming more certain as I spoke. 'Yes, that's right. I thought it would be popular with students and backpackers. I sold them all, made some good money.'

'You didn't come to meet Sarah in Chauron?'

'No of course not, I had no idea she was here.'

Cadieux met my eyes, looking thoughtful.

'My client is coming close to the end of the 24 hours you can hold her without further authorisation,' Madame Génin said, making me jump, and breaking the connection between me and Cadieux.

He nodded in acknowledgement. 'I don't think we will have too much trouble getting an extension from the Public Prosecutor based on the evidence we have.'

'Pah! From what I hear it is merely circumstantial,' Madame Génin's eyes flashed. 'I think we should ask for a break so I can advise my client…'

The door slammed open.

'Que se passe-t-il? Inspector Cadieux exclaimed with irritation.

A dark-haired man in uniform apologised for the interruption. I was surprised to see he look terrified of Cadieux. He must be a tougher boss than I had imagined. 'We thought you should see this.' He held out a file.

The inspector waved him away and once the door closed, began to read. The silence in the room was absolute. He took his time. Madame Génin and I stiffened. Was this good news or bad?

Cadieux tossed the file down and pressed his fingers into his eyes, shaking his head. He leaned back in his chair and gazed at the ceiling, thinking hard.

'What is it, Inspector?' I was grateful to Madame Génin, I wasn't sure I could have asked the question my mouth was so dry.

'A witness has come forward. His statement led to further forensic investigation.'

'What is it?' My voice was loud and urgent in the little interview room. The lawyer put her hand on my arm again. My muscles felt like concrete.

'The police in Chauron called for anyone who may have information on the body we found in the garden to come forward. Today, a gentleman who lived close by to Madame Heurteau's cottage reported seeing a man and a woman struggling in the woods, years ago. She was being beaten, he remembered her because of her hair. He described it as…' Cadieux looked down at his notes. '"Red as a winter sunset, the colour of autumn leaves." Most poetic, for a farmer.'

'Sarah,' I gasped.

Cadieux inclined his head in agreement. 'He thinks the woman was pulled into the cottage, but he can't be sure. His memory wasn't what it was. When asked why he didn't report this before he replied he didn't know.' The inspector dropped the paper with a contemptuous gesture.

'And the forensics?' Madame Génin's voice was sharp.

'They found a wallet…'

I sat up straight, my breathing fast and shallow. I put my hand over my heart to calm its jerky rhythm. The Oyster card, I thought, exhilarated.

'They identified a person of interest. The information we have matches the witness's description of the man he saw in the woods. We have also identified a car that sailed on the ferry between Calais and Dover around the relevant time.'

I could barely breathe. 'It's Alex, isn't. The name. It was him. The man I've been telling you about.'

'Yes.'

I closed my eyes. Relief burst like sunshine.

CHAPTER 21: AMBER

The afternoon in the pub stretched into the evening; it was torture for Amber. Her smile sat plastered on her face, heavy as concrete. She couldn't stop thinking about Brianna, and Katie, and all the others. Liz's face haunted her, and she kept looking at Alex as he chatted and laughed, getting increasingly drunk. Was he capable of that? Had he followed women and drugged them with the stuff Curly found for him? Even now she could see Curly passing wraps to a stream of people who approached their table to join the yelling throng.

How had she not seen this before? She knew he and Alex dabbled, and she'd seen them both smoke joints, but she had no idea he was selling. Was that where Alex's rolls of money had come from? Well, that would all have to stop if she did agree to try for a baby. How stupid he was! Why take such risks?

She wished she could go home but was conscious of Alex's eyes on her at all times. What could he see? She wanted to cover her face so he couldn't read the suspicion written there. By the time they got home he was so drunk he could barely stand. She helped him to bed and as he snored beside her she wondered if she could risk going and having another look in the bathroom but as she moved, Alex tightened his arm around her.

The night seemed to last forever, and Amber couldn't sleep. When Alex got out of bed she kept her eyes tight shut and her breathing even. More and more she worried he would be able to see what she was thinking in her eyes. She wished she could either prove he'd done something or be certain he hadn't, she couldn't stand this not knowing; it was splitting her in two.

She turned onto her back listening to the thrum of the shower. Closing her eyes she imagined walking up the path to her Mum's house, opening the door and walking through to the kitchen where her Mum would be sitting with a pot of tea, watching the dog roll in muddy puddles in the garden. An ache of loss curled her into a ball, and she buried her face into the pillow.

A waft of steam and citrusy shower gel dragged her eyes open. 'I know you're awake, Amber,' Alex said, towelling his wet hair.

Amber sat up, 'I didn't sleep very well, I was hoping to get another hour. It's not like I've got work to go to.'

'Well don't lie in bed all day, I don't want you getting fat. Get some food, will you? There's nothing to eat. Curly and I had to have fucking cereal this morning.'

'Sorry, Alex. Of course. I'll go this morning. The only thing is I haven't got much money. Paul hasn't paid me for the work I did before I got fired.'

Alex opened his wallet and counted out some notes, which he left on the dresser. 'Don't get any more fancy crap,' he said. 'It's too rich, gives me indigestion.'

'OK.'

He finished getting dressed and ran down the stairs calling for Curly. The door slammed and Amber stood at the window to watch them leave. Something was up; Alex's manner was offhand, dismissive. She was used to passionate affection or tormented rage. This detached stranger was frightening, but perhaps it was nothing – she mustn't get infected by Liz's paranoid fantasies.

As soon as the van left, Amber got dressed and went straight to the bathroom. She opened the cabinet and tugged at the shelf. It wouldn't move. Cursing in frustration at the single light gloom, she ran down the stairs to get the torch from the kitchen.

The shelf had been screwed back into place. Amber stared at the holes drilled so recently crumbs of sawdust lay in the bottom of the cupboard. She tried tugging it but it was fixed tight. She wanted to scream with frustration. When had he done this? How did he know she had stumbled across this secret space?

The pipes clanged again as she descended the steps leading to the basement. A gust of hot air blew her hair back as she got to the bottom so the heating must still be working. To her surprise she saw a little office had been set up in the corner of the room. A desk was pushed up against the wall. Piles of paper were strewn across it next to a slim lap top Amber had never seen before.

The screen brightened as she lifted the lid. Breath high in her chest, Amber tapped the keyboard. A password log in flashed up and she shut the lid in disappointment. There's no way she would be able to guess it, and if she tried Alex might be able to see what she'd done.

Sitting down on the office chair, she surveyed the papers. It looked like Alex was sorting his tax return, receipts were everywhere. She picked up a few random pieces of paper but nothing struck her as unusual. Maybe she should look for a life insurance policy in her name. One with a huge pay out to Alex if anything happened to her, she thought grimly.

If there was one, it wasn't in the desk. Their wills were in a top drawer, the ones they'd signed the day after they got married. Amber barely remembered it, she had been in such a daze with the wedding following on so soon after her Mum's funeral.

The wills were standard forms they'd bought from WH Smith. A simple statement leaving everything to each other. The deeds to the house lay beneath. It was in her name. Her Gran and Mum had left it to her on that condition; they wanted Amber to have security with assets of her own. Not that Amber saw the house as an asset. It still felt like a burden most days.

There was a funny smell. Amber remembered the basement as smelling of sawdust and fresh paint after Alex and Curly had finished, but now there was a strange tang, as if a toilet had leaked. She pushed the top drawer shut and opened the next one down. Empty. The third held stiff, white A4 envelopes marked with the logo of a variety of upmarket estate agents.

Amber picked up one and tipped out the contents. A glossy brochure slid into her hand and she gasped to see the house; the view from the street beautifully photographed on the front cover. Her pulse ticked up a notch as she leafed through the pages. Some photos had to be artist impressions as they showed a brand-new kitchen. It bore no resemblance to the room over her head - empty except for an old fridge and oven, a couple of battered units and a row of baked bean tins.

It looked amazing, like somewhere a footballer's wife would live, but Amber couldn't help a spasm of longing for her little warm flat with its views across the city. This glossy, perfectly designed mausoleum of a house wasn't for her.

There were five envelopes from expensive estate agents, all vying for the chance to sell the house. When had Alex done this? When did the agents come and measure up to create these detailed floor plans? Why didn't Alex tell her? She turned to the letters that accompanied the mock ups and almost fainted when she saw the sales prices they were suggesting.

Five million? She read through each letter. All said around the same. How was that possible? She couldn't begin to get her head around that amount of money. Head reeling, she forced herself to read through the first letter. Based on neighbouring sales… proximity to the common a big plus… a good sized house and garden with room for development…

Alex had said the house would fetch a lot of money, but this was more than she could possibly have imagined. She bundled everything back into the drawer and slammed it shut. She would talk to Alex about it as soon as he got back. A thought struck her. She opened the drawer again and took out one of the brochure mock-ups. It was important to have proof. Amber had got used to doubting herself, Alex had robbed her of any sense of certainty about anything.

The desk held nothing more of interest. The rest of the room was empty except for a few weights and a bench next to the barre Alex had been so keen to show off. Amber ran her hand along the smooth walls, working her way around looking for she wasn't sure what. A cupboard? A safe? A secret panel?

This was ridiculous, she thought. It was getting late and she had promised Alex she'd get to the shops. She slipped the brochure inside her shirt and made her way upstairs. In the bedroom she double checked Liz's envelope was still safely hidden and gathered up the cash Alex had left.

At Tesco, Amber stood in the gadget aisle, her basket heavy in her hand, scoring grooves into her fingers. She hated not having a phone but didn't have enough money in her account to buy even the cheapest one on the display. There was a cash machine by the entrance, and she'd checked her balance before she went in. She was right up to her overdraft limit.

Sighing, she put the basket down and rubbed the soreness from her hand. She really ought to go and see Paul at the salon, get him to give her what she was owed. Maybe tomorrow, she decided. Alex hadn't given her very much money, so she chose carefully. It struck her as absurd that she was sorting through shelves to find tins of beans on sale while was living in a house worth millions of pounds.

At the till, Amber calculated the cost of each item as she placed it on the conveyor belt. She only had the cash Alex had given her, what would she do if she didn't have enough? Her account was empty, and she had no other cards. She would have to put something back. She blushed with humiliation at the thought.

Amber sighed with relief when the total was just under £40, she could cover it with a few pence to spare. Not enough to buy a newspaper so she stopped at the rack before leaving and read as many front pages as she could. All of them featured pictures of Katie and Brianna. There was also a third woman Amber hadn't seen before. This must be the one Alex had mentioned.

On the bottom row Amber's eyes snagged on the local paper that carried a photofit of two men. Her heart stopped. Dropping her shopping bags, she grabbed it with trembling hands.

'*Police appeal for key witnesses to come forward after a woman's disappearance in Brighton,*' read the headline. Amber looked again at the sketches that accompanied the article. They were sickeningly familiar. '*The request comes after Brighton born*

Brianna Templeton (24) was reported missing. CCTV identified two men who were seen drinking with Ms Templeton at around 3.30 on the morning of Sunday 12th May, the last time she was seen. Officers believe the two men may have key information and appeal for them to come forward to help with their enquiries. Those from the Brighton policing team want the two potential witnesses to contact them by calling 101 with the reference 90EBT2383120.'

Blinking with disbelief, Amber checked the date of the newspaper. It had come out that morning, well after Alex and Curly had gone to the police. Why was the police still appealing for witnesses when they had already come forward?

It was only when the security guard touched her shoulder did she realise she had walked out of the shop, newspaper still in her hand.

'Miss. Miss. You've left your shopping.' He pointed back to the rack of newspapers where her bags lay on the floor.

'Oh, goodness, I'm so sorry.' Amber was mortified and hurried over to get them, balling the newspaper up in her hand.

'Are you OK, Miss?' The security guard followed and picked up a can that had rolled out of the bag.

'Yes! Of course! I'm fine!' But as she spoke, Amber swayed on her feet and the security guard jumped to grab her before she fell.

'Here, come and sit down at my desk for a minute. I'll get you some water.' He led her to his podium by the entrance and sat her down on a stool. 'Put your head down. You're as white as a sheet.' Gently, he pressed her shoulder until she bent forward. 'That's better.' He handed her a bottle of water. 'Do you want me to get the First Aid guy? I can call him.' He held up his radio.

Amber sat up. 'No, honestly I'm fine. You've been very kind, but I better get home…'

'Just wait a few minutes until I see some colour back in those cheeks. What happened? Did you see something bad?' He nodded at the paper crumpled up in her hand.

'Uh, no. Nothing like that. I just felt a bit faint. Probably something I ate.' She wanted to weep at his kindness but was frantic he would see the front page of the paper.

On automatic pilot, Amber walked home through the rain. She unpacked the bags in the kitchen and when she was done sat down on the floor and spread the newspaper out flat. For the first time in her life she had walked out of a shop without paying for something, she thought.

The article hadn't changed. No matter how often she read and re-read it, the facts stayed the same. Alex and Curly hadn't gone to the police as they had claimed, and Brianna hadn't been seen after they left to return to London.

Amber tried to remember exactly what happened that weekend. What time did Alex get back to the hotel? Again, she remembered the look on Alex's face as Brianna flirted with him. Had he done something to her? She scrambled to her feet, Liz's words ringing in her ears. 'You need to ask yourself what you've got that Alex needs… You're in danger, Amber. Make no mistake.'

Terrified, she ran upstairs. She had to leave. Call the police. She'd just pulled the suitcase out from under the bed when she heard the door slam. Her heart flew up and lodged her throat; she steadied herself with her hand on the floor.

'Amber! Where are you?'

'In the bedroom! I won't be a minute.' Her voice strangled. Breathing hard, Amber pushed the case back under the bed. She crossed the bedroom to the landing and looked down the stairs. Curly and Alex were looking up at her, drenched by the downpour that was now hammering against the roof.

'Fuck, I'm soaked,' said Curly, taking off his coat and shaking it.

'You're back early!' Amber said, gripping the bannister rail hard.

'Site got flooded. It's pissing down out there. Did you get to Tesco?' Alex pushed his hair back; it was so wet it lay flat against his head.

'Yes, it's all in the kitchen. I'll be down in a minute. Do you want to eat now?'

'I'm all right for the minute – you OK, Curly?'

'I can always eat,' Curly said with a laugh. 'But I'll have a shower first.'

He bounded up the stairs so quickly Amber took a frightened step back. She was still clutching the paper and hastily pushed it down the back of her jeans.

'All right, Amb?'

'Yeah, fine thanks, Curly.'

Alex disappeared into the sitting room and Amber walked down the stairs as slowly as she dared to get her breathing back to normal.

'Do you want a drink?' she asked Alex who was sitting, feet propped up on the coffee table, scrolling through the channels for Sky Sports.

'Yeah. Beer thanks.'

Amber was relieved he hadn't looked up at her, she didn't think she could hide what she was thinking from him anymore.

'I'm going to make a start on the potatoes,' she said as she handed over a foaming glass.

'I thought we said we weren't hungry,' Alex said, irritated.

'I know, but I thought I'd do a cottage pie, might as well do the potatoes now ready. I won't put it in until later.'

'Yeah, whatever. Move, Amb, I can't see the screen.'

Standing in the kitchen listening to Alex and Curly arguing about the football, Amber's thoughts jumped and collided together as she tried to decide what to do. Should she confront Alex? Maybe he had an explanation? Maybe the newspaper had outdated information? She would have to call the number to be sure.

She had copied the reference number onto a strip of paper that she pushed deep into her pocket. The newspaper she ripped into pieces and took outside, letting it soak into mush on the slick paving stones. Every word of the article was burned onto her brain, it wasn't like she needed to read it again.

She should just walk. If she left now, with no bag or coat, it might be a while before they realised she'd gone. The thought of shutting the door behind her and walking out into the rain was exhilarating. On autopilot, Amber peeled and boiled the potatoes and started chopping onions for the mince. The room began to fill with steam as she thought about what she would say to the police. She wouldn't be able to come back to the house afterwards, perhaps Amahle would put her up for a few nights.

'Amber!' It took a moment for her to realise Alex was calling her from the sitting room. She turned down the potatoes that were threatening to boil over. 'Amber!' he shouted again. 'Have you gone deaf?'

'What is it?'

'There's somebody at the door.'

Wiping her hands on a tea towel Amber left the kitchen. A loud rap on the door startled her, she was so on edge everything was making her heart race.

To her utter astonishment the door opened on two police officers, a man and a woman. It was as if Amber had conjured them into existence. She stared at them, open mouthed. Without moving, she called over her shoulder towards the sitting room.

'You'd better come here, it's the police.'

'What?'

Amber turned back to the door. 'Can I help you? Has something happened?' She sensed Alex and Curly moving behind her.

'We're looking for Alex Mortimer, is he here? We need to ask him a few questions.'

'Do you mean Alex Gray? That's my husband he's just here…'

But it was Curly who was stepping forward. 'That's me…'

'I didn't know your name was Alex,' Amber said in surprise, feeling stupid.

Curly ignored her. 'What can I do for you, Officers?'

'If you'd like to come with us, sir…'

Alex pushed Amber aside. 'What's this all about?'

'Nothing for you to worry about, we just need to ask Mr Mortimer some questions down at the station.'

'This is ridiculous!' Alex exclaimed. 'What about?'

'Is it about Brighton?' Amber asked before Alex shot her a look warning her to shut her mouth.

'I'm afraid we can't say, if you would come with me then, sir?'

Alex shot out his arm barring the way. 'No, this is ridiculous. Curly you don't have to go anywhere.'

Their radios crackled and the woman officer reached to hold it, her thumb over the button. 'Are you refusing to come with us, Mr Mortimer?'

'Yes, he is.' Alex reached to close the door but the officer moved forward, blocking the way with his body.

'If you could take a step back please, sir.' His words were courteous, but it was clear to Amber he was getting impatient. Alex sighed and got out of his way.

The officer put his hand on Curly's arm. 'Will you come in for questioning?'

'No!' Curly said. 'I haven't done anything.'

'Then I am arresting you on suspicion of the murder of Sarah Andrews. You do not have to say anything, but it may harm your defence if you do not mention when questioned something…'

The rest was drowned out by Alex shouting. Amber retreated up the stairs as an explosion of movement almost knocked her sideways. She heard the officer calling for back up and watched in horror as Curly was pulled out of the house.

CHAPTER 22: LIZ

I was free to go. I couldn't believe it. Within hours I was outside, standing on the pavement, marvelling at the warm sun on my face and the blast of fume filled air that zinged my senses into life. I could to return to the UK, although I had to report to my local police station in case the French police wanted to question me further.

'We still haven't a convincing explanation for the presence of your ring at the scene,' Cadieux said, his expression serious. 'But with this new evidence we will not get the authorisation to extend you stay any further.'

'And you're going to arrest him? Now?'

Cadieux nodded. 'We have asked the British police to call him in for questioning. I am told it will be a matter of hours. Ah! Your car is here. Goodbye, Madame Shaw.'

He stepped back as a police car drew up to the kerb. I got in and it pulled away, turning to say goodbye. Cadieux hadn't moved. He stood outside the police building and watched me until we turned out of sight.

I flopped back on the seat, relishing the sense of freedom and weightlessness. As we flew along the autoroute towards Chauron, I looked up at the clear blue sky and allowed the thick, filthy carapace of the past to flake away, bit by bit, disappearing into the French countryside.

After so many years I couldn't begin to imagine life without Alex's stalking shadow. The thought of the police arriving on his doorstep - his anger and bewilderment at being caught, the fact that Amber would now be safe - made me smile. Cadieux believed me. I knew he did. To be believed meant more to me than anything.

He saw the link between the women. He recognised it was more than a coincidence that the victims looked like sisters. I'd seen the way the people who worked for him responded to his authority. He was no pushover. Even Cartwright would have to accept those cases needed re-investigating. At last. At last the families would understand what really happened to their daughters. And no more women would vanish.

Back at Madame Betty's the little bag of belongings I had left there seemed pathetic. I thought of my empty flat. Time for things to change. My life had been on hold for too long. The police must have told her I was on my way as she was waiting for me at the door as we pulled up. As I got out, she charged down the path and hugged me. I was beginning to get used to it and hugged her back, which made her laugh.

Through pantomime she conveyed her sorrow about what had happened, and how glad she was I had been released. She hoped I would come and stay with her again, in the summer when the sun shone all day; and she had some food for my journey home.

I left with a bag bursting at the seams with bread, Tupperware pots of soup and stew, cakes, and thick slices of ham folded into greaseproof paper. There was also a cheese, but it smelled so bad I disposed of it in the station bin as soon as I got there. On the train home I thought about Alex. Was he in a police station right now? Had they charged him yet? Would he be on the news when I turned on the television in my cold little flat?

St Pancras was heaving. The noise and crowds of people were disorientating, and I lost my bearings for a moment. I felt insubstantial and frail amongst these commuters full of purpose before forcing myself to remember I was responsible for Alex being called in and questioned, finally meeting the justice he deserved, and I held my head up and gritted my teeth.

I had no money, but while I waited for my connection, I found a quiet corner with a bench and looked through Madame Betty's bag. Tearing off chunks of bread made fresh that morning, I worked through a whole pot of delicious chicken soup. It was good, and I savoured the simple pleasure of enjoying my food. I vowed to spend the rest of my life appreciating these moments.

Stuffed to bursting, I looked over at the station boards, I didn't have long. My eyes were beginning to close; exhaustion was catching up with me and with a full, warm belly all I wanted to do was climb into bed and sleep for days. I packed everything away and headed for the platform. I could sleep on the train.

I managed to find a window seat at a table and put my bag of food and rucksack on the shelf above my head. Before I sat down, I searched for my phone. For an awful minute I thought I'd left it back in France, but after taking everything out I found it wedged right at the bottom of the bag. It was flat and I had to rummage again to find the charger.

My heart sank when I plugged it in. The neck at the end of the wire had corrugated. Without much hope I connected it to my phone and spent ten minutes twisting it back and forth, but it was no good. It wouldn't charge. 'Oh, for fuck's sake.' I muttered.

I wanted to look up the news to see what was happening with Alex. I also wanted to phone Will. Had he read through the stuff I'd left him? Would he still want to see me when he found out the truth? I sighed and leaned against the window, letting the landscape ribbon away in ripples of green and blue. As the view became more familiar, my spirits lifted still further.

I needed money, that was a priority. I had to get back on my feet and order in more supplies so I could meet the hotel's contract. Having to make everything all over again was daunting, but the newly released positive side of my brain was having none of it. My designs would be better the second time around. I'd made them before, and I would make them more quickly now I knew the challenges.

It would take a lot of sweet talking to ask the hotel to wait. It had been a mistake to not respond to the manager's calls. A quiver of uncertainty threatened to stall me, but I shook it off. I'd convince them, I'm sure I could do it. My designs were good. Good enough to see off far more experienced and professional artists than I. The contract was mine, after all.

For the first time in months creative ideas were unfurling in my head. As I watched the greens and browns of the countryside roll past, I imagined a fine book of poetry bound with emerald leather contrasted with the richest walnut brown spine. It would suit a book of Romantic poetry with its earthy colours, I thought. Maybe Wordsworth, I'd always loved his writing.

It felt like a century since I'd handed the newly bound book of poems back to the woman whose father had read the book every day to remember his wife. Her face had lit up with delight; I smiled to remember it.

But this didn't help with the money situation. I slumped back and worried at my fingernail. I'd need a lot to sort out the workshop and get in materials to keep the hotel on side. There was nothing left of value except my bike and that wouldn't be nearly enough.

I couldn't remember if that bastard had destroyed my tools but picturing the carnage across the workshop floor I could only see materials and my designs destroyed. Hopefully my tools would still be intact, most were heavy and solid – difficult to harm. The leather. Those beautiful rolls of leather slashed with knives and torn into fluffy strips. My thoughts sped up, calculations chattering along like pages from a printer.

Was it possible? Excitement made my fingers tingle. Joyfully I allowed my ideas to jumble along, streamline and coalesce. I could use the leather still, I realised. I stood up so quickly to get my rucksack down the passenger next to me exclaimed with annoyance. I muttered an apology, but I didn't care. I had to get my ideas down.

I had a few pages left in the book and cursed the fact I hadn't brought more. I searched the pocket for my pencils and pulled out a handful. Wedged up against the window I began to draw. It was as I something had been released with Alex gone. Ideas appeared so fast I had trouble getting them all down. They filled two pages within twenty minutes, and I chose the best three and began to refine them on the last page.

Three different designs I could use with the shreds of leather I had left in my workshop. I would twine them together to produce something beautiful. I liked the idea of creating lovely things out of the ugly chaos Alex had wreaked.

One was a bracelet that plaited together many colours. With care I shaded in the design, outlining the loops and twists delighting to see the piece take shape. I still had those heavy drops of gold, I remembered, Alex couldn't have done much to them. I could incorporate them into the bracelet to give them a pleasing heft.

Second was a belt design I'd used when I first started out but now I embellished and developed it into something far more striking. The loops of leather in different textures and colours would look amazing; I pictured hippy girls wearing them like jewellery as they made their way to the beach.

As I started work refining my third idea, I became aware the woman next to me was peering over my shoulder.

'They're amazing,' she said. 'Did you think of them just now?'

'Er, yes. I'm a bookbinder really but I've got some leather I can't use so I thought I'd turn them into things I could sell, now the summer season is kicking off.' I was amazed how comfortable I was chatting about my work to this random woman on the train. It shook me to appreciate how disfiguring Alex's presence in my life had been; he'd forced me to put up a protective guard that had woven into my skin making it hard and scaled. Joy lit up my heart at the thought of what could grow in me now with that shell peeled away.

The woman leaned over and traced the curls and fronds of my belt design. 'I love this,' she said. 'What colours were you thinking?'

We chatted until the next stop when she got off, but not before insisting I give her my card so she could order one of my new belts.

'Have you a website?'

'No. But I'll get one up and running soon,' I said. 'Thank you, by the way. For being so nice about my pieces.'

'It was a pleasure. You're very talented.'

I grinned at her through the window as she stood on the platform and waved goodbye. The sunshine was dazzling, and I turned back to my final design.

As I sketched, I made calculations. All three designs could be made quickly. I'd use up the shredded leather I had left. The sun soaring high in the sky reminded me winter was over, before too long tourists would be flooding the beaches, lots of young people looking for fun and keen to salve their consciences by supporting local artists.

I'd add the label 'artisan', it was true after all. I could set up a stall on the main route down to the beach when the sun was out. I'd save up every penny and it wouldn't be too long before I could go back to the work I was doing for the hotel. Hope blossomed.

I couldn't wait to arrive, I leaned forward as we reached the outskirts of the city as if it would make the train go faster. The sketches looked complex, but they would be easy to make. I flexed the ache away from my fingers and leafed through the first pages of my sketch pad, stopping when I saw a little drawing I'd done of Will.

It had been the evening of our first date, the one when he'd taken me on his bike out along the coast. A day filled with sunshine and wind and a sort of wild elation, the possibility I could find something with Will, something I'd given up on ever feeling. The thought of seeing him again made me giddy.

The last ten minutes of the journey seemed to take forever. Way before we arrived, I gathered up my things and stood by the door, urging the train on. I joined the flood of commuters as they left the station and wondered what to do next.

My first instinct was to walk to Will's house. I wanted to tell him what happened, show him my designs, talk to him about my plans…

But I couldn't. I was a mess. My clothes were a state and I wanted to be beautiful for him, in my most flattering outfit with clean teeth and washed hair. I rubbed the bleached bristles. Perhaps it was time to let it grow out? Go back to my original colour. What would Will think of it?

I walked fast, happy to be back. I smiled at passers-by and they smiled back, the sunshine making friends of us all. It felt like I'd been away a decade and I had to reforge ties with old friends. I'd get my phone on charge, then take a shower and find some fresh clothes. Madame Betty had given me enough food to last a few days, so I didn't have to go shopping straightaway. My steps sped up as I reached the top of my street. I almost danced down it, so desperate to get started on the next stage of my life.

Something dark ran into the corner of my vision. A jogger on the other side of the road paused to fiddle with his AirPods. I hefted my rucksack back onto my shoulder thinking I'd buy some new trainers when the money came in. I'd take Will with me - we could run along the cliff path.

There was my door. Where had I put my keys? I stepped back as I heard the jogger approach, getting out of his way while I searched my coat pockets. A shadow fell across me, and I looked up.

'Hello, Lizzie.'

CHAPTER 23: AMBER

Alex and Amber looked at each other in shock. The house rang with the echoes of the violent scene of a few moments before.

'What the hell just happened?' Amber breathed. 'They've arrested him for murder? I don't understand. And who's Sarah Andrews?' Her stomach lurched. 'Oh my God, that's who that woman was talking about! She said she was going to find Sarah. I thought she was talking about you!'

Alex looked up. 'What are you talking about?'

Amber lowered herself to the stairs, grasping hold of the bannister. Her shoulders dropped as relief drained the tension from her body. 'That woman, Liz. I thought she was warning me about *you*. I didn't know Curly's name was Alex as well. She must have got mixed up – I *knew* there was something off about what she was saying.' She frowned, trying to remember what Liz had said. 'But wait, you said you went out with Sarah.'

'She went out with him just after me…' Alex said quickly. Realisation was dawning on his face. 'Jesus Christ, Amber, what are you on about? Did you think I had something to do with these missing girls?'

'No of course not!' she stood up. 'It was just I couldn't stop thinking about what happened in Brighton and with Brianna disappearing…'

He looked at her, open-mouthed. 'I don't believe this.'

'I'm sorry, but…'

'I've opened myself up to you in a way I haven't opened up to anyone in my LIFE and you think I'm a killer?'

Tears sprung to Amber's eyes. 'I know, it was stupid of me, I…'

His face crumpled. He raked his hands through his hair looking so desperate and haunted Amber's heart broke for him. 'My best mate has been arrested and my wife thinks I'm capable of the most horrible… the most awful… Oh, God. I feel sick.' Instinctively, Amber rushed to him, wrapping her arms tight around his body.

He stood rigid for a moment before collapsing onto her. 'I don't understand… I don't know what's happening. How could they accuse Curly? It doesn't make sense!' He gripped Amber so tight she could barely breathe. She held on, rubbing his back, pressing love and reassurance into his skin.

Alex pushed Amber away and rubbed his face, sniffing hard. 'We've got to do something,' he said. 'I should go down there. I need to get him a lawyer.'

'There's no point now,' Amber said. 'It's getting late. Why do you think they've arrested him? What possible reason can they think he did it?'

Alex's face swelled and anger flooded his skin dark red. 'It's that *bitch* Lizzie,' he said. 'She's set him up, got the police involved. She's trying to destroy us.'

His phone rang and he walked into the kitchen to answer it, keeping his back to Amber. 'Curly! Are you OK? What's happening?'

The call seemed to take forever. Amber tried to work out what was happening, but Alex's responses were monosyllabic. At last he hung up and stood for a moment staring at his phone screen.

'What's going on?'

'He's under arrest but they haven't charged him yet. He thinks the police will come and search the house tomorrow. He wants me to sort out a lawyer. Fuck!' Amber jumped as he smashed his fist into the wall.

'I'm sure it'll be fine,' she gabbled. 'There must have been some mistake.' But as she said the words Amber thought of Brianna, and poor Katie, her body thrown into the bushes only a few hundred yards from the house. Had Curly done something to them as well as Sarah?

The rest of the evening passed in a tense silence. Alex barely spoke through dinner and afterwards spent hours on the phone asking friends to recommend a lawyer for Curly. Amber, exhausted, went to bed but Alex didn't follow her for another hour. Side by side they lay, not speaking. Amber had no words to comfort him.

She fell into a fitful sleep, but Alex kept tossing and turning until eventually he threw back the covers and got out of bed.

'What is it?'

'I can't sleep. I'm going downstairs.'

'Do you want me to come with you?'

'No! You stay here, I'm fine.'

Amber sighed. She was just dozing off when she heard a sliding, scraping sound. She propped herself up on her elbow and tilted her head to listen. The house fell silent again. A shiver cooled her skin, but she rubbed it away and pulled the covers over her head.

When she woke up, the bed was empty and cold. Alex was in the kitchen, gnawing at his nails as he stared out of the window across the garden.

'Are you going into work?'

'Don't be fucking stupid.' He didn't turn round.

'Do you want anything to eat? A cup of tea?'

'No. I'm going out.'

'Where are you going?'

'Just out.'

Two days passed. Alex went out both mornings but refused to tell Amber where he was going. They had heard nothing more from Curly. The police had arrived and asked to be shown to his room. Amber watched as they walked out with his laptop and saw they had found his drugs and cash. She kicked herself for not thinking to go in and get rid of it, now he'd look even more guilty.

She was worried about Alex. She'd never seen him like this. He'd completely withdrawn from her and wouldn't talk about it. He was devastated by what had happened to Curly. Amber knew how close they were and how much the friendship had meant to Alex, but the news of Curly's arrest seemed to have destroyed him. He couldn't sit still, kept jumping up and pacing back and forth.

On the third day Alex walked in, his face carved from stone.

'They've charged him.'

'What!' Amber.

'For Sarah's murder… and Brianna's. Brighton police found her body last night.'

'I don't believe it. Oh, God, how awful.'

'The lawyer's trying to get him home on bail, but Christ knows what will happen. I don't know how it works if you've been charged with murder. Fuck!' He rubbed his face and ran his hands through his hair. 'I can't believe I'm even saying the words.'

'Do you…' Amber paused. 'Do you think he did it?'

Alex shrugged, his face wreathed with distress. 'I don't know. He's done some bad stuff but nothing like this. I can't believe he's even capable of…' He buried his head in his hands. Amber hugged him, pity for Curly mixed with terrible, terrible relief it wasn't Alex who had harmed those women.

'I've got to go,' he said at last. 'Curly's family don't know, I'm going to have to tell them what's happened. Curly didn't want them finding out through the police, he's asked me to see them.'

'Oh God, Alex. Do you have to do it?'

'There's nobody else who is as close to Curly as I am. His Mum and Dad know me, I'm the one who should tell them.'

'You're a good friend.'

'Yeah, maybe. But I'm not sure I knew him at all. Not if he did this.' He stood for a moment, his expression grave. 'I'll phone them now.'

Amber was making tea when Alex came in with his gym bag looped over his shoulder.

'How did it go?'

'I didn't tell them why I was coming to see them. I just said I was working nearby and thought I'd pop in. They live bloody miles away, so I'll stay overnight. I should be back tomorrow afternoon. Oh, and here's your phone. I found it when I emptied my gym bag to pack my stuff. It must have fallen in. Sorry, babe. At least I can call you now, let you know how I'm getting on. Phone me if you hear anything at all from Curly.'

'I will do. Oh, Alex. I'm so sorry about all of this.'

Alex gave a heavy sigh. 'Thanks... Look, I'm sorry if I've been a dick these last few days...'

She hugged him. 'Don't be silly. I can't imagine what you're going through.'

'I'll see you soon, OK?'

*

Amber walked aimlessly about the house, phone in hand. The local news had been full of Curly's arrest. It was reported a 'number of avenues' were being explored, which she took to mean that they thought he was responsible for the other missing women. She sighed; it didn't look like he would make bail.

Her phone took forever to charge. Sitting on the bed she watched the messages and voicemails ping in so quickly the phone almost vibrated off the locker. She couldn't face reading all the texts just yet, she'd wait until this was all over. There was no email from Paul about her wages, just a load of junk mail and the photo she'd sent herself from Curly's laptop. She saved it to her camera roll and then tapped to open it up so she could zoom in on Curly's face.

Amber stared at it for a long time. All those months they've lived in the same house and she had no idea what he was capable of. She jumped when the phone rang, replacing Curly's face with a photo of her and Alex together on their wedding day.

'Alex?'

'Just checking in to say I got here safely.'

'Good. How are they taking it?'

'I haven't told them yet. I'll let you know when I'm on my way home tomorrow.'

'OK. Love you.'

'Love you too.'

She put the phone down and stared into space. It was no good, she couldn't stop thinking about that shelf in the bathroom cabinet. It must have been Curly who'd screwed it up. She had to know.

Alex kept all the tools in the van, but there were a few bit and pieces littered round the house depending on where they were working. They'd spent the last few days laying floorboards in the attic rooms. Climbing up the top flight of stairs, Amber tried to remember the last time she had been up there. It must have been ages. When she last looked it had been crammed to the roof with old furniture and junk but that was now cleared.

Astonished, Amber turned slowly, taking it all in. The walls that had separated the top floor into four little rooms had been knocked down and now a huge space, like a penthouse, greeted her eyes. She imagined light flooding in through the big windows cut into the roof; the views across the common would be stunning. The new floorboards were nearly done; they were a beautiful, dark stained oak. It must have cost a fortune. Where was all the money coming from? Had Alex taken out a loan based on the value of the house? If he had, he hadn't told her.

She found a hammer and chisel and carried them down to the bathroom. In the mirror she was struck by her determined expression. Opening the cabinet, she removed the shampoo bottle and wedged the end of the chisel behind the shelf.

One blow from her hammer was all it took. The shelf splintered forward, and she tugged it out, dropping it on the floor, eager to see what lay behind it.

She needed more room. Growing impatient Amber used the chisel to prise the whole cabinet from the wall. She caught it in her arms before it fell and put it in the bath. She could now see the wall behind it, into which had been cut a neat, rectangular hole. Adrenalin began to surge into her blood. Clicking on her phone torch she held it in one hand and reached into the hole with the other.

A brick stood proud at the back of the space and along it were seven tiny glass bottles stoppered with a plastic cap. Underneath, a heap of objects. Stretching, she picked up a bottle and held it in her hands. Nothing identified it, but it was obvious what she had found. Was this what Curly used on his victims? Did he give it to Emma? Maybe she hadn't been lying about what happened that night. Amber felt like clouds were breaking away and disappearing in her head. If Curly had drugged Emma... then Alex... She shook her head. She couldn't think about that for the moment.

Amber put the glass bottle aside and reached for the jumble of objects wedged into the bottom of the space. She pulled them out and began to sort through them in the sink. Her stomach churned. A silk scarf, cheap looking necklaces knotted together into a tangle, a jewelled hair band and a tube of lipstick.

'Oh, Christ,' she muttered, swallowing hard to stop from retching. Were these trophies? From the victims?

Amber sat down with a thump on the edge of the bath, gripped with a compulsion to wash her hands. Should she put them back where she found them? Call the police? This was conclusive evidence connecting Curly to the murdered women, she was sure.

She tried calling Alex but there was no reply. Sending a text instead, she put her phone in her pocket and gathered up the stuff in the sink, pushing it back into the hole. She couldn't face looking at it and left the bathroom, closing the door shut tight behind her.

Amber sat on the bed, her eyes dry and a sense of great sadness hanging deep in her chest. Out of the window she could see the stretch of darkness that was the common, and her heart wrenched at the thought of Katie's body being bundled beneath the trees. The thought of that larky girl strangled and left for dead tore Amber apart.

Alone in the house with the drugs and trophies Curly had collected a few rooms away, when Amber finally fell asleep her dreams were filled with horrors. As soon as she woke up, she searched for the number of the police station, but just before she dialled Alex called.

'Oh, Alex. I'm so glad you called, I tried you over and over again last night, but you must have had your phone off. I found some terrible things Curly left in the bathroom and…'

'Where in the bathroom?' Alex's voice was sharp.

'Behind the cabinet, there was a space cut out behind it and I found some little bottles and some things…' she burst into tears. 'I think they are things he took from the women he killed,' Sobs tore into her sentences. 'I was just about to call the police so they can check for fingerprints or…'

'No. Don't. Let me deal with it, I'll talk to them. We need to tell them in the right way, the last thing I want to do is jeopardise Curly coming out on bail.'

'Oh… Well, if you think that's the best thing to do.'

'Of course it is. Trust me, Amber. I know it's awful. Just stay out of the bathroom, leave it how it is. Now look, babe, I need you to do something for me. Dom's just called, he's got a risk assessment form I've got to sign before he goes away, and I'm stuck in fucking awful traffic. I won't get back before he clocks off. Could you go and get it for me? I'll give you the address, it's not far from Chalk Farm underground.'

'That's miles away! It'll take me all morning.'

'Yeah, I know, sorry, but Dom's insisting – I can't look after the site while he's away without it.'

'All right Any news from Curly?'

'No, not yet. Got to go. See you later.'

*

It was a shock to see Curly's name on the front pages being read by passengers on the tube. Amber felt sick to see his face looming out at her and she fixed her eyes on the map above instead.

She checked the address Alex had given her, she hoped it wouldn't take too long to get to Dom's road from the station. The journey reminded her of the trip to Brighton and a lump pushed into her throat as she remembered how happy she'd been.

The day was mild but overcast as she emerged from the station. Twenty minutes later she was sweating and almost in tears with frustration. The address Alex had given her didn't exist – or she had written the number down wrong. Amber called him repeatedly, but he didn't pick up. He was probably driving still.

There was nothing she could do. Sighing with annoyance she made her way back to the tube and began the long trek home.

Alex was there when she arrived. He looked sullen and preoccupied. A livid scratch ran from his left eye to his jaw.

'Did you get it?' he said, seeing Amber in the doorway.

'No.' She dumped her bag on the sofa and sank down with a sigh. 'I think you gave me the wrong address. I couldn't find his house.'

'Shit, really? Amb I'm so sorry, let me see?'

She handed over the paper. He tutted, 'I'll have to ask Geoff to go over. You must have written it down wrong.'

Amber was about to protest but was too exhausted, there was no point. She couldn't even be bothered to get anything to eat, though she was starving. What a waste of a day. She must have spent five hours on that bloody train. Alex's phone screen lit up as he began to text.

'What have you done to your face?'

'Curly's mum's fucking cat. It was lying on my bed when I woke up and the bastard scratched me when I tried to move it.'

'It looks nasty, you should put some cream on it or something.'

He nodded absently, staring at the screen. He stood up and put his phone in his pocket. 'I've got to go out, Tim's recommended a lawyer and I need to meet with him.'

'What, now? You've only just got back!'

'He's doing me a favour. He's just finished work and will be going home soon. He can give me an hour if I go now.'

'Did you call the police? About the stuff I found?'

'Yeah. They said to leave it and they'd be over soon to collect everything.' He dropped a quick kiss on her forehead and stood to leave.

'Do you want to see them?'

'What?'

'The things in the bathroom.'

He shivered. 'No, I don't. I'm going to be late. I'll see you later. Won't be long.'

She was tired. The newly made bed was inviting, the table lamps casting warm pools of light across the pillows. Amber flopped onto the side of the bed, kicking Alex's gym bag which he'd left on the floor. She picked it up and put it on the bed, unzipping it to find it bulging with clothes. They stank of sweat.

The laundry basket was also full. With a sigh, Amber emptied it out onto the bed and started to sort everything into separate piles. Alex's gym kit went on top, it still felt damp. The black things went in first and Amber slammed the washing machine shut going up wearily for the other two loads, which she dumped on the floor in the kitchen.

Before putting it away she ran her hands around the gym bag to check she hadn't missed anything.

'Ow! she cried. Something sharp had slid under her fingernail and pierced the tender flesh beneath. 'Ooh,' she sucked on the end of her finger while feeling for what had cut her. A photograph. It had slipped under the lining and had caught her with its side giving her a papercut.

Amber pulled it out. For a heart stopping second, she thought it was a photo of Brianna but as she looked more closely she realised it wasn't her. The girl in the picture was much younger, and ten times more beautiful. On the back was one word. 'Lisa'.

Amber sat back on her heels. What did this mean? Who was this girl? Why was Alex hiding it in his bag? She shook her head. Suspicion riddled its way through her like a poison. Hadn't Alex done enough to convince her she could trust him? All that time she thought he had something to do with Brianna going missing and it was Curly all along. She put the photo back where she'd found it. There was nothing more in the bag but when she pulled out her hand, she noticed her finger was bleeding quite badly.

'Shit!' She grabbed some tissues from the box by her head and dabbed it away, wiping a wodge around the gym bag in case she'd bled into it. The tissue came out stained pink, and she reached for another handful and wiped round again until it came away clear. Throwing the pile of tissues in the bin, climbed under the covers fully dressed.

Her phone rang.

'Hi Amber. I'm still with the lawyer. It doesn't look good for Curly.' He sounded bewildered. 'Sarah's body was found in France. The police have said it's been there years. They searched

Curly's computer and found he'd hacked into Sarah's Facebook page and has been messaging her family and friends so they didn't realise she'd gone missing.'

'Jesus!' Amber was struck by a sudden memory of the smiling woman on Curly's laptop when she'd first used it. Was that Sarah? 'I can't believe it.'

'You and me both,' Alex sounded very young and Amber felt a surge of pity.

'Have you been able to visit him?'

'No, not a chance. We're trying to get bail so we can get him home. The lawyer's made an appointment to see Curly tomorrow. Until then he's advised that Curly doesn't say anything.'

'Alex...' Amber took a deep breath. She had to ask. 'What happened when you went to the police about Brianna? You know, after we saw it on the news? It's just...' The words burst out of her in a rush. '...I saw an article in the paper and they were asking for two men to come forwards and they looked like you and Curly, but I didn't understand why they were still asking when you'd already gone in.' There was a long pause. 'Alex?' She could hear him breathing.

'Shit,' he said softly.

'What?'

'I fucking trusted him.'

'What do you mean?'

'We went to the police, I promise you, Amber. But I let him go in first and when he came out, he told me I wasn't needed. That the police had said his statement was enough.'

'But he didn't talk to them.'

'No. I waited outside, he must have just gone in, hung about a bit, and come back out again. Fuck!' Amber winced as Alex's voice rose.

'What about the timing? You said she'd been seen in Brighton after we left, but I don't think that was right.'

'Yes, it was!' Alex said in surprise. 'She was last seen at 3.30 in the morning. I was back at the hotel with you before then. I don't know about Curly, though.' There was a muffled scratching noise as Alex put his hand over the mouthpiece. 'OK! Hang on.' His voice came back clear. 'I'm not sure when I'll be back.'

'OK but don't be too long. I don't like being on my own in the house.'

As she hung up, she tried to order her thoughts. Something was bothering her, but she couldn't grab it. The shock of what was happening was stopping her thinking clearly – it was all so surreal. She thought of all the work Alex and Curly had done on the house, hours they'd spent despite working full time. When had he murdered those women? He must have lied about staying with girlfriends, she decided. The house was nearly finished, only the kitchen and front sitting room to sort out. The proposed sales figure revolved around Amber's head again. Five million! It didn't seem possible.

Amber resolved to talk to Alex about the estate agent brochures as soon as she saw him again. He needed to be honest with her about his plans, why didn't he tell her he'd had agents in to do a valuation? She looked at her phone, with a few clicks she updated Alex's contact photo with the one she'd found on Curly's Facebook. Now she'd see it every time he called. She traced his open, laughing face; she needed to find her way back to this man – let go of the wall of suspicion she'd allowed to grow between them. She had to be there for him while his best friend was being tried. Whatever happened, he was her husband and he deserved her loyalty.

It wasn't late but Amber's eyelids were heavy and too many thoughts had crowded into her head and she couldn't find a clear path through them. Better to sleep on it.

*

A hammering on the door woke Amber up with a jerk, her mouth dry and heart beating fast. Totally disorientated, she reached for a phone. Only 45 minutes had passed since Alex had called; she must have fallen into a very deep sleep.

She staggered as she ran to the top of the stairs and clung to the bannister to stop from falling. Was it Alex? Why didn't he use his key? The house was in darkness, he wasn't back yet.

Her bare feet were cold on the tiles as she reached the door and she wished she'd brought her phone down with her. She stopped and stood in the darkness, listening hard. What if it was Curly? A great shudder of fear prickled her skin into goosebumps. She'd never been frightened of Curly, but what she'd discovered over the past few days had filled her with a creeping horror. The thought of letting him into the dark house while she was on her own was unbearable.

The door hammered again. It couldn't be Curly. He had a key. Amber flapped her hands with indecision. Another knock made up her mind. They weren't going away. She'd have to answer it.

Keeping the chain attached, she snapped on the porch light and opened the door. A tall, unshaven man with his hair in a ponytail was standing on the path surveying her with the brightest blue eyes Amber had ever seen.

CHAPTER 24: AMBER

'Who are you?' Amber asked, making sure the chain on the door was secure.

'My name's Will Dixon.' Seeing Amber's anxiety, he took another step away from the door. 'I'm so sorry to be knocking on your door so late but I…' he rubbed his jaw, 'I don't know what else to do.'

Amber studied him. In his faded jeans and pale blue chambray shirt he couldn't have looked less threatening. But muscles twisted in his forearms and his hands looked strong.

'I'm looking for Liz,' he said, his eyes steady on Amber's face.

'Liz?'

'Slim woman in her 30's, very short bleached hair…'

Amber nodded impatiently. 'Yes, I know who you mean. I haven't seen her – why do you think she's here?'

Will picked up a messenger bag and opened the flap. 'She left me this,' he said, his voice calm and slow; Amber found herself warming to him, there was something about him she trusted. 'It's where I found your address.'

'Her research! Into those women who disappeared. She gave me the same envelope.'

'To warn you against your husband.'

'Yes, but she got it wrong. It wasn't my husband that treated her so badly, it was his friend who had the same name… anyway, it doesn't matter. Why are you here?'

'I've read through all of this.' Will held up the envelope. 'Liz left it for me before she disappeared. I promised her if she didn't come back, I'd come find her.'

He was in love with Liz, Amber realised. That strange, intense, paranoid woman had inspired love in this man. She softened and took the chain from the door.

'I can't let you in,' she apologised. 'My husband wouldn't be impressed if I let a strange man into the house.'

'That's fine,' Will said with a slow smile. 'I promise I'm harmless.' His face fell back into seams of worry. 'Can you tell me what happened when she came to see you?'

'She told me she was going to find her friend, Sarah.' Realisation was beginning to dawn. 'That's what must have happened! Sarah's body was found, in France. She'd been dead for years apparently. They found evidence linking her murder to Curly, my husband's best friend, and he was arrested last night. He's also been charged with the disappearance of a woman in Brighton.'

Will's face grew still as he concentrated, his eyes intent. 'When did this happen?'

'She could only have been found a few days ago. Maybe Liz is still in France?'

Amber turned at the sound of faint banging.

'What's that?'

'Oh, nothing, it's the washing machine, I think. I put it on a while ago.'

'Well, thank you for your help. I didn't realise she'd left the country.'

Amber shrugged. 'Sorry I couldn't help more. You must be very worried.'

'I hope it's something stupid like she's lost her phone,' Will smiled. 'I'm sure she's fine. And you have been very helpful, I had no idea she'd gone to France. I'll call around and see what I can find out. I've already been to the police, but she's not been gone long enough for them to report her as a missing person.'

'Can I give you my number? I really want to know Liz is OK.'

'Please, it would be good to stay in touch.' He typed the numbers into his phone then dialled it; Amber heard it ring from the bedroom. 'Now you've got mine. I'll stay in touch, OK?'

'Thank you. I hope you hear something soon.'

He turned to walk away, and Amber was just shutting the door when he called out.

'Is this the guy they've arrested?' He was holding out a polaroid. Amber took it and recognised Liz as a younger woman. It must have been taken around the time of the photo Liz had shown

Amber the day she visited the crematorium; she was wearing the same green dress. But this time there was a man standing with her, his arm around her shoulders. 'Is that him?' Will said. 'It was right at the bottom of her pack of notes, I nearly missed it as it had stuck to the back of the map. I assumed it was her ex, the bastard who nearly killed her. Hey! Are you all right?'

Amber had gone deathly white, the polaroid fluttered to the floor and she touched her forehead with a shaking hand.

Will held Amber as her knees gave way, supporting her into the hall and settling her on the floor. 'What is it? Do you want water?'

'Where's the picture?' she said, her lips pale and dry.

'Here, it fell.' Will reached for it, holding Amber up at the same time. He passed it back to her. 'Is it him? What did you say his name was, Curly?'

But Amber was shaking her head, staring with such horror at the polaroid it made Will's skin creep.

'No.'

'Then who is it?'

'My husband.'

*

Will immediately tried to take control. 'You need to get out of here,' he said, pulling Amber to her feet. 'We need to go to the police. Right now.'

Amber, still knocked sideways with shock, shook her head. 'I can't, I've got to get my stuff, my phone…'

'No… sorry, I don't know your name.'

'Amber.'

'Amber, we really have to go.'

She didn't know what to do. This man was a stranger. Liz hadn't got the wrong man, she meant Alex. Her Alex. A tickertape of facts chattered through her head. Every detail Liz had told her. He wasn't fostered, he had a family somewhere. He was obsessed with women who looked like his first love. An obsession that led him to kill. He hadn't come back to bed in Brighton before Brianna had last been seen. He'd got back after it was light.

'Come with me, Amber. Please. We need to go to the police.'

Amber looked up at him, frowning. She spoke slowly as she tried to think things through. 'The police said they'd found stuff on Curly's computer. Curly had kept up messaging Sarah's family so they'd think she was still alive.'

'Doesn't mean he killed her.'

'No. That's true. He must have been covering for Alex. Look, Will, I'm sorry but I can't leave right now. I will, as soon as I've got my bag and things I'll go straightaway and spend the night with my friend. You go, find out what you can about Liz and text me, OK?'

Will wasn't happy. 'I don't want to leave you here on your own.'

'I'll be fine, I promise. You go.' She pushed the door shut and rested against it. She had to move quickly. Alex could be back any minute. She ran up the stairs past the bathroom, head reeling in horror at the realisation it was Alex who'd left those bottles and trophies behind the cupboard. She swallowed hard to stop herself from throwing up. Running into the bedroom, she grabbed her phone and charger. The screen flashed six notifications - texts from

Alex. Forcing herself to stay calm, she opened her phone to read them.

'Hi babe. Curly's out on bail!'

'You there?'

'Did you get my message? Bail set - a fucking fortune. His parents are paying.'

'?'

'??'

'I'm going to drive him up to his parents' house now. I'll be back in the morning xxx'

Amber took a shaky sigh. It gave her some breathing room and time to pack properly. She sent a text to Will passing that on, and reminded him to send an update as soon as he had one.

Her suitcase was still under the bed. Amber filled it with clothes and toiletries and packed her Mum's jewellery case at the bottom. There was no way she was leaving those precious pieces behind. They weren't worth much, but they meant everything.

At first, she thought it was her heart banging in her ears she could hear as she hurried towards the stairs. She stopped. Every nerve in her body stretched to snapping point. She was used to the noises of the house, the regular rattling of the pipes, but this was different. It was a regular, determined pounding.

The temptation to walk straight out of the front door was overwhelming, but Amber continued down the stairs and opened the door to the basement. The noise grew louder. Amber put her phone in her pocket and left her suitcase by the door.

She was so frightened it was almost an anti-climax when she reached the cellar and turned on the light. Everything was as she had left it a few days before. The papers on the desk were as she remembered, and the weights hadn't been touched.

Stepping lightly across the floorboards, Amber listened with every ounce of energy she had. She couldn't hear anything. Then a thud made the plaster shake. And another. She whipped her head round. It was coming from the area where the weights lay.

'Hello?' she called. Another thud, stronger this time. Amber put her hand on the wall, she could feel a distant vibration. Someone was there, trapped in a space built in behind the walls. The banging was becoming more desperate. Stress sent adrenalin pumping through Amber's veins.

Frantically, she felt for a seam or handle in the walls but there was nothing. There must be a door! Amber tore at her hair, this was hopeless. Sweat stung her eyes, she had to do something soon, she had to get out of the house in case Alex came back.

The weights. With a grunt Amber picked up the heaviest and pressed her palm against the wall again to work out exactly where the thudding was coming from. She didn't want to hurt whoever was behind there.

With a shout she hurled the weight at the wall, just to the left of where she judged the person to be trapped.

The weight smashed through the plaster exposing the wood and brick behind it but there was no space. She picked it up again, arms and shoulders screaming with the heaviness of the dumbbell and threw it a foot to the right. This time the weight disappeared into darkness and the air breathed a stench that made Amber gag.

A partition had been built, five feet away from the original cellar wall. Now she could see a space, as big as a room, had been created, accessed by a crawl space that led round under the stairs. With a strength she didn't know she had, Amber began smashing the wall all the way along to the corner. It was too dark for her to see anything, so she dropped the weight with a crash and turned on her phone light and stepped into the shadows, holding her shirt over her face.

What she saw made her retch. Metal rings and chains were screwed into the wall and glinted as she shone her light on them. Thick, soundproof insulation puffed out of the holes Amber had made, no wonder she hadn't heard anything.

She wanted to cry. How many women had he kept here? Scattered along the floor were scraps of cloth and dark stains. Two buckets pushed up against the wall were the source of the fetid stink. Shock glued her to the spot, any strength she had bled away into the ground. Sobbing, she ran the torch into the far corner.

Staring back at her, eyes glaring in the light, hands cuffed high behind her, lay Liz. A filthy wad of material had been shoved in her mouth. Dressed only in a shirt and pants her legs were covered in blood. Amber could see she'd been lifting her legs up and swinging them over and over again to smash into the wooden wall next to her. The insulation between that and the stud wall had muffled most of the sound, but such was Liz's strength she'd made enough noise for Amber to hear.

Gasping with horror, she stumbled over to where she lay and tried to pull at the chains that held her. They were fixed fast. Amber pulled the gag from Liz's mouth.

'The weights!' she croaked.

Amber ran back to the biggest dumbbell and used it as a hammer to break the links of the chains. The noise was incredible as she hit them repeatedly. Liz twisted beneath her, trying to wrench her hands free.

Amber's head was filled with nothing but the weight of the dumbbell, the thickness of the chains and the sound of the metal crashing together. Mindlessly she carried on until at last one of the links broke and fell away. In a flash Liz had pulled her hand free and she stood, taking the weight from Amber and working on the ring holding the other manacle.

At last, it detached from the wall and Liz and Amber fell together into the basement room. Liz recovered first and was on her feet grabbing Amber's hands to get her to stand.

'We need to get out,' she said, spitting dust onto the floor. She was filthy, and bruises were bloody and black all over her skin.

'Can you walk?' Amber offered her arm, worried about Liz's bleeding legs, one knee was terribly swollen.

Liz pushed it away. 'I'm fine. Come on.' She staggered and then righted herself. 'Where's the way out?' She rubbed her eyes and blinked, fierce as a mountain cat.

'This way,' Amber said, but as they approached the stairs, they stopped. Footsteps paced overhead. Immediately Liz snapped off the light and they stood in the darkness, looking up at the ceiling.

Barely breathing, Amber slid her phone from her pocket and turned off the sound. Notifications of missed calls and twenty texts appeared. Eyes wide, she read Alex's messages.

'Where are you?'

'Curly's dead'

'He took my car and drove away.'

'I couldn't stop him!'

'He was going crazy when I picked him up saying he couldn't go to jail and he couldn't face his parents.'

'He drove to a motorway bridge and jumped.'

'I'm coming home. I need you.'

Amber held up the phone and watched Liz read them. She shook her head. They jumped as the phone buzzed, Alex calling from upstairs. Amber shoved the phone into her armpit, terrified Alex would notice the vibrations.

In silence they looked up, following Alex's footsteps as he walked towards the kitchen.

In a voice that was barely a breath, Liz leaned into Amber. 'Where's the front door? How do we get out?'

'We can't go up!' Amber's eyes were wide with terror. 'He'll kill us.'

'He will come down here eventually,' whispered Liz. 'And there's no escape. We have to try. We'll wait until he moves and then we'll make a run for it.'

Mute, Amber shook her head, but Liz was resolute. Holding onto Amber's arm she took a step up the first few stairs, listening hard.

'Amber!' came the muffled shout from above. Fear liquefied her muscles and she couldn't move.

'He's moving upstairs,' Liz hissed. 'We need to go *now*!'

She grabbed a whimpering Amber and pulled her up the basement stairs. At the door she rested her ear close and gave a satisfied nod.

'He's upstairs. Now GO!'

She pushed Amber into the hall in front of her and followed her out. In their haste they didn't see Amber's suitcase and Liz's foot caught it and sent it skidding with a crash into the sitting room door.

'Amber?'

'RUN!' screamed Liz, and with shaking, clumsy hands, Amber tore at the door, sobbing at the thought it was locked, wasting precious seconds fiddling with the bolt before managing to get it open.

She cried out in terror as she heard Alex behind her thundering down the stairs. But Liz was already running, holding tight to Amber's hand. Without looking left or right, they tore across the road and into the darkness of the common beyond.

Amber could hear nothing beyond the panting of her breath and the thudding of feet. Liz swerved, heading for the undergrowth.

'Amber!' They heard a roar behind them. He was getting closer.

'Come on!' Liz called as Amber began to slow, her leg muscles burning.

Panting with terror, Amber cried out a warning as she saw a darkness flitting through the trees. He'd gone round and cut them off and was coming straight for them. She shrieked and dodged to the right, knocking against Liz who catapulted over a root and flew into the air, landing with a crash that knocked the air out of her lungs.

Amber ran to help her up but what felt like a wall knocked her aside and she skidded in the mud and fell, banging her hip hard against a rock.

She screamed to see Alex fall on Liz like an animal, his hands at her throat.

'You fucking bitch!' he snarled. 'You couldn't leave it alone. What have you done?' Amber heard Liz choking, frantically trying to peel Alex's hands away from her neck.

'No! Alex! Stop it!' A rushing sound filled Amber's ears and she jumped on Alex's back, trying to use her weight to get him off her.

It was no use. She might as well have been a fly, he twitched her off without effort. Liz stopped struggling and Amber moaned to see her lying, limp, in the muddy undergrowth. This is where Katie was found, she realised, appalled. He must have brought her here.

She took a step back as Alex stood and walked towards her, his step measured. He wiped his mouth, never taking his eyes from her.

'Amber,' he said. She backed away until a tree banged into her and within seconds, he had grabbed her by the collar. 'Little Amber. Little innocent Amber. What am I going to do with you?' She flinched as his spittle landed on her face. 'That bitch has messed everything up but luckily Curly took the fall. Stupid fucker, it never bothered him when I used his name. He had no idea what I was up to.'

'What happened to Curly?' Amber tried to keep her voice steady but the sound of Alex's voice and the madness in his eyes turned her bowels to water.

'He's dead. Jumped from a motorway bridge. Couldn't face jail or his mother knowing he was a serial killer.' He jerked Amber forward and whispered in her ear. 'A real tragedy. How will his poor old best mate cope without him? It was a hell of a struggle getting him over the side, fat bastard.'

'You killed him.' Amber searched his face but there was nothing there. Dead as a shark's eye.

'And what shall we do with you, my beauty? Don't think suicide is going to work this time, I'm going to have to be careful. Nothing like a good, old-fashioned accident.' With phenomenal strength he pushed her, one handed, down to the bed of leaves at the bottom of the tree. With the other he searched about picking up and discarding stones. 'A nice, clean broken neck,' he muttered. 'I could say you fell down the stair…'

Suddenly, as miraculous as a divine star, Amber saw Liz rearing up from the ground. In the moonlight Amber could see her body rippled with muscle, her face beautiful and cold as a Greek statue. In silence she dropped to her knees and searched the undergrowth. Amber daren't look at her in case it alerted Alex. She struggled again and Alex pressed harder until she lay still. Liz reappeared, carrying something which she weighed from one hand to the other.

With absolute grace, Liz lifted what looked like a giant club, took a moment to settle her balance, and swung with a movement filled with strength and beauty. Time slowed as Amber watched Alex stiffen. He started to stand up, releasing the terrible pressure on Amber's chest. Liz continued the long lovely curve of her swing and smashed the club into Alex's jaw. His head snapped back with a crunch and he threw his arms up in front of him. Without pausing, Liz gave a fierce cry and swung again. The impact knocked Alex over and he fell forward, face down in the earth and lay still.

CHAPTER 25: TWO MONTHS LATER

Amber smiled as Liz approached, the sea breeze ruffling her crimson skirt and tugging at her newly red hair. Behind her, Will waved and pointed at the bar. Amber nodded and got up to hug her new friend.

'God, it's gorgeous down here!' she said, looking out to the sea that danced and glittered in the late summer sun.

'I can't believe you haven't come earlier, it's not like I haven't asked.' Liz laughed. Her smile was wide, and her green eyes shone.

'You didn't have an exhibition on before now. Besides, I've been busy.'

'Ah, yes, The house sale.' Liz flopped into her seat. 'How's it going?'

'You're not going to believe it.'

'Five mil?'

'Six.'

'Fuck me, you're joking.' She looked at Amber in astonishment.

'I know, I can't get my head around it.'

'Especially considering it's been called the murder mansion for the past few months.'

Amber sighed. 'I think that's added value to it, to be honest. People are such awful ghouls.'

'So, what's next?' Liz leaned forward, her arms tanned and strong. Amber tried to reconcile this glowing, vivid woman with the wraith who had pounded on her door screaming impossible things. It felt like a century ago.

'I don't know. Nothing just yet. I'm only just getting over the dreams.'

Liz pushed her hair out of her eyes and turned her face to the sea. 'Me too.' She glanced back at Amber, her eyes soft with understanding. 'They will go, Amber, eventually. I've gone back to Jenny and she's been a real help.'

'It looks like he's been a help too,' Amber said grinning at Will as he waited to be served at the bar.

'He saved my life,' Liz said. 'I knew he was the man for me when he spent a month tracking down a very important book for me. I had to sell it as I was so broke, and he got it back. He gave it to me last night.' She smiled over at Will who was leaning on the bar looking out to the sea. Amber watched the strength of their connection. Liz grew more beautiful every day. A few months of eating properly, growing out her hair and time spent with Will had transformed her. Amber couldn't wait to see her exhibition.

The weeks following Alex's death were the worst of Amber's life. Every day brought news of more evidence of the number of women Alex had murdered. She shuddered now to remember their faces splashed across the news, the press interest became so intolerable she'd fled to live with Amahle, and Liz returned to Brighton.

Liz had spent a month selling the new designs she'd planned on her return from France. To her delight, a very well-known Instagram influencer had been spotted wearing one of her belts. Her popularity rocketed. The hotel who had refused to extend the contract changed their minds and Liz was working hard to meet the new deadline.

It had been Will's idea to take Liz's prototypes to an Art Gallery just off The Lanes. He'd thought them so beautiful he was the only one not surprised when they offered an exhibition and encouraged Liz to send them more. Now her sea-glass, calfskin leather bindings, and paper sculptures were on prominent display, catching the light streaming from the gallery's tall windows.

*

Liz and Amber spoke often, but rarely about Alex. They would carry the horror of that memory for the rest of their lives, but both had found the strength to hold it steady until the memories gradually shrunk and disappeared, leaving nothing but a bruise.

The last time they had talked about him was when the local girl, Milly Ryan, had been found. Her body wasn't far from where Katie's was discovered. Amber, living with Amahle while the police searched the house from top to bottom, had called Liz in floods of tears.

'They say she'd been kept in the basement for at least a week. The poor girl.'

'Christ.' Sitting on the sofa in Will's house, Dolly's head warm on her lap, Liz remembered the terror and fear she had felt waking up in that dreadful, stinking darkness of the basement room. She'd thought she was going to die.

Closing her eyes, she allowed the memory to drift into her mind and then let it drift away again as Jenny had taught her. Being with Will, walking the dog, working on her designs in her newly restored shop had brought Liz peace, at last, but there were still some nights when she woke up screaming.

'That's what I kept hearing when the pipes banged. I think it was Milly, trying to get help.'

Liz spoke soothing words, doing all she could to take the sting from Amber's guilt and shame. She would never forgive herself for the role she had played. 'You've got to stop thinking about it,' she said as Amber wept. 'It's over.'

*

Sitting in the sunshine with the chatter of tourists and locals surrounding them, Alex and the house felt a million miles away. A little woozy from the lunchtime wine, Amber waited until Will left to use the loo before turning to Liz.

'I've been meaning to tell you something.'

Liz looked at her, her eyebrows lifted. 'What is it?'

'I should have known, straight away it was Alex, not Curly who was responsible. It was right in front of me the whole time and I didn't see it.' She held up her phone and showed Liz the photo she usually kept hidden on her camera roll. The one she had loved so much of Alex and Curly on the beach. 'This picture, it was taken about a week before Sarah went to France.'

Liz leaned forward to peer at it. 'OK,' she said, puzzled.

'Look at Curly, look how he's holding his arm, he'd broken it. God, I'd heard Alex tell the story often enough. He'd done it challenging some bloke to an arm wrestle when he was drunk. Broke it in three places. There's no way he could have strangled Sarah - he was in a cast for three months. I should have known.'

'It wouldn't have made any difference,' Liz said. 'Not in the long run.'

'I know. But maybe Curly might still be alive if I'd seen it earlier.'

Liz reached across for Amber's hand and a moment of acknowledgement passed between them.

'Are you still going to give it all away? The money from the house?'

Amber nodded. 'I'm just keeping a bit to buy a new flat and put down a deposit on a salon. I've managed to persuade my friend Amahle to join me, I even tracked down my best friend, Emma. We fell out over Alex – turned out she was right all along. Shame I didn't listen to her.' She sighed and paused for a moment before collecting herself. 'It's nothing really special but it's always been my dream to run a salon. It's not too far from Crystal Palace. You'd better come and visit.'

'Of course I will. Do they know? The victim's families?'

'Not yet, I've got a lawyer who will contact them all for me. It's never going to make up for what's happened to them, but I had to do something.'

They sat in silence for a moment.

'I think about Sarah a lot,' Liz said at last, tears brimming.

Amber squeezed her hand. 'If you hadn't gone to look for her more women would have died.'

Wiping her eyes, giving a quick nod, Liz sat back and held up her glass.

'To Sarah.'

Amber touched the glass with her own, letting it chime. 'To Sarah,' she said.

THE END

ABOUT THE AUTHOR

Amanda Larkman was born in a hospital as it was being bombed during a revolution. The rest of her upbringing, in the countryside of Kent, has been relatively peaceful.

She graduated with an English degree and has taught English for over twenty years. *The Woman and the Witch* was her first novel, and it was followed by a collection called *Airy Cages and Other Stories*

Hobbies include trying to find the perfect way to make popcorn, watching her mad labradoodle run like a galloping horse, and reading brilliant novels that make her feel bitter and jealous.

She has a husband and two teenage children, all of whom are far nicer than the characters in her books.

Instagram: @Amanda_Larkman
Twitter: @MiddleageWar
Blog: middleagedwarrior.com
Facebook: Amanda Larkman: Middle Aged Warrior

Lightning Source UK Ltd.
Milton Keynes UK
UKHW021338310321
381313UK00008B/1689

Brandenburg-Prussia, 1466–1806

The Rise of a Composite State

Karin Friedrich

© Karin Friedrich 2012

All rights reserved. No reproduction, copy or transmission of this publication may be made without written permission.

No portion of this publication may be reproduced, copied or transmitted save with written permission or in accordance with the provisions of the Copyright, Designs and Patents Act 1988, or under the terms of any licence permitting limited copying issued by the Copyright Licensing Agency, Saffron House, 6–10 Kirby Street, London EC1N 8TS.

Any person who does any unauthorized act in relation to this publication may be liable to criminal prosecution and civil claims for damages.

The author has asserted her right to be identified as the author of this work in accordance with the Copyright, Designs and Patents Act 1988.

First published 2012 by
PALGRAVE MACMILLAN

Palgrave Macmillan in the UK is an imprint of Macmillan Publishers Limited, registered in England, company number 785998, of Houndmills, Basingstoke, Hampshire RG21 6XS.

Palgrave Macmillan in the US is a division of St Martin's Press LLC, 175 Fifth Avenue, New York, NY 10010.

Palgrave Macmillan is the global academic imprint of the above companies and has companies and representatives throughout the world.

Palgrave® and Macmillan® are registered trademarks in the United States, the United Kingdom, Europe and other countries.

ISBN 978–0–230–53565–7

This book is printed on paper suitable for recycling and made from fully managed and sustained forest sources. Logging, pulping and manufacturing processes are expected to conform to the environmental regulations of the country of origin.

A catalogue record for this book is available from the British Library.

A catalog record for this book is available from the Library of Congress.

10 9 8 7 6 5 4 3 2 1
21 20 19 18 17 16 15 14 13 12

Printed in China

For Robert

Contents

A Note on References	ix
Editors' Preface	x
Acknowledgements	xi
Glossary	xii
Gazetteer of Geographical and Place Names	xvi
Maps	xviii

Introduction		**1**
1	**The Teutonic Legacy**	**7**
	[i] Origins	7
	[ii] A Colonial Society	10
	[iii] The Idea of Prussia and the Development of Representative Bodies	14
	[iv] The Partition of Prussia, 1454–1466	19
2	**'State-building'**	**22**
	[i] Instruments of Integration	24
	[ii] The Military as an Instrument of State-building	30
	[iii] Territorial Integration – Confessional Division?	36
3	**Estate Society and Life in the Rural Economy**	**43**
	[i] Social Structures and Civil Society	43
	[ii] Noble Power in the Composite *Ständestaat*	47
	[iii] *Gutsherrschaft*	57
4	**From Baroque Court to Military Monarchy**	**64**
	[i] Coronation	64
	[ii] The Polycentric Kingdom	68

[iii]	The Court and Eighteenth-century Monarchy	70
[iv]	Military Monarchy and the Cities	73

5 Foreign Policies between East and West — **78**
- [i] Imperial Limitations: Brandenburg-Prussia in the Seventeenth Century — 79
- [ii] The Rise of Prussia in North-east Europe — 83
- [iii] Prussia's Greatest King? — 89

6 Enlightenment and the Public Sphere — **95**
- [i] Pietism, Educators and the Enlightenment — 98
- [ii] Toleration? — 101
- [iii] Law Reform — 108
- [iv] Prussian Enlightenment and the Public Sphere — 110

Conclusion — **114**

Appendix 1: A Selective Genealogy of the Brandenburg and Prussian Hohenzollern Lines, 1415–1797 — 118

Appendix 2: Table of Offices — 120

Select Bibliography — 122

Index — 149

A Note on References

References are cited throughout in brackets according to the numbering in the general bibliography, with page references, where necessary, indicated by a semi-colon after the bibliography number.

Editors' Preface

The Studies in European History series offers a guide to developments in a field of history that has become increasingly specialised with the sheer volume of new research and literature now produced. Each book has three main objectives. The primary purpose is to offer an informed assessment of opinion on a key episode or theme in European history. Second, each title presents a distinct interpretation and conclusions from someone who is closely involved with current debates in the field. Third, it provides students and teachers with a succinct introduction to the topic, with the essential information necessary to understand it and the literature being discussed. Equipped with an annotated bibliography and other aids to study, each book provides an ideal starting point to explore important events and processes that have shaped Europe's history to the present day.

Books in the series introduce students to historical approaches which in some cases are very new and which, in the normal course of things, would take many years to filter down to text-books. By presenting history's cutting edge, we hope that the series will demonstrate some of the excitement that historians, like scientists, feel as they work on the frontiers of their subject. The series also has an important contribution to make in publicising what historians are doing, and making it accessible to students and scholars in this and related disciplines.

JOHN BREUILLY
JULIAN JACKSON
PETER H. WILSON

Acknowledgements

The author would like to thank the Leverhulme Trust, which generously granted a fellowship during the 2000–1 academic year for a more comprehensive history of Prussia, then contracted with another publisher. Different personal and academic circumstances changed the focus of this project and explain its appearance in its current form. Thanks are also due to the University of Aberdeen for granting me a period of research leave to complete it; to the many colleagues who, over the years, encouraged my interest and research in early modern Prussia; to the Herzog August Bibliothek Wolfenbüttel, where much of this book was conceptualised, researched and written; to the Geheime Staatsarchiv Preussischer Kulturbesitz in Berlin-Dahlem and the Staatsbibliotheken in Berlin and Munich. My thanks also go to Sonya Barker, Felicity Noble and Juanita Bullough (Palgrave) for their support during the preparation of the typescript. Last but not least, I want to express gratitude to my family who patiently tolerated and supported my absences and self-imposed isolation to complete this work.

Glossary

Akzise (excise) — Consumption tax, mainly levelled on cities.

allodification — Abolition of the feudal elements of a contract of land appropriation, turning enfeoffed land into private property that could be freely disposed of.

Amt (pl. *Ämter*) — Administrative districts in the countryside, under the control of the General Directory and headed by a salaried official, with tax-collection powers and minor juridical responsibilities.

cameralism — Science of government based on the idea that the prosperity of the people would benefit the state.

cordon sanitaire — Quarantine cordon to prevent the spread of disease.

demesnes — Land under noble tenure, belonging to the manor house.

emphyteutic tenure — Tenure of land by civil contract, subject to payment of fees and other obligations, and granting land perpetually or temporarily on condition that the land is cultivated and protected.

fief — The grant of property (or tenure, office, legal rights, revenue, etc.) in legal possession by a lord to his vassal, in return for homage, usually connected to concrete obligations, e.g. to raise arms, send troops, etc.

Gutsherrschaft — Form of landed economy east of the Elbe where the landowner lives and works on the estate, farming his demesne through the labour service of an unfree peasantry.

Glossary

habeas corpus	Legal protection from being imprisoned or punished without due process.
Imperial Recess	The whole body of decisions passed by the Imperial Diet during one session.
Irenicism	Movement which sought to reconcile doctrinal differences between confessions and maintain religious peace.
ius indigenatus	The right of natives to be appointed to offices in their own province and territory, excluding foreigners.
ius reformandi	The right of political authorities to impose a particular religion on their territories.
Junker	Prussian nobleman, usually living on his estate.
Kanton system	Division of a territory into military recruitment districts from which soldiers were regularly drafted for intermittent service and training.
Komtur	Commander of a Teutonic Knight's castle, ruling over an administrative district.
Komturei	Administrative district commanded by a Komtur, high up in the hierarchy of the state of the Teutonic Knights.
Kreditwerk	Financial and credit administration run by the estates, taken over by the ruler in the second half of the seventeenth century.
Kulm Law	The law the Teutonic Knights used to found cities in Prussia; based on a mixture of Saxon, Flemish and customary law.
Kulturkampf	'Cultural struggle', nineteenth-century Prussian policies of discrimination against the Catholic population.
Landräte	Noble estates in the provincial assembly, nominated by the estates, but increasingly appointed exclusively by the prince.
Landtag	Diet, assembly of the estates of a territory.
margrave (of Brandenburg)	A ruler of a border territory (marches), here the Mark Brandenburg.

Glossary

monarchomachs	Political thinkers who argued that regicide is a justified means to resist tyrants.
Oberrat	Supreme Council of government in Ducal Prussia.
Ostforschung	Research by German scholars of Eastern Europe during the interwar and Nazi period, which propagated the allegedly superior role of German culture and ethnicity in eastern Europe.
Pfundgeld	Custom tolls levelled by the Hanseatic League on the weight of goods from and into Hanseatic ports.
Pruzzen	The native Baltic population of Prussia.
quit rent	Rent paid by peasants leasing land to free them of any obligations connected to the lease.
Reformed church	Calvinist church
Regimentsnottel	The 1542 fundamental law of Ducal Prussia.
Rétablissement	Policy of settlement and reconstruction in East Prussia after the famines of the early eighteenth century.
Sejm	Polish Diet, Polish-Lithuanian Diet after 1569.
Sonderweg	The concept of a 'particular path' of German history leading from absolute rulership, a weak bourgeoisie, and failed revolutions to Hitler's regime.
Stände/Ständestaat	Estates: privileged noble and urban corporate bodies/State of Estates: where these bodies participate in legislation, jurisdiction and government.
Tagfahrten	Assemblies of local urban and noble elites and representatives in Teutonic times, predecessor of the Prussian *Landtag*.
thaler (Reichsthaler)	Currency in the Holy Roman Empire, equivalent to one-twelfth of a mark of silver.
Tridentine Catholicism	Reformed Catholicism, based on the decisions of the Council of Trent, 1545–63.

Glossary

Vogt (also *Schulze* or *wójt*)	Official in charge of a village or town founded on German or Polish law, with jurisdiction and tax powers.
województwo (voievodship)	Palatinate: administrative and legal territorial unit.
Wendish Circle	A group of Hanseatic south-east Baltic cities under the leadership of Lübeck.
Westforschung	Research by German scholars on Western Europe during the interwar and Nazi period, which propagated the alleged superiority of German culture and ethnicity in territories lost to the former Holy Roman Empire (Alsace-Lorraine, the Netherlands). Polish *Westforschung* was the Polish response to German *Ostforschung*, with an interest in the autochthonous nature of Slavic populations West of the River Oder.
Zinsbauern	Free peasants who paid rent or labour dues in return for the right to lease land.

Gazetteer of Geographical and Place Names

German/English	*Polish*	*Other (indicated)*
Balga	Bałga	Balga (Russian)
Brandenburg (in East Prussia)	Pokarmin	
Bromberg	Bydgoszcz	
Bütow	Bytów	
Cammin	Kamień Pomorski	
Christburg	Kiszpork/Dzierzgoń	
Danzig	Gdańsk	
Draheim	Drahim	
Drewenz (river)	Drwęca	
Elbing	Elbląg	
Ermland	Warmia (bishopric of)	
Gnesen	Gniezno (archbishopric of)	
Grosspolen/Great Poland	Wielkopolska	
Kleinpolen/Little Poland	Małopolska	
Kleve/Cleves		
Kiev	Kiew	Ky'iv (Ukrainian)
Königsberg	Królewiec	Kaliningrad (Russian)
Krakau/Cracow	Kraków	
Kujawien/Cujavia	Kujawy	
Kulm/Culm	Chełmno	

Gazetteer of Geographical and Place Names

German/English	Polish	Other (indicated)
Lauenburg	Lębork	
Lausitz/Lusatia	Łużyce	
Leslau	Włocławek (bishopric of)	
Marienburg	Malbork	
Masowien/Mazovia	Mazowsze	
Masuren/Masurian Lakes	Masury	
Michelau	Ziemia Lubawska	
Netze (river)	Noteć	
Oder (river)	Odra	
Osterode	Ostróda	
Pommern/Pomerania (duchy of/later: East and West)	Pomorze (Wschodnie, Zachodnie)	
Pomerellen/Pomerelia	Pomorze (voievodship of)	
Posen	Poznań	
Pregel (river)	Pregoła	
Tannenberg (battle of)	Stębark/Grunwald (battle of)	Žalgiris (Lithuanian)
Thorn	Toruń	
Wehlau	Welawa	
Weichsel/Vistula (river)	Wisła	
Warschau/Warsaw	Warszawa	
Zips	Spisz	

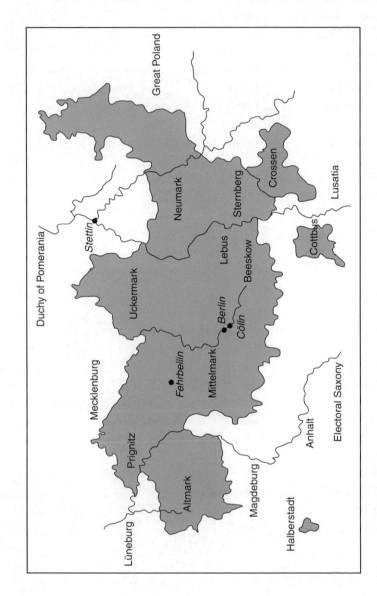

Map 1 Electoral Brandenburg, 1415–1608

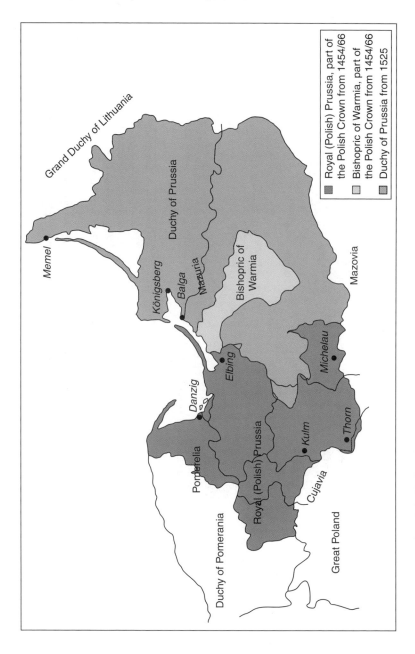

Map 2 Ducal and Royal (Polish) Prussia, 1525

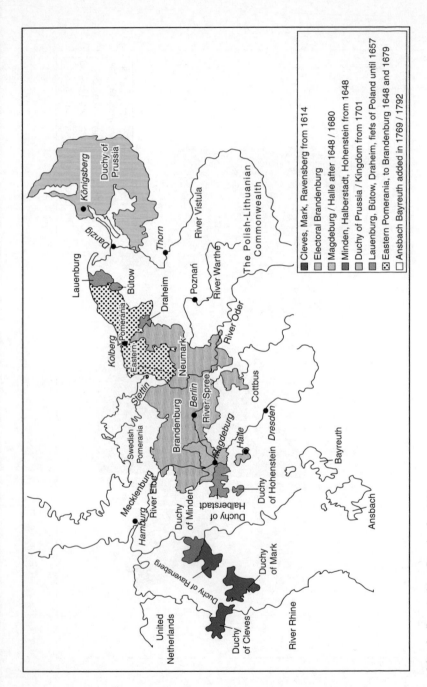

Map 3 Brandenburg-Prussia after 1614

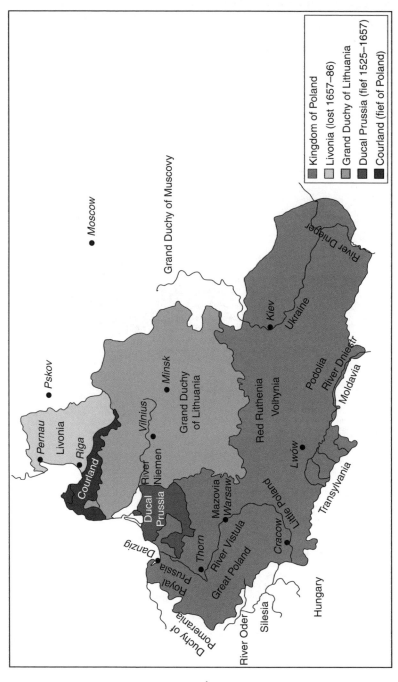

Map 4 The Polish-Lithuanian Commonwealth, c.1580

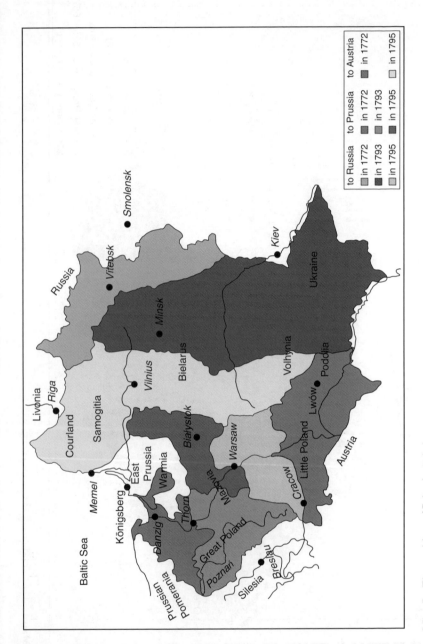

Map 5 The partitions of Poland, 1772–95

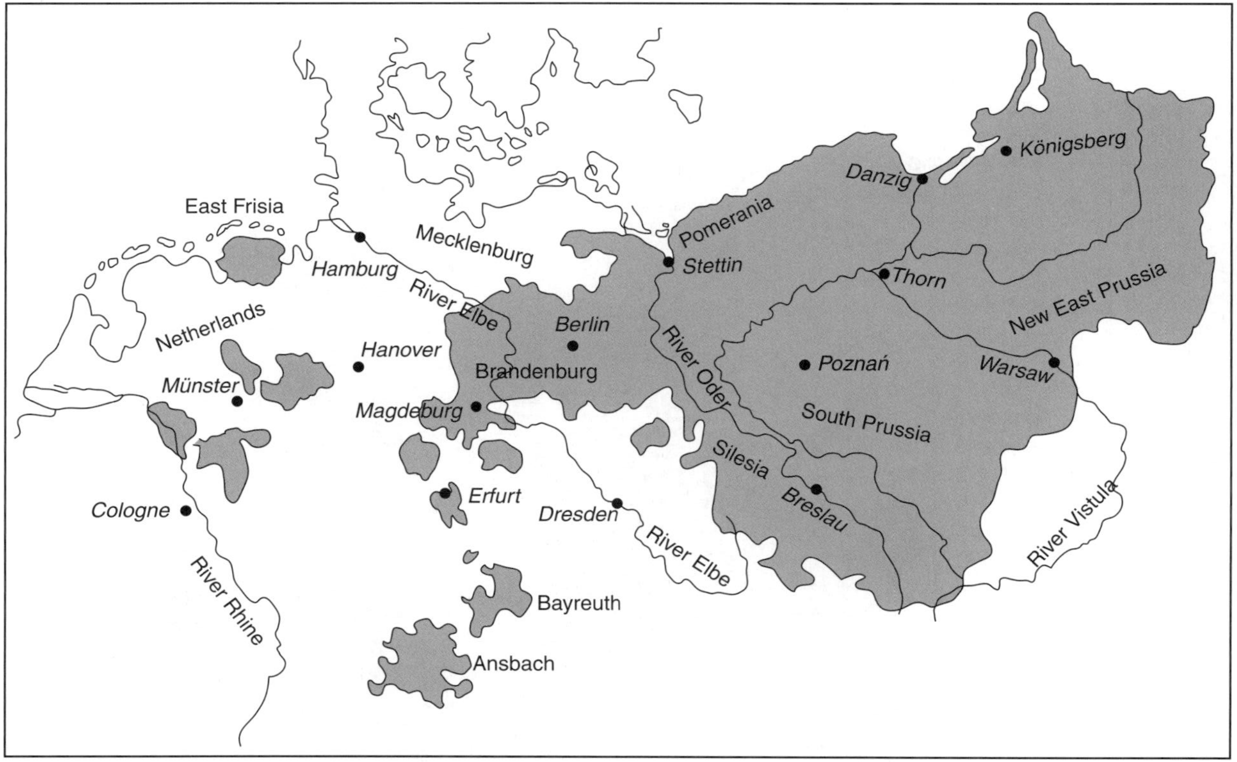

Map 6 Prussia in 1797

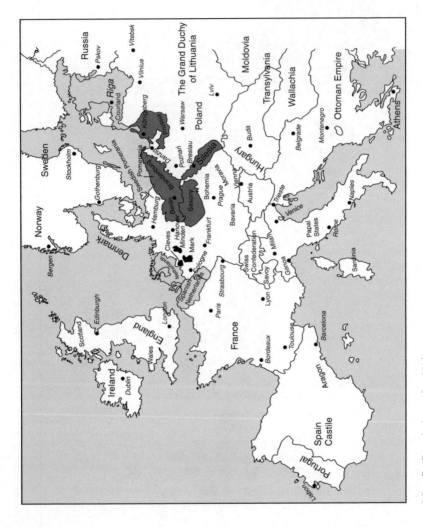

Map 7 Brandenburg after 1740

Introduction

A collection of territories under the rule of the Hohenzollern dynasty, Brandenburg-Prussia was one of the most complex political creations of late medieval and early modern Europe. It is the purpose of this book to stimulate students' interest in the pre-1800 history of Brandenburg-Prussia, when it was not a German great power but a collection of territories squarely located in an east-central European context. Helmut G. Koenigsberger characterised Brandenburg-Prussia as a composite state whose parts were separated from each other, which gave it a fragile constitution but also instilled in its rulers a particularly dynamic ambition [78]. The variety of titles borne by the Hohenzollern rulers in each of their territories over the centuries reflected the composite nature of these dominions. In his influential work on composite monarchies John Elliott differentiated between states which incorporated all their parts into one central body, and those in which the monarch ruled distinctly over each part. While Hohenzollern rulers usually wished to follow the first option, political reality and pragmatism forced them to accept the second. As Elliott pointed out, unions which permitted some self-government by their parts usually contributed to the strength and longevity of composite states [65]. In this light, the success of the Hohenzollern dynasty in gathering, augmenting and maintaining its territories followed a European model that has often been overlooked by older, Germano-centric historiography. Even in the early nineteenth century, Prussia was far from being the monolithic monarchy that nineteenth-century German historians would have liked it to be.

One of the main purposes of this book therefore is mythbusting. The most resistant of all myths was that of Prussia the 'maker of Germany', whose every move was supposedly aimed at German unification and the ultimate triumph over the legacy of the Holy Roman Empire. In his *Twelve Books of Prussian History* of 1847, the founder of the historicist school of history, Leopold von Ranke, praised Prussia as the model of a reforming, bureaucratic German state. More nationalist-oriented historians such as Johann Gustav Droysen, Heinrich von Treitschke and other nineteenth-century proponents of what was later called 'Borussian' historiography constructed a slick nationalist picture which promoted Prussia's 'German destiny' over all other aspects of its multifaceted history.

It was in the name of German nationalism that, between 1933 and 1945, the Nazis instrumentalised Prussian history, be it through the militant image of the Teutonic Knights or Frederick II's military aggression against his neighbours, which Hitler so admired. Even voices that supported republican and liberal models of the state, such as Friedrich Meinecke, defended Prussia's record of 'reforming' authoritarianism and emphasised the Prussian tradition – particularly its military power – as constitutive in the making of a united Germany. The finer points of Brandenburg-Prussia's composite character and traditions remained unexplored in favour of the 'Hohenzollern Legend', promoted by historians such as Gustav von Schmoller, who saw the dynasty as unifiers of the German nation [34]. It was not until long after 1945 that these views came to be questioned. In the 1970s Sebastian Haffner first pointed out that Prussia was absorbed and 'killed' by a new German imperial state and its aggressive German nationalism [6]. Scholars who, after 1945, have championed Germany's historical *Sonderweg* (particularism) share much with their Borussian predecessors: they usually leave the clichés attached to Prussia's legacy untouched but evaluate them negatively.

Scores of textbooks on the nineteenth century still obscure the fact that in the early modern period Prussia's direct neighbour in the East was not Russia, but Poland-Lithuania, whose three partitions by Prussia, Russia and Austria in 1772–95 drew borders through its heartlands and eliminated this state from the map of Europe until 1918. Why does this matter? As the European union is no longer an exclusively West European club, students of European history today need to look at the roots of modern Europe and the forces that formed it which pre-date the ideologies underpinning modern nationalism and the Cold War. Although vanished from the map of Europe, Prussia was an intrinsic part of this European history as a conduit between East and West: between Slavic, Germanic